Cassandra Parkin grew up in Hull, and now lives in East Yorkshire. Her debut novel *The Summer We All Ran Away* was published by Legend Press in 2013 and was shortlisted for the Amazon Rising Star Award. Her short story collection, *New World Fairy Tales* (Salt Publishing, 2011) was the winner of the 2011 Scott Prize for Short Stories. Cassandra's work has been published in numerous magazines and anthologies.

Visit Cassandra at
cassandraparkin.wordpress.com
or follow her @cassandrajaneuk

Acknowledgements

If you know the coast of North Cornwall at all, you'll recognise the place that inspired this book as Perranporth Beach, which has had my heart for as long as I can remember. As writers tend to do, I've made small changes to suit the purposes of the story, and filled it with fictional characters.

No-one in the book is real; but the beach really is that beautiful, and the tide really does come in that fast, and (if you were careless enough to get caught out) the caves really would be that dangerous. Never turn your back on the ocean.

Thank you to my wonderful editor Lauren Parsons and the rest of the team at Legend for all the amazing things you do for writers and readers.

Thank you to my brother Ian for being the most awesome little brother on the planet (and for being absolutely nothing like Finn), and to all of my amazing family down in the West Country. May Third Cubicle Jesus watch over us always.

Special thanks to my children Becky and Ben, for proudly taking my books in to Show and Tell (despite having to tell all your friends "You can't read this because it's got swearing in it") and for never once complaining when I huddle on the sofa, wild-haired and in my pyjamas, muttering over my keyboard like a witch.

Most of all, thank you to my amazing husband Tony for believing in me so entirely and supporting me so generously.

For big sisters and little brothers everywhere.

Chapter One: 1978

On this blazing afternoon the beach is home to both death and beauty, hiding its savage nature beneath a hot white welcome almost too bright for the eyes to bear. The retreating ocean has left tigery ripples in the bronze sand, and families with coloured windbreaks perch on the surface. Close to the top of the beach, billowy dunes bear witness to the power of the tide when it pours in, but now the waves are churning froth in the far distance and the dry sand dances in the wind. The children drop their buckets and stare in disbelief.

"What do you think?" their father asks.

"Struck dumb," says their mother, ruffling her son's hair. Her daughter, taller and older, frowns and pulls restlessly at the thin brown straps of her swimsuit. "Ava, will you leave those straps? They're fine."

"What shall we do first?" Their father looks around for a spot to settle. He selects a patch of sand, hesitates, walks on a few paces, pauses again, takes three steps more. The beach's scope is so vast – a bite from the black cliffs, taken by a mouth nearly two miles wide – that choosing any particular spot seems arbitrary. "Want to build a sandcastle? Dig a hole? Explore the caves?"

His daughter turns her frown towards him.

"I don't think we should go in the caves, Dad."

"Why not?"

"That sign, remember? And the tide?"

"Those signs are just to cover themselves," her father says. "They wouldn't leave them open if they were dangerous."

Ava looks disbelieving, but chooses to stay silent.

"So. What's it going to be, kids? Who fancies going caving? Come on, Finn, you'll love it."

"Can we run?" His son, who has been scrunching his toes into the sand and studying the results with interest, looks up eagerly, bright black eyes beneath thick lashes. His skin is already turning golden.

"Well, I suppose, but wouldn't you rather… "

"Come on!" Ava seizes her brother's hand and they charge off, roaring with delight, bare feet beating against the sand, the girl's long brown hair flying, the boy's black curls leaping. Their parents begin to claim their patch. The father hammers the windbreak with a rubber mallet. The mother tries to spread towels, but is foiled by the lick and curl of the wind.

"The lilo's going to blow away," she says.

"It'll be fine." He unfolds the lilo and begins to inflate it. His wife lays herself elegantly out on the towel and bastes herself with oil.

The children's run ends at a large square pillar of rock, as big as the hotel they left that morning.

"What's it for?" asks Finn.

"It's a rock," his sister tells him, enjoying the opportunity to patronise. "It's not *for* anything."

"There's people climbing on it." He points to three precarious figures teetering on a narrow path, yelling encouragement.

Ava is studying the ocean. She looks down at her brother, growing all the time, losing the baby roundness she has secretly cherished, but still small and vulnerable to her ten-year-old eyes. His armbands are at the bottom of their mother's beach-bag. He cannot yet swim without them.

8

"Shall we go back to Mum and Dad?" she asks heroically. "We can build a sandcastle if you like."

"Let's explore the rock first."

"How can you explore a rock?" she asks, then adds, "We're not climbing it, it's all right for me but you're too small," but he's already off, disappearing before her eyes, that steady sturdy tireless jogtrot she finds so hard to keep pace with. A second later and he's back.

"Come and look!" he's yelling. "It's this really ace weird thing!"

She's reluctant to get too excited, knowing his definition of an *ace weird thing* is not the same as hers.

"What is it?" she asks, not moving.

"I don't know, but it's ace! Come and see!"

Just in case she's being watched by anyone important, she rolls her eyes and sighs before following him. On the rock's seaward side, there's a large rectangular hollow, like a giant rock-pool. It's big enough to swim ten or fifteen strokes in. It's swimming-pool-shaped, but the bottom is sandy and greenish weed floats back and forth like drowned hair.

"What is it?" he asks.

"I don't know!" she snaps, annoyed because she likes knowing the answers and being able to tell him. "Why do you always expect me to know everything?"

He shrugs. "Mostly you do."

There are people in the pool, although they don't look as if they're enjoying it. A child floats precariously in a thin inflatable ring. The frill of her swimming costume flutters as she kicks. The child's father sits on the side and berates her for being scared.

"Let's go in," Finn says.

"You haven't got your armbands."

"I'll just go in a little bit," he replies, clambering up.

"You can't swim yet." She can't imagine why he wants to go in anyway. To her it seems like the worst of both worlds, the clinging communal oiliness of a public swimming pool combined with the chill and salt of the ocean. Why not just walk the extra ten feet and get into the proper water? "You're not allowed, Mum and Dad said so."

"I can swim without my armbands," he says. "Look, I can do it."

And to her astonishment, he almost can. His head bobs beneath the water and his foot slips secretly beneath him to push off from the bottom every few strokes, but he's undeniably making progress, huffing and breathless and jerky, but not sinking, not drowning. He's become a fledgling water-creature.

"You can!" she says. "You can swim. You're swimming! When did you learn that?"

The pride in his face as he glances shyly towards her squeezes her heart.

It takes them a long time to find their way back. She keeps up a bright artificial stream of chatter in case he's worried, this little boy she loves and tyrannises so fiercely. After a few minutes, she feels a warm hand slip trustingly into hers, and she squeezes it, breathless with responsibility.

"We'll find them soon," she says for the seventh time.

"You keep saying that, and we keep not finding them."

"Well, I can't help it, all right? We *will* find them – look, there they are."

She had imagined her parents sitting on the edge of their towels, anxiously searching, but her mother has unfastened the tie of her bikini and turned onto her front, and her father is sprawled across the lilo listening to the radio.

"You back?" Their father glances at them from beneath the hat that makes her embarrassed to be seen with him. "Want to dig that hole now?"

"Um… okay." Finn reaches for the spade and hands it to their father, who marks out a raggedy circle.

Ava's been so worried about getting them back safely that she's only just remembered the exciting news.

"Guess what?"

Her dad is busy with the spade. After a minute her mother stirs and turns her head.

"What?" she murmurs.

"We found this pool, and… "

"A rock-pool? That's lovely. Was there a crab in it?"

"No, not a rock-pool, like a sort of outside swimming pool thing, only with seawater in it, and… "

"Oh yes. They mentioned that at the hotel. It's covered at high tide. Did it look nice?"

"No, not really, it's all seaweedy, but listen… "

"If it's seaweedy be careful," says her mother. "You might slip."

Ava gives up. She will keep the knowledge to herself. They can find out for themselves that their son has (almost) learned to swim. Maybe Finn will tell them, later today perhaps, maybe even tomorrow, and she can say casually, 'Oh yes, didn't you know? He showed me yesterday morning.'

"Do you want to help dig this hole?" Her dad, already bored of his engineering project, offers her his spade.

"Can't I go in the sea?"

She can see from his expression that she's asked too soon. Her father feels rejected. He wants her to want to dig the hole. In his mind, digging a hole with her father and little brother will teach her teamwork and cooperation and be healthy, whereas going off to the sea by herself smacks of precocious pre-teen rebellion. Today a swim by herself, tomorrow cigarettes behind the bike-shed. Where will it end?

"It's too windy," her father says. "I don't want the lilo blowing away."

"I won't take the lilo."

"What if the waves are big?"

"The waves are fine."

"And we've only got three towels and your mother needs one."

"I'll dry off in the sun. Please, Dad."

11

"If you lie down in the sun for a bit you'll get a nice tan," her mother says. "You can have some of my oil."

She swallows the words that she wants to say, which are *What's the point of coming if I can't go in the water?*

"I'll bring back some seaweed," she suggests, suddenly inspired. Her father likes them to collect things.

"Love?" He nudges his wife with one toe. "What do you think?"

"She'll be fine," his wife mumbles from the edges of sleep.

"All right." He waves her off.

Finn watches wistfully as his big sister vanishes. He was hoping she would stay and dig the hole with him. He can already see that their dad was just pretending to be interested, and is about to leave him to get on with it "just for five minutes while I sit down". His mother won't want to get sand in her tanning-oil. Now he's stuck by himself with a big circle of sand to dig out.

If Ava was helping, she'd already have taken over. They'd be knee-deep beneath the surface, and he would have been assigned a specific menial task, such as building a surrounding wall to make the hole even deeper. While he periodically rebels against her bossiness, just so she doesn't get the idea she's in charge of him, he also secretly likes it. It's comforting to be told what to do.

Besides, however much he complains, Ava *is* in charge. She knows more than him. She can run faster than him. She can read harder books than him. She can swim in the ocean, breaking past the surf to slip between the wave's peaks like a mermaid, until he's afraid she'll swim on and on into the horizon. She can do anything. She is the person he admires the most in the whole world.

The only thing he doesn't understand is why she's so bad at managing their parents.

"This hole's going to be really great," Finn tells his dad, now back on the lilo.

"That's good."

"It might need decorating. To make it look even cooler."

"Ava's getting some seaweed."

"She might not get enough, though. It's going to be a really big hole. With a wall."

"A wall? That's nice."

"Yes. A really, *really* big wall."

"That sounds good."

"So, do you think I should get some more seaweed? Just in case she doesn't get enough?"

"Can you find your way back all right?"

"Easy. I just look for our windbreak."

His father smiles affectionately. "That's my boy."

The drowning begins gently. First, the shallows, seductive sheets of flat sun-warmed water. Then, the smallest breakers, little rolling waves that barely wet his knees, enticing him in further.

The swim in the pool was a test, a final experiment. He will join his big sister in the water, swim up behind her and say, 'Oh, hello,' calm and casual as if he's done this every summer of their lives, and she'll be even more surprised and impressed than when she saw him in the pool. He won't be stuck on the shore while she disappears off on her mysterious water-journeys. He'll be able to keep up with her at last. He's done this a thousand times in his dreams.

He rehearses how she does it in his mind. She wades out, gasping, until the water's up to her chest. Then she turns her back and lets a wave wash over her shoulders. Then she turns around again and starts swimming, and there's a moment when she stops gasping and starts laughing, as the cold holds her so tightly she doesn't feel it any more, and she disappears and reappears, disappears and reappears, until eventually she's glowing and filled with savage life.

He passes some critical point and the water-temperature drops abruptly, and a wave slaps roughly against his thighs and he holds his arms up high out of reach and gasps for breath. Slowly, he walks on. Then he turns around and waits for the wave.

When it comes it's a brutal slap right between his shoulders that knocks him off his feet. He had no idea water could be so solid. Then something else grabs him and drags him, away from the beach and deeper in. He splutters and fumbles for the bottom. Before he can find it, another wave hits him slap, and he's gone again, pull and drag away from safety, and he gets his head free for a minute and then slap, and this time he's right under the wave, they're taller than he is. How did the water get so deep so quickly? This isn't what he planned. He wants to fight but he can't. It's not giving him a chance. Every time he remembers what to do another wave comes, slap and drag, and he can't swim if he can't get started right, he needs to push off from the bottom and slap and drag, and a mouthful of air and he can't even scream and this wasn't what he planned, not at all.

Then a hand clutches his arm and a voice screams in his ear and he reaches out in terror and grabs a handful of what feels like seaweed. He grabs again and finds cold salvation, the limbs and torso of another person and someone's telling him, *Hold on, hold on to me, you idiot, what happened to your armbands?* He clings desperately, knowing this is his only chance. He's disoriented and lost but he thinks they must be getting closer to the shore, because now there's sunlight on his skin as well as water. And then the person holding him is Ava, staggering as she carries him into the shallows. She saw him struggling and came to save him – even though they argued all the way down in the car about who was making annoying noises and whose hand was over the line and whose turn it was to play I Spy. She's saved him from the ocean. He coughs up a mouthful of water and his breath begins to slow and the aftermath of fear is all through him and Ava, tall and stern, stands over him.

"What were you doing?" she screams.

14

"I was swimming," he mumbles. "Like in the pool."

"That wasn't swimming, not proper swimming, you were putting your foot down! You know you can't swim without your armbands!"

He doesn't want to cry, but it doesn't seem to be up to him. It's like trying not to be sick.

"Oh, don't cry," she says in despair, and holds her arms out.

He wants to crawl onto her lap but he knows it's babyish. He compromises by resting his head against her chest and letting her stroke his hair.

"I thought you were going to drown," she confesses. "I saw you go under – I didn't know if I could… " Her arms squeeze him in a fierce tight hug.

"I wanted to show you. I thought I could do it." The tears are spilling out again. He keeps his head against her chest. Maybe she hasn't noticed.

"It wasn't your fault," she says. "It was the undertow. It's really dangerous, there are signs everywhere. I don't know why Mum and Dad didn't stop you."

"I said I was going to get seaweed," he whispers.

Suddenly she smiles at him.

"You nearly had it, you know." She pats his back. "You were nearly doing it! You just need to practice in that awful – that ace pool thing. I'll make sure you can do it properly before you go back in the sea."

"Let's go back," he says, and she nods fervently. Her hold on his hand is tighter than usual.

Their parents have barely moved. Their mother gleams brown and beautiful on her towel. On the lilo, their father's face and chest are turning red.

"Shall we not tell them?" he says suddenly.

She stares at their clasped palms. "You've got hair all in your hand." She picks out tangled brown strands from between his fingers. He wonders where it came from.

"So, shall we not tell them?" he repeats.

She looks at their parents, oblivious and calm, and then back down at him. He wonders what she's thinking.

"Why did Mum and Dad let you go down there on your own?" She wipes her nose with the back of her hand. "Why weren't they with you?"

He shrugs. "You know what they're like."

She looks at him for a long time. He can see something changing in her, something deep and fundamental that squares her shoulders and lifts her chin.

"You stay with me from now on, okay? If you want to go swimming, come with me. And don't let them take you down to the caves, not today. If they try and make you, just say you want to build something instead. We'll go tomorrow morning if you want to see them."

"But can we not tell them? About… "

"Promise about the caves?"

"I promise."

"Then we won't tell them," she decides.

"And you won't tell them I cried?"

She touches the skin beneath his eyes with a tentative finger. "They might notice."

"We could say I fell over?"

"Okay. We won't say anything to start with, but if they notice, we'll say that."

Suddenly the whole episode takes on the dimensions of a tremendous adventure. He almost swam. His sister saved him. The day is magical once more. Overwhelmed by an irresistible impulse, he pulls her head down so he can kiss her.

"I love you," he confesses.

Her face remains close to his. He can see the freckles on her small straight nose, her brown eyes that are the same shape as his but lighter, mid-brown where his are black. Her hair hangs over her shoulders in long salty ropes. Her hand tightly grasps his and her eyes well with tears.

"Whatever happens," she says, "I'll always be your big

16

sister. I'll always look after you, whenever you need me, our whole lives. Okay? I'll always be here. I'll never let you drown."

The brother and sister who were lost

Once, a brother and sister lived with their mother and father. The sister was older than the brother and she had long hair that he loved to twirl his fingers in, and for a long time she was taller than him (and even when he finally overtook her, in his head she was still always in charge).

One day, someone asked the little brother, *What do you want to do when you grow up?* And he replied, *I'm going to live in a little house by the ocean. Just one room for me and my big sister, and we'll wake up every morning and look out at the beach and just be all by ourselves.*

But you have to have a job, the person told him. (It doesn't matter who the person was. Every story has some people in it who are unimportant. But just so they don't feel bad, let's say this person was a lady called Elinor, and she had a big house and servants and seventeen cats, and she always wore a turban in the afternoons and liked to take naps on a beautiful gold brocade chaise-longue.)

I'll write books, said the little brother.

And what about your big sister?

I'll make enough money for both of us, said the little brother, and the lady called Elinor with the big house and the servants and the seventeen cats laughed, and went home to put on her turban and take a nap.

But the little brother didn't mind. He and his sister had talked about their dream many times. They knew it was what they both wanted.

And they loved each other fiercely, even when they drove each other mad.

Then one day, the two children looked up and realised

they were lost. Exactly how this happened, it's impossible to say. Or perhaps it was simply too sad to talk about, so that part was always left out of their story, and after a long time, it was forgotten. Perhaps they took the wrong path on a long journey. Perhaps they were playing in a wood when darkness fell, or perhaps they sailed away in a nutshell and found themselves on a cold shore with no stars to navigate home by. Whatever the explanation, on that terrible dark day, they both looked up from whatever they were doing, and realised they no longer had a home.

And the little brother was frightened. But his big sister took his hand and said, *Don't worry, little brother. I promised I'd always look after you, and I always will. Whatever happens, I'll always, always take care of you.*

After that, the little brother knew there was nothing to be afraid of, because his big sister was holding his hand, and she would never let him go. Whatever happened, he would always be littler than she was, and she would always take care of him.

Chapter Two: Now

"So," said Donald, reaching for his daughter's hand. Alicia slid her hand in her pocket, then took it out again to pat his arm. He tried to be grateful for the pat, rather than hurt by the rejection. "Ready for the new term?"

"They'll all be talking about Newquay. And how good the surf was. They stayed up all night and had a barbecue. And went swimming by moonlight."

And went round the bars copping on like they're all eighteen, and Mattie Barker got in a fight and spent the night down the nick and was lucky to get off with a stern word, thought Donald, who knew the owner of the Kula Shaka and had heard the stories the parents weren't supposed to. If he said this out loud, she'd say he was spying. Was he? Possibly, but old habits died hard.

Alicia was looking at him sideways. "They're going again at half-term. For Emma's birthday."

"No."

"You don't have to pay for it."

"I know that, thank you."

"I just meant I'll do some shifts for you."

"No."

"I worked for Emma's dad at the café all summer."

"Yes, on the ice-cream stand, in the day. You're not working in the pub in the evenings."

She pounced on the opening. "I'll do weekends then."

"You work hard at school. Weekends are for having fun."

When she was angry she looked so much like her mother it hurt his heart. "How much fun can I have when they all go off without me?"

He didn't know what to say to that, so he resorted to silence. Ellen had always hated that too.

"Anyway," she said at last. "I've got my wages from the summer."

"You're not spending them on going to Newquay."

"Why not?"

"Because!" He didn't quite know where to start. "Because it's full of stags and idiots and you'll end up getting into trouble."

"I won't catch *idiot* off other people."

"You're fifteen."

"Exactly! Fifteen!" And the line that punctuated their lives: "I'm not a little kid, you know."

Oh, Lord, don't I just know. Ellen, if you're watching, I'm doing my best here, I swear. They'd made it together this far, just the two of them. He'd shown up for her, understudied for Ellen as best he could. He'd forced himself to learn tenderness as well as authority. He'd got them through the big milestones – first bra, first body-hair, first period – with stoic determination and grim humour. It wasn't the biology but the psychology that baffled him; the discovery that he was, once more, living with a woman.

He looked sideways at his daughter, wanting to see her as a stranger might. Round innocent face, hazel eyes, long fair hair. Pretty the way all young creatures were pretty. Pretty despite that absurd hairstyle they all wore, like a cottage-loaf made out of hair. Long, athletic legs – her best feature. The way men looked at her this summer – even the fathers, for Christ's sake – slow sly stares when their wives weren't watching, not with the intention of *doing* anything, just one for the wank-bank later on, but then they weren't horny teenage surfers or drunken stag-parties… no, he had to stop this, just thinking about it made him angry.

"So if I can't go to Newquay, can I swim here instead?"

He felt his heart contract.

"No."

"Just until half-term."

"No."

"Just when it's calm."

"It's never calm."

"Just when the waves aren't too big, then."

"No."

"But Dad!"

"You're not going in the water when the lifeguards aren't here," he told her.

"But… "

"But nothing."

"Then let me go to Newquay! I don't want to drink! I just want to swim before next Easter!"

"No."

"Please! I'm not a… "

"Little kid, I know. You're still not going."

"So let me swim here!"

"Will you please stop asking for things you know I'll say no to?"

They strode on together in angry silence.

"Emma didn't even ask her parents," Alicia said casually. "She just told them she was going away for the last weekend of the holidays."

Donald swallowed. His hold on her was so fragile. She did what he told her because she loved him. How much longer could that last?

"If you went off without telling me," he declared, "I'd come after you."

"What if you couldn't find me?"

"I'd bloody well look until I did."

She looked at him reproachfully. "Don't swear."

"You're not the boss of me." That made her smile a bit. "I'd go to the front desk of every hotel in Newquay, and I'd ask every single receptionist, 'Have you got a young woman called Alicia Emory staying here?' And I'd come up to your room dressed in my very worst dad clothes and I'd say, 'Sorry to disturb you children, but Alicia didn't tidy her room before she left so I'm afraid she's going to have to come home.' And you'd be so embarrassed you'd die of shame and never want to see any of them again."

She was trying not to give in, but he could see the corners of her mouth twitching. "We might be at the beach."

"Oh, even better. I'd come down to the beach wearing tiny little Speedos with my big fat gut hanging out over them."

She took his arm and cradled it protectively.

"You haven't got a big fat gut."

"Yes, I have." He stuck it out proudly. "Look at that. Great big wobbly publican's gut. Disgusting. You don't want your mates seeing that, do you?"

"Anyway," she told him, "you haven't got any Speedos."

"I'd buy some specially." He could feel her softening, relenting, and it evoked an answering tenderness in him. "Look, I'll think about it, okay? Maybe next spring."

She was on it like a cat on a mouse. "Or maybe this October."

"I only said… "

"Thanks, Dad. You're brilliant." She kissed his cheek, then dropped his arm and ran away before he could get in the crucial last words, 'I only said I'd think about it.'

Her footprints were already disappearing as she ran down to the waterline. This close to the ocean, nothing left an impression for long. He was about to follow her when he was distracted by two thin, wavering tracks meandering towards the dunes, like badly-laid tramlines, or sled-tracks in snow. Following them, he found a trolley stacked with planks and his friend George building – what was he building? – *something*, in a small sheltered spot between two tall sandbanks.

22

"Now then," Donald said to George's back.

George looked around, and nodded. "Hello," he said, and turned back to his task.

George had built what looked like a very small boardwalk, flat boards on stilts sunk deep into the sand. Donald knew without asking that George would have driven the stilts deeply and carefully enough to ensure the boards were perfectly flat and even. His meticulously drawn plans lay beside him, weighted with pebbles.

Donald had often thought he'd like to have some of George's drawings framed and hung on the pub wall. He asked once if he could buy some, but George had replied, 'No', no equivocation, no explanation, just a simple flat 'No', and then a minute later, 'Can I have a bottle of Heineken and a packet of pork scratchings, please', which was the thing George always asked for, and which he always consumed sitting in the same chair, at the same table. Donald glanced at the plans.

It looks perfect, Alicia thought longingly, watching the foamy wave spill over and crash against itself. *So perfect. And it's bloody months until Easter. And he hasn't really said yes to Newquay yet. All I can do until next year is bloody paddle. It's not fair.*

She sat down on the sand and tugged crossly at the laces on her trainers. Why was he so paranoid about her? Was it a dad thing? Or just a her-dad thing? Was it because he'd been a police officer? Or was it because she was all he had?

It's not like I want to do anything he wouldn't approve of. Alicia considered this for a minute, then conscientiously amended it: *It's not like I haven't been doing plenty of stuff he wouldn't approve of right here.* Her summer had passed in a haze of guilt and bliss and thievery. If her father ever found out…

She stood up to let the sea wash over her toes and wondered how her life would be different if her mother was still alive.

23

"George," said Donald, "this looks like a beach hut."

"It is a beach hut," said George.

"But – why are you building a beach hut?"

"I saw this television programme," said George. "A sort of kit you could order. I've been looking for a chance to try it out."

"You bought a kit? *You* did? I don't believe you."

"No," said George, patiently. "I *made* one of the kits. It's a very clever system."

"You can't build stuff on a public beach without permission."

"Look," said George, offering a long slab of wood. "You take out the groove on the bottom, then the tongue on the top. They stack onto the corner posts."

Donald looked. "Lovely, but George, you're going to get into trouble."

"It'll be fine," said George.

"Do you know how hard it is to get permission to put anything on this beach? Henry's spent years trying to get permission for a new storeroom at the back of the café, and has he got anywhere?"

"He could do it anyway," George suggested. "Just get on with it and see if anyone complains. I could do it for him. I was looking at it the other day and I've done some plans. I know he thinks he wants a new storeroom but he doesn't. What he wants is a sundeck. Then they can read newspapers and things, and their pop bottles won't blow over or get sandy, and the women won't get sand in that oil stuff they put on themselves."

Donald wondered when George had last been to the beach.

"And what would he say when someone asked to see the paperwork?" he asked.

"People worry too much about paperwork," said George, wrestling with a heavy wooden slab. He slotted it onto the groove of two poles forming the corners of the hut, and tapped it down with a rubber mallet.

"George, don't take this the wrong way. It looks brilliant. But they'll make you knock it down. I'm not trying to be mean but that's what's what's going to happen."

"Well, it's not mine, is it?" said George, picking up the next slab.

Cold curls of water kissed Alicia's ankles. With the season over, the beach's scale was so vast that it simply swallowed its few visitors, giving you the impression of being completely alone. She took two strides more, then shut her eyes and savoured the peace. The waves pawed at her knees and snatched at her jeans. She kept wading anyway.

One day soon, she'd have to leave the beach behind and go and find her real life, out in the rest of the world. The beach would shrink and fade and become part of her discarded childhood. Sometimes she almost wished her father had never brought them here to live. Why show her what it was like to live in Paradise when her only choice was to leave again?

A tall wave wet her to mid-thigh, and she swore, then looked over her shoulder, just in case her father had crept within earshot. To her surprise, he wasn't watching her. She shaded her eyes with her hands. She thought she could see him climbing into the dunes.

"Why would I want a beach hut?" asked George, laughing. "I can't stand it on the beach."

"Who's it for, then?"

George rummaged in his pocket, then held out a folded piece of paper. "I had a letter. There was a drawing in it." As if this explained everything, he returned to his building.

Donald unfolded the letter. The writing was spidery and excitable, with an excess of punctuation. Occasional words leaped out like ambushing soldiers. *Dunes,* he read. *One room. Bare. Sea.* What was this rubbish? On the back was a sketch of what was presumably the finished object. It had a little veranda and a large pot with a climbing plant growing out of it.

"You'll still be in trouble," said Donald, handing back the letter. "You're local. You ought to know better."

"It's not in anyone's way," said George. "Look at this place, it's huge. There's room for one little hut."

"What if everyone who wanted to just pitched up and built their own little hut?"

"But I'm not building a hut for everyone, I'm building a hut for just one person. That's a totally different thing."

"But it's really not – look, let me help you with that." Donald put out a hand and helped steady the slab of wood.

"No, it's all right," said George. "If you don't approve, you shouldn't feel like you have to help."

"You're my friend. I don't want you to die building it. Oh, hello, pet." Alicia's jeans were soaked, salt water wicking up the denim. Her trainers hung from her hand and her feet were white with cold. "Look at you, you're sopping. Come on. Home."

Alicia was looking at the beach hut. "What are you building?"

"Conversations start with *hello*," said Donald wearily.

"It's a beach hut," said George.

"Oh my God, really?" Alicia caught her breath. "Are there going to be more? Dad, can we get one? Could we sleep in it? I'd love that so much – like camping, but not so crap."

"Just one," said George.

"Just one? Why?"

"Because he only asked for one," said George, who could be fearfully literal at times.

"Who did?"

"My client," said George.

"But who? Who owns it? Was it expensive?"

"Never mind *was it expensive*," said Donald. "The important question is, *has he got permission*, and the answer, sadly, is *no*."

"Look at this." Alicia stood on the wooden floor and caressed the boards with her foot. "It's so smooth, no splinters or anything."

"Three different grades of sandpaper," said George.

"It feels gorgeous." She ran her fingers over the half-built walls.

"It won't last," said Donald. "Salt water rots wood."

"He said he wanted it left unfinished so he could paint it," said George.

"Can I help build it?" Alicia hopped out from behind the half-built walls and tugged at the trolley.

"I don't think George needs any help," said Donald.

"It'll go quicker with two people," said George.

"We need to get back," said Donald.

"Why?" Alicia was wrestling with a long plank. George took the other end and showed her how to lift it.

"I need to open up."

"You said weekends were for having fun." Alicia blew a strand of hair out of her mouth. "I've been working all summer."

"Mike called in sick this morning," he lied.

"But you said you didn't want me working behind the bar," said Alicia. "So I can't help, can I?"

Oh, for God's sake, thought Donald. *When did she get so ruthless? Is this what it's going to be like from now on?*

"I want you back for lunch."

"We'll be done in a couple of hours," said George. Donald swallowed the urge to hit him over the head with the rubber mallet.

"Come home for twelve," he said.

"Bye, Dad." Alicia was already reaching for the mallet.

"Did you hear me?"

"Yes."

"What time did I say?"

"Twelve." Alicia favoured him with a brief, brilliant smile. "Bye."

27

The trudge back up the beach seemed considerably longer. He had plenty of time to examine the anger that boiled within him. Why did he even care about the damn beach hut? He'd retired. It wasn't his job to keep people honest any more. And besides, it wasn't as if he was the only person who was going to notice. Plenty of people crossed the beach every hour.

(Although, now he thought about it, it was very well-positioned. It nestled into the dunes as if it had always been there. It would be out of reach of the highest spring tides, sheltered from the fiercest October storms. Had George chosen the spot, or was it buried somewhere in the letter?)

Who did they think they were, flouting the rules like this? What made them think they were so special that the law didn't apply to them?

He glanced at his wrist. God, ten to eleven. Mike would have been waiting since half-past ten. First weekend of the autumn staffing rota. Just three of them on today, including him. Trade would be a fifth of what it had been a month ago, but the weather and the waves would bring the surfers far into the autumn, even without the lifeguards. Alicia could plead all she wanted, but her board was in the back of the cupboard along with her wetsuit and they both knew it was staying there. He could relax until Easter Day next year. Mike was standing on the steps.

"Sorry." Donald fumbled with the keys. "Lost track of time. You won't believe what George is doing this time."

"He's not started on that sundeck for the café, has he?" asked Mike.

"He told you about that too?"

"Oh, you know George," said Mike gloomily. "Once he gets an idea in his head… he came in the other day looking for Henry, but Henry wasn't around and he was in the mood to tell someone, so I copped for the lot. Mind you," he added, "it's quite a good idea. But I could have done without hearing about it for three hours solid."

"Sorry about that."

"S'all right. He's always been like it. We're all used to him by now."

We, thought Donald, smiling to himself as he turned on lights and laid out clean towels. *How long do I have to live here before I get to be we?* It wasn't that he hadn't been made welcome. He was well-liked and respected, his daughter was popular and happy. But after nearly a decade, they still weren't part of the landscape.

He himself had no chance. If he lived here until the day he died, the opening words of his funeral oration would be, "Donald Emory wasn't born here, but…" Alicia was a hybrid – capable of fooling tourists, but still slightly foreign to the locals, a visitor who might or might not choose to remain. Maybe if she married a local man and had a child, their child would belong, or perhaps her grandchild… although even then, he could imagine any mild aberration being explained by the sage observation, 'Well, his grandmother wasn't from round here, you know.' He opened the cellar door and turned on the pumps.

Then again, if Alicia did stay, what kind of life would she have? Mike was a roofer by trade, his wife Anna was a nurse. Two skilled workers. But Mike couldn't get enough work locally and Anna's wage wouldn't cover a shift-worker's childcare if he worked away, so two years ago Mike had taken Donald's offer of head barman – flat-out with ten part-timers under him in the season just compensating for erratic shifts with casual extras in the off – and now he and Anna were clinging on by their fingernails. What would Alicia do for a job? The pub kept one adult and one child in modest comfort but it couldn't do more. And besides, he didn't want her to work in a pub.

"Blimey," said Mike, from by the door. "They get better every year."

"What get better every year?"

"The camper vans."

Donald carried the blackboard out and watched the van

pull into the beachside car park. Psychedelic flowers and mystic swirls, executed not with the smooth nasty airbrushing that always made him think of fairground rides, but with what looked like ordinary brushstrokes. The van even had a name: *The Jolly Deathtrap of Doom and Loveliness*. It was against the unwritten Code Of Being Local to stare, but he watched anyway.

The first person out was a man, tall and brown with a mop of wild curls. His jeans looked expensive, something which mystified Donald; how was it possible to make a pair of jeans so artfully that even a middle-aged publican could tell their value at fifty paces? His t-shirt had clearly been painted by whoever had done the van.

His companion was his shadowy feminine copy. Her hair was long and brown and wavy and her skin was pale, but they had the same-shaped face, the same wide eyes, the same build. Surely they couldn't be a couple. No-one could be that in love with their own appearance. Brother and sister, maybe? The woman's white peasant blouse blew in the wind. Her hair got into her mouth and she clawed it out impatiently. Then they both turned to face the beach and let the wind blow through them, holding their arms out to embrace it. Pair of oddballs. He realised he was staring, and went back inside.

As he turned the key in the till and emptied out coin-bags, two voices drifted through the open door.

"It looks just the same." A man's voice, not local.

"We're actually here!" They sounded like siblings as well as looking like it. "I wish the wind was in a different direction though. Damn it… "

"Have you got hair in your mouth again?"

"Yep."

"Do you remember the time you were unpacking that trolley in the supermarket?"

She began to laugh. "And I breathed in a big mouthful of hair… "

"And you were trying to claw it out and hawk it up at the

same time… "

"And you wrote to the supermarket afterwards and asked if they'd captured it on CCTV, *and they actually wrote back…* "

They stood just inside the pub doorway, leaning against each other, speechless with laughter. Was there anything more irritating than other people laughing at something that wasn't funny? The woman had little bells sewn on the frayed bottom of her jeans. What was the matter with him, that he was suddenly taking such a vast interest in other people's clothes?

"I'm still disappointed they didn't send it," the man said. "What shall we do now?"

"It's lunchtime," said the woman, with great authority.

"Is it? Hooray. What shall we have?"

"Let's get pasties and eat them on the wall."

"And Mr Kipling French Fancies." They were turning away now, their voices getting fainter.

"Oh, yes! Do they still make them?"

"Course they do. And then afterwards we can walk down and see… "

Their voices were fading as they disappeared down the street. They were going to the Oggy Oggy Pasty Shop. The Mr Kipling cakes they'd have to buy at the Londis next door.

"Fuck," said Donald out loud.

"What's up?" Mike's head popped round the door to the lounge-bar.

"Doesn't matter," said Donald.

"I could do with some pound coins if you've got them."

Donald fumbled for an unopened bag, tossed it over to Mike.

"Twenty enough?"

"Plenty. Do you want a note back?" Donald shook his head.

Mike disappeared. Donald stared madly into space, chewing his thumbnail. He guessed – no, the hell with guessing, he *knew*, with the bone-deep certainty of infallible intuition – that the brother and sister with their ridiculous clothes and their strange hilarity and their plan to buy pasties and Mr Kipling French Fancies were the people who had commissioned George to build the beach hut down in the dunes. Which meant that, however much he'd liked their camper van, they were now his implacable enemies.

Chapter Three: 1983

Finn was lying quietly under the blanket staring at the ceiling when he heard the soft click of the door opening. He sat up at once.

"Ava?"

He could see her by the light in the corridor, tall and thin and pretty, her long hair tousled, flapping frantically at him to be quiet.

"Sorry," he whispered. She rolled her eyes and put her finger to her lips. "What?"

"Shh! The house mothers are going to hear you!"

"I'm whispering! This is as quiet as I can be!"

She scurried into his room, pushed the door shut and sat on the narrow bed.

"You've got the loudest whisper of anyone I know," she told him. "I bet there are people who can't shout as loud as you can whisper. Can I get in with you? My feet are freezing."

Finn obligingly held the covers open for her and she slid in beneath the sheets.

"What did you have for tea?" Ava asked.

"Fish fingers."

"With chips?"

"Jacket potato. And baked beans. And ice-cream with sauce on afterwards. How about you?"

"Stew."

"Was it nice?"

"No. The meat was grey and the dumplings were chewy. When we live by ourselves, I won't ever make dumplings. They're horrible and unnecessary. And when I make stew, it won't have grey meat, it'll be all pink and tender inside."

"And no carrots."

"You need carrots to be healthy."

"Can't I eat an apple instead?"

"I don't think it works like – oh, all right. No carrots."

"You're brilliant."

"But you've got to eat some vegetables. You've got to eat broccoli at least once a week, all right? Finn? Are you listening?"

Finn moved closer to Ava and put his head against her shoulder. She winced and pushed his chin into a more comfortable position.

"Your chin's bony," she told him.

"So's yours."

"Yes, but I'm not digging it into you."

"Dig it into my head. I want to see what it's like."

"No, it'll hurt."

"Please. I'll be quiet."

"But why – oh, all right then – " She jabbed hard at the top of his curly head with the point of her chin. Finn jabbed her shoulder in return. They smothered their giggles in the pillow.

"I was asleep before you came in," said Finn, when their laughter subsided.

"No you weren't, you saw me outside."

"No, before that. I woke up because I had the dream."

"The dream about the beach?"

"Yes."

"Did the wave get you?"

"It never gets me. You always come. Then I woke up and I knew you'd come and see me. You always do that too. Are you all right?" Ava swallowed hard and scrubbed at her nose

34

with the back of her hand. "Why are you crying? Are you thinking about... "

"No, don't. And I'm not. I'm not crying."

"Can't we ever talk about it?"

"We agreed, remember?" said Ava. "It's easier if we never do."

"We could pretend something. We could pretend they're on a long journey. Sailing over the ocean in a little boat."

"Like Moominpappa?"

"Yes."

"That woman they made us see said that's a bad idea," said Ava. "Making stuff up, I mean. We're supposed to accept the reality." Finn shrugged. "I know you don't like her but we've got to look like we're listening and paying attention or they won't... "

"Ever let us live by ourselves," Finn said with her.

"I'm really sorry we ended up here." Ava thumped Finn's pillow into shape and lay back down. "Why do they call it a *home*, anyway? It's like the opposite of a home."

They lay quietly for a while and watched the pattern made by the headlights of passing cars moving over the ceiling. The curtains were a little too short for the high window, the fabric a little too thin to shut out the street lights outside.

"What did you have for breakfast?" asked Ava.

"Toast and cornflakes."

"And a glass of milk?"

"No, just water."

"You're supposed to have milk every day," said Ava. "It's good for you."

"I had milk on my cornflakes."

"That's not enough."

"How do you know?"

"I just do," said Ava.

"I don't like milk just to drink. Anyway, you have to wait for milk. I wanted to do some more drawing." He reached under his bed and scrabbled for a piece of paper.

"What's that?" Ava turned the paper into the orangey light so she could see it better. "Is it a jellyfish? It's really good."

"It's the cushion," said Finn reproachfully. "The round one with the… "

"… button in the middle. The one that used to be in the middle of the sofa. Sorry, of course it's the cushion, I can see it now. It was just the frill around the edge."

Finn looked critically at his drawing. "It does look a bit like a jellyfish."

"It doesn't look anything like a jellyfish. Once you put the button on, you'll see."

Finn put his drawing back under the bed and looked into Ava's face. "Where do you think the cushion is now?"

Ava looked back at him wordlessly.

"Because I had a dream last night," he said. "Everything from our old house was washed out to sea. A big wave came and it went right over the house, and it was all floating away."

"Was it a frightening dream?"

Finn thought about this. "No," he said. "I think all our stuff was quite happy about it really. It was going on an adventure." He hesitated. "So, maybe one day it can all come back to us. Like when things get washed up on the tide. Not boring stuff like wardrobes and tables and things. Just – you know – the important things."

"Like the cushion," said Ava.

"And the books."

"And those brown mugs with the white tops." Ava sighed.

"And the knives with yellow handles."

"And the biscuit tin."

"What biscuit tin?"

"You know," Ava said. "The one with the picture of Winston Churchill."

"I don't remember that."

"Yes, you do. It used to be at Gran's, we got it when she died." Finn looked blank. "It had his picture on the lid, you must remember! He's sort of old, and fat, and bald."

"Is that who it was?" said Finn, amazed.

"Gran used to keep mini-rolls in it."

"I don't remember that either."

"Maybe you were too little. But that's okay," Ava added hastily, seeing his face. "You don't need to remember everything, neither of us do. We've got each other. If we each remember different things, we won't ever forget anything important."

"I was thinking," said Finn. "When we live by ourselves, maybe we could live by the sea. Near the beach. Our beach."

"I don't know, Finn. They might not let us go that far to start with."

"But in the end."

"And it's expensive. Everyone wants to live by the sea, the houses are all really… "

"Could we live in just one room?" asked Finn.

"Could we what?"

"I bet we could live in just one room," said Finn.

"I don't think so. You need a kitchen and a bathroom and a bedroom each and a living room. That's five rooms just to start with."

"I bet we could live in a beach hut," said Finn.

"A beach hut?"

"We could build it ourselves. It can't be very hard. They're only made of wood."

"But… " Ava sat up and wrapped her arms around her knees, pulling the blankets off Finn. "Where would we fit everything?"

"We'd have the bunk beds on one side," said Finn. "That's the bedroom. And a table on the other side. That's the dining room. And a little cooking stove at the back. That's the kitchen. And we can cook outside on the beach whenever it's not raining."

"But what about the bathroom?" Ava was chewing her thumbnail, frowning with concentration.

"We could get one of those toilets they have in caravans

and put it in a little tent."

"They get full up."

"We could empty it at the toilet-block. You know the one at the top of the beach? And we could swim in the sea to get clean."

"What about washing clothes?"

"We could go to one of those places with those massive washing machines. You know, the shop ones."

"Oh my God," said Ava.

"You're not supposed to say *Oh my God*."

"Oh my bloody sodding God," said Ava.

"So what do you think?"

Ava grinned. "We could have bookshelves on the walls."

"And folding chairs to sit in. And a biscuit tin with only nice biscuits in, no malted milks or fruit shortbreads ever."

"And we'll dig a fire-pit and fill it with driftwood and bake potatoes in the embers and have them with sausages cooked on sticks."

"And will you go swimming?"

"Yes. Every day and every night."

"But won't it be too dark to see?"

"I'll swim by moonlight." Finn shifted restlessly in the bed beside her, and she stroked his forehead gently. "And when there isn't any moon you'll have to come and hold a torch so I don't forget which way the land is."

"You promise you won't drown?"

"I won't ever drown," Ava told him. "Promise. Once we get our beach hut, we'll be together for always."

Chapter Four: Now

Donald tramped across the sand and wished he had a uniform. Not a police uniform necessarily, a parking-warden would do it, a jumper with an embroidered council logo maybe, maybe just a badge on a lariat around his neck. Just *something* that would make him seem more like a man with a job to do and less like a...

Like an interfering wanker, he thought, despising himself for his weakness. A decade ago he hadn't needed the signs and signifiers of authority. Just him and his backbone were all he'd needed to get done what needed doing. And it was time he remembered that, because he was on his own with his crusade. Despite the murmurs around the bar and the mutters in the street and the shaken heads over shop counters, no-one else seemed inclined to deal with it. How could they all be so indifferent? Everything about the beach hut filled him with rage.

Maybe they simply trusted him to sort it out? One of those mysterious assignments of responsibility that happened without anyone saying a word. He'd noticed the same thing when it came to the town fete. Perhaps some local junta had met in a room somewhere and decreed, *Yep, Donald's the man to deal with those beach hut nutters. He's got the experience and he knows how to handle himself. Everyone concentrate hard and send out those vibrations. He'll be down there in a week giving them what-for...*

It didn't help that the weather was perfect today. Bright September sunshine warmed his back. The sea was like a box of spilled diamonds, almost too bright to look at. A spaniel leapt past him, its ears streaming in the wind like the hair of a beautiful girl. The surf wasn't up to much, but there were people going in anyway. No lifeguards now until next Easter. Please God they wouldn't wash up drowned and dead on the next tide. His feet were too hot, but it was hard to look authoritative while dangling a pair of Caterpillar boots by their laces. He strode on.

The sound of their laughter reached out to him from within the dunes – two deep throaty chuckles, one tenor, one alto. They were painting the outside of the hut a powdery blue and it was already drying in the warm lick of the wind. The paint was freckled with sand, and fat drops fell onto the billowy dunes below.

"I'm having paint remorse," said the woman, studying the half-painted outer wall.

"You always get paint remorse," said the man. He lay on his back, painting the underside of the tiny veranda.

"The wood looked so nice and clean," she said. "Now I've ruined it. Look, it's like a motorway road sign. What if it stays this colour when it dries?"

"Let's see." The man rolled out from the veranda and rose to his feet in one smooth, fluid movement that Donald envied. "It'll be fine. See? Those dry bits? All pale and pretty."

"But it's all in streaks!"

"That's how paint always dries. If it looks funny we can put another coat on."

"Remember our flat?" said the woman. "In Barley Court? And that massive blue stripe right around the middle of the living room wall? It took us about... "

"... fifteen coats to cover it," he interrupted, "and we kept going back and back and back for more and more paint, and... "

"... in the end it was like it was haunting us, nobody else could even see it, but *we* could still see it, and... "

"Do you remember the flat-warming? And you drank a massive pint glass of that punch I made because we only had pint glasses, and you kept dragging people over to look at the wall and going, *Can you see the blue stripe? Can you see the blue stripe? It's still there, isn't it? The blue stripe's still there,* and no-one could understand what you were on about."

"I shouldn't have left you in charge of the punch. What did you put in it?"

"All the alcohol we had, and some fruit juice. Why did we even have some of that stuff? We can't ever have gone out and bought sherry, can we?"

"When I get to Thailand," said the woman, "I'm going to sit in a bar on the beach for about three days, and make the barman recreate that punch for me. And I'll tell him, 'One day I'm coming back here with my little brother and he's going to order one too. So you'd better get it right.'"

The man put his hand on her shoulder and squeezed it.

"Damn right I will," he said. "One day years from now. We'll get drunk together and point at the walls and go on about blue stripes and drive everyone else mad. And you can show me all the best places to eat. It'll be brilliant. Oh, hi there."

"Hello." Donald realised he had made no plan for how to open the conversation.

"I'm Finn." The man held out a hand, then dropped it. "Actually, best not shake my hand, I'm covered in paint."

"I'm his sister, Ava. Also covered in paint."

Freckles of blue dotted her nose and cheeks and a long stiff strand of blue hung sharp and rigid among the rough tangle of her hair. A sudden painful memory of an afternoon with Ellen, painting Alicia's nursery, paint dripping on her head. She'd had to chop a chunk out of her fringe. She'd frowned into the mirror and said, 'I look ridiculous.' He'd said, 'You look beautiful.' She'd said, 'You're just a man, what would

41

you know.' And he'd said, 'I knew enough to knock you up,' and put his hand on the stretched white dome of her belly. She'd said…

Not here. Not now.

"I'm Donald."

"Nice to meet you," said Ava, sounding alarmingly friendly. "Do you fancy a drink?"

"Um… "

The beach hut door was still bare of paint. Her fingers left little blue smudges as she pushed it open. "We've got Diet Coke, cider, white wine or water. We might even have some ice cubes by now. Or tea and coffee if you fancy something hot."

"How?" Donald demanded. From the corner of his eye, he could see Finn trying not to laugh.

"Camping fridge," said Ava from inside. "And a camping stove. Run off a gas bottle. What can I get you?"

He peeked quietly inside, telling himself that he wasn't being idly nosy, he was gathering useful information and scoping out the enemy. Two folding chairs and a folding table, boxes of books, stacks of paper, an ancient brown suitcase with clothes peeking out. A bunk bed, fitting so perfectly against the wall it must surely have been built by George. Two mounds of bedding topped by pretty patchwork quilts. An upturned wooden tea-chest with one side prised off. A stash of saucepans and a coffee-can crammed with cutlery. On top of the tea-chest, a two-ring gas stove. A blue glazed plant-pot with a miniature sprout of green curling from the black soil. The world's most perfect Wendy house.

"No, really, nothing, thank you," said Donald. What was this strange pair doing about washing? About using the toilet? The public conveniences were locked at 8pm.

"Are you sure?" Ava's smile was quick and pretty. "It's no trouble. We've got biscuits too." Her biscuit tin had a picture of Winston Churchill on it. The chocolate HobNobs looked delicious. "They were only opened this morning, I promise they're not soggy."

"I should tell you I'm not here as a friend," said Donald desperately, then blushed.

"An enemy!" Her laugh jangled down his spine. "Even better. But you can still have a biscuit if you like."

"Look," said Donald. "This isn't a joke. You can't build a beach hut here without permission. You'll have to take it down."

Finn opened his mouth to say something, but Ava shook her head slightly and he subsided.

"We're a tourist town," Donald continued. "The beach is how we make a living. We can't let you ruin it."

"We won't make a mess, you know," said Ava. "We love this beach too. We came here when we were children."

How old was she? In her forties? Her fifties? Her thirties? He was terrible at guessing women's ages, especially when they were dressed like refugees from Glastonbury and had no make-up on.

"It's nothing personal," he went on. "If you don't want to live in a house, that's up to you. But we can't have a shanty town on the beach."

"We won't be here for long," said Finn. He looked reproachfully at his sister. "Ava's going travelling."

"Round the world," said Ava. "India, Thailand, Tibet, Bhutan… "

"Don't forget the cold places. Iceland, Denmark, Alaska, Svalbard, Nova Zembla."

"Then somewhere hot again, but lazy this time. Maybe the Maldives."

"The Maldives? Won't that be a bit boring and full of yachting types?"

"Good point. Okay then, Jamaica. And Haiti."

"Haiti?"

"Haiti looks interesting. Birthplace of voodoo."

"I always thought that was just in Bond movies," said Finn.

"That's why I want to go. To find out."

"Okay, that's a good argument. I'm convinced. Haiti's in. And then… " Finn caught the expression on Donald's face. "Sorry, we're rambling. But the thing is, this is our last few months together before Ava leaves. So we thought we'd spend them here."

"And what are you going to do while you're here?" (Unnecessary question, but he couldn't stop himself. Surely no-one would give them a job. Surely not.)

"Swim. Sleep. Eat. Read. Walk. Look at the sea." Finn shrugged.

"We don't want to make life difficult for you," said Donald. "I'm sure you're… " *(a pair of over-privileged time-wasting layabouts)* "… nice people. But if you want to stay here, there are plenty of hotels. This beach hut has to go."

"Are you the planning officer?" asked Finn, sounding interested.

"What? No, I just live here."

"You live here? Do you own the pub, by any chance?"

"I – well, yes, as it happens I do. Does it matter?"

"I just have this theory," said Finn. "Sorry, I didn't mean to interrupt."

"Actually, I've finished," said Donald. "That's all I came to say. You want a holiday, book a cottage or a guest-house like everyone else. I can give you plenty of people to ask. But you can't stay here, neither can the beach hut, so I'm hoping you'll see sense and take it down without going through the courts."

"That would be a bit pointless," Finn agreed.

"Really?"

"Oh, yes. Massive time-waster for everyone."

"Well, good. I'm glad you agree."

"Because apart from anything else," said Finn, infuriatingly cheerful, "going through the courts will take months and months. Maybe years. Remember Dale Farm? And we won't be here anything like that long. We'll be gone by midwinter night."

Moonstruck hippies, Donald thought.

"Also," Finn continued, "it'll cost a fortune, and take up hours of your time, and make everyone sad and angry. And the end result will be the same whatever you do. We'll be here for a few months, then we'll be gone. I'll clean up, there won't be anything left behind. So you might as well save yourself the hassle and just put up with us for a bit."

"You actually think you can live in a small wooden hut? Right through the autumn gales? Getting cut off at every high tide? With no running water or sewerage?" Donald snorted. "Do you have any idea how cold it gets down here?"

"The wind won't be a problem because we're in the lee of two big dunes," said Finn, "and we've got a heater, and plenty of warm clothes. We have a chemical toilet with bamboo screens, which we'll be emptying at the campsite and taking with us when we go. And a mate of mine built me a portable shower from a garden hose. You can have a go on it if you like. But thank you for thinking of us."

"If I have to come back with someone from the council, I will," said Donald. "Just so you know."

"Fair enough," said Finn. "It's a free country. If you want to waste your time, I can't stop you."

"Look, mate," Donald continued doggedly, "however much you want to think this is okay, you are actually breaking the law. You need to take this seriously."

"I am taking this seriously," said Finn. "I'm taking it very seriously indeed. I'm just not worried. I've done my research, and I know how long it'll take you to evict us. Time's on our side."

"Finn," said Ava, frowning.

Finn gave her a quick, secret smile and a wink.

"And how about you?" Donald asked Ava. (Her travel plans meant she must have money. She couldn't want to live in a one-room shack with autumn coming on.) "Do you want to be dragged through the courts and hassled by the locals? Just because your brother's an idiot doesn't mean you have to be."

He saw instantly this had touched a nerve. When she

looked at him she was channelling that secret female power that made grown men feel like naughty little boys. Ellen used to be able to do it too. Any threat to Alicia and she would transform into an angry Goddess –

"I'd back off if I were you," said Finn to Donald. "Don't anger the Gods and all that."

"By the way," said Donald, maddened by this unwelcome sympathy between them, "that camper van of yours. It's been in the car park for a week. Didn't you know there's no overnight camping allowed?"

"No need to worry," said Finn. "We bought a resident's permit."

"How did you get hold of a… " He stopped himself. His own fault for not checking. *Never ask a question you don't know the answer to.*

"Besides," said Finn, "we're not sleeping in the van. We're sleeping down here."

Donald took a breath. He didn't need to get angry. This was just the opening move. He had the power. The law was on his side.

"You don't need to worry, you know," said Ava, very gently. "We're not trying to start a commune. We'll be gone by midwinter. Finn will take the beach hut down when I leave. And then you'll never have to see either of us again."

When she pushed her hair back from her face, her t-shirt rode up and exposed a slender inch of skin. Was she doing it on purpose? Did she think he'd give in and drop the issue, in gratitude for a glimpse of female flesh? For God's sake, why was he even looking? If he had a type, she was the opposite of it. He loved seeing women dressed and groomed, fresh and scented and lovely. It was an old-fashioned taste but he couldn't help it.

"You'll be hearing from us officially soon," he said.

"Is that the Royal *us*?" Finn asked.

"Good luck getting the paint out of your hair," Donald snapped. It wasn't much of an exit line, but it was the best he could do under the circumstances.

As he strode off across the sand, he heard Finn say idly to Ava, "He fancied you, you know… where are the biscuits?"

Donald straightened his shoulders and walked faster.

Holding her breath, Alicia stood in the deserted café and watched through the gaps in the storm-shutters as her father walked by. Would he guess she was in here? She'd always struggled to keep secrets from him. Wherever she stashed her contraband, he always found it – homing unerringly in on the stolen chocolate in her dressing-up box, the copy of *Cosmopolitan* stashed behind her notice board, the library copy of *Interview with the Vampire* in her underwear drawer. It had even crossed her mind that he had hidden a camera in her room.

But surely, she thought, *surely he won't check for me in here.*

Was she breaking the law? She had been given a key by Emma's dad, and in the bustle of closing up for the season he'd forgotten to ask for it back. Or perhaps it had simply not occurred to him that, with the whole world to choose from, she might elect to spend time in a dark, cold, dusty room, with chairs stacked onto tables, and smelling of old chip-fat.

I'm not doing anything, she thought. *I'm just… being alone in the dark. That's all.*

Nonetheless, she knew she wasn't supposed to be here, standing statue-rigid behind the shutters and watching her father's remorseless progress up the beach.

Emma's dad came in once a week, to turn the lights on and off and check for leaks and make sure everything was in order. She'd taken the time to learn his schedule so she could be sure of her stolen haven. Now, she stood alone in the large cluttered space and felt bliss running through her veins. The plastic gingham covers, still subtly scented with antibacterial spray, were gathering a coat of sand that crept in past the storm-shutters.

Her father glanced towards the café and she felt an electric jolt of fear. Had she done something to give herself away? What if he came round the back and saw the rolled-up shutter?

He was passing the café. He wasn't coming in. She was safe.

What was her dad doing down here anyway? She'd worked out long ago that he didn't like the sea. Left to himself, he'd never venture past the car park. He only came down to the waterline when she dragged him there for exercise, or when she wanted him to watch her swim or surf, or when she was late back and he came to look for her. So where had he been?

Snippets of conversation, overheard in the bar on her way in or out, or as she bought something from the shop, or passed a clump of mothers on the street. *Camper van. Beach hut. Down in the – really? Cold? Draughty? Sheltered spot. Besides, George – Married? Brother and sister. Really? Oh yes. Saw them in the – In here yesterday, buying – Donald said – Did he? Has a point. Maybe, though – Seem nice. Oh yes, lovely. But still –* Her dad's tight-lipped rage whenever they were mentioned.

He's been to see those beach hut people, she thought, *to tell them to move on.*

She hadn't been down there since she and George had stood back and smiled at each other, admiring the small piece of perfection they'd created. She could still feel the smooth wood against her fingers. That night she'd dreamed about it, and about herself living in it, a singular existence in a haven that was hers alone. She held this dream in her head like a pearl in an oyster. She was afraid of losing it to envious reality.

Heart pounding, she made herself count to twenty before leaving the café. She hadn't been forbidden to visit the beach hut for the same reason she hadn't been told not to let herself into Emma's dad's café when it was closed; it had simply not occurred to her father that he needed to tell her these things.

I'm not disobeying, she told herself, in rhythm to her

strides. *It's not disobeying if he hasn't said not to.*

But the truth was she would have gone anyway.

But it's blue, she thought as she approached. In her mind, the beach hut was the bleached-bone colour of sanded wood. And there they were, the man and the woman, not married and not a couple but brother and sister, hippie-looking, flower children, nice manners though, the one thing everyone insisted on… these were the two people whose house she'd helped to build. The two people who were living inside her dream.

"Hi there." The man smiled and raised a hand, a passing greeting rather than an invitation. She stopped and stared anyway. The man was painting the roof now, standing on a chair to reach. The woman was inside, half-hidden by the door.

If they invited her in, would she say yes or no? And if she said yes, what would happen next?

"Do you remember," said the woman from inside the hut, "that time when Ianto got his car stuck on that beach? Tell me about that again, please."

"He said he'd seen someone do it in a film," said the man, dipping his brush into the paint pot. "I can't remember what film it was, but I know it wasn't about people driving cars on beaches. I think it happened one time in the whole two hours. But it got right into his head. He said he wanted to drive *his* car onto the beach and see if he could drive it off again, or if the wheels would sink into the sand. So we drove onto the beach at Ynyslas, and of course it got stuck."

"Instantly?" The woman came out of the hut with two blue-and-white-striped mugs.

The man began to laugh. "Instantly. It wasn't like we were fine for a couple of minutes and then we went a bit too far – he just rolled onto the beach, and as soon as all four wheels were on the sand, like, the *very second* all four wheels were on, we were stuck."

49

"And the tide was coming in?" the woman prompted.

"And the tide was coming in." The man jumped off the chair, put down the paint pot and took the mug from her hand. When he laughed, a slop of tea fell out over the side. "We couldn't call the police because his tax disc had expired. So we just did the best we could with what we had. I think we had the car mats, and Sam and Jenny, and a kid's plastic spade Jenny found in a sand dune, and that was it. We finally got it off just as the waves were washing round the front tyres."

"Now tell me the best bit," the woman said.

The man was laughing so much he had to put his mug down.

"The best bit," he said, "was that Ianto's whole point was you *couldn't* drive an ordinary car onto a beach, because it *would* just get stuck and it *would* take hours to get it off again. He risked his car getting washed away by the sea, just so he could prove that sometimes stuff you see in films isn't strictly accurate." The man was looking at Alicia, keeping a friendly distance between them but obviously aware that she was standing there, watching them. "Are you okay there?"

"I helped George build your beach hut," said Alicia, then felt stupid.

"Really?" The man looked delighted. "You both did a brilliant job. It's perfect. I'm Finn, by the way, this is my sister Ava. Want a cup of tea and a biscuit and a look around?"

She reached into her heart for the image she'd cherished, but already it was shifting, fading, changing. The walls were blue now, not a colour she'd have chosen. It was becoming somebody else's haven. "I'm not sure." If she crossed over the threshold, what would she find inside?

"Do you mind us being here?" Ava asked her unexpectedly.

"What? I mean, pardon?"

"I wondered if you minded us building a beach hut on your beach. If you don't like us being here, you can say, I won't be upset." There were crow's feet at the corners of her eyes. "Well, I might be a bit upset, but we're not going to shout at you or anything. This is your place much more than it is ours."

"No, I don't mind," said Alicia. "I don't mind at all. In fact I wish – I mean, I know I can't, but if I could… " She stopped, desperately wanting to be treated as an equal, a member of the tribe of *Adult* rather than a gawky teenager.

Finn looked tactfully away to let the pink drain from her cheeks and neck.

"We came here when were kids, you see," he said. "We had this dream that we'd build a little hut and come and live here, right by the sea, and wake up every morning and see the gulls and the breakers." In spite of herself, Alicia caught her breath. "Then we grew up a bit and realised it probably wasn't going to happen."

"Only Finn never really grew up," said Ava. "He always insisted we were going to do it. And now here we are. For a few months, anyway."

"Not for good?"

"Until midwinter."

"What happens at midwinter?"

"Finn's going home."

"What about you?"

"I'm going travelling."

"By yourself?"

"By herself," said Finn. "I'd go with her but she won't let me."

"That's because he's got work to do," said Ava.

"What sort of work?"

Finn smiled evasively. Alicia wondered wildly if it was rude to ask.

"He's a writer," said Ava. Alicia could hear the subdued possessive pride in her voice.

"Not really," Finn said.

"Yes, really."

"What books do you write?"

"Fairy   tales,"   said   Ava,   without   the   slightest

51

embarrassment. "A children's book called *Urban Fairy Tales*. He's illustrating it himself. It's beautiful."

"That's so cool," said Alicia. (Did every word out of her mouth have to make her sound like the very worst kind of teenage cliché? Why couldn't she sound normal?) "My dad just owns a pub. And before that he was a policeman." (No! Why did she say that? Ava and Finn were glancing at each other.) "No, please, he doesn't know I'm here. I don't care what he thinks anyway, I think it's brilliant – I mean, more than brilliant – it's – oh – you know… " She kicked crossly at the sand. "I pick my own friends." (If they asked how old she was she'd die of shame.)

"You know, it's really quite possible your dad hates me," said Finn.

"Us," said Ava.

"Oh, no, not you, just me. I told you, he… "

"Finn," said Ava warningly, and Finn subsided.

"So can I see inside?" Alicia asked.

"Fraternising with the enemy?" Ava smiled.

"And have a cup of tea? You said I could have a cup of tea."

"How about I bring you a cup of tea outside?" Ava suggested.

"The politics of tea," said Finn. "Important stuff. Come on Ava, let's live a little. Fraternise away. What's the worst that can happen?"

"Oh, well… here." With sudden decision, Ava unfolded a deck chair and offered it to Alicia. "Sit down and I'll get the biscuit tin."

When she left two hours later, aware that she was now officially late for lunch, Alicia glanced longingly at the beach hut. The paint was just a shell, a millimetre-thick coat that could surely be peeled away. They'd take their stuff with them. They would be here, and then they'd be gone, but the beach hut would remain. Then it would be all hers again, smooth and white and empty, and she could come down with a sleeping bag and lie on the tiny veranda and gaze up through thick blackness at the cold white winter stars.

Chapter Five: Now

She was suddenly so tall, Donald thought, watching Alicia's long hair swinging as she padded around the kitchen. Yesterday, he'd filled sippy-cups and coaxed Rice Krispies into her round, smiling face. Today, she poured Cheerios and coffee in silence and perched at the breakfast-bar with her back to him, as if the process of leaving had already begun and all that remained were the formalities. Another blink and she'd be gone altogether.

"What are you doing today?" Annoying question but he couldn't stop it. "If you need a lift, I'm going to the Cash and Carry."

"No, thanks."

"I'm not going for a bit. You've got time to get ready."

"No, I'm fine. Thanks."

"Have you got other stuff planned?"

"Dad," said Alicia, oozing patience, "I've just woken up, okay? I haven't finished my coffee yet."

Wasn't that supposed to be his line? Mornings used to begin with Alicia assaulting him with a bright relentless torrent of words, while he stumbled round the kitchen in a caffeine-hungry daze. Now she was the one who sat on the stool and buried her nose in her coffee mug while he hovered around her, desperate for a reaction – any reaction – even a negative one.

"Sorry, love." He risked a quick stroke of her hair. "You know, you're growing up so fast. I can't get used to it." Silence. "So you'll be in most of the morning?"

"I don't know."

"Have you got homework?"

"It's not due 'till Tuesday."

"So you have got some?"

"Dad! Stop fussing!"

"This is an important year."

"I know that! They're *my* exams, okay?"

"Well, you're *my* daughter, okay?" (Was she refusing to answer because she was struggling? Or was it just a teenage reflex?) "If I hear from your teachers that you're behind… " (He hadn't meant to start a fight. How had they ended up here?)

"Dad, for God's sake! I've done my homework! I'm getting good grades! I'm not pregnant! What more do you want?" She slipped off the breakfast-stool, her mug still clutched in her hand.

"Don't leave your… "

"Mug in my room. Yes! I know!" She stalked out, her bare feet slapping against the tiled floor. Donald thought about following her, to…

(to what? To apologise? To berate her further?)

(to carry on the conversation and see if he could drag it back into a better place?)

… but instead he put the kettle on to boil and spooned out a mound of Nescafé.

What had she meant, 'I'm not pregnant'? Why throw that in? Was it a coy way of telling him she was now having sex? Please God, she couldn't be. She was still a child.

Outside he saw Mike parking his ancient Peugeot 106, low-slung suspension and sporty seats, a relic of someone else's youth resurrected to serve as a second car. Anna would have the underpowered people-carrier filled with crumbs and socks and ice-cream wrappers. Things were tough for them, he knew. But at least Mike had Anna, her pretty face and her curves and her cynical laugh and her tight budgeting and her no-nonsense way with the children.

Would he swap his life for Mike's? Would he give up his stable, sterile, two-dimensional existence for the near-bankrupt improvidence of three children and two working parents and the deep familiar peace of a shared bed, animal comfort tempered with the knowledge that the wolves prowled a few feet from the door?

He'd often pictured Anna naked. Not with any intentions, just because she was a reasonably attractive woman who he saw reasonably often and who occasionally figured in his dreams. He could imagine her in bed, making love with that combination of crisp efficiency and unexpected earthiness he associated with nurses. She'd be good at it, he was sure. Skilled and deft and self-assured, knowing what she liked and what she didn't, willing to speak up, bold and unafraid. It would never happen. He would never want it to happen. But it was a pleasant fantasy to indulge in.

On the street, a woman walked past wearing blue jeans and a white cheesecloth shirt. She looked like the woman from the beach hut, Ava. Outrage stabbed him deep in his belly – how dare they? His daydream about Anna dissolved, leaving him ashamed of the ten minutes he'd spent fantasising about going to bed with his mate's wife, with his teenage daughter two rooms away.

Would he change his life if he could? Who did he envy most? The man with the loving wife and the surfeit of children, scrabbling every month to pay the bills? Or those cheerful reckless travellers in their illegal encampment? Which would he choose?

"I'd choose you," he said to the empty air.

He had no pictures of Ellen on the walls, just a thick folder of snapshots that he kept locked away in his cabinet with the rest of his past. He didn't need photographs. She was with him every day. The life they should have had. The siblings

Alicia should have argued with and told to stay out of her room. The dishwasher always overflowing. The endlessly-replenished mountains of washing. The clutter of shoes in the doorway.

He'd already phoned the planning department ('Thank you for calling. Your call is important to us and will be answered as soon as a member of staff is available. You are at position… *nine*… in the queue'), and sent an email ('Thank you for your email. Your message is important to us and we will respond within twenty working days'). He'd have to make the time to visit in person.

He'd spoken to the local coppers too, and seen the look of resignation in their eyes. They'd already been down to see them, the officer said. They weren't littering, or causing a nuisance. They'd seemed like nice, reasonable people and they swore up and down they'd be gone again in a few months. It was council land and the dispute would have to go through council channels. He was really very sorry, but…

The kettle had boiled, but he didn't want the coffee after all. He put the mug back in the cupboard instead, making a mental note to remember which one it was so he could use up the coffee-granules next time.

"I'd choose you," he repeated to Ellen as he went downstairs.

Alicia heard her father speak as he passed her door, but couldn't make out the words. He often talked out loud to himself – not often, and thank God never in front of her friends, but enough for it to seem normal. When she was little, she'd sometimes pretended her mother had come back and what she could hear was one side of their conversation. Once or twice she'd even heard her mother's replies, muffled but unmistakeably her voice. She listened hard, hoping for another kindly haunting, but there was only silence.

Her biology teacher had once told her that every cell in the human body was replaced in a seven-year cycle, which meant there was now no part of her remaining that had known her mother. As she blew out the candles on her fifteenth birthday, she marked the moment with the secret thought: *From now on, I'll always have lived longer without her than with her.*

Her diary lay open on her bed, but she wasn't happy with anything she'd written. She'd begun it with the vague idea of creating a new persona, an acceptable alternate for the person she suspected she really was. But when she read her entries back, they sounded stilted and strange. *This morning in class Jake was looking at me and whenever I tried to catch his eye he looked away. What if he asks me out? I don't like him like that, but maybe I should give him a chance.* Alicia slammed the book shut in disgust and tossed it away, then retrieved it and hid it carefully under a stack of sanitary towels. She wouldn't put it past her dad to read it. Would her mother have looked? And if she was somehow still with Alicia and could read what she'd written, would she even recognise the girl she'd left behind?

At least she had the whole weekend ahead of her.

She dressed slowly and carefully. Getting dressed was like putting on armour; it was important not to leave any chinks for people to get at the core of you. Her skin was quite good today, just a couple of spots at her hairline. Make-up made them worse but she smoothed it on anyway, unconvinced by her skin's ability to face the world naked. Why was she bothering? A few years ago she wouldn't have cared. It was pointless, she looked how she looked, it would have to be good enough for everyone else.

She looked in the mirror and saw a fifteen-year-old girl staring back from behind a smooth beige mask, the eyeholes lined black.

"Shit," she said, and rummaged beneath the sanitary towels for her diary.

I'm sick of trying to look how I think I ought to look. I'm sick of trying to act how I think ought to act. I'm sick of trying to sound like I think I ought to sound. From now on I'm writing this diary for ME. I'm writing about what's real.

So. I might see him today. I don't know. It depends on whether I can get away. My dad's supposed to be going out, so...

Just thinking about it makes my stomach churn. Is that what love's like? When your stomach won't stop churning?

She chewed the end of her pen thoughtfully.

I wish it was still summer. I wish there was still a lifeguard on the beach. I wish I could go in the water.

Donald was down on his knees in the lounge-bar counting packets of crisps when he heard George's voice out front. They weren't open for another ten minutes, but George had never got the hang of opening hours. If the door was unlocked, that meant he was allowed to come in. And now here he was, wandering about the place and looking for someone to talk to.

"Hello, Mike." George's voice, loud and cheerful and slightly irritating, made Donald's spine tense up. Some days he got on fine with George. Some days the man drove him insane. He already knew what sort of day today was going to be.

"All right, George." (Mike was going to talk to him, thank God. Maybe when he'd finished counting crisps he could crawl to the lobby and escape upstairs.) "What you up to?"

"I was just passing so I thought I'd come in," said George. (That was the hardest thing about George; when he got bored he'd just turn up and expect you to entertain him.)

"Anything doing?"

"Just those beach hut people," said George. "I can't understand what all the fuss is about, myself. It's a good beach hut."

(The way she'd smiled at him when she said he was her enemy. Why couldn't he shake the memory? Two packets of Cheese and Onion. Six of Salt and Vinegar. Nineteen of Prawn Cocktail...)

"Heard you built it, mate."

"It was this new construction system I saw," said George, his voice taking on that slightly hectoring tone he used to talk about stuff he'd made. "It's based on the tongue-and-groove principle. It's a challenge to get the joints just right, but it makes for a very quick build."

"That right?"

(Had she managed to get the paint out of her hair yet? Did she even care? Seven packs of Scampi Fries. Who ate Scampi Fries? They didn't smell like anything a human being should consume.)

"I don't know how well it'll last, mind you. But they're only going to be there until midwinter."

"I heard that too. Reckon they mean it?"

Silence. Donald could picture the look on George's face. A man who always said exactly what he thought and stuck rigidly to his word, he had difficulty with the concept of other people not doing the same.

"Seem nice enough," said Mike, into the silence.

"They're very nice indeed," said George, with great authority. "Extremely polite."

"That's good." Mike laughed. "Maybe they'll start a trend. Things carry on the way they are, reckon a few of us'll end up living in beach huts. I was saying to Anna last night… "

"Can you go and see if Alicia's here?"

(Donald banged his head on the top of the shelf.)

"Sorry, mate?"

"Alicia. Donald's daughter."

"Do you mind me asking why?"

"She helped me build the beach hut the other day. She did a good job for a beginner. I've got some work she can come and help with if she likes."

"I'm not sure she's in." Mike's voice had got louder and slower, making sure Donald would hear him. Donald began to crawl along the bar.

"Then can you go and look, please?"

"'Fraid I just work here, mate. Upstairs is their flat."

"Oh, I'm sure Donald won't mind," said George. "I've seen you go upstairs before for things."

"Ange isn't here until twelve. I can't leave the bar empty."

(Just out of George's eyeline, Donald reached the connecting lobby, gave Mike a grateful thumbs-up, and crept up the staircase, placing his feet at the edges to minimise the creak.)

"I'll watch it for you."

"If you hang on five minutes Donald should be back soon." (Thank God for Mike, straight and honest and reliable as the tides. Donald was at the top of the stairs now, but he could still hear their voices.)

"I've got quite a lot to be getting on with, so now would be better. It'll only take you a minute."

"No, George, I don't think I can do that… "

"Alicia!" Donald tapped on her door. "Alicia. You decent, pet?"

She was writing in a flowery-covered notebook that she closed when he saw him. Poetry? Diary? Vampire novel? Kids these days didn't seem to do much actual writing, it was all on computers. Odd to see her with that long black smudge down her ring-finger. He'd almost forgotten she was left-handed.

"What is it?"

"George is downstairs," he said. "He's got some mad idea you're going to help him in the yard." Alicia looked horrified. "It's all right. He doesn't know you're here."

"But he'll be here for ages, he always is." Alicia sighed dramatically. "So now I'm trapped up here. Brilliant."

"So you have got plans, then?"

"Dad!"

"What? I'm only asking."

He hated seeing her look at him as if he was her gaoler. Suddenly inspired, he held out his hand.

"I know what," he said. "But you'll have to be quiet."

She put her notebook (Short stories? Alter ego? Letters to her friends?) in the oilcloth backpack he'd bought her for her birthday, bemused by its seventy-pound price tag, and scuffled into her trainers.

"What are we doing?"

"You'll see."

They crept down the corridor, treading gently, avoiding creaky floorboards, Alicia trying not to giggle. He hadn't used these skills for years, but it was true what they said, whatever they said, something about never forgetting how to fall off a log… He opened the bathroom door and ushered her inside.

"Don't ever, ever do this again," he warned, opening the window. Outside was the flat roof of the back porch, a thick ugly slab of concrete but easily strong enough to take twice his weight, never mind Alicia's. "Down onto the porch. Onto the bins, then down. Don't jump, you hear me? Do not jump. Just sit down, dangle your legs over, then drop."

"Are you serious?"

"Before I change my mind."

He thought she might be frightened, but she hooked her leg coolly over the windowsill and dropped onto the porch in one smooth movement. Then she leaned in through the window and gave him a quick kiss.

"You're the best," she told him.

"I'm the worst," he said. "If Social Services ever hear I let you climb out the bathroom window… "

"You saved me from George," Alicia insisted. "You're my hero. Bye."

He swallowed the lump in his throat and watched with pride and terror as his teenage daughter slipped over the edge of the concrete roof, onto the bins, then down and across the car park and out of sight. Her hero. The perfect dad who vanquished monsters and took her on adventures.

Feeling slightly ashamed of the pleasure it gave him to thwart George, he decided it was now his duty to go back into the bar and take over from Mike the task of keeping their visitor entertained. He rehearsed the sentences in his head, bracing himself for the conversation. 'Now then, George. How are you? Having a good day? Alicia? She's gone out with her friends. No, I don't know where, they'll probably be out for the day… '

As he thumped back down the stairs, he realised that, actually, he really didn't know where Alicia had gone, or who she'd gone with.

That's why they have mobile phones, stupid.

Nevertheless, he would have preferred her to tell him something – even a comforting lie. Her insistence on keeping vast swathes of her life a careful blank made him unsettled and nervous, convinced she must have something to hide.

Alone on the seafront, Alicia replayed the window incident in her head. She'd forgotten he could be like that. Earlier he'd driven her mad with his questions and questions and questions. Now, he was her hero. Which was the real dad? Perhaps he was many people, uneasily sharing one body. She'd had the same thought about herself.

The tide was on its way out, making the sea look smaller and flatter and safer than it really was. It wasn't the size of the waves that would get you, it was the undertow. Most days it just tugged at your legs a bit. Some days it knocked over the small and the unwary. Very occasionally it would drag you out and out and out, finally depositing your pale bloated body ten miles down the coast. The undertow was the reason the lifeguards prowled the shoreline and yelled through the megaphone. The undertow was the reason she was strictly forbidden to swim outside the season. The undertow, or maybe her father – who didn't like the water and had never understood her need to be in it whenever possible – did he have a point?

At least she could paddle. She stuffed her socks and trainers into her rucksack. Damp sand shimmied into the clutter, where it would get into her hairbrush and scratch her phone and ruin her lipstick. She secretly liked the loose grains, dancing gold-dust at the bottom of her bag. Wherever she went, the beach was always with her. She knew where she was going, even as she pretended she didn't.

"Hey there." Finn and Ava were on the veranda, lounging comfortably in canvas chairs. Finn was adjusting a gigantic umbrella to cast a shadow over his battered laptop. Ava was reading *The Rough Guide to Shanghai*.

"Hello." Alicia normally hated hovering on other people's doorsteps, trying to find the right words to convey *I'd like to join you* without looking pushy or rude. But the nice thing about Ava and Finn was they never seemed to expect this. They just assumed you were joining them, and that you wanted whatever they were having, and got out the biscuit tin and the kettle, or even a bottle of wine or cider, without any fuss or questions or complicated etiquette of refusal and repetition.

"Grab a chair," said Ava, gesturing towards the beach hut as if it contained thousands of rooms. "They're inside somewhere."

With the door half-closed, Alicia could pretend she was alone and this was her space to do as she liked with. She looked around proprietorially. She'd take down the top bunk bed, of course; no-one but her would ever sleep here. But she liked the extravagant bright colours of the patchwork quilts, one all pinks and reds and greens, one blues and purples and yellows. Perhaps they'd forget and leave the quilts behind.

The tea-chest dresser could go, although she liked its ingenious neatness. But it just wasn't strong enough to last. Maybe she'd get George to make her a more robust version. The bookshelf on the wall she'd keep, and the yellow table and the green chairs, but she'd sand them down to expose the beautiful pale wood. They were obsessed with colours, everything in here was bright and clashing and the walls were covered with maps. How strange that countries as different as Madagascar and Iceland looked so alike when seen from above.

Maybe she'd keep them, as a memento.

On the table, a sheaf of paper was weighted down with a beautiful smooth rock – the kind of beach-treasure you picked up and carried home, kept for a while, then realised you had absolutely no use for and threw away. If she moved the pebble that would be snooping, but flicking through the pages was probably all right. She riffled furtively through.

Words and pictures. This must be Finn's book. It was impossible to pick up the story, but she read the chapter titles. *The children who were lost. The boy who went to find himself. The man in the paper cave. The girl who was caught between two worlds. The sleeping dog. The bloody compliment.* The drawings were quirky and disturbing, people and creatures with heads slightly too big for their bodies and elongated limbs. Their fingers looked like talons. She didn't like them, but she couldn't look away. They were too frightening for kids, surely. She thought about her diary, the struggle to get six lines down on paper, and felt embarrassed to be judging someone else's work.

"Need a hand?" Ava was standing in the doorway. Alicia felt herself turn hot and ashamed, but Ava didn't seem to think there was anything wrong with her guest looking through her papers. "That's the latest draft. The story's finished but he's still working on the illustrations."

"How long did it take to write?"

"A while," said Ava, picking up the chair.

"Too long," said Finn, trying to take the chair from Ava. Ava resisted. "No, come on, put it down. What's the point of having me around if you're going to do the heavy lifting?"

"I can manage," said Ava.

"Yes I know, but I can manage better. Step away from the chair. Hands where I can see them." Ava reluctantly let go of the chair. "Good. Now, I'm going to pick it up... easy, easy, no need to get upset... and keep moving... keep moving...

out we go… and now sit down in *your* chair… perfect. Now you just keep sitting there… and I go back over *here*… and Alicia distracts you with wry observational stories of modern living while I put the kettle on."

"We need a new gas bottle," said Ava. "I put the spare one on this morning."

"I'm on it like a knife. Alicia, get distracting, please, she's going to try and say she's going for it."

"What shall I talk about?" Alicia asked.

"Tell her about that time you were busted for arms dealing coming back from Kazakhstan."

"I've never been… "

Finn pointed a long finger at her. "Kazakhstan. Go."

"Okay," said Alicia. "So, um… I was coming back through the airport, and I got to the check-in counter, and as well as the check-in lady there were these two soldiers with guns, and they said… no, it's no good, I can't think of anything."

"No, that was going well," said Finn, busy with the tin of teabags. Alicia's dad kept the teabags in a ceramic jar that said "TEA", but Finn and Ava had chosen a tall black tin with small people in wide trousers and coolie hats, dancing among dragons and cherry-blossoms. The tin was scratched and old, as if they'd had it for a very long time. Her dad would have said it was unhygienic and thrown it away."Did they speak English? Or do you speak Kazakh?"

"I speak Kazakh," said Alicia.

"Course you do. Only if I ask you to, you won't, because every word of the Kazakh tongue contains at least one syllable that's a swear word in English." The kettle whistled impatiently. Finn filled the mugs. "There you go."

Alicia took a chocolate HobNob from the Winston Churchill tin (another wonderful thing about these two… all their biscuits were nice) and dunked it in her tea. If anyone had asked her to explain the pleasure in sitting in silence with two people, decades older than her and whose surnames she didn't even know, she would have been unable to begin. But

Ava and Finn never asked her to explain.

Clutching boiling mugs of tea, they sat on the veranda and stared out at the ocean.

"Right," said Finn. "I'm off to get a new gas bottle. If the Foreign Legion come looking for me, don't tell them anything."

"It's my turn to go," said Ava.

"Too late, I'm gone." Finn heaved the bottle over his shoulder. "Remember, you ain't seen nothing and you don't know nothing and there ain't nobody called Finn round these parts. Got it?"

"It should be me," said Ava.

"But then I'd be here when the Legion come calling." Finn strode away.

Alicia watched Finn leave with a sense of loss. Finn was fun and silly – easy to listen to, easy to be around. But Ava was beautiful and compelling and intimidating, and she was living inside Alicia's dream apparently without effort, whiling her days away watching the water and talking to her brother. Did she even like Ava? Or did she resent her for having the life she craved? Alicia wasn't sure.

"What does he mean about the Foreign Legion?" Alicia asked, for something to say. Ava laughed.

"Okay, so there was this guy Finn knew once. Andy something. He worked for a circus for a while, and something offshore, and a bit of time as a mercenary – all sorts. Anyway, one time they were talking about travel, and Andy mentioned he hated travelling in Europe because he couldn't use Charles de Gaulle airport. So we asked him why, and he said, 'I joined the bloody Foreign Legion, didn't I, and then I got pissed off with it and left again, and the buggers are still looking for me.' Apparently they're like the Mob, they absolutely never ever forget, and if he ever lands in French territory his passport will trigger an alarm somewhere and they'll arrest him for desertion. Finn spent weeks trying to find out if he really had joined up and deserted, or if it was just a brilliant cover story for not liking France. So ever since, Finn's been pretending he's a Foreign Legion deserter, too. And whenever anything bad happens, he always says, 'Never mind, we can always run away and join the Foreign Legion.'" She laughed at Alicia's expression. "Well, it was funny at the time." She put down her mug, and stretched. "Fancy a swim?"

"In the – in the sea?"

"Why not?"

Because there's no lifeguards and I'll never get away with it and my dad will kill me. "I haven't got a cossie."

"I can lend you one." Ava looked Alicia up and down. "You're slimmer than me but we'll manage."

My dad will kill me. He's bound to find out.

"My mascara will run." *And my dad will kill me.*

"I've got make-up remover. It's okay, you don't have to, I just thought I'd ask."

"Are you going to?"

Ava laughed. "Why do you think I moved here?"

He'll absolutely kill me.

"Go on, then."

It felt strange to wear Ava's costume, stranger still to see her undressed. From a distance, and with clothes on, Ava looked younger than she really was. But in the strong sunlight Alicia saw the lines in Ava's face, the silver threads in her hair, the downward pull of gravity on her body, the lived-in texture of her skin. Alicia secretly stroked the smooth firmness of her own thighs. If her mother had lived, would she look like that too? It was hard to imagine. The costume Ava had lent her was pretty but demure, navy-blue and cut in an old-fashioned shape with a skirt-like panel covering the tops of her thighs. Ava herself wore a black one-piece, plain and workmanlike. A wave slapped hard against Alicia's belly and she gasped.

"You don't have to swim if you don't want to," said Ava. "Don't let me bully you."

"You're not – oh!" Another wave, puckering her nipples

68

and splashing her neck. "You're not bullying me at all, I want to, it's just – cold!"

Ava was ahead of her now, pushing eagerly through the water. Her arms were brown gooseflesh but she plunged deep into the heart of a wave and out the other side, gasping for breath but laughing too. Alicia hesitated a moment, then threw herself after Ava, feeling her entire body contract and resist and protest and then suddenly accept the icy embrace of the ocean, the salt lifting her and the weed clutching at her and the sun sparkling so bright it hurt to look, and when she screamed aloud, wild and forgetful, she heard Ava screaming too, a savage joyful noise to frighten the seagulls, the very opposite of Sirens.

It was about their usual for a lunchtime; just enough to keep him and Mike and Angie busy. A few old regulars in for a pint, filling the hours before a snooze in front of *Bargain Hunt*. A handful of tourists, making the most of childlessness by booking in the off-season. Five tough old ladies with a gleam in their eye who called Donald 'young man' and winked at Mike until he blushed, and sat in the corner drinking gin and cackling lewdly to each other (would he ever be that old, Donald wondered? Would Alicia?). All leaving plenty of time for him to check his phone every few minutes, to see if Alicia had replied to his text.

She still hadn't.

He looked again at what he'd sent.

Hey pet, tea at six so I'll see you then, okay? Dad x

Maybe she hadn't thought it needed a reply. Maybe silence meant she would be back for six. Maybe she hadn't read it yet.

Maybe she was in the boot of a car, plastic ties around her wrists, duct tape across her mouth.

Of course she wasn't. That image was just a hangover from his old job. Nothing like that happened here. And even in the city of their previous life, it happened to hardly anyone.

Check again. Still no reply. He beckoned Mike over.

"You and Ange okay to mind the shop for half an hour?"

"No worries."

"I've got to embarrass Alicia by turning up and talking to her in front of her mates. I mean, she's been out for a whole three hours and hasn't answered her text messages, so of course I've got to track her down and make a show of both of us. That's just the rules, right?" Mike looked embarrassed. "Teenagers. Don't have 'em, mate."

"Bit late now, boss. You should have said about six years ago. Might have made a difference then."

"Hindsight's a beautiful thing. See you in half an hour max, all right?"

"No rush." Mike flicked the pump and began to pour a pint of lager.

A quick scope of the High Street, scanning the usual teenage haunts. Not in the bus shelter, not in the car park, not in the shop, not on the wall. Not on the benches. Not on the chip-shop quiz machine. Other people's teenagers, yes, but not his teenager. His teenager had to be different. What could you expect with a dad who taught her to climb out of windows to escape unwelcome visitors? Her bag slapping rhythmically against her shoulder as she jogged across the car park.

Of course. She'd be down by the ocean, wading into the water as far as she dared. And why not? It was strange, but harmless. It was hours and hours until high tide. She'd be fine. He'd just walk down far enough to see her and then he'd come back again.

Sand blew into his eyes and he blinked it out impatiently. He didn't have to break in on her solitude. He'd just go a little further, just far enough to make sure she was there by the shoreline, and then he'd turn around and go back and she'd never know he'd been checking on her.

Two distant figures were walking out of the sea. Two women, long hair streaming. One of them looked like…

"Alicia!" He had to force himself to knock on the blue door like a normal person rather than beat it in with his fists. He felt as if he could take it off its hinges with a single blow. "Alicia!"

"Dad." The panic in her voice told him everything he needed to know. "I'm just… "

"How dare you disobey me?"

"Dad, I just – I was only… "

The fury erupted. The door flew open under his hands. He stared into the hut. Two women stared back. One young and in her underwear, her jeans draped over her arm, skin like a golden pearl, the unexpected innocent beauty of young wild things everywhere. One much older, wearing plain white cotton knickers, hair tumbled about her face, white bra half-fastened, pale breasts exposed. A temple of female mysteries. The sight tugged hard and painfully at his loins. He stared, transfixed.

"Dad!" Alicia's voice, coming from a woman's mouth. "Dad, get out! We're getting dressed!"

"Fuck." Now he'd cursed in front of her, perfect. "Sorry." He closed his eyes, then the door, turned away, stared madly at the ocean, trying to forget what he'd seen. He'd burst in on them, but he was the one who felt invaded. How could he possibly reclaim the high ground from here?

A fragment of time, and they were beside him on the veranda, Ava's face calm and unreadable, Alicia's angry and mutinous and streaked with make-up. Ava looked at the make-up and smiled.

"Wait a minute," she said, and went inside. Alicia and Donald stared at each other.

"Here." Ava poured something from a bottle onto a pad of cotton-wool and smoothed it over Alicia's face. The make-up melted away under her gentle touch. Donald fought to stop his anger doing the same thing. It was such a tender gesture.

"Now," said Ava to Alicia. "Why don't you go home, and I'll talk to your dad?" Alicia's lip trembled. "It'll be all right, you'll see. Go on. Wash the salt out of your hair or it'll be like straw tomorrow."

"But… "

"Remember, if it doesn't work out, you can always join the Foreign Legion."

This clearly meant something to Alicia; she smiled tremulously and picked up her bag.

"Bye, then."

Donald drew breath beside her.

"Hang on," said Ava. Her hand on his arm was an assault, an insult. "No, keep hanging on… bit longer… bit longer… just 'till she's out of earshot… there." She turned to him and smiled. "Okay, go."

Letting his temper fly loose was a wicked pleasure.

"Do you have any bloody idea how dangerous this beach is to swim off?"

"Yes. Finn nearly drowned here when he was five."

Her answer, like everything she did, threw him off balance.

"Then why the hell did you take my daughter in? I don't care about you, I couldn't care less if you fucking drown. But you've got no right to make decisions for Alicia."

"I rescued him," said Ava. "I know how to keep swimmers safe. I was watching her the whole time. Besides, she's a brilliant swimmer. She could probably rescue me if she had to."

"So the lifeguards we have all summer are just for fun, are they?"

"They're looking out for people who think swimming is twenty lengths in the swimming-bath every three months."

"People drown on this beach. They die. There was one last year."

"People die everywhere. Do you let her cross the road on her own? Get in other people's cars?"

"She knows the rules."

"Teenagers like to break rules," said Ava.

"You don't know the first bloody thing about parenting,"

Donald offered, realising halfway through the sentence that he had no idea if this was true or not.

Ava didn't answer, but he could see the question had touched her. The pain in her eyes gnawed at his own heart.

"That was rude of me," he said reluctantly. "I don't know anything about you."

"I don't have children," she said.

Her hair was rough and laden with salt. It needed a good wash. If he tried to stroke it, his fingers would get caught in the tangles. Ellen had always been so clean, so groomed.

"I won't take her in the water again," said Ava. "I'm sorry, I didn't know you'd mind so much. I should have thought. She just looked so wistful."

"Well, good."

She turned restlessly away from him, closing the beach hut door with a firm little twist of the door-knob. There were no rings on her fingers.

"You should be careful of yourself too," he said, half-reluctantly. "The autumn storms will come in soon. Look, is Alicia making a nuisance of herself?"

"No, of course not, she's lovely."

"She is. That's why I don't want her... "

"Going in the water. Yes, I know. I understand now. I won't take her again."

"Well, thank you."

It was hard not to look back as he left her, but he managed it somehow. He was glad of the slow trudge through the sand, giving him time to think as he walked. Time to wonder.

The man who lived in the cave made of paper

"But where are we going to live?" the brother asked.

"We'll live together," said the sister. "Just the two of us."

"Will they let us?" he asked.

"Not at first. At first we'll have to live with other people.

But when I'm old enough, we can go and ask permission."

"Who do we ask?"

"There's a very old man who lives in a cave made out of paper. His cave is surrounded by guardians, and they work very hard to keep everyone out so that no-one will go in and disturb the old man unless they have something really, really important to say. He's lived in the cave for so long he's forgotten what the sunshine looks like, but every piece of paper is covered in words, and he can remember every single word that's written on them, and every single word is a spell. If we can get in to see him and tell him the right words of the right spell, he'll set us both free and we can live wherever we want."

"But how will we get past the guardians?"

The big sister took her little brother's hand. In her heart, she was very worried. She knew it would take a long time and be terribly difficult to get past the guardians, and finding the right words of the right spell to set them both free would be almost impossible. She knew that, to do this, she would have to give up everything she'd ever wanted for herself. But when she looked down at her brother's face and remembered the promise she'd made him, she knew she would try.

"I'll find a way," said the big sister. "You'll see."

"I knew that really," said the little brother, and smiled.

Of course, the little brother had no idea of how hard it was going to be, or how hard his big sister would have to work, or how much it would cost her. He only knew that they loved each other and she would look after him no matter what. He was just little, and it would be a long long time before he understood.

Chapter Six: 1986

"Let me get those." Finn pushed Ava out of the way and began lifting boxes out of the cab. His voice was beginning to break and the first faint shadow of hair dusted his upper lip.

"It's not very big," Ava warned.

"So? This is the best adventure ever."

"Don't say that to anyone important. We've got to look like we're taking it seriously. They think I'm too young to look after you."

Finn looked disbelieving. "You're a grown up."

"They'd have preferred you to stay with Steve and Marie."

"Can we see inside? Where's the key?"

"Here." Ava rummaged, and found a Yale key.

A clutter of dried leaves lay in the hollow where in better times the doormat would have nestled, and a gust of wind blew in a swirl of dust and three more leaves to join them. The stairs were uncarpeted and spattered with paint, and the walls were a dark textured brown.

"The flat's a bit nicer than the hall," said Ava. Finn was already running up the stairs, his trainers squeaking against the wood.

"Is it this one here?"

"Next one up."

"We're right at the top? Cool." The second staircase was narrower, the patch of floorboards outside the doorway barely big enough for two. Finn tried the handle.

"It's locked." Ava held up a second key. "We need to watch that. It's not a very good area."

"It's a brilliant area." Finn took the key and scrabbled impatiently with the lock and bounded over the threshold. "Hey, this is ace!"

"I know it's small."

The flat's four rooms, cream-walled and brown-carpeted, were crammed into the eaves. An oddly-shaped living room with a miniature kitchen area. A tiny bathroom with a half-sized yellow bath. Two slivers of bedroom separated by a thin stud-wall. When a double-decker bus lumbered past, the windows rattled.

"We can paint it," said Ava. "Once we can afford the paint, I mean. There's not much furniture yet but we can try the second-hand shops… "

Finn wasn't listening. In two giant strides he was across the living room and into the bathroom.

"It needs cleaning," Ava called. "Sorry, I only got the keys this afternoon… "

"Oh my God, no way!"

"What?"

"Come and look at this!"

"What is it? Is it a spider? If it's a spider you have to put it out for me. I can do everything else but you're in charge of spiders."

"No," said Finn, from the bathroom. "Come and look at the wallpaper."

In the damp place behind the toilet, the cream-painted wallpaper was black with mould and peeling away from the wall.

"I know," said Ava despairingly. "We'll fix it, I promise. As soon as I get my first month's pay."

"No, you don't understand." Finn took hold of the edges and, with one smooth quick movement, tore it away and threw it on the floor. "Not that wallpaper. *This* wallpaper."

The tear exposed a shiny brown approximation of wood panelling, like a bad photograph endlessly replicated, marked with patches of adhesive. Ava touched it gently with her fingertips.

"I'd forgotten that," she whispered. "I can't even remember which room it was in."

"The bathroom," said Finn.

"Was it? Oh my God yes, it was! How come you can remember? You must have only been about three or four."

"Our baths used to take hours. I used to wonder if they'd gone to sleep downstairs."

"They'd put us in together," said Ava. "And we argued over who got which towel. We both wanted the one with the whale on it."

"And the one with the orange circles was the worst one. It was always a bad day when one of us had to have the worst towel."

"Then one day," said Ava, "there was a new towel. Do you remember? With… "

"Pawprints! And the whole towel ranking changed overnight."

Ava looked again at the battered panel of wallpaper. "Maybe it's a sign."

"Course it's a sign," said Finn. "This is where we're meant to be."

Ava leaned back against the bath. "What have I done? You were better off before, you had a proper big bathroom with decent towels and a nice bedroom and – all right, I'm sorry, I'm sorry." Finn was looking at her as if she'd grown an extra head. "You're right. It'll be great. Won't it? We'll manage."

"And then they'll get bored of checking on us and leave us alone."

"I wouldn't count on that. Fuck, we need to get our stuff in off the pavement before someone nicks everything." Finn grinned. Ava pointed a stern finger. "Don't say that word. Not ever."

"You can swear in front of me, I don't mind."

"I'm supposed to set a good example."

"You do set a good example."

"No I don't. But I'll try."

Miraculously, their possessions were where they'd left them, neatly stacked into cardboard boxes and ancient suitcases. They brought everything inside in slow, cumbersome shifts – first into the lower hallway, then up the stairs. On the street the collection had seemed insignificant, but once inside, the boxes filled the living room floor.

"We should unpack," said Ava.

"Let's have a picnic," said Finn.

"There isn't anywhere to go."

"An inside picnic."

"The floor's covered with boxes."

"We can sit on the landing outside."

"We really should – oh, you know…" Ava hesitated. "I'm supposed to be acting like a grown up, it's not a proper meal really."

Finn was rummaging in the food box.

"Oh, yes! You bought stuff for ham sandwiches! Result!"

They ate their sandwiches sitting side-by-side on the narrow stairs, leaning against each other for warmth. A dirty dormer window let in grudging amounts of light, and the stairs creaked when they moved. In the flat below, someone inside rattled impatiently at the door, then fell silent.

"Maybe they're shut in," said Finn. "Trapped in their flat."

"Or maybe they're scared."

"Or on the run from the FBI."

"Or from Social Services." Ava put down her glass of water. "You know… "

Finn nodded. "Course I know."

"This isn't just an adventure."

"I know. This is real life."

"And it's really important we don't do anything terrible.

They're watching. If I lose my job or get behind with the bills, or if you miss school or get into trouble, or even if the flat just gets too dirty… "

"I really do get it, I swear."

"I know it seems like I'm worrying about nothing but it was so hard to convince them and I know they'll take you away again."

"Look," said Finn firmly. "I know all that. And I'll do my bit. Promise. I won't bunk off school or forget to do my homework or take up smoking or sell drugs or anything. You can give me a list of jobs to do and I'll make sure they get done. I won't complain."

"I wish you didn't have to worry about it."

"Look, I'll start right now. Let's unpack."

"We haven't got anything to unpack into," said Ava.

"Then let's put boxes in the right rooms," said Finn.

They didn't have a television, so they opened up the rickety sash-window and perched on tea-chests and watched the raggedy stream of people pass by. As dusk fell, the colours turned murky beneath the sodium lamps and the mood of the street shifted from resigned drudgery to a brittle and violent festivity. Two floors beneath them, the takeaway did a steady business.

"This is great," said Finn. "Hey, see that dog? It's going to eat that big mound of dog shit the other dog's left behind and its owner hasn't noticed."

"Urgh. Why do dogs do that? Look at that man there. He's got a t-shirt that says SPAM on it."

"I think he heard you. Quick, he's looking round." The man stared up at the sky as if he'd heard the voice of God. "Duck down."

They hid beneath the windowsill, smothering their giggles.

"So what's your job like?" Finn asked, when they were sure the SPAM man had left.

Ava shrugged. "It's a job. I turn up. I do stuff. They pay me."

"Yes, but what do you do?"

"Typing, filing, answering phones, making coffees. They sit around in suits looking important and smoking. I suppose they must do some actual work sometimes. But whenever I see them that's what they're doing. Look at that man in the Volkswagen. He's wearing a hat. An actual trilby hat. I didn't know you could still buy trilby hats. Do you think he inherited it?"

"Maybe he just got out of jail and that's the hat he was wearing when he went in. Do you want some chips?"

"We can't afford them," said Ava reluctantly. "Sorry."

"I can afford them."

"What are you talking about?"

"I've been saving my pocket money."

"You can't spend your pocket money on food. You should save it for things you want, like trainers and stuff."

"Why would I want trainers and stuff? Steve and Marie gave me five pounds a week."

"Then books or something."

"I wanted to help," said Finn. "We've got nearly three hundred pounds."

"Three hundred! That's a fortune."

"I was aiming for more, but they wouldn't let me get a paper round."

"How can it be three hundred pounds?" Ava was doing sums in her head. "That must be literally every penny they ever gave you."

"I knew we'd need it. We're a team."

"Yes we are."

"So let's celebrate with chips."

"I'll go."

"You will not. Have you seen the people going in?"

"I'm a grown up. You're just a kid."

"That's why they won't take any notice of me."

Finn raced down the stairs, his feet thundering against the wood. A minute later, Ava saw his curly head disappearing into the takeaway. It was ten-thirty, peak business hour for salty greasy food. Ava rested her chin on the windowsill and watched the customers pour in. Three big men with no necks and shaven heads. A minute later, two skinny rat-faced teens. Three girls her own age, tumbling off tall heels. A middle-aged man came out and untied a quivering dog from a lamppost. Two more men went in, loud shirts and loud voices. A couple came out. Then a woman with gigantic boots and dreadlocks. Then Finn, clutching paper-wrapped treasure. His footsteps echoed ahead of him.

"I'll tell you what," said Ava, taking the warm package gratefully. "We'll never have anyone sneak up on that staircase. We don't have to get plates dirty, do we?"

"Course not."

They ate their chips and smiled at each other. Halfway through her portion, Ava dropped the bag onto the floor and screamed with joy.

"We did it!" she yelled out of the open window. "We actually bloody did it!"

On the street outside, people stopped and stared. A no-necked muscle-man gave her a friendly wink and yelled back "Bloody good for you, love."

"We really did," Finn told them. "Well, she did, anyway."

"That your girlfriend, mate?" The man with no neck had made up for it with tattoos. Thick sleeves of ink covered both arms from beefy shoulder to tree-trunk wrist. "Bit young for her, ain't you?"

"My sister," said Finn.

"Yeah? She got a boyfriend? Hey, darling, you got a boyfriend? Fancy a drink? We can get one in before last orders."

"Good night," said Ava firmly, and closed the window.

"You've broken his heart," said Finn.

"I don't think his heart was very involved there."

"Maybe he'll come back tomorrow and bring you roses."

"I hate roses. I'd rather have sunflowers."

"Hang on, I'll tell him." Finn threw the window up. "Hey, mate! Mate! If you want to buy my sister flowers, get sunflowers, not roses! Okay?"

"I'll bear that in mind, mate!" The reply drifted faintly up on a cloud of exhaust fumes and leaf-dust.

"We should go to bed," Ava said, yawning. "Give me those wrappers, I'll put them in the bin. What's that?"

"Present." Finn was grinning from ear to ear.

"What is it?" Ava tore impatiently at the thin brown paper. "Oh, no way! Oh my God! Oh, Finn, where did you find this?"

"At a jumble sale. It was some church thing. I was looking at the bric-a-brac, I moved a Bruce Springsteen LP and there was Winston looking up at me. I couldn't believe it when I saw it."

"It's the exact same picture." Ava caressed the biscuit tin, and then shook it. "And it's even – has it got biscuits in it? It has! It has got biscuits in it! Finn, this is the best thing!"

"I took the packet out of the cupboard while Marie and Steve were putting boxes in the car."

"So they're stolen biscuits?"

"Sorry."

"Don't be," said Ava with her mouth full. "You found Winston! After all these years."

"You don't think it could be the exact same one, do you?" said Finn. "I mean, it's in the same area – and when – when – you know."

"Yep."

"Well, they, you know – they cleared everything out, and – I mean, it *could* be, couldn't it? I know they must have made millions of them, but… "

"Let's say it is," said Ava, putting her hand on the lid. "This is our Winston Churchill biscuit tin. Owned by our grandmother. Passed down through the generations."

"And these," said Finn with his mouth full, "are definitely our biscuits."

"Definitely."

They munched biscuits by the light of the sodium-lamp outside.

"Did you ever wonder if this wouldn't happen?" Ava asked.

"Nope."

"Not for a minute?"

"Not for a minute," said Finn. "I knew you'd sort it. You're amazing."

"I don't know about that."

"You're amazing," Finn repeated. "And one day – I promise – one day I'll do something amazing in return, okay? I mean, I don't know what I'll ever manage that's as good as this."

"It's not much," said Ava. "It's just a grotty little city-centre flat. But we won't be here forever. And we'll get curtains and furniture, and we won't have to sit on tea-chests and we'll have a television."

"Don't say that, it's great! But I didn't mean that. I meant everything else, you know, after Mum and Dad."

"No, don't, we promised we wouldn't."

"No, I won't, I promise, I just meant – I appreciate it. I really do. I don't want to take it for granted."

"You're my little brother," said Ava, stroking his hair. "What else was I going to do?"

Finn wiped his face fiercely with the back of his hand.

"Besides," said Ava, "how do you think I'd cope without you? There is literally no-one else on the entire planet who would think to buy me a Winston Churchill biscuit tin."

"Actually, I nicked it. I waited until the woman went for a cup of tea and then I walked out with it."

"But it's huge! How did you get away with it?"

"I pretended to put some money in the pot and I walked out with it under my arm. No-one said anything. Well, Marie asked why I wanted it, but I said I'd keep pencils in it, and she was happy with that."

"A criminal mastermind. I should probably tell you off."

"If anyone asks, I'll tell them you were really severe."

"It's a deal."

"Together we're invincible," Finn said.

Ava nodded. "Us two against the world."

The sleeping dog

The wild wood was the secret home of many strange people. There was an elderly couple with tangled grey hair who lived in a cave and never wore clothes. They spent their days digging tunnels deep, deep underground, and then they filled the tunnels with secret bonfires to warm the soil, so they could welcome the Winter Solstice with armfuls of daffodils. There was a tall bony woman with the head of a parrot, who kept sparrows in silver cages. The sparrows had miniature men's heads and sang operatic arias in deep, mournful voices. There was a huge white tiger, said to have the power of speech (although apparently it had never yet met anyone interesting enough to talk to).

And in the wood's tangled heart was a clearing, and in the clearing was a house built from smooth white pebbles and a thick coat of whitewash. It was the cleanest, emptiest house in the whole world – so clean and empty you'd almost think it was deserted.

Almost, but not entirely, because you're far too clever to actually think that. If you ever came across this house, you'd quickly deduce that:

A house with no people never stays deserted for long. Before sunset on the first day, a thousand creatures creep in and make their own dusty, grassy, webby, leafy homes in there, turning the house into a busy miniature city. And therefore:

The house must have at least one person living in it, sweeping the house free of all the life that creeps through the window-frames and scuttles down the chimney and blows in through the open doorway.

And, of course, you'd be right.

The man who owned the house lived alone, and nobody knew his name or anything about him, although he was perfectly polite and always well-mannered. He wore white clothes, ate only vegetables and grains, and had almost no possessions. There were no books in the corners and no pictures on the walls. His bed was a washed white flour-sack stuffed with pale dry straw and covered with a soft cream woollen blanket. He had a chair made from bleached wood and clean bones, and a table of cool unmarked marble. He kept his cooking-fire shut up in an iron stove so it couldn't escape and cause trouble, and every Sunday he scrubbed the walls down to the bare stone and applied a new coat of whitewash.

If you met this man, you might think perhaps he was a monk, or a philosopher, or at the very worst a harmless eccentric whose house you could call into when the world was too much to bear and you just needed to be somewhere clean and quiet for a while. (Although naturally, you'd take off your shoes at the entrance.) But in fact, people rarely came to visit. The reason was simple. They were afraid of the man's dog.

The dog was glossy black, and its coat was so thick and lustrous you could plunge your hands in halfway up to your elbows. It was eight feet long from the tip of its nose to the feathery fringe of its tail, and its paws were the size of dinner-plates and its ears were lined with fur. When it groaned and yawned in its sleep, its huge teeth were sharp and white, and its tongue was like red velvet. It slept in a corner where the sun never shone, and no-one knew what colour its eyes were, because no-one had ever seen the dog awake. It simply slumbered on and on in the darkness, breathing slowly and deeply, while the man whitewashed the walls and polished his marble table and stuffed his flour-sack bed with clean straw.

Once, a woman came to the door selling ribbons and laces. She looked at the dog as it twitched and sighed and dreamed, and it looked so soft and glossy that she reached out towards it to stroke its fur. But the man leapt across the room and took her by the hand and begged her not to wake the dog up.

The man was perfectly gentle. But the look in his eyes frightened the woman so much that she ran away and married a fisherman who lived aboard his boat all the days of the year, and never set foot on land again.

After that, the man had considerably fewer visitors.

And then one day a brother and his sister stood in the doorway and looked at the man inside his house, and a terrible and curious thing happened. All by itself, the dog woke up. It yawned and stretched and licked its lips, and raised its muzzle high in the air, sniffing, sniffing, sniffing. Flecks of drool fell from its rosy tongue as its claws tac-tac-tacced across the stone floor towards them.

The man begged, *No, no, go back to sleep, go back to sleep!* But the dog took no notice. Its wild gold eyes were fixed on the brother and sister, its ears pricked and alert. And even when it was close enough for them to smell each other, it was impossible to say if the dog meant to lick their hands, or tear their throats out.

Chapter Seven: Now

Don't be arsey, Donald told himself as he pulled into the car park. *You need them on your side.*

He glimpsed his reflection in the plate-glass doors, and sighed. It was no good. No matter how he dressed or how much he tried to alter his body language, he just naturally looked intimidating. Not aggressive, thank God – he'd known a few scrappy, rat-faced men who could start a fight simply by walking into a room – more a looming physical presence that made everyone else a bit quieter, a bit more well-behaved. He shouldn't complain. On balance it had worked well for him. It was an asset in his current job, an asset as a father. It had been an asset in his former life.

'You've got the face for it,' his former guvnor always said when sending Donald out on a tough job. 'Born to be a copper, you were.' And Donald would swear and Harry would laugh and Donald would say one day soon he'd quit and Harry would tell him he'd never quit, it was in his bones and all of that was before Ellen was sick, before there was something in *her* bones, and Jesus Christ, surely he should be past this now? The sudden blindsiding memory boiled up out of his stomach and grabbed him by the throat, dragging him back into a past he still missed, still longed for. Damn it. Did it show in his face? He turned away from the doors so as not to frighten the people inside.

And he saw Ellen, getting off a bus.

It had been months since he'd seen her – maybe even as long as a year – and the shock was almost as sharp as the first time. Coming home from the cemetery, glancing out of the car window and there she was, bent down to talk to a scrappy terrier. The urge to yell *No, don't touch it – germs, remember?* was so consuming he'd wound down the window before he could remind himself that was all in the past now, she was beyond infection control precautions, beyond all of it, and he closed the window and pulled over and stared at his wife until she saw him watching and her face dissolved into that of a stranger, suspicious and frightened of the strange man watching her over the steering wheel of his Mercedes. Back then, these glimpses of her had torn at his heart. Now he missed them and was grateful when they came to him.

He knew it was out of order to stare at strange women, but he watched anyway, wanting to hold onto the illusion. She wore the kind of outfit he associated with heavy linen napkins and long-stemmed glasses of chilled white wine; a beige trouser-suit, a white blouse, shiny pinky-beige heels that he thought vaguely might be described as *nude*. Her hair was pinned into a shining chignon.

He suddenly remembered his dream from the night before. He stood on the beach at night, watching Ava walking out of the water. Her hair hung down her back and her skin gleamed in the moonlight. He suspected he'd borrowed the image from *Dr No*. When he woke, aroused and unsettled, he felt as if he'd been unfaithful to Ellen.

Was that why he was seeing Ellen now? Had she come back to warn him? That was ridiculous. He had no interest in Ava. She was on his mind because of the whole beach hut situation, because of what he'd come here to do. Ellen was walking away from him now, towards the town centre. If she knew why he was here, would she disapprove? Surely not. She'd liked things to be tidy and orderly. She would never have taken off with her brother to live in a beach hut. A man

88

with a dog blocked his view, and then a horde of teens. Ellen was out of sight.

"Morning," he said, leaning over the desk in what he hoped was a friendly fashion. He could tell from the way the girl shrank back that it wasn't working, and straightened up hastily. That made it worse – now he was blocking the light, his shadow falling across her personal space like the harbinger of an assault. *Next time I'll wear a cheap black suit and sunglasses,* he thought wryly.

"What can I do for you?"

"I'd like to make a complaint," he said.

"Can I ask what the complaint's about?" Her smile was brittle and professional. *Stop being so paranoid; she must be used to difficult people. And besides, damn it, I'm not being difficult! I'm not even getting angry –*

"I'm reporting a case of trespass on council land."

"Can I ask which site? If it's the car park in Trevenna, we appreciate you taking the time but we are actually already aware, and we're going through the process right now to… "

"No, no, this is on a beach." Huge, giant mistake. He was too big and too loud and too male to get away with talking over a young, pretty woman. Now he was the gobby misogynist oik with no manners. What did it matter? He had a valid complaint, she couldn't ignore him; and besides, once the complaint was filed he'd never see her again.

"I see." Her mouth drawn tight and prim. Assigning him to the category of *you won't believe what I had to deal with at work today!* Something for her fiancé to get mad about. The ring on her finger was smaller than the one he'd given Ellen. "Why don't you give me some details and we'll take it from there."

Half an hour later and he was back outside in the car park. Thirty minutes of his life gone, and for what? Ellen, at the end of a bad movie: *Well, that's ninety minutes of my life I'm never getting back.* Her leg brushing casually against his as they stood up to leave, back when such jokes were funny, when they thought they had a wide ocean of years and months and weeks washing at their feet. Back when there was time to be cross or bored with each other, time to waste on bickering and sighs and being mad because the other one had forgotten to put on the dishwasher. The time they'd wasted; the years they'd been robbed of. He thought he'd made his peace with all this years ago but now here it was again, grinning and chattering like a monkey on his shoulder. He swiped angrily at his eyes. His hands were shaking.

It was their fault. That couple of idiots down on the beach, with their crazy cheerfulness and their impossible lifestyle and her scheme to travel the world. He'd been planning to take Ellen to Bangkok when she got ill. Then he'd planned to take her when she got well again. They'd taken a brochure with them to the hospital, wild distraction from the horror they knew was coming. *When they tell us the bad news,* Ellen had said, and he'd interrupted, *If, if they tell us, it could still be good, you've got to think positive,* and she'd shaken her head – *I don't think they tell you to bring someone with you when it's good news, love. So, when they tell us, the first question we're going to ask is, 'How soon will I be well enough to go to Bangkok?' Okay?* There were tears in her eyes as she said it.

God, this was killing him. Why was he doing it to himself? So what if Ava would see the city he'd planned to take his wife to and now would never visit, so what if the pair of them were a couple of spoilt rich kids with no idea of how brutal real life could be. He couldn't drive like this. He'd have to walk into town and buy a coffee.

> *Hey Mike been held up sorry. Are you okay to hold the fort for another hour or so? Angie's due on at lunchtime so you're not on your own.*

Within seconds, the reply flashed up on his screen:

> *No problem take your time. See you when you get back.*

Donald put his phone away and offered up a tiny guilty prayer of thanks for the downturn in the building trade that had delivered Mike to him. Mike was the kind of employee you dreamed about but never quite believed in – dependable, unflappable, unemotional. He couldn't imagine how he'd ever managed to run the pub without him. He turned in the direction of the town.

The town centre was an ersatz copy of the London of his former life. They did say it took a decade for the rest of the country to catch up. Here were the arty boutiques, windows dressed with old mirrors and battered Victorian mannequins. Here were the wine bars that also served a million different coffees, blonde wood and olive paint and square plates on tall tables. Here were the women conspiring over plates of salad and wine glasses large enough to keep a goldfish in. Glancing through a plate-glass window, he saw a faintly familiar figure in tall heels and a beige trouser-suit.

The woman he'd seen earlier, masquerading as Ellen. Across the table from her, his back to the window, was a man in a dark suit. So his vision of her lunchtime had been right. Were they having a nice lunch? The man's back looked tense and angry. Bet they were having a huge whispered argument; too posh to let go in public and really scream at each other. He grinned to himself and went inside to take a closer look.

He ordered a double espresso, enjoying the rich bitter scent even before he took his first mouthful, and then the dirty pleasure of the coffee itself, the way it prickled your throat like cigarette smoke and shot into your bloodstream like nicotine. The couple in the window were drinking wine. A frosty glass of white for him, and, rather unexpectedly, a rich glass of red for her. He'd have thought she'd be afraid of spills.

As if his thought had jinxed her, her fingers grasped clumsily for the stem of her glass and sloshed a luscious red-black glob into her biscuit-coloured lap. He expected her to panic and call for napkins and salt and ice-cold water. Instead, she shrugged and drank from her glass. It was her companion who was angry, handing her napkins and a water glass. Maybe he'd paid for the suit.

"Would you like to order some food from us at all today, sir?" A smooth young man hovered at his elbow, the faintest hint of patronage in his voice as he took in Donald's crumpled suit and crumpled face. Donald took in his opponent with one smooth swift glance (pretty-boy face, gym-bunny physique, flawlessly encased in a tight white t-shirt and tighter black jeans) and felt a surprising wickedness stir within him.

"Would I like to order some food from you at all today," Donald repeated. "Would I like… to order… some food… from you… at all… today."

"Our specials today are the scallops with ginger and spring onion for the starter, and the Thai crab cakes with sweet chilli sauce for the main, and our soup of the day is ham hock with split peas."

"Ham hock and split peas. Imagine."

The boy was looking at him differently now, his smile tight and frantic. "Or, um, maybe just another coffee?"

"Or," said Donald, "and this is just an idea, mind you – is it okay if I suggest an idea?"

"Of course, by all means."

"Thank you." Donald deliberately stretched his lips a little wider than was comfortable. "So, here's my idea. My idea is that you leave me with the menu, and then come back in a few minutes, and ask me once I've had time to take in what's on offer. Is that okay?"

"Absolutely."

"So we're both happy, then?"

"Yes, definitely happy."

"Good. I'm glad we're both happy." Donald took the menu, enjoying the way the boy flinched. His years of being professionally slightly scary were so far behind him that he'd forgotten how much fun it could be to do it on an amateur basis. The boy scuttled away to the bar, where Donald could see him commiserating with the girl who'd sold him his coffee. Frightening a boy that young and green was like shooting fish in a barrel. No challenge to it, but amusing enough if you'd had a bad day. *You have to make your own fun in this world,* he thought, and peered at the menu.

He was getting old; he'd reached the age where he had to adjust the distance before he could focus. Fancy soups, fancy sandwiches, overpriced steak, chicken wrapped in one thing and stuffed with something else. He wasn't sure if he was hungry or not – that annoying in-between state where you could eat, but would regret it later, because by three in the afternoon you'd be starving again and you'd end the day having crammed in a whole extra meal. He was definitely putting on weight. The husband on the other table was trim and rangy. Donald glimpsed his own reflection in the window – a grim-faced thug hunched over a menu as if it was the first time he'd seen such a thing.

Oh, what the hell. He'd have the ham sandwich, plus chips and a side order of guilt. At the other table, the man tried to take his wife's hand.

The waiter was edging closer, trying to work out if it would be worse to bother Donald a second time, or to keep Donald waiting when he wanted to order. Donald beckoned him over.

"Now then," he said. "I've had a good look at this menu of yours, and I think I would like to order a ham sandwich with a side order of rustic chips – but only as long as those rustic chips won't turn out to be oven fries. They're won't turn out to be oven fries, will they?"

"No, sir."

"Excellent. Oh, and before you go, there's one more thing I'd like you to do for me."

"Yes, of course."

"If it's not too much trouble."

"Oh, no, definitely not."

"You don't know what I'm going to ask for yet," said Donald. The boy looked on the verge of tears, and the savour vanished from the game. "Don't worry, lad. I just want to move tables."

"Which table would you… "

"That couple," said Donald, pointing. "They're having a row. I want to eavesdrop while I'm having my lunch."

The boy blinked, but held his tongue. He moved Donald's coffee cup with reverential care, then ran for the kitchen. Donald settled into his new position. His improved table came with improved seating arrangements: a padded leather bar-stool with a low back instead of the high wooden chair. It reminded him of dawn raids, the smells of stale tobacco and spilled alcohol. Of course, he'd never got to sit down on a dawn raid. Maybe this was a sign he'd gone up in the world… his coffee was cold, but he drank it anyway, listening to his neighbours.

"… must be something," the man said. "Is it because we never – because it's still not too late, we could… "

His companion, rather splendidly, said nothing. Donald could see her back stretched straight and tall as she sat in her uncomfortable wooden chair and her ruined beige trousers. A rustic chip fell from her fingers and landed on the floor.

"… you even listening?" Her companion was growing angry again. "This is why we always end up… " his voice sank to a furious whisper. Donald, straining his ears, caught little fragments like scraps of glass. "… believe you're doing… ridiculous… at our age… should be able to… " Donald's sandwich arrived and he seized it from the waiter's hand, making a furious gesture for silence. This was the good bit, he could tell. The waiter dropped the knife and fork.

"I do apologise," the waiter bleated. Donald shushed him again. The boy looked at him with hurt in his eyes. Donald sighed and beckoned him closer in. The boy hesitated. Donald expertly grabbed his arm and pulled him downwards so that his ear was next to Donald's mouth.

"Now I'm going to predict the future," Donald said. The waiter winced, but stayed obediently still. "I predict that the man at that table is going to throw a wad of money on the table and then walk out on his wife. He's going to do it in five, four, three, two… "

"Well then – fuck you!" The husband stood up, reaching blindly into his pocket. "I can't do this any more, okay? I've tried everything and none of it's good enough. I haven't got the energy. See you around." To Donald's deep satisfaction, the man threw a bundle of notes onto his plate, and left.

"I am an unappreciated genius," Donald declared, and let go of the waiter. The wife sighed and put her knife and fork neatly on her plate, but showed no signs of following her husband. Instead she checked carefully through the sheaf of notes before tucking them underneath her wine glass. Donald could see there was at least eighty pounds there. The rustic chips were very good. He ate three in one mouthful, then applied himself seriously to his sandwich.

Between the chips, the waiter and the arguing couple, it had been a surprisingly enjoyable couple of hours. The guilt he felt at leaving Mike to hold the fort while he gallivanted around eating poncey chips was just enough to add spice to the occasion, like adding a little too much Tabasco to a bowl of chilli.

It wasn't until he got back to the car park that he remembered why he'd come. Those bloody idiots in their bloody beach hut, and the bloody council with their bloody list of questions. *Are they causing a noise nuisance?* Well, no, he had to admit they weren't. *Are they causing a litter nuisance?* Actually, he had to give them that, there didn't seem to be any. *Are there more than two people in their party?* No, he'd already said; there were just the two of them, brother and sister. *Are there more than six vehicles parked illegally?* There weren't *any* vehicles. Look, this wasn't just a bunch of travellers – they'd paid some bloke to build them a beach hut! A patient pause. *Are they behaving in an abusive or threatening manner?*

Never mind. He'd reported them. Wheels were in motion. Visits would be paid. Discussions would be had. Eventually, if necessary, court orders would be issued. Finn and Ava would be moved on and life would return to normal. It was time he got back to work. There was his car. It was a long walk round to the entrance. Laboriously, he climbed over the barrier. His coat caught on a bush and his keys fell out of his trouser pocket.

And there, bafflingly, was the woman from the café again, standing at the bus stop, checking the timetable. Everywhere he looked, there she was – slim and elegant in her beige trouser-suit and nude heels. Unless it was someone else, of course. Maybe it was a popular look for women this autumn.

She turned slightly to look up the road for the bus, and he saw the splash of red wine across her thigh. He'd never imagined a woman who dressed like that would be seen wearing stained clothing. Surely she'd just go and buy a new outfit? Come to think of it, he'd never imagined a woman who dressed like that catching a bus.

Then the woman looked towards him, and he saw that it was Ava.

They looked cautiously at each other across the barrier.

"Hello," she said at last, and smiled. He felt his chest tighten, and forced himself to relax. She looked older today, with her hair brushed neatly back from her face and her good but damaged clothes.

"Hi."

"Busy day?"

Why did he feel ashamed? He had nothing to feel bad about.

"That's a bit different," he said, gesturing to the trouser-suit.

"I'm in disguise."

"As a WAG?"

She laughed. He liked that she was laughing. Why did it feel good to make her laugh? They were enemies.

"Something like that. Would I pass?"

"Not with that wine stain."

"No, I suppose not. Never mind. I'll never wear it again after today."

"Not much call for expensive trouser-suits in Bali, then?" What would the council officer say if he dragged her out here and pointed to Ava and said, *Look, this is the woman I'm talking about, the one who lives in the beach hut?* Would she believe him?

"Not really."

"Where's that brother of yours?"

"He's meeting his editor in London."

"It's a real thing, then? His book, I mean?" Donald found it uncomfortable to consider that anyone as odd and feckless as Finn might be capable of producing a finished manuscript, never mind getting a book deal.

"Of course it's a real thing."

"Would you like a lift?" he asked, before he could stop himself.

"The bus is fine."

"No it's not." Why was he trying to talk her round? "The bus is crap, you could be here for hours. And those heels must be murder to stand in. Ellen used to say…."

In the suddenly charged silence, they stared at each other.

Then Ava took three steps towards the barrier and put her hand on the pole. The heels made her clumsy; she stumbled, winced, slipped her feet out of the shoes and tried again. The scissoring of her legs as she climbed over reminded him of a game the girls played in the playgrounds of his youth. Two girls held a tight-stretched skein of elastic bands, a third girl jumped over and over as the barrier crept higher: *floor, ankle, kneesies, bumsies, waisties, armsies,* and the always-impossible *necksies…* the quince bush had dropped stems like caltraps, and he winced as she coolly picked one out of the sole of her foot.

"It's this one," he said, wishing he still had his old

97

Mercedes. Why did he care what she thought of his car? She fumbled with the door handle. "Sorry, it's a bit stiff, I'll do it for you."

As he closed the door on her, he realised she'd left her shoes on the pavement, standing neatly side by side, like watchful sentries at a long-abandoned post.

He hadn't even left the car park before he was regretting his invitation. What could they talk about for the next forty minutes? It was like being tortured. Trying too hard to look relaxed and confident, he was driving like it was his first time behind the wheel. He stalled the engine at the traffic lights.

"When Finn and I were little," said Ava, looking out of the window, "my grandfather had this really terrible car."

He restarted the engine and inched elaborately forward.

"Also," Ava went on, "he was a really terrible driver."

The Focus in front of him dithered between lanes. He fought the urge to swear and honk the horn.

"He used to take us to church sometimes," Ava said, still looking out of the window, "and every time he stopped the car, for any reason, the engine would stall. Every single time. And he'd get really embarrassed. And Finn would look at me and grin."

Just pick a lane.

"And because we knew he was embarrassed," Ava continued, "we knew we shouldn't laugh. But at the same time, it was really funny. And the more Finn looked at me, the funnier it was, and the harder it was not to laugh, and in the end, we had to spend all our journeys to church in total silence and not look at each other or speak at all, and our uncle got really worried and told our aunt he thought we were taking the whole church thing a bit too seriously."

He manoeuvred carefully past the Focus and forced himself not to glare at the driver. "I thought you said your grandfather."

"Actually he wasn't a relative at all. He was just part of a couple Finn lived with for a while, until I was eighteen and they let us live by ourselves. Our childhood was like that, you see."

"Eighteen?" He tried to imagine a girl barely older than Alicia in sole charge of another human being's welfare. What must that have even been like? It had happened to him when he was thirty-eight and he still hadn't felt ready for it. "But what happened to your… "

"This is a game," Ava said. "It's a long drive back home so we might as well. We take it in turns to say something about ourselves the other person doesn't know."

"A game? So it's not true?"

"No, it's definitely true. That's the rules. It's a game, but it has to be true. Your turn."

His conscious mind went blank, but some other part of him that seemed to know how to do this took over. To his horror, the words that came out of his mouth were, "I was sitting behind you in the café where you had lunch. I didn't recognise you though."

She sat very still. The hands folded in her lap were crusted with diamonds.

"Your turn," he said.

"I was talking to my husband," she said.

"I already know that."

"How do you know?"

He glanced at the heavy rings weighing down her left hand.

"He might have been my lover."

"Lovers don't have rows like that. I know what a domestic looks like, I had enough of them when… " He swallowed. "The way you were hissing at each other over the menus – that was marriage, all right."

She considered this.

"Okay, fair enough. So. We were arguing because he wanted me to come back to him. He doesn't understand why I left."

"I already know that too."

"How do you know? Are you sure you're not cheating?"

"No man ever understands why a woman leaves him."

"Is that what happened to you?"

He changed up a gear. "It's still your turn."

"I ran away from him in the middle of a dinner party," she said. "Until I phoned him yesterday, he didn't have any idea where I was."

"That was cruel." Was that too much? He overtook a caravan.

"Maybe he deserved it."

"If he deserved it you wouldn't have got in touch."

"No, that's true," said Ava. "He didn't deserve it. But I couldn't stand being in the same house as him any longer. And someone I trust told me it was time to stop putting him first."

"Was that Finn?"

"Your turn."

"I'll have to think."

Several miles passed in silence.

"I went down to the council offices to report you," he said as they turned off the dual carriageway.

"Doesn't count. I already knew."

"No you didn't."

"Yes I did. You told us you were going to, and now that's what you've done. At least you warned us first. As deadly enemies go, you're a pretty nice guy really."

"Are we deadly enemies?" He was surprised by how much he minded.

"You want my home torn down, you don't like your daughter spending time with me and you absolutely hate my brother. I'd say that qualifies."

"That's not the same as hating you. Maybe we could still… "

"Be friends?"

He pressed hard on the accelerator. "Forget it."

"It's still your turn."

"I don't want my turn."

"I suppose we'll just have to sit in awkward silence, then."

"I suppose we will."

The miles unfurled beneath the tyres and the gorse sped past. After a few minutes, Ava opened her window and held her left hand out, palm upward, to the breeze.

Someone had parked in his usual spot in the car park. He parked next to it instead, and made a mental note to move his car later. Then he caught himself thinking this and told himself to stop being such an old man. Ava was struggling with the door handle. Despite his anger he found himself going round to the passenger side to free her.

With her bare feet and her hair beginning to unravel from its chignon, she looked more like the flower-child with the softly chiming ribbon-trimmed jeans who had stood outside his pub planning lunch with her brother. He looked her up and down.

"That stain's going to set soon," he said.

"I told you, I'm never wearing this suit again."

"How about when you come home from travelling?"

"I won't ever come back either. I'll find the perfect beach and sit in the sunshine and wait for Finn to come and join me." She was trying to sound light-hearted but her mouth looked tense, and as she turned away from him to let the breeze blow her hair away from her face, he thought he glimpsed tears. "Thanks for the lift."

"No problem."

"We used to talk about this, you see," Ava said. "When Finn – when we – you know, when things were tough. About coming to live on the beach. No-one to disturb us. Could you do something else for me?"

"I thought we weren't going to be friends."

"Please."

He was tired of this now. "What is it?"

"Could you not tell Finn where I was and who I met?"

"Sorry, what?"

"Please. If you wouldn't mind. Don't tell him I went to meet my husband. Finn wouldn't understand."

"When would I ever even speak to him to tell him?"

"Just if he happened to come and see you or anything."

The wind was tugging at her hair again. He checked the impulse to tuck the strands behind her ear. "Look, are you – are you in trouble? Do you need help? Because I can put you in touch with people who… "

"Oh, oceans of trouble," said Ava. "More trouble than you can possibly imagine. But I'll get out of it all right."

"Why would your brother mind you talking to your husband? Why would he care? What the hell did he do to you?"

"Finn? Or Paul?"

"Either of them."

"It's still your turn," she told him.

He stood with his car keys in his hand and watched as she picked her way delicately across the car park.

Chapter Eight: 1995

The car park was rammed and the queue was seventeen cars long, but the battered Vauxhall waited patiently for forty minutes, finally squeezing between two Fiestas. After a minute, the doors opened and four people clambered out. The car's engine ticked softly as it cooled.

"Look at that," said Finn, gazing at the beach and sighing with pleasure.

"It's fabulous," Ava agreed.

"It's crowded," ventured Paul.

"I'm going to the loo," said Caroline. "Then let's find the hotel and unpack."

"Let's go down to the beach first," said Finn.

"I've been in the car for seven hours. I want a bath."

"You can wash in the sea," coaxed Finn, following Caroline across the car park.

"I don't want to wash in the sea, I want a bath in a proper bathroom. I feel grubby."

"You look fine," Finn told her.

"Fine?"

"Beautiful. You look beautiful."

"Look, we'll talk about it in a minute, all right?"

"Your brother," Paul said to Ava, "is hopeless with women."

"It's Caroline's fault," said Ava. "What's the matter with

her? Who comes on holiday to sit in a bath?"

"I wouldn't mind sitting in a bath with you," Paul murmured.

"Well, I don't think that was the sort of bath Caroline meant."

Paul put an arm around Ava's shoulder and tried to pull her towards him. She didn't push him away exactly, but she remained separate and still, gazing across the spill of people towards the ocean.

"At least the weather's nice," he said after a minute.

"What do you mean, *at least?*"

Paul looked at the battered parade of seaside shops. Faded postcards on wire racks, flaky sticks of elderly pink rock, buckets and spades dangling from torn canopies like rabbits in a butcher's shop. The pebble-dashed concrete of the public toilets. "It's not exactly Alicante, is it?"

"Of course it's not Alicante. That's the whole point." Ava shrugged his arm off and reached into the car for a floppy straw hat.

"The plane to Alicante wouldn't have to stop every hour to top up the radiator. If you'd let me drive us down… "

"We wouldn't all fit in your car."

"So? Finn and Caroline could have come in his car, we could have come in mine. I don't get why we all had to come in one big mob like a bunch of students. Look, I'm sorry, I'm not trying to start an argument, okay?"

Ava shrugged and turned away from him, as if Paul wasn't important enough to be worth arguing with. She saw Finn and waved eagerly.

"He's still there," Finn called.

"Really?" Ava laughed. "That's brilliant."

"I know. You'd have thought he might have gone by now, but no, he's still going strong."

"How long must he have been there?"

"Well, I *noticed* him when I was five, so it's been at least seventeen years, but he might have come a long time before

104

that. It would be awful if they'd painted over him."

"They wouldn't dare."

"What are you talking about?" asked Paul.

"The stain on the wall of the third cubicle in the Gents," said Finn. "It looks like an upside-down Jesus."

"I'm sorry, what?"

"Well, it doesn't have to be Jesus, to be fair," said Ava. "It could be any old bloke with a beard."

"Course it's Jesus. Who else would manifest himself like that?"

"Good point. And it does look just like him."

"You've seen this too?" asked Paul, bewildered.

"In a photograph." Ava's lips were curving irresistibly upwards. "Finn borrowed the camera and took one secretly. Do you remember? When we got the photos back? And Roy and Janet were looking through them and there were all those photos of the beach and the sea and so on… "

"… and then they got to that one of Third Cubicle Jesus, and they just stopped and looked at it, and… "

"… and you said, 'Oh, that's Jesus,' and they just nodded and kept looking through the pictures… "

"What on earth are you talking about?" Paul demanded. "What's so funny?"

"I'm sorry," said Ava, wiping her eyes.

"I'm not," said Finn. "Third Cubicle Jesus is important. He needs recognition. Shall we go down to the beach?"

"Shouldn't we wait for Caroline?" Paul said to Finn and Ava's backs.

"Oh God, yes," said Finn, looking guilty. When Caroline came out from the Ladies, he put an arm around her and kissed her hair. After a minute, Caroline nuzzled him affectionately.

The sand was crowded and crossed with invisible lines of possession. Finn and Ava picked their way cheerfully through, ignoring tuts and mutters and dark looks. Paul and Caroline trailed apologetically in their wake.

As they got closer to the water, Ava began to shed her clothes. She took off her hat and dropped it on the sand. She peeled off her flimsy cheesecloth shirt (Paul, holding his breath between arousal and embarrassment, was relieved to see the bikini underneath). A quick pause and an awkward shimmy, and her jeans lay like a shed snake-skin, her flip-flops caught in the ends.

"What's she doing?" asked Paul, picking up Ava's clothes. The scent of her made him catch his breath.

"Going for a swim," said Finn.

"She could have said."

"She'll be back soon. Do you want to see the caves?"

"Can't we just sunbathe?" asked Caroline. She had spread a towel on the sand, and she sat down to undress. Until now, Paul hadn't realised there was a right and a wrong way to take your clothes off on a beach. Caroline, sitting on a towel and shrugging awkwardly out of her t-shirt, was the epitome of modesty. Ava's unwrapping had been more like a strip-tease.

"The caves are great," said Finn. "All cold and spooky."

"In a bit," said Caroline. "Can you look after my hairclip?"

Finn took the chunky plastic clip, inspected it dubiously, then stowed it in his pocket. "If we don't go now we'll miss the tide."

"Oh, all right." Caroline sighed. "Are you coming, Paul?"

"I'll wait here for Ava," said Paul. "You kids have fun, okay?"

"I love how you make it sound like we're actually your children," said Finn.

The wind was too strong. The beach was too crowded. It was too far to the bar, and when you got to the bar it probably wouldn't sell you a real drink anyway. Finn's car was uncomfortable, old and unreliable. The hotel would be damp and in need of redecorating, with nylon sheets and luke-warm bathwater. Finn and Caroline would be in the next room, and they'd have to listen to them having noisy enthusiastic sex.

106

Paul sat on the towel and thought about all the things that were wrong with this holiday.

Then he saw Ava, blue-lipped and glowing, and decided he didn't care. He was here for Ava. If, for some inexplicable reason, she was happy here, he'd make himself be happy too.

"How was the water?" He offered her a towel. She smiled, but didn't speak. "You know, the water in Alicante's much warmer."

"The swimming pool's still there," she told him.

"What?"

"It's a sort of lido built into the rock. It's pretty horrible really, like the world's biggest rock-pool. It's covered up every high tide so the water must get changed at least twice a day. But it still looks like every kid on the beach peed in it."

"Then why did you want to go and see it?"

"Because it's always been there."

"Like Third Cubicle Jesus?"

"Like Third Cubicle Jesus."

"Look," said Paul, then stopped.

"What?"

"The thing is, I know you and Finn came here before… "

"That dog's stolen an ice-cream, look."

"Don't try and change the… "

"Would you like an ice-cream?"

"I'm not trying to make you talk about… "

"We always used to get ninety-nines, but once Finn got this thing called a Screwball with a glob of chewing-gum right in the end of… "

"I just don't know how much more I can stand of all this reminiscing," Paul blurted out. "All the way here, you and Finn – oh, look, it's that restaurant that used to be a Wimpy! Do you remember, when you had the ketchup and it fell on the floor? Hey, look, there's that crack in the concrete that looks like that dog we saw once that had those ears… "

"Do we really sound like that?" said Ava, laughing. "Sorry. I'll try and stop."

"Thank you." He looked at Ava, nearly naked in her bikini, the towel slipping from her shoulders, and swallowed. "Can we go and find the hotel now?"

"Shouldn't we wait for the others?"

"No," said Paul firmly, "we shouldn't. They'll work it out for themselves."

"But what's the hurry? We've only just got here."

Paul pulled Ava against him.

"Do you have any idea," he whispered, "how sexy you look in that bikini? No, God, please don't move, you have to stay there for a minute while I get myself back under control."

"Won't I make it worse if I stay here?"

"Good point. Yes, definitely worse. Oh, shit, this is embarrassing." He really was embarrassed, but she was laughing with him, she was focused on him. "Do you have any cold water?"

"Apart from the cold water that's all over me?"

"Talking about how naked and wet you are isn't helping."

"There's the whole Atlantic ocean over there. Knock yourself out."

"Too far. I need to think of something really unsexy. Talk clean to me."

"Saggy grey knickers on the washing-line. Your parents having sex. Third Cubicle Jesus."

"Oh, for God's sake, not that again."

"You said to talk clean."

"I did. Okay, that's done the trick. Third Cubicle Jesus obviously has his uses. Let's go."

The hotel was as run-down as he'd feared, and the bed had a flowery bedspread and thin blue sheets that felt damp against his skin. He straightened his shoulders and told himself he'd survive. He was alone with Ava, and who cared if the bed they tumbled onto was small and unpleasantly soft? When she finally married him he'd take her somewhere beautiful and luxurious, and lay her tenderly down in crisp white linen.

And within a few minutes of closing the door, he didn't care, he was lost and breathless and aching with need, and her hair was in his mouth and her legs were around the small of his back and nothing else mattered.

It was only afterwards, when Ava got up to go to the tiny bathroom and he tried to open the window and realised it was painted shut, that his irritation with the cheapskate shoddiness of this trip returned.

It's Finn's fault, he thought to himself. *This whole thing was Finn's idea.* He tried to suppress the uneasy feeling that, if he hadn't agreed to come on holiday as a foursome, Ava would simply have gone away with her brother without him.

"It's a bit cold," Caroline ventured, peering into the cave.

"We're not far from the old mine workings," said Finn. "There's a massive streak of iron ore – yep, it's still here, come and see."

"Lovely."

"If you lick it you can taste the iron."

"I'm not licking a cave wall, Finn."

"It's all right, it's only rainwater. Come on, live a little." Caroline put out a doubtful pink tip of tongue. "It won't hurt you. The arsenic workings are further up the coast."

"What? Have I just licked a wall with arsenic in it? Why did you make me do that? Ugh, I feel sick."

"No, it's all right, it really is, I promise, I read a book about it. Look, I'll lick it too if you like."

"Why would I want *you* to lick a cave wall? Now what are you doing?"

"I'm going through that pool to see what's on the other side." Finn rolled his jeans up above his knees and waded into the clean blue stillness of the cave-pool. "Man, that's cold."

"Are you sure it's safe?"

"It's probably all right."

"Probably?"

"Well, everyone does it but you can never be totally sure in a cave."

"Finn," said Caroline, "come back. Right now."

"It's fine."

"Finn," Caroline repeated, her voice trembling slightly, "please, come back outside. I'm cold and I'm frightened and I want to go back to the beach and enjoy the sunshine."

"What? Oh no, you are as well. I'm sorry, I didn't realise." Finn splashed back through the pool and put his arm around Caroline's shoulders. "All right, let's go."

"But you haven't finished."

"I'll come back another day."

"You'd rather be poking around in a smelly old cave by yourself than relaxing with me?"

"They're not smelly. They're actually very clean. They get a good washout every high tide and the rainwater drains through them." Caroline looked at him. "I think they're interesting, that's all. But you don't have to come back with me."

"You'll get lonely."

"No, I won't, I'll just bring… "

"Ava," said Caroline.

Finn looked confused. "Why is that a problem?"

"Because… !" Caroline threw up her arms. "Because you'd rather spend time with your older sister messing around in some poxy bloody cave than sunbathing with your girlfriend! Normal people come to the beach to get a suntan!"

"You can get a suntan. I don't mind."

"But I mind. I feel like I'm competing with Ava all the time."

"That's ridiculous," said Finn. "She's just my sister."

"Exactly! Just your sister! I don't know why you even wanted to come on holiday with her and Paul. He doesn't want to be here either."

"Yes, I know," said Finn. "That's sort of why I asked them. I think he wants to marry her. So I thought I'd bring them both down here and see what happens."

110

"You're trying to split them up?"

"I'm not trying to do anything. I just thought it would be an interesting experiment, that's all."

"Look," said Caroline. "How is it even your problem? She's a grown woman. She can make up her own mind. I mean, I know she looked after you when… "

Finn took her hand. "Let's go back to the beach."

"No, we should talk about this."

"I'm sorry, you're right, I'm a terrible boyfriend."

"No, you're not. I just wish you wouldn't keep changing the subject whenever I mention… "

"I'm lucky you put up with me, I really am." He tucked her hair carefully behind her ears. "So lucky. What would you like to do?"

"All right, I get the message… what do *you* want to do?"

"I want you to have a nice time."

"I know you do," said Caroline despairingly. "That's the problem. You actually think I might enjoy being dragged miles across a crowded beach to get cold and damp and miserable."

"You said you liked me because I'm spontaneous."

"Maybe not quite this spontaneous, okay?"

Finn put his arms around Caroline and nuzzled her neck. After a minute, she relaxed against him.

"That feels nice," she murmured.

"I really am sorry I made you lick the wall."

"You should be. Mmm." Finn's fingers were stroking her back beneath her t-shirt, lightly scratching with his fingernails. "That's lovely."

"Lovely enough to forgive me?"

"It's a start."

"Can I kiss you? Or will I taste of cave?"

"Let's risk it. No, not too cave-y."

"Hooray."

"So." Caroline smiled at him. "Shall we go back to the beach now? And get some sun?"

"If you like. Hey, did I ever tell you about Third Cubicle Jesus?"

"Ava! It's me! Are you awake?"

"Well, *now* we both are," muttered Paul, pulling the pillow over his head. It smelled musty. "For fuck's sake, what time is it?"

"Yes, hello, definitely here! Hang on, I'm coming out." Ava pulled on her damp, sandy jeans and a crumpled t-shirt. She closed the bedroom door carefully behind her.

"It's dinner time," Finn announced.

"God, so it is. What shall we have?"

"Remember that fish and chip shop?"

"Oh, yes! Excellent plan." Ava banged on the door. "Come on, Paul, we're going out for fish and chips."

There was an ominous silence from behind the door.

"Food," Ava said.

Still silence.

"He hasn't died, has he?" Finn asked. He knocked on the door. "Paul, are you dead?"

The floorboards groaned, then Paul stood in the doorway in his boxer shorts.

"What?"

"Just checking you're not dead."

"A night in that room and I might be."

"I've got the answer to that," Finn told him. "We're going out for fish and chips."

"You and Caroline might be. Ava and I are going to a restaurant. There's a decent-looking one on the high street."

"It won't be better than the fish and chip shop," said Finn, with the air of one making a biblical pronouncement. "At the fish and chip shop, they sell Qualipies."

"The name says it all," said Ava. "Come on, Paul, you'll like the fish and chips."

"No. Thank you."

"We'll take them down to the seafront and eat them on the

112

beach," said Finn.

"You have to watch out for the seagulls, though," said Ava. "They're bastards, they really are. They have one wingman seagull who walks up and down in front of you and looks hopeful, and then the others swoop from behind and make you drop your chips."

"Is that supposed to make me want to come with you?"

"It's part of the experience," Finn insisted.

"Says who?"

"Paul," said Ava coaxingly.

"Oh, for God's sake," said Paul. "All right. We'll go to the damn chip shop. They'd just better have mushy peas, that's all."

"They have mushy peas," said Finn. "They have everything."

"Including Qualipies," said Ava.

"What's a Qualipie?" asked Caroline, from the doorway.

"No idea," said Finn. "Never had one."

"So why are we talking about them? Is this another one of your stupid jokes?"

"It was a sign," said Finn.

"In the window of the fish and chip shop," Ava added.

"And it said… "

"Qualipies."

"The name says it all!" Finn and Ava were laughing now, enclosed in a warm bright circle of remembrance.

Is it just me? Caroline wondered.

I'm going to kill Finn in a minute, Paul thought to himself. *If I have to listen to him braying with laughter about nothing one more bloody time…*

"Um," said Caroline.

"Let's just go, shall we," said Paul wearily.

The fish and chips, unexpectedly, were marvellous. Paul broke open crisp light golden batter to reveal thick white flakes within, steaming and firm and savoury. Beside him on the wall, Finn squeezed a neat blob of ketchup from a packet and dipped a chip into it.

"These are fantastic," said Paul.

"Finn always knows where the best food is," said Ava, putting her head on Finn's shoulder for a moment. Paul hadn't noticed until then that Ava wasn't sitting next to him.

"That's true, actually," said Caroline. Her hair blew into her ketchup. She pushed it impatiently away. "I hadn't noticed before, but you're right."

"Everyone's blessed with one special thing," said Finn. "The restaurant would have been rubbish."

"You don't know that," said Paul. "You haven't eaten there, it could be brilliant for all you know."

"I don't need to eat there," Finn insisted. "I already know what it's like."

"Because you went there once back in the nineteen-seventies when you were five?"

Ava stirred uneasily, but Finn patted her shoulder.

"Firstly, it's eight o'clock on a Saturday night and the only full tables are the ones in the windows. Secondly, the extractor fan smells funny."

"How can you know the extractor fan… "

"Because I went round the back and smelled it."

"For the love of God, why?"

Finn held up a hand. "Don't interrupt. Thirdly, the chef's too thin. Never trust a skinny chef, it's unnatural. And fourthly, I asked the guy on reception what he thought of the restaurant, and he said it was awful and no-one with any sense would eat there."

"When I talked to him," Paul protested, "he told me it was a great place to eat and he'd book me a table."

Finn shrugged. "I suppose he must have liked me more than he liked you."

"Or maybe he remembered selling you an ice-cream as a child?"

"Paul," said Ava.

"I'm sorry, but – actually no, I'm not sorry. I've just had enough of this whole attitude – *I know this shitty little place better than you do because I used to come here ten years ago when my parents were still...* "

"But the fish and chips are really good," said Ava very loudly. "I'd much rather be here than in the restaurant. Caroline, did you get a drink? Do you want some of my Coke?"

"I'm fine," said Caroline. "You're not supposed to drink with meals."

Finn snorted with laughter. "Where did you hear that?"

"It's true," Caroline insisted.

"Is that a rule for everyone, or just for you? What happens if you forget? Do you explode?"

"If you drink with your meal," Caroline insisted, "you get fat."

"But you're not fat," said Paul.

"That's because I don't drink with my meals."

"Or turn into a Gremlin," said Finn.

"Or melt," suggested Ava.

"Melt?"

"Yes, you know, like the Wicked Witch of the West."

"Oh, yes. Do you remember the time we stayed up all night looking for the Hanged Munchkin?"

"Was that the night we drank that awful cider?"

"That's the one," said Finn. "That really was disgusting. South Western Gold. Ugh. I wonder if you can still get it anywhere?"

"We're in the land of the cider-apple," said Ava. "We'll have a look tomorrow."

"Good plan. Does anyone want to go for a swim?"

"Yes." Ava crumpled up her chip papers and stuffed them in the nearest bin.

"Brilliant. Caroline?"

"You know," said Caroline, "I think I'm going back to the hotel now."

"Me too," said Paul. "Ava, it's really late."

"It is not really late, it's about nine o'clock in the evening."

"Well, it's really late to swim. Anyway, it'll be freezing."

"I don't mind the cold," said Ava.

"And there aren't any lifeguards."

"We'll manage without the lifeguards," said Finn.

"Finn," said Caroline despairingly.

"What?" said Finn, astonished.

"We'd better go back to the hotel," said Ava.

"Had we? Why?"

"Because," said Ava.

Holding hands in the dark, Paul and Ava lay next to each other in the saggy double bed and listened to the muffled voices through the wall.

"They're arguing," whispered Ava.

"Oh, you think?"

("… don't want you to… I just want… ")

("Caroline, come on… ")

Paul put a hand on Ava's thigh, then took it off again.

"Shut up," he ordered her.

"I didn't say a word!"

"You're talking to yourself in your head."

"Sorry, am I not allowed to think now?"

"Not when you're thinking *I hope Finn's all right and I hope she's not upsetting Finn and I wish Finn could just find someone to be happy with and…* "

"Good Lord, you're a mind-reader. Let's see if I can do you." Ava put a hand on his face. He shrugged it off.

"Stop it. I'm really angry, Ava. We're supposed to be on holiday with each other. You're supposed to be paying attention to me. And all I'm getting is a poor second best to your kid brother!"

"You don't understand," said Ava.

"Yes, I do. You think I don't, but I do. I understand a lot more than you think. He's not little any more, he's six

116

foot one and he's out of his teens and he's old enough to do everything legal. You gave up your whole childhood for him, Ava. I won't watch you give up your adulthood as well."

"It wasn't like that! We were… " Ava stopped.

"You were what? What was it like?"

"Never mind."

"Why won't you ever talk to me about this? We've been together eight months and you never bloody let me in. What's the big secret? For God's sake, I don't even know how your parents – where are you going?"

"To knock on their door and make sure they're all right," said Ava, wrapping herself in burgundy silk.

"Are you insane? Get back into bed right now."

"But… "

"But nothing. Dressing gown off. Bed. Right now."

Slowly, Ava peeled off her silky outer layer and climbed back in beside him. Paul wondered if she'd even been planning to go, or if she'd just done it to stop him asking questions.

("… don't know if I can… ")

("… please don't be… I do love… ")

("Ha!… you know… love?")

A door slam and angry feet passing their door. Through the wall, a stream of muffled syllables with the short angry rhythm of fluent cursing, and the sound of someone shuffling around. Another slam of the door, and more footsteps. Silence.

"Well, that's that then," said Paul cheerfully. "Give me a cuddle." He slapped Ava's hand gently away from her mouth. "And stop chewing your nails, I want them long enough to scratch my back. Now where are you going?"

"To preserve the public trust, protect the innocent and uphold the law."

"What?"

"Swimming. I won't be long."

"Liar. Please listen. He's an adult. Leave him be – look,

I can't understand you if you talk to me with a jumper over your head. What did you say?"

"I said," said Ava, emerging from the depths of her polo neck, "I'm not going for Finn. I'm going for me."

The tide had crept close to the top of the beach. On the slender sliver of sand remaining, Finn was writing with a stick.

"I heard Caroline leaving," said Ava, treading carefully around the edge of the words.

"Oh, no, did you? Sorry about that. I didn't mean to disturb you. I think she's gone home."

"I'm sorry."

"It's all right, I don't mind." Finn's teeth gleamed sharp and white in the twilight. "She's been getting sick of me for a while. Doesn't Paul mind you coming down here?"

"Probably." Ava kicked off her flip-flops and dipped a cautious toe into the sea.

"That's what he gets for stopping you from swimming earlier."

"If I drown he'll never let me forget it."

"You won't drown. You're a mermaid in disguise."

"And it's really cold."

"Yes but the hotel rooms are like blast-furnaces. Or mine is, anyway."

"And I haven't got a swimming costume."

Finn glanced around. "Just go for it. Underwear's fine. No-one's watching. Go on, you know you want to."

"Oh, you know what… " Ava was already pulling her jumper off over her head. Seconds later she was gasping and muttering as she waded through the flat, glassy water. Finn folded her jeans and jumper out of the way of the sea, and carried on writing.

Twenty minutes later she was back, dripping and shivering.

"I forgot to bring a towel," she said.

"I didn't." Finn handed her a thin white sheet.

"You went after Caroline with a towel?"

"I didn't go after Caroline at all. I just came down here to do some writing, and I sort of thought you might be along later, so I brought a towel just in case."

"How did you know?"

"Message from Third Cubicle Jesus." Finn turned round and stared at the car park while Ava peeled off her wet underwear and put on her jeans and jumper.

"I must be freezing but I can't feel it," Ava said. "I can only tell because my fingers won't work properly. If I don't go back soon, Paul's probably going to leave too. Why aren't I going back?"

"Because you're not sure if you care," said Finn. "I'm sorry, but it's true. You don't know if you really like him, or if you just feel like you ought to."

"Damn it," said Ava, and sat down on the sand. After a minute, Finn began writing with his stick again.

"What are you doing?" Ava asked.

"It's a story," said Finn. "A story for the sea. It's about a mermaid who tries to live in Birmingham. In the end she realises it won't work, and goes back to the sea, but it takes a long time. There, it's finished." Finn sat down beside her in the sand. "It'll dry out overnight and blow away by morning. And the sea will take the rest."

"Why write it on the sand? Why not on paper?"

"Because," said Finn, and threw away his stick.

"I can't believe how long it's been since we came here," said Ava, gazing regretfully at the glitter of the streetlights reflected in the water.

"Look, the dunes are nearly an island. One day we'll live there."

"When we're old, you mean?"

"Or when everyone's sick of us laughing about stuff only we think's funny." Ava wrapped her arms around herself and shivered. "Are you cold? Have my jacket."

"Then you'll be cold. Besides, it'll never fit."

"Course it'll fit, you dimwit." He wrapped the shabby military jacket around her shoulders. "I could wrap this around you twice if I had to."

"Do you think," said Ava, "I completely fucked us both up when we were kids, and now we'll never be able to sustain proper adult relationships?"

"Don't be daft."

"But… "

"But nothing," said Finn firmly, and tossed Caroline's hairclip into the sea.

Chapter Nine: Now

Today might be the last time, or it might not.

Sometimes I see him and I can't believe it. Not like he's a movie star or anything. It just seems weird. Like I made it up, or dreamed it. Except if it really was a story or a dream, we'd both be the bad guys.

Until she saw him standing in the shadows, Alicia was convinced in her bones he wouldn't be there. It would be like when she'd been younger and thought that if her dad would just take her to London she'd definitely, definitely meet Rihanna. Then their train had pulled into Paddington and she'd suddenly understood how very big the world was and how many people there were in it.

And even if she hadn't constructed it all from daydreams and wishful thinking, there were a million other reasons why he wouldn't be there. He was weighed down with the trappings of adulthood. A home to go to, a car to drive home in, people who needed him. He wasn't even hers to take. She was stealing him.

And yet there he was, leaning against the blank wall of the deserted holiday apartments and watching for her, a miracle in the dark.

It seemed simple at the start but it's not now. Every time we meet it's a risk. I don't want him to get caught. Or me either, actually. I don't want us to get caught.

They didn't speak. That was the first rule, although quite how they'd agreed it was difficult to say. But in his face she saw the faint question: where shall we go? The second rule: he never initiated anything.

Sometimes his passivity irritated and even upset her. But it also made her feel powerful. She could stop it any time she wanted, for days or for weeks or for ever, and he'd never demand to see her, or shame her in front of her mates, or even ask why.

She wanted to take his hand, but she didn't dare. She had more freedom than her friends, who were tangled in a tight network of aunts and uncles and parents' friends from schooldays who had been each other's bridesmaids and best men and best mates for all of their lives. Meanwhile, she floated free and unencumbered, just herself and her father. Nonetheless, the town was always watching. She was careful, to protect him as much as herself. She was fifteen. She was innocent. It would be him her father came for.

She turned the key over and over in her jacket pocket.

You think it'll be simpler when one of you's older, but it was easier when I was going out with Ewan. I mean, people expect teenagers to snog in bus shelters. The town's full of hotel rooms, but we can't exactly book one. I can't bring him home. He can't take me to his place.

She was in control, except she wasn't. Someone else was working the levers when she slipped into the storeroom and whispered "tonight" in his ear. It had been on her all day, a heavy weight of expectation and need, the desire to prove – what? – something. That she could have him. That he was hers. That he wanted her so much, needed her so much, that he'd risk everything he had, just to be with her.

She rolled up the shutter a scant couple of feet and slipped beneath. The air in the café was cool and damp against her cheek. The power was on, but she didn't dare turn on the lights. The harsh electric glow of the strips would seep past the shutters and tell someone, somewhere, that there were people up to no good in the Beach Café. If anyone had seen Alicia slipping off, they'd let her go, because as much as everyone liked her and her father they still didn't really belong here, and telling Donald would be interfering. But business was business, and a potential break-in at the café would be passed on instantly to Emma's dad, Henry. She knew this instinctively, without ever being told.

Anyway, I don't think I'd like it at his house. Too much like cheating. And I'm not a cheater. Except I am. I'm stealing someone else's husband. What's wrong with me? How can I even live with it? Never mind like it. God. I don't want to think about this.

In her pocket were five tea-lights, stolen from the emergency power-cut kit. If there was a power-cut in the next two hours, her dad would go to the box and open it and realise the tea-lights were missing. Somehow he'd divine from this that she was up to no good, not at some undefined point in the past or future but right now, this minute, and he'd come raging out of the pub towards the café, unerringly drawn to the spot where she cowered in the darkness.

Except that, in a whole lifetime of being caught – exposure of everything from stolen biscuits in bed to stolen kisses at the back of the playing-field – this was the one thing she'd kept hidden. Maybe her father wasn't infallible. Maybe she was cleverer than she imagined. The thought gave her confidence as she lifted a chair down and set it in the centre of the tea-lights.

It's like I'm two people. Alicia that hangs out with her mates and texts under the covers and wonders about sex and doesn't know how to talk to boys. And Alicia that sneaks out and meets a married man and does... things. And loves it.

When I was going out with Ewan and we'd kiss or touch or whatever, I was worried the whole time about how it looked. Like, if my legs looked fat, if my stomach was sticking out, if I looked sexy. So it was dead hard to concentrate on what it felt like. I mean, I remember that I liked thinking how I probably looked really cool and sexy for this imaginary audience. But I don't remember ever thinking about if I was enjoying it.

But the stuff I do now...

Sand stuck to his shirt and his jeans and he brushed it off, unselfconscious and at ease in his skin. His hair was untidy and his chin was covered with stubble, black flecked with grey. He seemed completely unconcerned with how he looked, and because of this, she found he looked beautiful.

I mean, my generation's got sex on tap. We've grown up with it. The other day there was this clip going around - My Little Ponies *having sex, for God's sake. We've probably seen more sex than any generation before. But I still only just found out sex isn't about how it looks on camera. It's about how it feels. How messed up is that?*

He was watching her by the candlelight, his hands by his sides, waiting to be told what to do. She felt the blood beating in her ears. What would happen if she did nothing at all? If she just stood in silence, watching him watching her, until the tea-lights burned out and the darkness swarmed back in and it was time for them to leave?

His eyes met hers, and she felt a flash of fear in case she saw anger, resentment, any hint that he thought she was a tease, or – worse – a silly girl who wasn't worth bothering with. If she saw that, ever, even for a second, the whole thing would be over, and worse than over, it would be ruined, smashed, even the memories turned toxic and radioactive.

You're beautiful, his gaze told her.

She pointed to the chair.

Most of us have never had proper sex, but we all know what an orgasm looks like. You open your eyes and your mouth really wide, and you yell 'yes' and 'fuck me' and all that stuff, and then you scream 'YESSSS!' Job done. You don't get sweaty or mess up your make-up or put yourself at an angle where you look fat or ugly. Also, it only takes, like, a few minutes, and it happens dead easily or else you're frigid. Thanks, YouTube.

I mean, I used to think the same.

He watched breathlessly as she unbuttoned her shirt, then his. She saw the tip of his tongue as he licked his lower lip. She could feel the heat in his skin. His chest was hairy. She was never sure if she liked that or not. Some days she enjoyed how smooth and silky she felt by contrast. On other days, the memory turned her stomach and made her vow never to see him again.

There was this one time with Ewan. We were indoors for once, in his bedroom. I thought I'd do a strip for him. So he put on some music and lay down on his bed and I started trying to take my clothes off.

It felt really weird. I didn't know if I was doing it right and I wished I'd practiced in front of a mirror. Then I got really mad with myself because it seemed so pathetic, worrying if I was taking my top off properly. And whether it looked sexy or just really dumb that I was stood with my shirt and bra off, but my skirt and tights and shoes still on. And whether he could tell that my right boob's bigger than my left. And I felt like such a massive twat, but I kept going anyway. Then when I was naked I let him feel me all over and rub against me, and he was really into it and I just wasn't, it was like being humped by a Labrador or something, only he didn't notice.

Two weeks after that, he dumped me. And I wasn't sure if it was because of that day in his room. Like it might be my fault for taking my clothes off and letting him get himself off and not enjoying it.

It was intoxicating, knowing she could do anything she liked. She put her hands on his chest to feel his heartbeat. He half-raised his hands to touch her, then stopped. She waited a minute, wilful, even though she wanted him to touch her. It was still a shock to discover she could want as well as be wanted, that her body could feel pleasure as well as inspire it.

She put his hands on her breasts. He pinched her nipple, slow and firm. It hurt, and then it was blissful. His eyes were half-closed. With his shirt off she could see the middle-aged slackness in his skin and muscles, and she closed her eyes, not wanting to be reminded.

I don't know why I feel guilty when it's him that's cheating. I'm not married. If we got caught they'd blame him, not me.

Grooming. What a stupid word for it. Grooming's lovely. Grooming makes me get all happy and sleepy and relaxed so you can do whatever you want with me. Like that time Caitlin brushed my hair and painted my fingers and toes and gave me a facial, and I was so chilled I didn't realise she'd done my nails old-lady beige. I didn't care even when I realised. She could have painted it all over my face and I still wouldn't have minded. Well, actually I'd have been pretty pissed off when I came out of the grooming trance, but it would have been too late then, wouldn't it?

Actually, maybe grooming is quite a good word for it.

She was sitting astride him now, pressed tightly against him, rocking herself against the rigidity of his body. Afterwards, the word *dry-humping* would make her squirm and cringe. She put his hands around her waist and felt his fingers splay across her skin. They were so big they almost covered her. If he squeezed, he might be able to make his fingertips meet.

Did she enjoy feeling this dainty, this delicate, this small and fragile? Was it erotic or terrifying to be cradled like a porcelain doll? Later this memory would send her bolting out of her chair, hands flying up to cover her face, dyed scarlet with shame. Right now, she liked it. Soon she wouldn't be thinking at all.

Afterwards I feel dirty and disgusting. Is it because I am dirty and disgusting? I'm cheating with a married man, so I must be. Why can't I stop? What's wrong with me? Why do I like it so much? Where does it even come from? Just because he makes me...

I don't even like writing the word down. That's how messed up I am about it.

This was the best moment, when all she could think about was the unbearable sweetness unravelling within her. The first time she'd been completely silent, astonished by the physical truth of something she'd begun to suspect was just a gigantic female conspiracy to make men feel happier about themselves. As it faded, she wondered wildly if she'd done it right – if she'd been too quiet, if he'd be angry, if he'd laugh. Then she'd seen his own expression – face contorted, eyes scrunched tight – and thought for a minute he was having a heart attack.

Look, I'll write it down. He makes me come, cum, have an orgasm, hit the peak, get there, get it on, get it off. Whatever I'm supposed to call it. Why do I have to call it anything? And I love how it feels. I really really do. It's, like, a million times better than I ever imagined. So why do I feel so bad afterwards?

Afterwards there was the awkward part, tissues and mopping up and clumsiness and the sticky feeling and worse than the sticky feeling, the grubby sensation that she'd done something wrong, that between them they had destroyed something rare and precious. She looked away as Mike rummaged in his boxer shorts and, using a clump of tissues from his back pocket, mopped up what she presumed was his sperm. The tissues looked worn and grubby. Why couldn't he at least bring clean tissues? The candlelit glamour was gone, and he was just a tired spent man more than twenty years older than her, performing a graceless ablution in the dark.

When he'd finished wiping and arranging and tucking in, he glanced at the tissues, grimaced, looked towards the bin. She tried not to shudder and shook her head sternly. Emma's father might see them and realise someone had been in over the winter, maybe even have the tissue DNA-analysed (okay, that was absurd... even her own father wouldn't go that far. And besides, it wasn't her... stuff... on the tissue, it was his). Still, the bin wouldn't be emptied until Easter. What was the matter with him?

She could hardly look at him, but she was desperate for him to speak. She wanted him to make sense of the encounter. She wanted him to make it glorious instead of grubby. But what could he say? She'd sometimes imagined the word 'love', but where could love take them? She dug her fingernails into the soft flesh at the base of her thumbs.

The worst thing is I can't talk to anyone about this. Not anyone at all. I mean, Katie and Emma and me, we all say we can tell each other anything, but we can't really. Not this. What would I say? 'Hey, you know what? I've got something going on with this married man'? They'd – actually I don't know what they'd do. Look at me funny. Never talk to me again. Say it's probably because my mother died when I was little, like that's the only thing that's ever happened to me that mattered.

Oh God, I really hope my mum can't see me when I'm with him. What would she even think of me? And why doesn't that stop me? I must be the worst person in the world.

He slotted the chair into its spot in the dust. She blew out the tea-lights and was about to pick them up when he grabbed her wrist and shook his head. The tea-lights were clear hot pools of melted wax. She would have to wait for them to cool.

Did she want him to wait with her? She was sick of his presence now, sick to her stomach, but she didn't want him to leave. She wanted him to be the one left behind, tidying up, rolling the shutter down, while she scurried off to her bedroom and tried to forget. But he wouldn't. That wasn't how it worked. He was treating her like a woman, not a child. It was her job to pick up the mess. Maybe this was her punishment.

Maybe this will be the last time. I ought to stop but I can't. It's like I'm addicted. I can't stop even though I know it's bad. Okay, that's exactly me being addicted.

He leaned towards her, wanting to kiss her. Even this, she thought, even this he wouldn't do without her permission. She didn't want to let him but she did it anyway. How could she despise the taste of his lips when not ten minutes ago her mouth had opened wide to welcome in his tongue, greedy for the closeness? She wanted him to speak but he wouldn't. Then he was gone, ducking beneath the shutter, disappearing into the dark.

She sat on the floor and dabbed angrily at the cooling wax, burning her finger. The wax set instantly into a soft pale blob. When she peeled it off, its identical twin remained behind, a fat white blister that she longed to puncture even though she knew it would hurt more. She stared at the blister and thought about the day it began.

It was the middle of August. The whole town was bleached dry and pale by the hard bright sunshine, a fierce light that took the moisture from your hair and the colour from your curtains, compelling you to strip down to the briefest approximation of modesty your wardrobe possessed. The beach was a writhing maggoty mass of well-oiled bodies. At the café, they were run off their feet. She had done two extra hours and taken three hundred and ninety-six pounds at the ice-cream stall.

"Quitting time," Emma's dad told her once the mid-afternoon rush was over and the queue had reduced to a mere seven customers.

"I don't mind staying."

"Go on with you." He moved her aside and smiled at the harassed-looking lady in the Dolce and Gabbana sunglasses. "What can I get you?"

"Three ninety-nines, please."

"I'll do another hour."

"No you won't, your dad'll kill me. There we go, that's one… "

"Another half an hour."

"You've done a great day's work. Now off you go. And two… "

"But… "

"And three. Six pounds thirty, please… and three pounds seventy back to you, enjoy. Go on. Skedaddle."

"See you tomorrow, then." Alicia slipped out of the ice-cream booth.

She wanted to swim, but the sea wasn't hers today. Today it belonged to the mob, who descended like locusts but left money in their wake, and were therefore necessary. She went home instead, to take a lazy shower and lie on her bed and dream. Mike was heading a busy team behind the bar, efficient and unflappable, tolerating George's lecture on the subject of where the clinker-building technique had originated. Mike was a good worker, they'd be lost without him. That's what Dad always said. She enjoyed the shower, her second of the day. The hot water felt like an outrageous luxury.

Cocooned in her towel, she padded into her bedroom. A fat oblong of sun warmed the polished floorboards. She dropped her towel and stood in the sunshine, wondering if she was actually steaming as she dried. She put on her knickers, then her bra, then her jeans, reached for her t-shirt, and saw Mike standing on the landing, rooted to the spot, gazing speechlessly in through her bedroom door. She had no idea how long he'd been there. When he saw her seeing him, his hands twitched in a helpless gesture that could have been either an apology, or a summons.

She could have screamed. She could have slammed her door shut. She could have picked up her phone and called her father, or the police, or even, with some thought and investigation, his wife. She could have ended his life. She had the power. She was in control.

Why, then, did she not do any of these things? Why, instead of fear or outrage, did she feel a strange thrill of discovery, as if his gaze had remade her into someone else entirely? Why did she cross the landing to where he stood, take his hands in hers, put them on her waist, and hold up her face for him to kiss her?

The candles were cool enough to handle. She swept them recklessly into her bag and crawled out beneath the shutter. The pub was still open, her father still safe behind the bar. The shadows sheltered her as she made her silent way back, up over the bins to the porch roof and back in through the bathroom window. As she pulled it shut, she heard the faint chime of the bell for last orders. She wiped salt from her cheeks and reached into her rucksack for her diary.

So, I saw him. Did I love it, or did I hate it? Am I exploiting him? Is he exploiting me? Why can't these things just be fucking simple?

Today might have been the last time, or it might not.

The bloody compliment

As they travelled, the brother and sister met a very rich powerful man, with a very rich powerful house. It was the sort of house that looks lovely from the outside, and when you see it, you think that the people inside it must be very special in all ways – richer and taller and cleverer and more beautiful and more amusing and more tragic and just generally *more*, in every possible way.

Perhaps one day you might be invited inside a house like this one, and if you're lucky, you'll just be a guest, because once you're on the inside you'll quickly realise that the people inside these houses are just as lost and confused as you, and they've only invited you in because they hope you'll see them in the way they wish they truly were.

Or perhaps they'll be something worse than lost and confused. They may actually believe they are richer and taller and cleverer and more beautiful and more amusing and more tragic and just generally *more*. Those people are very hard to be around. If you happen to find yourself in a house of any description with people like that, I suggest you leave quickly.

But the man the brother and sister met was the most dangerous kind of all. He was the kind of person who looks at someone else and sees, not who they really are, but who the person doing the looking wants them to be.

He looked at the boy's sister and he didn't see all the things about her that were true. He didn't see that she was fierce and brave and wild and strange and dangerous and strong in all the ways she'd had to learn to be, to keep her little brother safe as they wandered through the world. He looked at her and thought, *She's beautiful.* He looked at her and thought, *She needs protecting.* He looked at her and thought, *She'd make the perfect wife for me.*

Only one of these things was true. But it never occurred to the man that he might be wrong, because when he was very young, he'd had a silver spoon glued to his mouth and a pair of rose-coloured spectacles welded into his face, and now he couldn't see anything he didn't want to see. (He was also a rotten kisser, but that's a story for another time.)

And so the man began to give the sister compliments. He wrote them in violet ink on slips of creamy paper and tied them to the collars of small slim creatures with whiskery faces and slender bodies, and he posted them through the door of their tent at night. The notes were so lovely that the sister hardly noticed that, with every compliment he sent her, the small slim creatures would tear off a piece of her flesh and eat it, nibbling her into a different shape.

Chapter Ten: 1996

"Ava, can I come in? There's some bloke here with a load of flowers."

"What? Really? What kind of flowers?"

Finn stuck his head round the bedroom door of his tiny flat.

"Great big ones. Aren't you supposed to be running round like a headless chicken and worrying about shoes?"

"I told Paul I didn't want flowers."

"Well, now's your chance to lose your shit and tear them up and stamp on them. Or we could give them away in the street. Or leave them on a stranger's grave."

"Hang on." Ava wrapped her dressing gown around her and padded down to the communal hallway.

"Hi." The delivery boy was in his teens and, seemingly, deeply ashamed to be delivering a trailing cascade of ivy, white roses and calla lilies to a woman in a dressing gown. "Um, you just sign here, if that's okay?"

"She won't bite," Finn said helpfully. "She sometimes does, but today's her wedding day so she's promised to lay off biting people until after the honeymoon."

"It's true," said Ava. "No biting today."

"I've got a pen." The delivery boy's neck was red. "Um, congratulations on your wedding."

"Steady," said Finn. "It hasn't happened yet. She might

still change her mind. Then I'd have to marry the groom instead, since there aren't any bridesmaids."

"Or the groom might run away," the delivery boy suggested.

"There's no chance of that. He told me once that I'm stuck with him as a brother-in-law because my sister's got his heart locked away in a cabinet, and if he jilts her she'll take it out and burn it, and then he'll die." The delivery boy laughed nervously. "I think that's what he said, anyway. It was either that, or *I've waited for your sister my whole life and I'm going to marry her if it's the last thing I do.* I was a bit drunk at the time." Finn looked at the delivery boy severely. "Are these from her Portuguese lover? Because if they are, then we might as well call the whole thing off."

"I don't know, they just give me the name and the address."

"So they could be from anybody? Maybe they're from that millionaire whose heart you broke when you ran away from him in Rio." Finn took a tarnished silver hip-flask from his pocket and held it out. "Brandy?"

"There's a thing. With the flowers. A card. And I can't drink on the job. Thanks." The delivery boy backed away.

"You can come to the wedding if you like!" Finn called after him. "You could sit next to Ava's future mother-in-law and offer her slices of lemon to suck!"

"He's gone." Ava sighed happily. "Who am I going to tease delivery boys with once I'm married?"

"I think you'll still be allowed to visit," said Finn.

"Yes, but then I'll have Paul with me."

"You could leave him at home. Or he can sit inside and sigh and read the paper like he does now, and we'll go off and be annoying somewhere else."

"Isn't it supposed to be different once you're married?"

"I don't know, I've never been married. Are you supposed to be putting on your dress or something?"

"Oh, probably. Can you hold these for me?" Finn held the flowers while Ava opened the tiny white envelope. She looked at the message for a long time.

"It says," she said at last, "*I know you said you didn't want flowers but I couldn't help myself. I want to take care of you for ever. Love always, Paul.* And it's in his handwriting as well."

Finn inspected the bouquet critically.

"I should hope so. Even someone as rich as Paul shouldn't pay other people to do his handwriting for him."

"I mean he must have gone to the shop himself. Not just phoned it in." Her voice broke on the last word and she scrubbed fiercely at her face with her dressing gown sleeve.

"Oh, hey." Finn put his arm around her shoulder. "I was only teasing. I don't actually think he pays someone else to do his handwriting for him."

"It's not that. It's just – it's just… " she glanced at the clock on the wall. "No, I haven't got time to be upset, I've got to do my make-up."

"Of course you've got time, you daft article. They can't start without you, can they?" Finn laid the bouquet down on the bare floorboards of the hallway. "Come on. We're going to get to the bottom of this."

In the tiny living room, Ava sat on the battered sofa that Finn had re-covered in purple velvet. Finn sat beside her. After a minute, he handed her the hip-flask.

"Drink," he told her.

"I'm driving."

"We'll get the bus."

"In a long white frock?"

"It'll make everyone's day. They'll probably let you on for free. The number 15 stops right by the church. Everything looks better with brandy. Drink."

Ava took a swig.

"Besides," said Finn, just as she was swallowing, "Paul's probably built you a whole new church just outside to save you the walk." Ava choked, and looked at him disapprovingly. "Come on, that was funny."

"I wish you didn't hate him," said Ava, trying to get her breath back.

"I don't hate him, I think he's a decent bloke. *He* hates *me*, but that's because he thinks I'm a bad influence. Have some more brandy."

"I can't. I'll be reeling drunk and his mother will hate me even more than she does now."

"So what if she does? She just feels threatened. You're better than all of them and they know it."

"He's way richer than… "

Finn pointed a stern finger at her. "Don't you dare say it."

"But it makes a difference."

"Right, forfeit." He passed her the hip-flask again. "Two fingers."

"I shouldn't. Oh, what the hell."

They sat in silence for a while and watched the sunlight shine through the sycamore leaves and make patterns on the wallpaper.

"You were up late," Ava said eventually.

"Did I keep you awake?"

"No. I just woke up and saw the living room light was on."

"I had an idea for a short story about a hunter who catches a goat in the woods."

"Does he eat it?"

"No. It's a very beautiful goat, so he decides to keep it as a pet. But the goat knows there's a bad winter coming, and when things get hard enough the hunter's going to eat it anyway. On the other hand, the hunter has a really tight hold on the goat, and he has some quite good vegetables in his bag. And back at home, the goat has a family that needs feeding."

"Carry on."

"So what the goat does is, it pretends to be delighted and to go along with everything the hunter wants. The hunter says he's going to build the goat a beautiful cage to live in, with silk cushions and a gold water-bowl and all the cauliflower it can eat."

"The goat likes cauliflower?"

"Someone has to. And the goat goes along with all of this.

But it's a really long way back to the hunter's house, and they get a bit lost, and then they're out in the dark and the cold. So when night falls, they snuggle together under the hunter's fur cloak."

"Really? Eww."

"This is a fairy tale, so it's okay. Goats are lovely and warm, they run a bit hotter than people, so after a few minutes, the hunter's really comfortable. He falls asleep feeling safe and cosy, and has the most beautiful dreams. The goat stays with him until dawn, so he doesn't freeze to death. Then it creeps out from beneath the fur cloak, grabs the hunter's sack and trots away again. And when he wakes up in the morning, the goat's gone and all that's left is a note: *Thanks for the vegetables.*"

"So now the goat can write?"

"It's a fairy tale."

"It might work better with a deer," said Ava. "Deer are prettier."

"Deer are thick. Besides, goats can be pretty too."

"You didn't say if it was a boy goat or a girl goat. And its family aren't in it very much."

"It's only a first draft. You don't have to marry him, you know."

"Sorry?"

"You don't have to marry Paul," said Finn. "You can still run for it."

"We live together," said Ava. "We own a house. It's the morning of my wedding day. Those are my flowers in the hall. That's my dress on the back of the door. Everyone will be on their way to the church. I'm supposed to be there in forty minutes."

"So what? You can sell the house and bin the flowers and wear the dress to go to the beach in. I'll go and tell everyone. In fact, I insist."

"But I love him."

"But you're not sure."

"Wedding day jitters. I'm nervous about walking down the aisle with all those people looking at me."

"Remember the time we got drunk with those guys from that band? We came down on the coach for the weekend and went to a lock-in in Covent Garden and drank absinthe until two in the morning? And then we got a taxi and broke into that lido? And you took your dress off and went swimming? And even the policemen cheered when you climbed out?"

"Oh God," said Ava, smiling faintly. "Don't tell Paul. He'd be horrified if he knew I'd been arrested for disorderly conduct."

"If he loves you he won't care," said Finn. "I sometimes think he's got this idea of you in his head and he's trying to turn you into it."

"But," said Ava, "the thing is… the trouble is… I think I *want* to be the person he's got in his head. I want to be serene and mysterious and sleek and groomed and well-off. And, and, this is awful, but it's true; it's so lovely not having to worry about money. We were so broke for such a long time… "

"But it was great," Finn interrupted. "You were great. It didn't matter how much of a dump we were living in, you always made it fantastic."

"No, *you* made it fantastic," said Ava. "You still do. Look at this place. It costs half nothing, but I'd still rather be here than – oh, shit."

"So don't get married," said Finn. "You can stay with me while you sort things out."

"But we work at the same office. I can't just not marry him on Saturday, then turn up for work on Monday."

"Get another job."

Ava shook her head. "It's too complicated. I'd have to work my notice and they might not give me a reference and – no, it's no good, I've got to go through with it now. We're a couple, it's all decided anyway. This is just the paperwork. It'll be fine. We're a good team. We get on well. You can't expect to be all excited and happy on your wedding day when

139

you've lived with someone for two years and washed their underwear and seen them sit on the sofa picking their nose." She stood up. "Can you hand me my dress?"

Folds of frail white silk shimmied around her as she pulled the dress over her head. When her face emerged, it was smudged but smiling.

"Just promise me one thing," said Finn, pulling the zip up in one smooth, long tug. "And then I'll shut up about it for the rest of time."

"What's that?"

"Promise you're not marrying him so you'll have enough money to look after me if I need it."

She opened her mouth to reply, then closed it again. Their eyes met in the mirror for a moment, then she quickly looked away.

"No," Finn said passionately. "No, I'm not having this."

"Finn… "

"I'm an adult. You don't have to worry and plan and marry some twatty rich bloke."

"It's not that," said Ava. "It's not. It's not. I promise it's not. I'm sorry. You just took me by surprise."

"You're sure?"

"Get me my make-up bag," she ordered, turning towards the mirror.

"She's late." Nate looked at Paul uneasily. Paul stood tall in his morning-suit, attractive and confident; but then, he'd seen Paul looking like that in front of clients when he'd been throwing up with nerves in a lay-by half an hour before.

"Bride's privilege," said Paul. "Five minutes."

"The vicar's trying to catch your eye."

"Why do you think I'm looking serenely into the distance and admiring the stained glass windows?"

"You don't think – no, never mind. Your mother's hat's amazing. Makes her look like the missing member of Mel and Kim."

140

"You think she's changed her mind, don't you," said Paul.

"What are you talking about?"

"You think she's not going to turn up. Oh God, what am I going to tell everyone?"

"Of course she'll be here, you lunatic," said Nate, a little too robustly to be believable. "She loves you to bits. You're the match made in heaven. Everyone says so."

"Do they?" Paul looked heartened.

"Is she at home? I can nip out and give her a call."

"She's at her brother's place. He probably hasn't even got a phone."

"Her brother?"

"Yeah, you know. Finn. Looks a lot like her, but darker. I can't stand him. She's like a different person with him, they get off into corners and giggle like a couple of mad people." Paul bit at the skin around his fingers. "He's giving her away."

Nate looked at the front left-hand pew, empty even though there would be no-one coming to fill it.

"What happened to her parents, anyway?"

"Don't know. She's never said."

"What, never?" Nate blinked. "Is that – is that normal?"

"Are you saying Ava's not normal?" Paul's glare was so fierce that the vicar looked at them in alarm.

"No! It's just – well. A bit odd. Or maybe not. I don't know. Why are we talking about this? Why haven't you laid on any bridesmaids for me to shag?"

Paul forced a laugh. "Ava wanted a really simple wedding. Half an hour, a couple of witnesses and everyone piles down to the pub after. My mum wanted the full bells and whistles. So we agreed, we'd divide everything up and I'd organise the bits I was in charge of exactly how I wanted them."

"You mean how your mum wanted them."

"Well yes *obviously*, but the point is, the bridesmaids were on Ava's list. And she said she wasn't having any. So you're out of luck."

"I'm never being your best man again."

141

"Think I'd ask you anyway?" Paul checked his watch. "Ten minutes. Ten minutes is normal, right?"

"You look gorgeous." Finn gave Ava a hug.

"You don't think I should have got my hair put up?"

"All in a pile and frizzy like a poodle? I do not."

Ava looked at herself critically in the mirror.

"Stop that," said Finn. "You look amazing. He'd marry you even if you turned up in jeans."

"If we'd got married at the Registry Office, I'd have worn jeans. Those jeans you made me years ago. Do you remember?"

"Course I do."

"But we're getting married in a church, so I'm wearing a long white dress. And it's a very pretty dress, so that's all right. Let's go."

In the hall, flowers trailed magnificently over the dusty floorboards

"I know what," said Finn. He plucked off a long trail of ivy and tucked it into Ava's hair, coiling it around her ears like an Alice band. He picked off a rose and put it behind her ear, then drew three more out of the slightly collapsing cascade and put them in her hand. Then he knocked on the door of the ground-floor flat.

"Quick, let's go," he said, as shuffling feet approached the door. "She thinks I steal stuff out of her bins."

"So why have you given her my flowers?"

"When she was younger she was a fantastic beauty, and men gave her flowers every night and begged her to dance. But they were all so lovely, she couldn't possibly choose one to marry. So she just kept on accepting dances from strangers and letting them bring her flowers. And now she's old and she doesn't get flowers any more, so I thought it would be nice for her to have some. There's the bus, we'll have to run."

"I can't run in these shoes," said Ava, struggling.

"Take them off. I'll hold the bus up." Finn ran wildly

142

down the street to the bus stop and stood in front of the bus, his arms held out. Ava took off the high-heeled slippers and ran in her bare feet.

"Thank you," she said gratefully to the bus driver, who looked at her dress and grinned.

"Two, please," said Finn, dropping the coins into the slot.

"Twenty minutes." Paul chewed his lip. "Maybe I should go outside and look?"

"It'll be fine," said Nate.

"I know!" snapped Paul. "Shit. The vicar's coming to talk to me. What do I say? What do I say?"

"Don't worry," said the vicar cheerfully. "I had a wedding last Saturday, the bride was an hour late. The wedding car had a flat tyre. I'll have a word with the guests, let them know this is all very normal and expected."

"There you go," said Nate, falsely hearty.

"If she doesn't show, I bet he'll tell us *that* happens all the time too and he had a wedding last Saturday where the bride ran away to Bolivia," said Paul.

The bus was full, so Ava and Finn stood at the front, much to everyone's approval. Several passengers began singing hymns. An old lady in a hat told Ava that her first child would be a boy "because you've got the hips for it, dear". Finn gave his top-hat away to a small boy in a yellow coat, then offered round the hip-flask to anyone who wanted some. Since no-one did, he passed it to Ava. Ava took a deep swallow, then steadied herself against the pole to put her shoes back on. When they got off at the church, the passengers gave them three cheers.

In the churchyard, Finn stopped and put his hands on Ava's shoulders.

"Absolutely sure?" he asked.

Ava's cheeks were flushed and radiant with brandy.

"Is it true?" she asked. "About the old lady who lives

143

downstairs? And all the men who bought her flowers and danced with her?"

"Course it's not. Well, I say that. I never asked. She only ever speaks to me to shout about the bins."

"But it sounds true," said Ava. "Yes, I'm absolutely sure."

"Where is she?" Paul looked past his mother, thin and beige under a disapproving hat, towards the door.

"It's only half an hour," said Nate.

The vicar's twinkly gaze was flagging. His face was subtly rearranging itself into a bracing configuration of *these things happen, it isn't the end of the world.* Paul's palms were damp. He resisted the urge to wipe them on the silvery trousers. The hat felt ridiculous, heavy and oppressive. Why had he let his mother talk them into morning-suits? The congregation were beginning to rustle and mutter.

Then, blessedly, there was a stir of expectation in the back pews. The door opened a crack to admit Finn's head, tousled and curly. When Nate caught his eye, Finn gave him a highly visible thumbs-up. The congregation's shoulders dropped by a relieved/disappointed half-inch. The organist struck up the wedding-march, the doors opened and there was Ava, in a simple white frock, three white roses in her hand and a strand of ivy tucked into her hair. (What had happened to the bouquet? If the florist had lost the order, he'd burn their shop down.) Finn's morning-suit fitted, although his hair was the same mop-like mess it always was and he appeared to have forgotten his hat. The vicar's cassocked body expressed nothing but broad satisfaction. His mother looked at Ava's dress, at her flowers, her hair, judging, assessing, sighing, whispering, wishing. His aunt patted his mother's hand consolingly. His father caught Paul's eye and winked.

Ava looked beautiful.

Afterwards, Paul remembered just two things about the moment when he finally bagged the prize he'd been pursuing since the night he'd looked up, half-cut with his tie in his

144

pocket, and seen the girl from the office, subtly isolated and subtly out of place, watching the party with a cool, amused gaze.

The first memory was the vicar speaking the words: *Speak now, or forever hold your peace.*

No-one spoke. When did that ever happen, outside of Gothic novels and romantic comedies? But he'd been aware of a slight movement from Finn, a glance passing between him and Ava, which Paul in his heightened state instantly interpreted as meaning, *Want me to?* and Ava's wordless reply, *It's fine.* And at almost the same time, Nate on his right-hand side stirred and coughed and when Paul frowned at him, he saw the same question written on Nate's face. *You sure?* And then the moment was past, and the ceremony rolled on, the vicar seemingly unaware of the supporting parties for both the bride and the groom subtly implying that perhaps this marriage was, after all, a mistake.

The second memory was how it felt when the vicar told him to kiss the bride. Ava's lips beneath his, tasting faintly of chemical strawberries, and the knowledge that he'd finally done it; he'd made her his.

"Lovely reception." "Fabulous reception." "Brilliant choice for the reception." Compliments fluttered like confetti as the guests streamed through the elegant Georgian portico, pale and ornate like the wedding-cake. "Glorious place for a reception."

Paul's mother, who had been swollen with anger since Finn had cheerfully explained that he and Ava had come on the bus, relaxed and began to smile. "Our wedding present to them," she told the guests, and after her third glass of champagne, "My wedding present to Paul."

"Thought she wasn't going to show," Paul's uncle murmured in the startling glossy white of the tiled bathroom.

"Christine said that." Paul's father rinsed his hands beneath huge brass taps. "Mind you, I think she might have found the silver lining."

"Still not keen?" Peter grimaced.

"Still not keen. Thinks she's not good enough." David reached for a fluffy square of towel. "Well, no, that's not it. She just – you know, Ava – difficult background. Skeletons in the closet." He inspected the towel. "D'you know, these things look just like Paul's old nappies."

"Meant to ask," said Peter. "Where were all her family?"

"You saw it. Her brother. That scruffy pillock who walked her down the aisle."

"And that's it?"

"Yep. The parents – well, now I come to think of it, I'm not sure what happened to the parents. I mean, I assume they're dead. Anyway, Ava pretty much brought him up. They were in some sort of foster care for a while. Then it was just the two of them."

"Huh."

"I mean," said David, "it's pretty impressive. The way she took responsibility. But still." He shrugged. "Maybe Christine's got a point. You never quite know what goes on in her head… "

"Ah well. Too late now."

David laughed. "Just the next forty years of sighs and looks and awkwardness to get through. God, what an awful conversation to have on your son's wedding day. Let's get another drink."

Peter clapped him on the shoulder with a slightly damp hand. "It'll settle down once there's a sprog on the way."

The residual awkwardness drowned gloriously in a lake of champagne. Men took off their ties and women took off their heels. Girls in bright frocks leaned flirtily against boys in conservative suits. Paul and Ava clung to each other's hands like dazed survivors of a shipwreck.

Nate wanted to get Paul on his own, but there was always another relative who'd known him and Paul when they were at school, another tipsy girl gushing about how much she loved weddings. He smiled and got rid of them as fast as he decently could. All he wanted was to talk to his best friend and make sure he was still his best friend – that he hadn't fucked up too profoundly in that moment when the commanding impulse had risen up in him, *Man up and say something*.

It was Paul's look of disbelief that quelled him to silence. Then the impulse subsided and the ceremony had gone on and why was he panicking anyway? There was Paul, and Ava had been snaffled by some great-uncle who wanted to kiss her... no, Paul had rescued her, and they were together again. Was Paul avoiding him? No, he was being paranoid. But when he'd handed the rings over, Paul hadn't caught his eye.

He checked his Rolex. Two hours until his speech. Maybe he should lay low for a bit, let the champagne do its work. Beyond a pair of tall French windows was a small enclosed garden. Fresh air, that's what he needed.

The clean quiet of the garden filled him with a paradoxical craving for nicotine. He took the Marlboros from his inside pocket and stepped discreetly behind a tall shrub.

The shrub had already been claimed by the lad who'd walked Ava down the aisle – Ava's brother – what was his name? Flynn, no, Finn, and he was smoking – could it be? Yes, it definitely was – smoking a spliff.

"Hi." Finn seemed entirely unembarrassed to be caught getting stoned at his sister's wedding. "Are you hiding from Paul too?"

Nate stared at the spliff.

"Sorry," said Finn. "Would you like some?"

"No!"

"Fair enough." Finn took another contented lungful, held it, let it go. Nate lit a Marlboro and watched enviously. Amazing to see him doing this, calm and peaceful, as if it was as normal as his own tobacco. The scent conjured memories of that long lazy summer between Lower and Upper Sixth...

147

"Seriously." Finn put the joint into his hand. "I've got plenty. Chill out a bit. Then when Paul catches up with us later we won't mind when he's angry."

"Why would he be angry? It's his wedding day."

"I haven't been to a lot of weddings," said Finn, "but I think it's usually considered poor form for the witnesses to try and stop it. Are you all right?"

"It's been a while," said Nate, between coughs. "It's good, though."

"I've been saving it for a special occasion."

They stood quietly behind the bush and let the smoke do its work.

"What do you do for a living, then?" Nate demanded.

"I raise alligators for meat and sell them to restaurants."

"Really?" Nate tried to think if he'd ever seen Alligator listed on a restaurant menu. "Which restaurants? Anywhere I'd have been?"

"A few of the sushi bars use it. Most customers probably think it's tuna with a Japanese name, but they don't hide it or anything. It's a delicacy in Asian cuisine. Oh, and Le Gavroche. They have it on as a seasonal specialty."

"Bollocks they do," said Nate crossly. "What do you really do for a living?"

"This and that." Nate looked at the joint with faint alarm. "No – well, not much, anyway. I sell to a few friends, but I don't make much off it. At the moment, I work in a bar. And I write."

"Not much like your sister."

"No, I know." Finn suddenly looked very young and vulnerable, and Nate – unexpectedly – felt mean.

"What are you writing?" (Why had he asked that? Please God he wouldn't have to listen to the boring plot of some angsty novel. If it got dull he'd go to get them both a drink, then never come back.)

"Fairy tales."

Nate struggled to think of something positive to say.

148

"What's the point of that?" he demanded. "Some German blokes already wrote down all the fairy tales."

"No, they didn't. There are loads more."

"Well, I don't think there's much of a market," said Nate. "Sorry."

"Are you?"

"You should write horror. Stephen King does all right."

"Fairy tales are often horrible."

"No they're not."

"Did your mother not read you the ending of *Snow White*?"

"All right then," said Nate crossly. "Let's hear a horrible one."

"Once," said Finn, watching the smoke twirl into the dirty sky, "there was a Prince who was raised so that he had no idea he could ever be wrong."

"Can I have some more of that?" asked Nate, taking the spliff from Finn's hand.

"The King loved how confident and proud his son was," said Finn, while Nate inhaled deeply. "And he thought it would be wonderful if he could stay that way as he grew. So he told his wise men that they had to raise the young Prince to believe he was always right, because then he would become a proud, confident leader."

"Here." Nate handed the spliff reluctantly back to Finn.

"He was clever, and he was an only child, and he was the King's son," Finn went on, "and a lot of the time when the King's wise men answered him a question he got it right, and even when he was wrong, no-one ever dared stand up to him. And the more he was never wrong, the more he assumed he never would be wrong, and the more frightening the idea of being wrong started to become."

Nate found it was quite soothing to stand in the cool afternoon air, smoking a joint and listening to this amiable child of the universe prattle in his ear.

"One morning in the garden, he heard a blackbird singing. It was the most beautiful sound he'd ever heard, so he decided to have the bird caught so he could keep it as a pet. He got his Master Falconer up from the mews and told him, 'Catch me that blackbird and bring it to me in a cage.' And the Master Falconer said, 'Blackbirds can't live in cages. It'll pine away and die, and then you'll be under a curse and die too, because bad things happen to people who kill blackbirds.' And the Prince was astounded, because it was literally the first time in his life anyone had suggested he might be wrong."

"So what happened next?" asked Nate, since Finn seemed to be waiting for him to say something.

"The Prince killed him," said Finn. "And got a new Master Falconer who knew which side his bread was buttered. So the Falconer caught the blackbird, and it went to live in a cage in the Prince's bedroom. But it wouldn't sing, and it got sadder and sadder and sadder, and everyone knew it was going to die, including the Prince, but he was too frightened to admit he was wrong, even to himself. Then one morning he woke up and it was lying cold and dead on the bottom of the cage."

"Brilliant."

"Hang on, I haven't finished yet. That night, the Prince had a nightmare. He dreamed that the blackbird had flown back into his room and was stealing away his teeth to build a fortress. When he woke up, he looked in the mirror and found a brown spot on his front tooth, and from then on he didn't dare speak in public or even open his mouth too much. The second night, he dreamed that the blackbird was stealing his hair to weave itself a warm nest. When he woke up the next morning, he saw that his hair was beginning to thin on top, and from then on he wore a hat, day and night, until everyone began to whisper and wonder. And the third night he dreamed he was in bed with a beautiful woman, but as they were making love, that part of her turned into a gigantic golden beak that tore it off and swallowed it whole. So after that he didn't dare go to bed with anyone – even though he was supposed to get married and produce an heir.

"And so it went on, with the Prince becoming more and

more frightened because he'd finally discovered he could fail. Eventually it was clear he could never be allowed to inherit the kingdom, so his own father arranged to have him slaughtered and his body thrown on the midden. And the King and all his wise men looked at each other and said, 'What did we do wrong?'"

"That's stupid," said Nate.

"I've had three glasses of champagne and half a spliff. Sorry."

"You'll never get a publishing deal if that's the sort of crap you write." He took another drag on the joint. "And this is shit as well."

"Would you like some coke instead? Just a couple of lines before your speech?"

"And furthermore," said Nate, "your sister's bloody lucky Paul looked her way twice. If it goes tits up it'll be because of her, not him, and the only person who thinks they shouldn't be together is you, because you're a weird little freak with issues."

"If you're going to be rude then I'm going to have to ask for my joint back," said Finn gravely.

Nate threw it on the ground and shredded it to pieces with the toe of his shiny shoe.

"Are you happy?" Paul took Ava's hand and turned it so that the light caught the hoop of diamonds. Ava's smile was tired. "I know I keep asking."

"You don't really need to ask, do you?"

"What happened to your flowers?"

"I've got them here."

"Some of them."

"These were all I needed. The rest have gone to a good home."

"I wanted you to have them."

"Let's not fight about flowers."

"I'm not trying to fight, I'd just have liked to see them."

"You mean your mother would have liked to see them."

"What's my mother got to do with anything?" Paul demanded.

Ava glanced at Paul's mother, who was nibbling a strawberry and laughing. "She looks a bit happier."

"Oh, she's in her element," said Paul gloomily. "She's been planning this since I asked out Amanda Allbright when we were fourteen."

Ava leaned her head against his shoulder. "Nate's speech was interesting."

"I never thought he was the crying type," Paul agreed. "Do you know… " he stopped himself.

"Yes, I do actually."

"No you don't, you can't possibly know what I was going to say and it wasn't important anyway."

"Finn did the same thing. You don't think they're right, do you?"

"Of course they're not bloody well right." Paul's voice was quite a lot louder than he'd expected. He lowered it hastily. Rowing on their wedding day was bad enough, but rowing in front of his mother would be unforgivable. "What's the matter with you?"

"The two people who know us best both thought… "

"They're not the two people who know us best," said Paul fiercely. "Finn's just your kid brother, and Nate's a bloke I know from school. The two people who know us best are you and me. Okay? And we know it's a brilliant idea to get married." He kissed her. "Let's go and dance."

Chapter Eleven: Now

The phone's ring came from everywhere and nowhere. Donald scrabbled frantically among the papers on his bureau. No sign of it. His bedroom? The kitchen? How could he lose anything in a small flat? He stood on the landing and listened, then dived triumphantly into Alicia's bedroom.

"Don't hang up, don't hang up, don't hang up," he chanted, trying to sort through Alicia's desk in a way that would show her he'd been looking for the phone, rather than spying. T-shirts, underwear, some sort of journal, the phone. He stabbed triumphantly at the answer button.

"Sorry," he said. "I mean, hello." Discouraging silence. "Hello?"

"Hello?" A woman's voice, wearily professional. "Could I speak to Mr Donald... "

"Yes, speaking, speaking."

Another little pause, and from this martyred silence he realised it must be the girl from the council offices.

"I'm calling in regards to your complaint," she said.

"Yes."

"As part of our open communications policy, we provide regular updates to all complainants on the progress of issues... " She sounded as if she was reading from a script. "... can't always share all the details due to confidentiality for... "

His fingers mechanically scrabbled through Alicia's things, fumbled open her Maths book. Notes and calculations. That rounded cursive script, so reminiscent of Ellen's. Was handwriting a hereditary trait? Was it Alicia's oblique way of keeping her mum's memory alive? Or was it just the way they'd both been taught? She seemed to be doing okay; there were plenty of red ticks, a few corrections. The woman talking in his ear had finished her scripted introduction. He closed the book and made himself concentrate.

"… paying a site visit in the next couple of days to complete a welfare assessment."

"Sorry, a what?"

"A welfare assessment," she repeated, patient and chilly. "As a public body, we have a statutory duty to assess the welfare needs of anyone occupying council land to ensure we're considering all relevant circumstances."

"What sort of relevant circumstances?"

A tiny sigh. He wished he could make his voice less impatient, less loud.

"For example, if there are children involved."

"They don't have any children, they're brother and sister."

"Or if either of them has a significant health need."

"Oh, for God's sake."

"And whether they have the ability to access other accommodation."

"She's got a house." (Her husband had wanted her back, he was sure of it. He'd walked out of the restaurant, but Ava had been in control.) "She's just decided not to live in it." (But why had she left him? What had he done to make her leave him? He hadn't looked like the violent type. But then if violent men *did* look like who they really were, how would they get women to marry them?)

"… for the Welfare Officer to determine, sir." The honorific annoyed him because it was a technique he recognised. *I'm not getting angry, sir. Why are you getting angry? Don't speak to me like that please, it's not necessary.*

154

Beneath Alicia's Maths book was a hardbacked, flower-patterned journal. "I'm just keeping you informed as part of the council's commitment to… "

"Open communication, yes, you said." He flicked blankly through the journal. Page after page of loopy handwriting. Strange, in this digital age, to see so many handwritten words. Sometimes she left him post-its on the fridge. *We needed more milk so I bought it, now you owe me £1.59! Don't forget I'm late tom – goin out w da girlz! :)* The spelling done on purpose to tease him. Occasionally, when she was younger, *Dad, you're the best!* He'd kept those in a drawer somewhere. "So when is this welfare inspection due to take place?"

"I can't confirm the exact date," the woman said, her tone suggesting she might have told him if he'd been less snotty. "I would imagine within the next two days. But of course it depends on other commitments."

"So you have a lot of people illegally camping on council land, then." Words leapt out of Alicia's notebook. *Alone. Feeling. When we're together.* She must have a boyfriend. He hadn't realised. "Or is there some sort of emergency that might take precedence over these two jokers who've been living here for nearly two months now?"

"Sir, I'm calling as a courtesy to give you some information. There's no point shouting."

"I'm not shouting, I'm just asking."

"If I feel you're being abusive or threatening, I'm entitled to end the call." She sounded almost smug about this. He forced himself not to take the bait.

"I see. Well, thank you for giving me the information your policy states I'm entitled to. I'll look forward to receiving more informative updates in the future." He was going to hang up without saying goodbye, but she beat him to it. The click of the receiver was loud in his ear.

He flicked randomly through another couple of pages of Alicia's journal. He'd kill anyone else who looked, but he was her father. She'd never know. He'd keep his best poker face on and act properly surprised when she told him there was a new man in her life. He just wanted to know who it was. He turned over several pages, but confusingly, there was no mention of a name. Just a pronoun, *he*, repeated endlessly, occasionally emphasised with capitals or underlining. He had to look, how else was he supposed to find out what they were up to? The constant spectre of a teenage pregnancy, although surely these days all young girls would know better than to – he paused on an entry dated just a few days ago, transfixed by the phrase, *I love how it feels.* Would it be easier or harder to parent a girl who liked other girls instead? The word *orgasm* leapt off the page, shrieking like a mandrake. He heard Alicia's footsteps on the stairs, slammed the book closed and leapt away.

"Dad?" She stood frowning in the doorway.

"You had the house phone on your desk," he said, waving it like a talisman.

"I was out of credit." She was good at looking casual, but so was he. Maybe it hadn't said *orgasm* at all, maybe it was *organic*.

"I'll top you up. Get a tenner from my wallet." Of course it hadn't said *organic*, why would she be writing about organic food in a journal about a boy?

"No, it's fine, I've done it."

"It's all right, I'll sub you a tenner."

"It's fine. You give me plenty. I just didn't get round to it."

He should be pleased that she wasn't grasping and greedy like teenagers were supposed to be. He should be pleased she was managing her own finances, saving her summer wages, making her allowance last. Why did he feel like she was trying to placate him?

"Well, if you use the landline, make sure you put it back, okay? I don't want to be rummaging through all your girlie stuff."

"Dad." She was smiling now. "It's not *girlie stuff*, it's just make-up and clothes and… "

"Don't you say that word." He was edging away from her desk as she edged towards it. "It's bad enough having to buy them for you."

"Real men aren't scared of Tampax," she called as he retreated.

"I can't hear you," he called back, putting the phone back on its base-station. Out of nowhere, a flash of memory: Ellen, bandana-shrouded and grimacing with nausea, asking him to pick up some sanitary towels. He'd been flattened by amazement that her cycle still functioned when so much else about her was broken – by the illness and by the treatment that was supposed to burn it out of her. How could her body possibly believe it was in any shape to nurture a new life? If she'd felt remotely like having sex, if they'd managed to get pregnant, if it had somehow withstood the poisonous cocktail poured in through the drugs port, what hideous monster would have been brought to birth nine months later? Why was all this rubbish coming back to him now? Was Ellen haunting him? Could she see into his head? Did she suspect him of forgetting her? Of wanting to betray her with… ? He leaned his head against the wall and tried to breathe.

"I'm going out." Alicia was watching him. Her bag was slung over her shoulder.

"Where are you going?" To meet the mystery boy from her journal?

"Just out."

"Yes, but where?"

"Dad! It's half-term! Just you know, around!" Her temper flared so easily these days. The joys of having a teenager. "I might go for a walk across the sands. I'll be out for lunch."

"Will you?"

"If that's all right, I mean." He looked at her sternly. "Dad, is it all right if I stay out for lunch?" A pause. "Please?"

It was almost a relief to know she was only going to hang around that bloody beach hut. Maybe the Welfare Officer would come while she was there. Make her see that they were nothing more than a couple of charming freeloaders. "All right, then. Dinner at… "

"Six, I know."

"And you've definitely got phone credit?"

"Yes!" A quick, reluctant kiss at his jawline, her arms around him for a perfunctory second. "Bye."

Once he was sure she'd gone, he went back and examined the clutter on her desk, being careful not to touch anything. As he'd half-expected, the journal was gone. That told him something important – in fact, two things. She didn't want him to read it. And she didn't trust him to keep his nose out. He was surprised to find he was hurt by this.

Of course, she really couldn't trust him, but she didn't know that. She'd never caught him looking. And besides, he wouldn't say a word. She was entitled to the illusion of privacy. Who was it, though? Which boys' names had she mentioned? None.

He went downstairs to open up.

About two in the afternoon, in the empty hours between the lunchtime and evening shifts when he had the pub entirely to himself, the Welfare Officer turned up. Donald knew instantly he was from the council. He had that unmistakeable public-sector air about him, a combination of anorak plus file-of-papers plus grey-slacks-and-shirt-with-short-sleeves. He looked harassed and tired, and the way he fumbled with his papers told Donald this was an official visit.

"Hi. Um, are you Mr Emory?"

"I am." Donald felt a faint tingle of anticipation.

"Am I right that you registered a complaint about some illegal campers on the beach?"

"That's me." The tingle grew stronger.

"Great." The man awkwardly shuffled his paperwork under one armpit, then stuck out a warm, damp hand. "I'm Steve. Steve Jones."

"Good to meet you. Can I get you a drink?"

"No thanks, I'm fine. Look, I'm sorry to ask, but I wondered if I could get your help locating them?"

"I'm sorry?"

"I was due to make a welfare visit. We have a statutory duty to assess any welfare issues before going any further with the… "

"I know. Some girl called from your office and explained. What's the problem?"

"And they're on the beach, is that right?"

"Yes, just in the lee of the dunes – look, you can't possibly miss it. It's a beach hut. You walk out across the sands and there it is."

"The thing is, I can't seem to find them."

Donald stared at him.

"Is it possible they've moved on by themselves?" Steve suggested.

"Absolutely not."

"Do they have any transport?"

"Wait here a minute."

Donald marched out into the street and stared at the car park, mostly empty now. The Jolly Death trap of Doom and Loveliness was missing. They must have gone out for the day. He marched back inside.

"I think I'd better show you."

"If you've got time that would be brilliant." Steve looked relieved.

"One more minute." Donald grabbed his coat from its hook in the lobby. Then he reached under the bar for the cardboard sign he'd made the day the dishwasher suffered a sudden existential crisis and flooded the whole ground floor with warm, greasy suds. He locked the door and hung the sign on the handle. *Closed due to unforeseen circumstances.*

"Let's go."

The walk was made in awkward silence, punctuated with a series of conversational offers from Steve. When Donald had grunted brief replies to the weather, the previous season, the prospects for the winter, the premier league and the state of the tide, Steve finally gave up and followed a respectful couple of paces behind.

Their boots left clean sharp impressions. To pass the time, Donald tried to divine the footprints that crisscrossed their path. A neat line of dog-prints next to a set of boots, the sudden change in pace as the dog was set free. Small, meandering welly-prints reminded him of walking with Alicia, the way she would splash through puddles then press hard with every step, looking back to see how far she could get before the water ran out.

He hadn't thought to tell her where he was. He'd completely forgotten. Christ, what was wrong with him? What if she went back home and – he scrabbled in his pocket for his phone.

"Got to text my daughter," he explained to Steve, stabbing frantically at the buttons.

> *Alicia pet, had to go out for an hour. Pub is locked. Have you got your key? Love Dad xxxxx*

Sometimes it took her hours to reply, but this time she answered instantly.

> *No probs Dad tx for letting me no Axxxx*
> *Where are you? xxxxx*

Again her reply was almost instant.

> *Just out with friends like I said remember!!!*
> *Love you loads see you l8er xxxx*

Yes, but which friends? He'd thought she was down at the beach hut. That mystery boy, no name, no face, just a collection of acts and sensations. *Keep her safe. Let her go.* Competing impulses, wrestling for supremacy. He put his phone away and strode on. He could hear Steve breathing hard as he tried to keep up.

"Just round here," said Donald, in the faintly accusing tone of one pointing out the obvious. "It's just… "

The place where the beach hut had stood was empty. In

this grassless landscape there was no yellow faded patch to mark its vanishing, no flattened plants springing sturdily back to life. Not a scrap of rubbish; no indentation where the gas bottle had rested. It was as if they'd only been there in his dreams.

Loss coiled painfully in his belly. He told himself it was simply because he'd imagined a triumphant confrontation.

"Looks like they've moved on by themselves," said Steve.

"Not a chance," said Donald.

"This is definitely where they were?"

"Oh yes. This is the place. But they haven't gone. They said they'd be here until midwinter."

"We do find travellers' plans can be quite fluid," said Steve. "They may have decided on the spur of the moment."

"Not a chance," Donald repeated. "They'll be back. I know it."

"Well, I can't really complete a welfare assessment if they're not here for me to assess them," said Steve. "And since they seem to have gone, it looks like we can close off the case." He looked round at the smooth gold curves of the dunes. The topmost dusting of sand riffled in the breeze. "They've left it very clean."

"They'll be back," said Donald stubbornly. When Steve glanced at him, Donald saw in his eyes the faint suspicion that these beach hut dwellers had never existed. "If you come again tomorrow, you'll find they're right back where they were."

"Thanks for showing me, anyway," said Steve. "To be honest, it's always better when these things resolve themselves. But if you have any more trouble, with them or anyone else, give us a call and we'll start again. Okay?"

Donald heard the unspoken message: *This is now over.* He watched Steve walking away. A stout black Labrador pranced heavily towards him, and Steve pulled its ears in a friendly manner. Perhaps he and the girl who'd phoned him would laugh. Perhaps Steve was the fiancé. The Labrador's owner called a sharp syllable and the dog nosed greedily in her hand. How had they got the beach hut down so fast and left so little trace? A butterfly, out of season and improbably blue, fluttered around Donald's ear, then settled on his shoulder. Looking more closely, he saw it was a large flake of blue paint.

"George," said Donald, into the silence. "What have you done?"

"Oh, hello." George looked at Donald in honest astonishment. He was pottering in the place he and everyone else still called the boat-yard, even though the days of boats being built here were long gone and most of his trade was in garden sheds.

"George." Donald wasn't sure where to begin.

"What?"

"George."

"What?"

Donald spotted a stack of neatly-piled, blue-painted wood. "*George.*"

"What?" George was getting exasperated. "What do you want? I keep asking you."

Donald couldn't trust himself to speak, so instead he pointed.

"That's the beach hut I built," said George. "I took it down for them. There was someone coming to look at it and Finn didn't want them to see. It's a good thing I used properly seasoned timber or we'd never have got it down without breaking it. It was enough of a job as it was. The paint didn't help."

Donald continued to stare blankly at George.

"So would it be all right for Alicia to come and help out when she's finished her schoolwork, then?" asked George, bafflingly.

"What?"

"Maybe you don't remember, I mentioned it to you, let's see… seven weeks and two days ago. I said she could help out in the yard. You said she was out. So when I saw her this morning, I asked her again. She said she'd have to ask you because she had a lot of schoolwork. So, now I'm asking you."

"Hang on. Back up. When did you see Alicia?"

"This morning. She helped with the take-down. She was very useful." George beamed at Donald.

"And what happens to the beach hut now?" asked Donald.

"Ah, now, that depends if whoever it was has been to see them," said George. "Do you know if whoever it was has been to see them?"

"Oh yes," said Donald. He knelt by the pile of stacked timber and picked at a large, loose flake of blue paint. It felt rubbery and flexible. He tore it carefully in two, then into four. "He's been down to see them. And they weren't there. So they've closed off the case."

"Good," said George. "Then we can go down there tomorrow and put it back."

"Brilliant," said Donald. "George, can I just ask one thing? Did Alicia just happen to turn up this morning? Or was it arranged?"

"How would I know that?"

"You might have – she might have – oh, never mind," said Donald wretchedly. "It doesn't matter. I'll ask when I see her."

"She won't be back until later."

"What?"

"They went up the coast in the camper van. All three of them. Alicia was in the front seat. Do you know," said George, thoughtfully, "camper vans only have one front seat-belt that goes right across everyone, regardless of how many people there are? I never knew that. It doesn't look very safe to me. Finn was driving but I don't know how good he is. Are you all right?"

"Fine."

"You've gone very red."

Donald took a deep breath.

"So if Alicia's free tomorrow," said George, "she can come down if she likes. Rebuilding the hut shouldn't take long. And then she can give me a hand with… "

"No, I don't think so," said Donald. "I'll see you later, George."

"I'm busy later. Come and have a look at this, it's really interesting."

"George," said Donald very loudly. "I'm leaving now. I'll see you the next time you come in for a drink. Goodbye."

"Bye, then," said George, and picked up his steel tape measure.

It was just before six o'clock when the camper van rolled back into the car park. The windows were down. Irritating music thumped out. They tumbled out of the van, wrapped up and laughing. Alicia was wearing a beanie hat he hadn't seen before and a pair of mismatched gloves. Did they know he was watching? Did they care?

Donald stood quietly in the shadow of the bus shelter and waited. Alicia took off her hat and shook her hair loose as she ran. It was clotted with seawater. Had she been swimming again? Which beach had they been to? She looked like a different person disguised in Alicia's skin, and as he stared at her it occurred to him that this was because there was a kind of wild joy in her face and her body, in her bright eyes and reckless movements, that he'd never seen before.

Mike must have been watching too. A familiar figure waved from the door of the pub. When he looked back at Alicia, she was once again the girl he knew, his quiet and slightly withdrawn daughter, contained and wary, mysterious and beloved. Her pace slowed and she folded the hat carefully into her coat pocket.

What would he do if she ran away with them?

Ava was stretching in the twilight, fingers reaching for the sky. A bulky coat hid the shape of her and she shivered and pulled it close. No wonder, swimming on a day like today. Was she pale and smooth like she was in his dreams? Was her skin chilly beneath the coat, or warm? The thought provoked a kind of treacherous tenderness, a weakness that crept through his stomach and outwards, threatening to turn him soft and feeble. He gritted his teeth and forced himself to picture her goose-pimpled and drowned and ugly, to remember that she was flouting the law and had spent her morning skilfully evading justice. She lowered her arms again, stamped her feet a few times, then walked towards the toilet-block.

Finn stuck his hands in his pockets, wandering aimlessly about in the way men did while waiting for women. Donald forced himself to wait too, for the right moment. The moment when Finn would be behind the van, screened from Ava's view. Waiting was hard, but it came with the territory. If you couldn't be patient, you couldn't do the job. The moment might come, or it might not. Sometimes you got lucky. Sometimes you didn't. Finn whistled and muttered, scuffling at a stone with an ancient work-boot. Donald breathed in, then out, in, then out. Finn moved behind the van.

It was a moment of pure savage pleasure fired straight from the base of his brain. He hadn't done this in years but his muscles leapt at the chance to relive old glories. Finn struggled, a reflex action driven by instinct, not thought. Would he fight until his strength gave out, or accept the battle was already lost? After a moment, Donald felt Finn go quiet and still. Now there was just the sound of their breathing, and the tick of the engine as it cooled.

"That was quite clever," said Donald. "Taking down the beach hut so the Welfare Officer couldn't assess you. It must have taken a lot of work. Did it take a lot of work?"

"A reasonable amount, yes," said Finn, around Donald's fingers. He sounded scared but calm.

"And now they've closed the case," said Donald. "Of course, I could go down and report you again. But it's taken weeks to get this far. By the time they get around to you, it could be your time to move on anyway. And since you cleaned everything up so nicely, they might just write me off as a nutcase with a bee in my bonnet." His tone was confiding, fatherly. "Not that I have an actual bonnet. I'm speaking metaphorically. You do know what I mean by *metaphorically*, don't you?"

"Pretty clear on that one."

"You have made one mistake, though," said Donald.

"It certainly looks that way," Finn agreed.

No, Donald commanded his hands, which were eager to fold around Finn's throat.

"You see," said Donald, "you haven't understood who you're dealing with. You think I'm just your average retired copper. Maybe not the very brightest, maybe a little bit too hung up on the rules, but a grafter. A decent chap. You think because you beat me using the rules, that means you're safe, and you can forget me and enjoy your winter." His right hand was slipping from his control, inching down towards the spot where Finn's carotid artery fluttered like the heart of a hummingbird, the only outward sign of his fear. "But the truth is, mate – that whole decent-chap act I put on every day – that's not me. The truth is that I'm a very, very bad man."

A pause, to give his message time to sink in. Donald counted the time by the ticking of the engine, and used it to force his fingers to obey.

"So," said Donald, when he had counted nine ticks and watched Finn attempt to swallow, "do you think we understand each other?"

"I'd say so, yes," said Finn, his voice cracking on the last syllable.

"Good. Because now I'm going to tell you what I know about you. I know you're not much of a man. I know you're happy to live off other people. I know you've got a past you're not proud of." Actually he hadn't known that for sure until he felt Finn flinch as he said the words. "I know you've been hanging around my daughter. My beautiful, vulnerable

166

fifteen-year-old daughter."

"My God," said Finn, sounding shocked for the first time. "She's just a kid. Surely you can't think I… "

"If you hurt my daughter," said Donald, "if you do anything to hurt her, in any way, I'm going to drown you. I'll take you down to the caves and tie you up and leave you in there for the tide. Do you understand what I'm saying?"

Finn was looking through the window of the camper van.

"Ava's coming back," he said. "If you want her to ever speak to you again you might want to let me go now."

In the moment when Donald hesitated, Finn slid to the ground and was suddenly free. He stood up, wincing. Then he looked Donald right in the eye and smiled.

"It's all right," he said. "Proper grown ups can never stand me. You should hear Ava's husband on the subject."

"You little bastard." Donald lurched forward. Finn climbed hastily into the van and shut the door.

"We're sleeping in the van tonight," Finn told him. He looked frightened but determined. "Somewhere up the coast, so you won't have to do anything about it. And I promise Alicia's safe when she's with us, okay?" Donald's fist thundered clumsily through the open window, missing by half a foot. The engine throbbed into life. "Look, I won't tell Ava about any of this. She doesn't want to admit it but she likes you really. And just so you know, I think you'd probably be a lot better for her than that prick she married."

Chapter Twelve: 2006

"I'm quitting," Donald told Harry.

Harry looked at him over his mug of coffee.

"He's lost the fucking plot."

"He lost his wife. Give him time."

"Time. It's been months."

"Yeah, well, she was sick for months, wasn't she? Remember that job on the Appleton Road? Last bloody minute, he bailed and we had to bring Dave instead? They were at the hospital, getting her diagnosis. Then he had a year of her dying. Give him a chance."

"He's finished. Can't do this job if your heart's not in it. He should walk before he's pushed. Must have the cash. He's been in for fucking ever."

"You after his job? Come on, back to it."

You never hear anything good by eavesdropping, Donald told himself, resting his forehead against the cold white tiles of the stall.

"So we've got the Niewinski job, then the Blue Crocodile. Andy's not happy. The Brixton boys. Getting all up in his face with their bad selves, or some such thing. Show your faces, let them know we're keeping an eye. If it gets tricky, don't be afraid to step in. Donald, you all right for that? Donald?"

"Got it."

"Sure you're up for it?"

Donald felt himself redden. Normally, Harry punished inattention with at least five minutes of banter. He hated that Harry still had the kid gloves on. He'd been widowed, not bloody incapacitated.

"Donald?"

"Yes. Sure."

"I could give it to someone else?"

"You could," Donald agreed. "Or I could kill you and eat your liver for dinner?"

The laughter was a bit too loud, a bit too appreciative. He didn't want their sympathy. He just wanted – he just wanted – no, he was absolutely not going to cry in front of the lads, he'd never hear the end of it –

"What else?" he demanded. Beneath the table, he tried to press his nails into his palms. But he'd already bitten them down beyond the quick.

"Boss." Donald tapped on the door.

"Donald."

"Need a word."

"Sod off and stop disturbing me. There you go, that's… four, five, six."

"I'm serious."

Harry beckoned Donald into the room. "Let's have it."

"The Blue Croc job. I can't take it." Harry's flinch of annoyance wasn't quite covered by the sympathetic smile. "Childcare problem. Sorry."

Harry shrugged. "These things happen. I'll call Ricky."

"Ricky? That little prick?" The whisper overheard in the Gents, the poison dripping in his ear. *He's lost the fucking plot.*

"What? He's available. He wants the job."

"He told you that, did he?" Angry even though he couldn't justify it.

Harry frowned. "Why do you care anyway?"

169

"He's not ready."

"No-one's ever ready. He'll have to step up."

"The Croc needs calming down, not stirring up. Ricky's spoiling for a fight."

"Maybe a fight's what we need. The Brixton boys are getting cocky. About time we showed them they're on our radar."

That rattled him. He'd always handled The Croc. He took pride in keeping things smooth. The door staff knew they could call him when things kicked off. He kept an eye out for the girls, too, making sure they got as much respect from the punters as was possible when you took your clothes off and shook your tits and bits for a living.

"Anything else you need, mate?" Harry was clicking his pen against the desk, a sure sign that he'd had enough.

"No, nothing else. Look, I really am sorry."

"Don't sweat it, these things happen. Take the time you need."

"It won't happen again."

"I said don't sweat it." A moment's hesitation, then an evil grin, like in the old days. "You sure there's nothing else I can do for you? You getting lonely at night? You want to bend over the desk and I'll do you up the arse?"

"Wash your filthy mouth out," said Donald, grinning back.

Driving to the school, his Mercedes sliding all slick and smooth through the dusty traffic, he tried to make himself care about what would be going down at The Croc. But his heart felt light and empty.

Alicia was sitting outside the school office. He could see her through the glass doors. Whenever he'd been collected early it was because he'd done something terrible, and his mother would chivvy him home with little slaps and pushes and he'd know he was in for a proper walloping when they got home. Alicia was never in trouble. A good girl. Took after her mother, not her father. What else had Ellen passed on to her?

Please God let these things not be hereditary, let her live her life without having to face that hell. Her face was streaked with tears. As soon as she laid eyes on him, her lip began to quiver and within moments he was kneeling in front of her while she howled into his shirt front.

"Sorry to bother you at work, Mr Emory." The school nurse's mouth was tight and disapproving.

"Donald, please. And it's no problem." Every time they met he tried to build a rapport with her, but it was hard; his face and his job worked against him.

"She was fine all day," the nurse said. "And then at about two o'clock, it was all just a bit too much, wasn't it pet?" She stroked Alicia's hair, encountered Donald's hand doing the same thing and flinched away.

"What lesson were you in?"

"Science." The word came out indistinctly from beneath his chin. He pushed her gently away so he could look into her face.

"What sort of science?"

"Just – just science," hiccuped Alicia. Her eyes were huge and pleading.

"Come on, pet, you must know what sort of science."

"I don't," she insisted, through sobs. She was trying to hide in his shirt front again, but he held her away, determined to get to the bottom of it.

"What was it that upset you?"

"It doesn't matter."

"Of course it matters! Of course it matters," he repeated, trying to soften his tone, knowing he sounded angry. He *was* angry, that was the trouble. Not with Alicia, but with whoever it was who had done something, said something, to remind Alicia of what she'd lost. He wanted to fight them. He wanted to beat them into submission.

"We were talking about how plants grow," said Alicia.

This stumped him. "How did talking about how plants grow upset you?"

"It just… " Her nose was running. The nurse stepped in with a tissue. By the way she carefully didn't look at him, he knew she thought he was handling this all wrong. Alicia's face was crumpling again, grief welling up in her chest. "It just did!" The staff room door opened and an irritated face looked out. Donald put his arms around Alicia and held her, rough and tight.

"It's hockey club tonight," he said. "You can't play in this state, though, can you?" He stroked her hair again. It felt rough. Had he remembered to brush it? Ellen, brushing and brushing and brushing, and Alicia twisting and complaining beneath her touch, *Mum, you're hurting, stop it, it's finished, it looks fine.* "Get yourself calmed down, then you can go and get your kit on. I'll come and get you at five."

"She might be better off at home for today," said the nurse, in a tone that was clearly an instruction.

"Alicia? Pet? Is that what you want?"

As he looked into her face, he saw something terrible. She wasn't trying to decide what she wanted. She was trying to work out what he wanted her to say.

"Come on," he said, hauling her to her feet.

"Where are we going?"

"We," he said, "are going to blow this joint and go and find some fun. Have you got your stuff?"

"It's on my peg, but what about hockey club?"

"You worry about the fighters, I'll worry about the tower."

"Da-ad." She was smiling reluctantly now.

"What?"

"It's embarrassing when you talk like that."

"Where do you fancy going? The world's our oyster."

"Can we go to the seaside?"

"Well, not quite that far, pet. It's work and school tomorrow." Her face fell. "But we could go to the pictures? And then McDonald's for tea?"

"It's just I was thinking we could go swimming," she said.

"Okay, we can go swimming. We'll pick up our gear and

172

go to the pool."

"No, I meant outside swimming."

"We'll go to an outside swimming pool."

"There aren't any outside swimming pools. Are there?"

"Course there are." The nurse was smiling a little and holding out Alicia's bag and coat. "We'll find one. And we'll freeze ourselves to – we'll get really cold, then we'll get a greasy fry-up in a café for tea. Okay?"

His calm was a façade. His shoulders were tense. He wanted to know what had upset her, in the middle of a lesson about how plants grow. He wanted to kill someone.

"Bit of excitement at The Croc yesterday." Ricky, swaggering a little, fingers in his belt-loops, absurd but somehow commanding the room.

"Heard it got messy." Sean, the bloke he'd heard gossiping with Ricky in the bogs.

"We handled it. The Brixton boys got the message." Ricky inspected his fingernails, and glanced at Donald, a sly challenging look. "Been coming a while."

"Fair enough," said Donald, turning the page of his newspaper.

"You ask me," said Ricky, "it needed handling a while ago."

"Ah," said Donald, nodding.

"All this light-touch stuff," said Ricky, looking at Donald directly now, trying to catch his eye. "That's had its day, that has."

The room began to subtly rearrange itself, everyone getting ready for a fight. Donald was heartened to see that most of the movement was in his direction. The lads still had his back. Or maybe they were just enjoying the show?

"You might be right," said Donald.

"Time for some new blood, maybe," said Ricky.

"New blood's always useful." Donald turned another page, then looked right at Ricky and bared his teeth. "If you're looking for a transfer, Ricky lad, I could give you some tips. Work hard and stay focused and in a couple of years, you might be ready to come and work for me."

A moment while the words sank in, and then laughter and a scattering of respectful applause. Donald resisted the urge to take a bow, and instead turned back to his paper. *Just play it cool, boy...* he'd heard that advice in a song years ago. Ricky was visibly struggling to keep the lid on, but managed not to storm out. Instead he smiled and joined in the applause, acknowledging the massive slap Donald had administered, then sat down and flipped through the girlie calendar on the table.

Shouldn't have done that, Donald thought. *Now I've let him know we're enemies.* A few years ago, he would have relished the fight. Now all he felt was a huge weariness, a creeping disgust at these stupid jostlings for power.

"... and we need to look at The Croc. Again." Harry looking tense and edgy. The situation with the Brixton boys clearly giving him grief. Donald suspected he was getting hassle from higher up, which in turn meant pressure from Civvie Street. Girlie clubs were tolerated if they stayed quiet, classy and trouble-free. It didn't look good to have a bunch of anxious, cocky rude boys rolling into town, flashing their cash and their blades, making the girls jittery and skittish and the (exclusively white, exclusively rich, usually middle-aged) punters uncomfortable. The whole situation was coming to a head nicely. If he'd been watching The Croc the way it needed watching, the Brixton boys would never have dared show their faces.

"It's time we turned up the heat," he said out loud. "Let these angry young men know where they stand. There's only so much the door crew can do. What with political correctness and all." He cracked his knuckles. "I'll drop by this evening. Have a little talk."

"What about The Lamp?" asked Harry.

"I'll pick up The Lamp as well."

"You after my job, Donald?"

"If I wanted it I'd already have it."

"You sure you won't have another childcare issue?" This, incredibly, from Ricky. The silence in the room was sour and tense. Ricky raised his hand to his mouth to bite his nail, then instead folded his arms across his chest. Donald glanced at Harry and saw, for a brief unforgivable moment, a flicker of doubt on his boss' face.

"If I have a problem," said Donald at last, "I'll call on you, Ricky. You can come round to my house and do your monkey impression for my daughter. She'd like that very much." He looked at Harry. "You happy, boss?"

Harry was still hesitating. This was not good. This was not good at all. This was potentially career-ending stuff.

"Sounds like a plan," he said at last, and Donald could breathe again. "But Ricky, I want you along with Donald at The Croc, okay? Since you two are getting on so incredibly well today."

The release of laughter, and everyone took deep breaths as their shoulders loosened up. Donald and Ricky glared at each other, then shrugged. Only one thing to be done: man up and cooperate.

In the alleyway opposite the unmarked door of the Blue Crocodile Club, Donald and Ricky stood and watched the nightlife and waited for the Brixton boys. The streets were full of pretty young things in silly little frocks, and handsome fresh-shaved city slickers trying to get into their knickers. A night full of promise, as long as what you'd been promised was sour wine and easy sex and a fistful of regrets in the morning. The air tasted warm and dusty.

"There." Ricky nudged Donald hard in the arm. Five young men, bright-eyed and sharp-gestured, tracksuits and gold jewellery, a bad parody of gangsta chic. They weren't the only black men on the street, but they were the only ones of whom you'd say, *a gang of black youths.*

"I see them."

"Fuck me. They're right there." Ricky was quivering with excitement.

"Let's get a drink," said Donald.

"But… "

Donald grabbed Ricky's arm and forced him onto the street. "The Laughing Monkey looks good. Reasonable prices too."

"But they're right fucking there!"

"Yes," said Donald. "They are right fucking there. Right near the fucking entrance to this fucking alleyway. And if they fucking see us guarding the fucking door like fucking Cerberus, they are going to smell what's coming quicker than your fucking dad ran for the door after he got your mum up the fucking spout. So now we are going to the fucking Laughing Monkey, where we will buy a fucking drink like any other punter, thus making sure they go into the fucking Croc and start some fucking trouble and save us the fucking effort of coming back down here every night for the next fucking week. Was that fucking clear enough for you, or should I curse a little bit more before it sinks in?"

Ricky's face was sullen, but he nodded.

"Excellent. Then what can I get you?"

The racket in the bar made his head spin. Had it ever been fun to come to places like this? He was too old for this game. No, he couldn't afford to think like that. This was just a temporary blip while he got over – lock it down, Donald, or you won't survive the night.

He squeezed through the crowd and caught the eye of the barmaid. The brandy was rough and hot in his throat. Beside him, Ricky pushed a sliver of lime into the neck of his beer and took down a long swallow.

How many years had he been doing this? Too long to like the answer. Working his way up from walking the beat to

176

working the patch. This should have been the year he put his bid in for promotion, Harry moving either upwards or outwards, making room for the next man in the chair, and if his life had gone differently the chair would have been his. What would that have been like? A bigger better house in a greener leafier suburb. A flasher car on the driveway. That school for Alicia they'd been talking about. His mind was following two trains of thought: one picturing the life that had been stolen from him, the other counting mechanically in his head, giving the Brixton boys the time they needed to banter with the doormen, get inside, order their drinks, make themselves at home.

"Time to go."

"Can I finish this first?"

"No you can't." He waited for Ricky to argue, but of course Ricky had his eye on the main prize here, which was to be part of the operation that took down the Brixton boys. Ricky abandoned his bottle on a table and followed Donald outside.

The doorman grinned when he saw them and opened his mouth to speak, but Donald silenced him with a fierce gesture and he subsided into the shadows. Inside The Croc, a blonde, a brunette and a redhead worked the stage, their bodies bumping and grinding, their faces a smooth absent blank. The boys were sprawled all over a corner table, two walls to their backs and the whole room under their gaze. They beckoned a girl over – Katya, he thought, or maybe Veronica. She went reluctantly, knowing trouble when she saw it. He watched them enjoying her discomfort.

"Nearly there," said Donald. "You ready, Ricky my boy?"

"Born fucking ready."

"Here it comes. In five, four, three, two… "

The table turned over; the sparkle of spilled ice and alcohol; the shriek of the girls; the gasps and shouts from the other punters; the music that, unlike in the movies, kept pounding over the sound system, slow and sultry, incongruous. It felt like he was watching himself through glass. The gleam of metal. He felt his mouth move, heard his voice produce the words he was supposed to say. Ricky quivering at his side. The words that would set things in motion, keep the dance going, the dance they were all here to do. The arrival of the doormen, sweaty and eager. Both of them wannabes who hadn't made the grade. The blade at the girl's throat. The boys bunched together, tense and eager, a tight circle of warriors. The demands for wallets, watches, cash; for recognition, status, ownership. The dance he'd been doing his whole adult life. He remembered the scent of Alicia's hair as he kissed her goodnight and tucked Bad Bear in beside her. *Daddy's got to go and get some bad guys, sweetheart. No, of course they won't get me, they never do.* He had to concentrate, had to get in touch with this moment.

And then the dance exploded into life, and he was too busy to think about anything but getting his moves right.

They were racing through the streets, the boy leading, him following. Alleyways and passages, sudden corners and unexpected courtyards, all the secret ways of the city opening before them. He remembered Alicia sobbing into his shirt-front as they sat outside the school office the week before. Driving away that afternoon, he'd wanted to kill someone. A bad impulse, but a hard one to conquer. His chest tight and angry, breath burning his throat. Was he ever going to catch this kid or were they just going to run until one of them dropped? A stroke of luck as the kid glanced over his shoulder and, looking, slipped on a McDonald's wrapper. A moment more, and they lay on the warm dry stone together, close as lovers. The heat of the boy's body radiated through his tracksuit. His eyes were huge and liquid.

"All right," said Donald. "Calm down now, it's over. I've got you."

The boy writhed frantically beneath him and gathered a hawk of phlegm in the back of his throat. Donald wriggled a hand free and slapped it over the boy's mouth.

"Don't spit at me, please," he told the boy. "Have some respect for your elders. It'll stand you in good stead later."

The boy gazed defiantly up at him. Silenced and flattened like this, he looked very young. Perhaps only a few years older than Alicia. Thinking of his daughter should make him feel gentler, more paternal, but it didn't. He had to move very carefully now, very slowly, so as not to do anything stupid.

"We're going back to my place," Donald confided. "For a nice little chat."

Fear in the boy's face now. Fear of the locked room, the men who came in pairs, the hard conversations and the silence after. Or was it just fear of Donald himself, of the rage that had squatted on his shoulder since the day he watched Ellen descend into the pit?

"It's all right," Donald said, to himself as much as to the boy. "It's all right. Nothing bad's going to happen. We just need to ask you some questions. Just a few… "

Beneath him, the boy flexed his strong young body up in a powerful curve, then collapsed and tried to roll sideways and outwards and free. Donald could hold onto either his captive or his own temper. A sharp blink of anger, and then he felt pain in his hand and saw the boy bent double over a handful of red spittle and small white bones and knew which he had chosen.

"Shit," said Donald, almost to himself, and hauled the boy to his feet. The boy wailed and gasped through a gappy red grimace. The rage was still there but he had control of it now, he could tell his hand to stay by his side and it would obey.

"Please," said the boy. "Please. Fuck. Please."

Again those dark eyes pleading. Again that reminder of Alicia. Or was it Ellen, the way she'd looked at him from the hospital bed? He was too old for this game. He had to get out while he still could, before he did something he could never put right.

"I think you'd better go," he told the boy.

"I'm quitting," he repeated, staring at the spot on the wall just to the left of Harry's left ear.

Harry sighed, and picked absent-mindedly at the edge of his desk, and in that moment of hesitation Donald knew he'd made the right choice.

"Where are we going?" Alicia asked. It was the seventeenth time she had asked since they set off.

"To live by the sea, sweetheart," he told her.

"Really? It's not just a story?"

"It's not just a story."

"No, really," said Donald into the silence. "Please don't try and talk me out of it."

"Oh come on, Donald, I didn't mean… "

"It's all right." Donald shrugged. "It's time."

"You don't have to. Take a few days. Give it some thought."

"I've given it some thought."

"You were the best, Donald. You still could be. Could be in my place one day."

"You see," said Donald, "I'm not who I used to be."

"Look, that night at The Croc. Those kids are like Olympians. No-one could catch them. They're just made differently."

"I caught him," said Donald.

"You what?"

"And then I let him go." Harry stared at him. "Things have changed. I'm a liability to you now."

The decision settled over them both like fog.

"You all right for money?" asked Harry.

"I've got enough put by."

"Security?"

Donald grinned. "I've got insurance."

"You sly old bugger." Harry sighed. "What you going to do instead?"

"I'm going to open a pub," said Donald, and Harry gave a

180

great snore of laughter.

"But of course you are. What else could you possibly do? Every copper's dream. A pub, he tells me."

"I'll be leaving next week," said Donald.

Harry stopped laughing. "Next week. You are taking the piss."

"Give my jobs to Ricky. He'll be like a dog with two dicks."

"Three days. I give you nearly twenty years and you give me three bloody days. Look, I know it was tough with Ellen, it makes you re-evaluate, but… "

"You see," said Donald desperately, "If I hadn't let him go, I would have killed him." A pause. "I wanted to kill him. I wanted to kill him more than you can possibly imagine. I still do. It doesn't have to be him. Just anyone who gets in my way will do me fine. And I don't think that's going to go away. If you keep me on, Harry, I'm going to start a war for you."

Harry rested his chin on his hands and looked at him for a long time.

"What about Mum?" asked Alicia. A new question. His heart stuttered.

"What do you mean?"

"We're leaving her behind. At the – at the graveyard."

"Oh, darling." He reached clumsily back between the seats and grabbed her hand hard. "Oh, sweetheart. Darling. That – what we're leaving – that's not Mum. Okay? Wherever she is, I promise, she's not there. If she's anywhere, she's here with us." He managed a watery smile. "Telling me to keep both hands on the steering wheel and watch the road."

"So she's coming with us? Sort of, I mean?"

"She's coming with us," Donald agreed, and squeezed her fingers between his.

A cool female voice was reading the headlines. Out of a background hum of *talks aimed at restoring* and *meeting* in Frankfurt to discuss and *proposed privatisation will now go before the*, a name he recognised. Drive-by shooting. Possible revenge attack. Officers have vowed to leave no stone unturned. Sleep peacefully, Ricky. You were a prick and you wanted my job, but you didn't deserve that.

"Dad, when we next stop, can I come and sit in the front with you?"

"That sounds like a plan to me," he said, and turned off the radio.

The daughters of mermaids

Sometimes, when a sailor or a fisherman has been out at sea for too many cold lonely salty days, he might glimpse a shoal of mermaids playing in the waves.

He sees their human parts first – long coarse spirally hair, stiff with salt and adorned with shells and seaweed, and their fierce faces, slim bare arms and backs that are strong enough to drag a boat and everyone aboard it down beneath the waves. Then one of them will turn over in the water, and he'll see the sharp flash of sunlight on their silvery scales.

If he's wise, he turns away then, and busies himself with his nets or his sails or with calculating how much longer his fresh water will hold out – for nothing good ever happens to a man who gets too close to a mermaid. But if he's too foolish to realise that *beautiful* isn't the same as *friendly* or *gentle* or even *safe to go near*, he'll steer a little nearer, and call out to get their attention.

Then the mermaids will turn their faces towards him, and he'll see that behind their crimson lips their teeth grow in jaggedy backward-slanting rows, and their nails are long and sharp, and their eyes are black with hunger. Then, even a moderately foolish seafarer will turn into the wind or (if the wind is flat) reach for his oars and row as hard and fast as he can without looking back. Once the mermaids have you in their sights, they don't give up easily.

But if he's very foolish indeed, he'll notice that the faces and bodies of the mermaids have the perfect beauty of hunting animals in their prime, and his heart and his hands will begin to ache with longing. Just beneath the surface, the tails of the mermaids will twitch and flicker. And as they circle his boat, slowly first and then faster, creating a whirlpool, he'll let his hand dip into the water to try and touch them as they pass.

The boats of these most foolish seafarers are never seen again, and even Davey Jones – who is just a man himself, and has learned the hard way not to interfere – can't say precisely what happens to them. Most people say that the mermaids eat them, and then turn their vertebrae into cups and the tops of their skulls into bowls, and carve their shoulder blades into combs for their hair.

But for every nine people who swear one thing is true, there'll always be a tenth who swears the opposite. In this case, the tenth person was an old blind man with a bald head and a waxed moustache and one leg and a hook for a hand, and a taste for the unspeakable black ale served in the sailor's tavern at the very end of the world. When he got good and drunk he'd sing sea-shanties in spine-tingling harmonies, and when he began to sober up again he'd chew tobacco and tell stories about the things he'd seen in his seagoing days. And this man always said that sometimes, in the autumn and under a low hunter's moon, a baby would come to shore in a basket made from driftwood, naked and new and screaming with hunger; and sometimes there'd be a gold armband or a raggedy hunk of whale blubber tucked in alongside, like a present, or perhaps like payment.

These babies, he said (between gobs of tobacco-spit) were the daughters of men and mermaids (always daughters, never sons), and they would be taken in and raised by the lonely fishermen's wives who prowled the shore and waited for their men to come home to them.

And in this way, from time to time, there would be a girl or a woman who looked human, and who sounded human, but whose blood was saltier than human blood, and whose innermost heart would always belong to the ocean.

Most of the time – so the blind old man said – these daughters of mermaids would live their lives almost like everyone else. But when times were hard, the mermaids' daughters would go down to the shore and stare longingly out to sea. And sometimes, when one mermaid's daughter met another, they would dive into the water together and swim and swim and swim, summoning each other one with their fierce cries, never glancing back to shore, no matter how hard their loved ones called to them.

Chapter Thirteen: Now

Alicia shivered and pulled her hands inside her sleeves. She'd had gloves last winter, but of course they'd vanished now. In the shoe cupboard, in a drawer, in the pocket of the coat that didn't fit her any more but which was somehow still in the house, in a pair of wellies, down the back of the sofa. Possibly separated, possibly wrapped tightly together. When she lived in the beach hut, she wouldn't lose anything because there was nowhere to lose it. When she lived in the beach hut – if she could move in right now – if she could get down there and find they'd moved on...

She pictured them not being there, and was surprised to find the image hurt her heart.

They'd go soon anyway. It was nearly Halloween already. The gales were beginning to blow in from the top of the world. Two months left. When she was little, a year was an impossible journey. Now every time she looked up, another week was gone. Her dad always said time got faster with age, although maybe that was because he lived such a boring life anyway. Someone had been this way before her. She followed their footprints as they turned towards the dunes. Another ten weeks until Ava flew south chasing the sunshine like a bright bird, and Finn went... somewhere... and the hut would be hers.

Something was happening. The beach hut's slender possessions were spread across the sand – a tea-chest, two suitcases, a miscellaneous pile. The reed screens that shielded the chemical toilet, and which she secretly hated (when it was her beach hut, she vowed, she would build another hut, a hut with soundproofing. Either that, or she'd live entirely alone and never allow anyone to visit for longer than thirty minutes) were weighed down by the folding chairs. The clean water-tank gurgled quietly and emptied its precious cargo into the sand. Worst of all, George, standing on a wooden work-bench, had pried off the ridge-pole and was taking off the roof, while Finn stacked the pieces in a neat pile.

"What's happening?" Finn gave her a friendly wave. Her throat was almost too tight to speak. "Why are you breaking the beach hut?"

"I'm not breaking it," said George. "I'm taking it to pieces."

She found her voice. "That *is* breaking! Stop it! You can't!"

"It's all right." Finn climbed up beside George and peered through the hole in the roof. "Ava, how's it going in there?"

"The screws are stuck," said Ava, from inside the beach hut.

"I'll give you a hand." Finn jumped down from the bench.

"No, there's no need, just give me a minute."

"If you go inside," said George, "I'll have to stop doing the roof. And if you want to get it down before eleven o'clock, we need to keep working on the roof."

"Shit!" Ava appeared in the doorway. "Have we packed the first-aid kit? I've just stabbed myself with the screwdriver."

"What did you do that for?" Finn pried open her fingers. Fat crimson droplets soaked into the sand. "Okay, that's bad. Alicia, could you look in that suitcase for the first-aid kit?"

"Oh, hi," said Ava, smiling at Alicia. "Finn, it's fine, don't fuss."

"No, it's not fine. Sit down. Alicia's getting a plaster. I'll do the bunks."

"If you go inside," George repeated patiently, "I'll have to stop doing the roof. And if you want it down before eleven o'clock... "

"What's going on?" Alicia wailed. Tears collected in her

throat. "Why is all your stuff packed? Where are you going? Why are you wrecking everything?"

Finn looked hard at Alicia. She stared defiantly back, praying he'd put her flushed cheeks and swimming eyes down to the breeze.

"I'm not supposed to tell you."

"Finn," said Ava, struggling with the zip of the suitcase. "Damn it, I'm bleeding on everything."

"That's because you didn't do what I told you. Sit down. Sit. Down. There. On the bench. Mind the tools. Sit. Right now. That's better." Finn rummaged in a battered tin box and found some Elastoplast. "Give me your hand." He smoothed the plaster carefully over. "Of course, what I should really do is wrap it in a strip of fluffy orange toilet paper that someone's blown their nose on."

"That would be the authentic thing to do," Ava agreed.

"But we'll stick to the hygienic solution for now." Finn looked at Alicia thoughtfully. "George, have you got another screwdriver?"

"I've got lots of other screwdrivers," said George. "Whether I've got the *right* sort of screwdriver is another question."

"I need another one the same size as Ava's. Have you got another one of those?"

"Let me see." George, apparently forgetful of the importance of getting on with the roof, climbed down and peered into his toolbox. "Now. I don't have another with a Phillips head on it. But if you're careful – *if* you're careful – you might manage with this one. But you'll have to be really careful not to strip the screws, because it's not really designed for the job and… "

"Brilliant, thanks. Why don't you sit with Ava and make sure she doesn't get up and start doing stuff until the bleeding's stopped. Alicia, here's a screwdriver. Come on."

"I'm not helping you wreck it." Alicia followed him inside. It looked bare and desolate. "If you're going then fine, but don't wreck it, please, just leave it up."

"No, you don't understand," said Finn, laughing. "We're not *going*. We're not leaving until midwinter night. We're hiding."

"What?"

"We're hiding." Finn lowered his voice. "From your dad. I think he's set the council onto us. Don't tell Ava I told you."

"Why can't you tell me?"

"She thinks it'll upset you to be put between us and your dad." Alicia snorted. "I know, but she's older than me, she worries about these things."

"Aren't you both just grown up by now – no, forget it. How are you hiding?"

"Help me take the bunks down and you'll see. We have to be quick. I reckon they'll be here by lunchtime."

Once she got the hang of it, it was surprisingly exciting. There was a select thrill to hastily stacking the deconstructed beach hut onto George's trolley, neatly and in order at George's insistence. ('But we can sort it out later,' from Alicia, and George, hectoring and firm: 'Now, that's a common mistake. But if you get everything out of order, then identifying each piece can be almost impossible… ') A tense fifty-minute pause while George and Finn dragged the trolley laboriously across the sand, which was not quite damp enough to stop the wheels from sinking in every fifty yards. When they finally disappeared, Alicia and Ava sat serenely on the pile of possessions and watched the dog-walkers making a path down to the caves and back.

"What if the council man comes before we've packed up the van?" Alicia asked.

"We'll club him over the head with a rock and drag him down to the sea."

"Really?"

Ava laughed. "What do you think?"

"I don't know."

"You think I might be a murderer?"

"No, I didn't mean that."

"Hey, don't feel bad, it beats being boring. Do you mind if I go for a swim?"

"Can I come too?" Alicia asked, without much hope.

"I promised your father."

"So? He's an idiot."

"Don't say that. He's doing his best."

"He's trying to have you evicted."

"But at least he warned us first," said Ava, smiling to herself.

"He'd never know," said Alicia.

"Ah, but you and I both would."

Ava peeled off her boots and her socks. Her coat and her jumper. Her t-shirt and her jeans. Finally she stood on the beach in a black cotton bra and knickers. Alicia looked away in embarrassment, but then turned back to watch.

After all, what was the difference between that and a bikini? Why shouldn't Ava go swimming in her underwear? Cold and slightly jealous, Alicia found the biscuit tin and consoled herself with the Cadbury's Chocolate Fingers.

She meant to stop at two, but they were the good ones with three layers of chocolate on them, and they fitted so neatly into her mouth – just under half a finger for the first bite, then the second half crammed in sideways – that she couldn't make herself stop. Before she knew it, she'd wolfed down the entire packet. Ava was coming back. Alicia crammed the empty box into her pocket. A woman with a dog, wrapped up like a Matryoshka doll, looked Ava up and down, then stopped to deliver what looked like a few words of approval.

"Was it cold?" Alicia wished she'd got a towel ready instead of stealing biscuits.

Ava was speechless and shivering. Her fingers were clumsy as she scrabbled through the suitcase. Zipping it closed again, she tore a thumbnail. Alicia winced as Ava bit it impatiently off and let it flutter away on the breeze. The plaster on her palm flapped like a broken wing. Alicia took the towel and patted water from Ava's back.

"The water's lovely," Ava explained, through blue lips. "It's the walk back that finishes you off." She peeled off her underwear and dropped it to the sand, then wriggled clumsily into her t-shirt. "God, am I putting on weight or something? Why can't I get this stupid thing on?"

"Of course you're not." Alicia picked gingerly at the cotton, trying to unroll it without scratching Ava's skin, which looked thin and shrivelled. For the first time, Alicia understood what her dad meant when he said it wasn't attractive to be too skinny. "It's because your hands are cold." She handed Ava her jumper, then her jeans. Ava wrestled with the chilly, damp denim, then sat down hard on the sand, half-laughing, half-embarrassed.

"I can't do the button," she admitted.

Shyly, Alicia took hold of Ava's whitened fingers. "We need to get the blood flowing."

"It's okay, I just need a minute."

"No, this works, I promise." Alicia rubbed Ava's fingers between her own, gently at first, then vigorously. "It gets the circulation going. My dad used to do this when I was little. When we used to go to the park – actually no, it can't have been my dad, he was always at work – oh!" The sudden memory was overwhelming. She was engulfed by her mother's presence, the glossy dark hair, the glow of her cheeks, the scent of her face-powder. The shock was so great that she dropped Ava's hands into her lap. Her own hands flew to her cheeks.

Ava flexed her fingers. "That's much better. You're a life-saver." Her gaze was on Alicia's face, but not looking directly into her eyes. "I might actually manage to dress myself now." She stood up and turned away, wrestling with the button. "Yep, that's done it. Just in time. There's Finn with George's trolley. Wish we'd had it when we moved down here. Can you pass me that carrier bag?"

She crammed her underwear clumsily into the bag and shoved it into her coat pocket. Alicia blinked hard several times and turned to let the wind blow away the expression from her face. By the time Finn arrived with the trolley, she was able to look at him and grin.

"This is a wicked plan," she told him. "Where are you going now?"

"Up the coast." Finn glanced at Ava. Ava smiled. "Want to come with us?"

Finn stowed Alicia carefully in the centre of the single wide seat. "You have to sit here because it's the safest place. Well, I'm saying that. To be honest, I'm not sure any of it's all that good. But if someone side-beams us you'll have me and Ava for padding."

"Why is there only one seat-belt?"

"Oh, because of President Truman, I should think," said Finn. He opened the door for Ava and she climbed in. When Ava leaned briefly against her, Alicia felt the faint residual vibration of the sea's chill in Ava's flesh. On the other side, Finn was warm and comforting. The seat-belt threaded across their laps and Finn clicked it into place.

"It's amazing they're still allowed to sell these really," said Finn, backing the van slowly out. "It's got no turning-circle to speak of, it tips over if you look at it funny, and this bit… " he kicked gently above the pedals "… this bit is basically just plywood. So if we crash, that's us dead."

"Seriously?" Alicia blinked.

"Seriously."

"Why drive it, then?"

A little boy in a red hat was watching their progress up the hill. Finn waved. The boy stuck his finger in his mouth and stared back. "Because right up until the moment you die, you look really really cool and little kids wave at you when you go past. Well, sometimes they do. But it's all right. Today I'm feeling lucky. We got everything off the beach before

191

the council officer came, and the tide was in our favour so we didn't have to do a moonlight flit. Today, the Gods are smiling on us. Let's go somewhere we don't know about yet and get some fish and chips. Ava, left or right?"

Ava peered up and down the road.

"Right."

"Where are we going?" Alicia asked again.

"Anywhere. Don't you ever go somewhere on a whim?"

"Have you actually met my dad?" said Alicia.

Ava looked at her reproachfully.

"Don't mention the war," said Finn. "Here's how it works. We take it in turns to pick a direction at each junction. We drive until we find somewhere we like. Then we stop, and pretend that's where we were going all along."

"What if you run out of petrol?"

"We did once," said Ava. "Do you remember? That time in that little village? It was about half-past nine but everyone had basically just gone to bed. And you went into the pub to ask if they had a phone we could use."

"Oh yes," said Finn, laughing. "And he was really suspicious and kept asking questions, and all my answers were terrible because I didn't know where we were going or what we were going to do when we got there, and he obviously thought I was planning a crime spree. And then you came in and talked to him for about five seconds and he took off his apron and offered to drive you to the garage. You've got a way with men who own pubs."

"Shush."

"You're allowed to like him, you know. I bet he'd be more fun than… "

"That's the end of that conversation," said Ava firmly. "Which way now? Left or right?"

"Right," said Alicia at random.

Right led down a steep hill. The van raced joyfully along, resisting Finn's attempts to hold it back with the brakes. Alicia leaned shyly against Ava. When Ava made no objection, she closed her eyes so she could think.

What would it be like if, hypothetically, Ava was to start going out with her dad? She'd watched friends at school go through the cycle of arguing parents, separating parents, divorced parents, new boyfriends and girlfriends. She'd been part of supportive conversations, agreeing that their parents were selfish bastards and if they ever had kids, they'd never put them through it. But she herself had never been the one alternately frowny and casual, switching between violent hatred and elaborate shoulder-shrugging.

Was it because her mother had died, rather than left them? Was her dad still so in love with her that he couldn't bear to think of anyone else that way?

"Left or right?" Finn asked.

"She's asleep, I think," said Ava. "Right." Alicia started tell them she wasn't, but the van was already making a slow wide circle, so she went back to her train of thought.

How did grown ups go out, anyway? On TV they went to restaurants and drank wine on sofas before falling into bed together. Would Ava put on a demure black dress and pin her hair up? Would her father take his blue suit from its hanger and shave for the second time that day? Where would they go? And afterwards, would they – ugh, no, it was too horrible to think about.

The movement of the van was soothing. She let herself drift into a warm doze, intermittently aware of the van pausing and moving on, winding through narrow lanes and reversing back to passing places.

When she woke, they were by the sea once more, on a tall cliff over a deserted bay. The ocean was subtly different, bluer, softer, gentler, the waves breaking against black rocks and white sand.

"Where are we?" asked Alicia, stretching.

"Somewhere awful," said Finn, turning off the engine. "The houses have got corrugated roofs. Why do people do that? But the beach is nice and they sell fish and chips.

Hopefully the crime rate's quite low as well."

"Why does that matter?" asked Alicia.

"We're leaving everything we own in a van that doesn't lock properly."

"Aren't you worried?"

"What good would worrying do?" Finn led the way down the quiet seafront to a side-street billowing with the scent of hot fat and vinegar.

The path down to the beach was treacherous and crumbly. Alicia looked at it doubtfully.

"Should we be doing this?" she asked.

"Probably not," said Finn, testing the path with one foot.

"It looks dangerous," said Alicia.

"True." Finn's feet sent a rattle of stones ahead of him.

"And if we get stuck and have to call the coastguard, we won't know where we are to tell them," said Ava, edging down the path and wincing at the dry rattle of falling soil.

Finn grabbed at a clump of grass for support. "On the plus side, we don't have a mobile phone, so we don't have to worry about what we'd say to them."

"I've got a mobile phone," said Alicia.

"Have you? Damn. Still, maybe you could lose it on the way down. Or not get any signal."

"Are we going down, then?" asked Alicia, from the clifftop.

Finn slithered down a few feet further. "Well, aren't we?"

"Yes," said Alicia recklessly, and scrabbled after them.

The cove's high black cliffs were like cathedral walls. They had nothing to sit on, but there was a thick band of smooth grey pebbles that were all right as long as you didn't want to lie down, so they sat on that, and watched the sea wash against the crisp fringe of seaweed.

"Bet there's a cave," said Finn. "I'm going to have a look. Behave yourselves while I'm gone."

"Don't lick the walls," said Ava, yawning.

"How else am I supposed to decide whether to open an arsenic mine?" Finn shambled away.

"Should we go with him?" asked Alicia.

"If you like."

"Aren't you going to?"

"I'm going to swim," said Ava.

"Again?"

"Is there a rule about swimming too often?"

"No, but you haven't got any… "

Ava was already undressing. "Life's short. You've got to make the most of every opportunity."

Another minute and Ava was naked on the beach. Alicia thought her face might burst with embarrassment. Ava walked into the water and the waves closed around her. Alicia heard her gasp and swear. Her body vanished beneath the water and only her head was visible.

"Can I come too?" Alicia begged. "Please."

"You're not supposed to."

"There's no undertow here."

"Not that we know of."

"My dad won't ever know unless you tell him." Ava had turned back onto her front and was swimming towards the horizon with strong, clean strokes of her arms. "Please let me come in with you."

Ava turned back to shore for a minute. She was too far away for Alicia to read her expression.

"Why do you need my permission?"

Alicia took a deep breath, then began to undress. Running down the beach, one arm holding her breasts and the other cupped over her groin, she prayed Finn was absorbed in his cave and wouldn't see her making this wild dash for freedom, wearing nothing but her own skin. The cold took her breath, then gave it back again as she became a water-creature, reborn clean and free. The horizon was calling her. She wanted to swim out and out and out and never come back.

"Alicia." Ava swam after her. "Don't go too far."

"Don't be boring."

"Boring!" Ava laughed.

"I didn't mean it like that."

"I don't mind, it's just… " she laughed again. "Look at me, being all grown up and responsible. That'd show my husband."

"Have you got a husband?" Alicia was startled.

"I had one, but I think I've probably lost him now."

"Really?"

"Does it seem so unlikely?"

"Is that why you're living in the beach hut? Did he get the house?"

"Are you getting tired yet? I don't want to drown you."

"I'm not a kid, you don't need to change the subject. What happened? Did he leave you?"

"No, I left him."

"But why? Did he have someone else?"

"So cynical! No, he didn't. Or not as far as I know, anyway. I suppose anything's possible."

"I don't ever want to get married," said Alicia.

"Fair enough. You might feel differently when you're older though."

"No I won't. Men are horrible. And the ones that aren't horrible are boring. That's the only two kinds of men there are. Boring ones like my dad and horrible ones like – like your husband."

"He was probably more in the boring camp actually, but it's an interesting theory. Maybe I'll try a horrible one next time."

"Don't laugh at me."

"I'm not laughing, I'm giving it some serious thought."

"Let's swim out further."

Ava glanced back towards the beach. "We're a long way out. Are you sure you want to?"

"Are you scared?"

"No, of course not, but… "

"Then let's keep swimming," said Alicia.

She had never swum this far from shore, ever. She should be freezing, but she only felt it when her arms or shoulders broke through to the air. If she stayed beneath the waves she'd be safe. Ava's arms and legs moved with the smooth confident strokes of a machine, scissoring and flexing, scissoring and flexing. How far would they go? Her arms were growing heavy.

"I know this married man," said Alicia suddenly. "He's cheating on his wife. She doesn't have any idea."

"That's a pretty shitty way to behave."

"He is shitty, that's just the right word for it. They both are, him and his – his lover. They must be, both of them, to do that. And they both know it too. Well, she does, anyway. But she can't make herself stop."

"How do you know? Surely she hasn't told you all this? Alicia, are you all right?"

"It's just it's a long way back," Alicia quavered.

"Oh Alicia, I'm so sorry. I'm so selfish. I wasn't thinking." Ava trod water and looked at Alicia's face. "Are you scared?"

"No. Yes. Yes, I'm scared. We've come too far."

"No we haven't. It's all right, I'm here with you."

"I can't get back, I can't. I've come too far, it's too late."

"There's always a way back."

"Look how far away the beach is. Look at it. How am I going to swim back all that way? I can't do it on my own."

"But you're not on your own, you're with me." Ava grabbed her hand and held it tight. Alicia clung to her desperately. "We'll get back together. Come on, swim with me. Just five strokes."

"I can't do it. I can't swim back."

"You can swim five strokes. There you are. Now another five. And now another five. Good girl."

The rhythm of swimming calmed Alicia's panic. She forced herself to breathe.

197

"What if we can't make it?"

"We'll make it."

"But what if we can't?"

"I swear I won't let you drown. Five more. That's it. Now five more."

They swam slowly on. The ebbing tide clutched at their legs like a tired child.

"I thought you were leaving this morning," Alicia confessed. "I mean, I know you're going in the end, but I thought you were leaving today. I always thought you'd leave the beach hut behind you. I want to live in it. Don't laugh, don't you dare laugh."

"I'm not laughing. But you know it's not really practical, don't you?"

"Why not? You do." Ava was silent. "I know it's not mine but I thought I could have it anyway. I didn't even like you when you first came. I just wanted the beach hut. I suppose that's stealing, isn't it?"

"Is it? I don't know."

"Actually I don't mind even if it is stealing. It wouldn't be the worst thing I've… " Alicia splashed at a seagull floating curiously nearby. "Go away, stupid! Get out of the way!"

"Hey." Ava's hand reached through the water to clasp Alicia's. "It's okay. We're going to make it."

"I can't do it. It's too far."

"Yes you can."

"No I can't."

"How about I tell you a story while we swim?"

"What good will that do?"

"Keep swimming and we'll see."

Alicia's arms dragged slowly at the water, the seagull bobbing beside her.

"When Finn was about seven," said Ava, "he went through a phase of squashing Christmas baubles. He used to stand by the Christmas tree, pick a bauble, and squeeze it."

The seagull studied Alicia from one round, yellow eye.

The scarlet spot on its beak was very bright.

"He used to squeeze and squeeze and squeeze," said Ava, "until in the end, the bauble would collapse into pieces."

"Why?"

"Keep swimming. And remember to breathe. That's it. He said he wanted to know how hard he could squeeze before it broke. And unfortunately, the only way to find out was to go past that point, and actually break it. So he'd stand there, squeezing and squeezing, and in the end it *would* break, and there would be bits of glass everywhere. Then I used to sweep up the bits for him so he wouldn't get into trouble."

"That was nice of you."

"He never asked me to, mind you. He would have sorted it out for himself. But he was only little, and I didn't want him to cut his fingers."

"Didn't your mum and dad… " Alicia was going to ask if her mum and dad had noticed their Christmas baubles disappearing, but Ava kept talking.

"Then one day, he squeezed a really big silver bauble, and it broke all over the place. And when I fetched the brush and dustpan, I stood on a massive piece of glass and cut my foot."

Alicia shuddered. "Did it hurt?"

"Like you wouldn't believe. There was blood everywhere. It wasn't serious, I didn't need stitches or anything, but Finn was horrified. I kept saying it was all right, he didn't need to worry, but he said it wasn't all right, and he was sorry, and what could he do?" The seagull spread its wings and flapped heavily off. "After that, he never squeezed baubles again."

"Did he miss doing it? Squeezing the baubles, I mean?"

"I don't know," said Ava. "I never asked."

In the end, the shore was closer than it had seemed. Fifty strokes more, and they felt sand beneath their feet and cold air against their skin. Alicia slipped and shivered her way up the beach on feet too numb to feel the pebbles. Ava put an arm around her shoulder.

"It's all right," she said. "This is the worst bit. Get a couple of layers on and you'll start to feel better. Then you'll be all high and giddy for at least the next six hours."

"I wish we lived somewhere warmer," said Alicia. Her teeth chattered so hard she could hardly speak. "Can't I come with you when you go?"

"Go? Go where?"

"To Thailand," said Alicia, struggling with her t-shirt. "To the beach, and the place with – ow, my fingers hurt – with the beach huts with straw roofs and the cocktails in coconuts."

"Alicia."

"I'm not asking you to pay or anything. I've got savings. How much is a ticket?"

"Far too much." Ava picked up Alicia's jumper and pulled it over Alicia's head. Then she helped Alicia get her hands down the sleeves and out again, before grabbing her own clothes.

"More than a thousand pounds?" She hadn't got a thousand pounds, but her dad kept a stack of cash in a box in the bottom of his wardrobe.

"I can't take anyone. I'm sorry."

"But Finn said he didn't think it would be long till he came out… "

"It will be," said Ava, her voice suddenly fierce. "A very, very long time. His book's coming out soon, he's got to stay for that, and then afterwards… " she stopped. "He needs to get old first. Like me."

"You're not old."

"I am. Old and dried up. I'll frighten all the locals when I walk out onto the beach in my swimming costume."

"That's stupid, you wear your swimming costume all the time and you don't care what anyone thinks. I don't have to share your hotel room, I could sleep on the beach."

"Damn it." Ava put her arms around Alicia and held her tight. "I'm sorry. But no."

Alicia let her arms fall to her side and went stiff and rigid. After a minute, Ava let her go and tried to look into her face.

200

Alicia sat down to put on her trainers.

"Are you warming up yet?" Ava sat down beside her.

"A bit."

"Want to borrow my jacket?"

"No thanks."

"I'm sorry."

"What for?"

"Alicia," said Ava patiently, "don't sulk."

"I'm not sulking."

"Yes, you are. I hate it when people tell me *no* as well. But – oh look, there's Finn."

Finn shambled across the beach with his hands in his pockets and his trainers hanging around his neck. Ava waved, and Alicia saw his arm go up in response.

"You two are like sea goddesses," he told them. "I had to paddle to the cave and it was so cold it hurt. How do you do it?"

"Mind over matter," said Ava.

"You just have to go for it," said Alicia, wrapping her arms around herself.

"Well, I'm freezing," said Finn. "Let's see if the heater's working today."

A few minutes into their return journey, Alicia sat bolt upright.

"Oh my God," she said, beaming.

Ava laughed.

"I feel great," Alicia announced. "Oh wow!"

"And that," said Ava to Finn, "is why I go cold-water swimming in October."

"And not a single pill in sight." Finn patted Alicia's shoulder.

"Why didn't you come in?" Alicia asked, grinning from ear to ear. "You should try it, everyone should. Next time you are totally coming in with us, seriously… "

"Can't. I have an obscure skin condition that means my skin melts in salt water. True story."

"Your feet didn't melt."

"I had them treated with a special coating so I can paddle in the ocean and pass for normal. But it was too expensive to get my whole body done. Also, it turns my skin an unattractive shade of green, and I think that might be why I find it hard to get girls to talk to me. It's also why I can never have children."

"Don't say that," said Ava.

"It's all right. I'll steal one out of an orphanage and raise it in a life of luxury. It'll work out fine. You'll see."

"Where will you sleep tonight?" Alicia asked. "Are we rebuilding the beach hut?"

"Tomorrow," said Finn. "Tonight we sleep in the van. Or maybe with the fishes. Depends how angry your dad is with me when we get back."

"With us," said Ava.

"Nope. With me. I told you, he… "

"*Pas devant les domestiques*," said Ava.

"I'm not a *domestique*," Alicia protested.

"No, I know, but you'd be even madder if I called you an *enfant*."

"I'm going swimming every single day from now on," Alicia announced. "I'll get up before school and swim in the dark."

"Don't go in on your own," warned Ava.

"Remember to watch out for sharks," said Finn.

The engine hummed to itself as the van drove back up the slow winding hill.

Chapter Fourteen: 2010

"This is a dystopian future," said Ava, stroking Finn's hair away from his forehead. "We're living in a dystopian future."

"I'm sorry."

"Don't be, this is great."

The airport was a gleaming empty space of white and chrome and glass. Finn lay with his head in Ava's lap while she leaned against a tall pillar. A fellow traveller might have paused to wonder at the conservatively dressed woman with her expensive shoes and handbag, and the thin scruffy figure in t-shirt and jeans who lay in her lap as if it was the only haven he had ever known. But in these silent early hours, there were no other travellers.

Occasionally they glimpsed tiny figures scurrying between destinations, bringing the tools of their trade (a cleaning cart, a gun, a wheeled suitcase in the colours of their airline). Whenever one of these figures approached an escalator or a travelator, it began to roll, inviting them to change floors or traverse a few hundred feet of floor-space with eerie speed. When their target vanished, they lapsed back into stillness.

"I didn't want you to have to do this," mumbled Finn. "I didn't even write to you in case I put something that made you think… "

"That's how I knew. You always write." Finn stirred restlessly in her lap. "Shh. Lie still. You need to rest."

"I had that dream again," said Finn. "We were on the beach, just down from the dunes. I think we were living there. Do you remember when we were kids… "

"Of course I do."

"There was a huge wave coming in, just rolling in like a tsunami. I was terrified, but you were totally calm. You said, 'Don't worry, I'll protect you.' And just as it was about to break over us, I woke up and the police officer was leaning over me and grinning and telling me I'd got a visitor. Ava, I'm so sorry."

"Look at that escalator. It's gone quiet again. How does it know?"

"There must be a sensor."

"Yes I know, but is it in the ground or on the ceiling or what? Or maybe there's a gnome in the basement with CCTV and a big red button." She stroked his hair again. "Do they have gnomes here?"

"I don't know. Yes, I think they do, but they're not called gnomes, they're called something else, I can't remember."

"Don't be so angry with yourself."

"But I am angry with myself. I'm furious. I'm too old to need rescuing. And you've got better things to do than chase after me. You need to live your life and let me get on with living mine."

"D'you know, you sound exactly like… "

"Like Paul?" Finn's smile was like the faint sad ghost of his younger self. "How about that? It's almost like he wrote me a letter and put it in my backpack for me to find and I've been carrying it around ever since."

"He did that?"

"Only sensible thing he's ever done. That and marrying you, of course."

"But why would he?"

"Because just for once, he had a point and every word he wrote was true."

"Of course it's not true. He just… "

"… doesn't like me, I know. No, it's all right. I know he doesn't. He never has. He thinks I'm a bad influence. Does he know where you are?"

"Not exactly. I told him I'd be gone about a week."

"But he knows you're chasing round the world trying to find your idiot little brother."

"You're not an idiot."

"Course I'm an idiot." Finn shivered and coughed. Ava laid a hand on his forehead.

"Your temperature's going up again. As soon as we get back you're going to the doctor."

"I'll be fine, I've had it for weeks. It'll go in the end."

"Are you taking anything for it?"

"Nothing I can bring through airport security. It's all right, don't look like that, I haven't got anything on me, of course I haven't. You don't think I'd do that to you, do you?"

Ava stroked the faint tracery of scars on his arms.

"You're not in trouble with it, are you?"

"You mean, am I addicted? No, I don't think so."

"How sure are you?"

"Pretty sure." He closed his eyes. "I mean, I do miss it. If you offered me some right now I don't think I could say no. But I'm not plotting to run away from you and go find a dealer. Oh, Ava, don't cry, I don't want to make you cry, this is why I didn't call you or write to you, you should be at home being happy with Paul." He sat up and put his arms awkwardly around her.

"Don't be sorry, you don't have anything to be sorry about. Finn, tell me the truth, did I do this to you? Was it my fault?"

"How can it be your fault?"

"I brought you up. I was supposed to look after you."

"And you did. You were great."

"But we lived in such shitty places for such a long time."

"They were not shitty places," said Finn fiercely. "They were our homes and they were perfect. That last foster home, that was shitty. Squashy sofas and floral borders with

205

matching curtains. And every ninth tile in the kitchen had a picture of a mortar and pestle with a pear next to it."

"But at least the roof didn't leak."

"And," said Finn, smiling for real now, "in their bedroom, they had a massive horrible picture of horses running across some beach somewhere, insanely pretty horses with big eyes and floaty hair. Like horse pornography. And above that horrible picture, they had a big peach satin bow. With the ends tucked behind the picture and poking out of the bottom. And a little v cut into the ends."

"They didn't. Did they?"

"They did 'till I stole the ribbon. Do you remember that hairclip I gave you? With the big peach bow?"

"You didn't!"

"It looked much nicer in your hair than on their wall."

"Do you think they ever knew?"

"Well, if they did they never said anything."

"Still," said Ava, "they didn't ever give you tinned ravioli for dinner."

"That's because they were idiots. Tinned ravioli is the food of the Gods."

"What kind of God encourages his followers to eat tinned ravioli?"

"The let-it-all-hang-out kind of a God. A God who's not afraid to embrace His inner slob. You didn't only feed me tinned ravioli. Once you made that thing with raspberries and meringues and cream cheese."

"They were all from the reduced shelf. Is that a policeman?"

"Oh, shit, is it?" Finn sat bolt upright.

"What? What have you done?"

"Oh, you know. Forged bank notes and a highly convincing cow-suit and a guy selling fake magic beans. The main thing is, we all got equally ripped off. No, I'm kidding. The police are absolutely not looking for me over some forged bank notes and a highly convincing cow-suit and fake magic beans. Look, he's going now anyway."

"That's good."

"Unless he's gone to get reinforcements."

"I used to be able to tell when you were kidding."

"I used to be able to tell myself."

"Never mind. We'll be on another plane in an hour." Ava yawned and stretched. "Does this count as coming to Malaysia? Can I say I've been here on the basis of five hours in an airport terminal?"

"Definitely. You could start conversations with, *When I was in Malaysia last Thursday,* and then look embarrassed and refuse to say any more."

"I never get to have conversations," said Ava. "That's not how it works with the people Paul and I know. We stand in bars or sit around dinner tables or get together for drinks parties, and competitively exchange facts. *We're going to Tenerife for a few weeks this summer. Annabel's taking her dance exams next week. We can't decide whether to use Adrian's bonus to go mortgage-free, or stretch ourselves and invest in somewhere bigger.* If I said, *I was over in Kuala Lumpur the other week,* they wouldn't say, *Oh, that's interesting, what were you doing?* If they'd been there themselves they'd say, *Malaysia's fun for a couple of days, isn't it? Although I prefer Bali myself.* And if they hadn't been there they'd say, *I must get round to Malaysia some time. Somehow we always seem to end up going somewhere else* – and then we'd be back onto the competitive facts exchange without missing a beat."

"They need livening up," said Finn. "Start making up outrageous lies and see if they fall for them. Tell them you're going to look round Blenheim Palace with a view to buying a little place there. Just seventeen rooms plus a service apartment."

"Paul would have a fit."

"Do him good."

"Do you know," Ava said thoughtfully, "I used to think Paul was a great conversationalist because we never seemed to stop talking. Then one day I realised he's not great at conversations at all. He's great at monologues. We drove up to Manchester once and as an experiment I decided not to speak until he asked me a direct question. It took us five hours, and he never did. And he didn't notice."

Finn was silent.

"Even our arguments are like monologues. He says what he thinks, and I disagree with him, and he restates what he thinks in a more elaborate way. And I get more and more frustrated until I end up in tears, and then he apologises for upsetting me, and that's the end of it. But he never actually changes his mind."

Finn squeezed her hand where it lay on his hair.

"This is the part where you say, *Ah well, husbands, eh? Never mind, how many other men would stand for their wives leaving them a note saying, Gone to get Finn, back in a week or so?* And then we change the subject and talk about something else."

"How about I say, *You could leave him?*"

"I can't do that."

"Course you can. It's easy. People leave each other all the time. Well, people leave me all the time, anyway. Maybe I'm just inherently quite leave-able."

"You're lovely."

"I can't be or they wouldn't keep leaving. It goes all right for a few months, then I get boring or something."

"I'm sorry it didn't work out with Claire."

"Claire?"

"Do I mean Claire?"

Finn closed his eyes and thought. "Well, the most recent girl to leave me was Helen, but there was probably a Claire in there somewhere – oh, yes, Claire. She got mad because I wanted to go to the knob museum in Iceland." Ava laughed so loudly it echoed off the walls. "Ava, can I ask something? Why don't you and Paul have children?"

"Wow."

"Okay, bad question."

"No, it's a good question. I just don't really know the answer."

"You do know where they come from though, right? Because I can get you a book or something. I owe you a Christmas present."

Ava closed her eyes and leaned back against the pillar.

"I've got a story for you," Finn said.

"I'm listening."

"It's about a woman who went for a walk in a dark wood, and met a witch."

"How did she know she was a witch?"

"How did the woman know? Or how did the witch know?"

"Too jetlagged to understand. Do both."

"Okay. The woman knew because the witch lived in a beautiful caravan, and on the wall of the caravan there was a certificate with a massive great red wax seal that said, *Certified Witch.* And the witch knew because she'd worked hard for years, taking crappy jobs and studying so she could get qualified."

"Why was the woman in the woods in the first place?"

"She was having a difficult time and she needed to be by herself for a while. So she wasn't all that pleased when she saw the witch's caravan. But the witch smiled at her and said, *Come inside and we'll talk,* and because it was a witch asking, she had to do it. So she went inside and sat down at the table."

Ava shifted against the pillar to get comfortable.

"The witch had a crystal ball and a deck of tarot cards and a magnifying glass for looking at palms. She took one look at the woman and knew she wouldn't need any of it. But she got the crystal ball out anyway, because it's nice to put on a good show.

"So she took the purple silk cover off the crystal ball, and looked into it, and hummed for a while. The woman sat and looked round the caravan and enjoyed the peace and quiet. And she thought, *Actually, this is quite a nice place to live.*

Not too much to clean. Plenty of storage. You can up sticks and move whenever you want.

"The witch said, 'You're at a crossroads in your life.'

"The woman looked at the wooden walls and thought, *Bet it's cold in the winter.* And she thought about her central heating. Then she looked at the wood-burning stove and thought, *On the other hand...*

"The witch said, 'You have some difficult choices to make.'

"The woman thought, *And imagine, not having to clean if you didn't feel like it. In fact, a bit of dirt is probably what everyone expects. Imagine living in a grubby house where nothing matches and everyone thinks it's charmingly bohemian.*

"The witch said, 'You want to be happy, but you don't want to hurt others to achieve it.'

"The woman said, 'You know, you could probably say that about pretty much anyone, anywhere, in the whole of human history.'

"The witch replied, 'I know, but it frightens people if I just get straight down to it. Here's what I think, I think you're bored and you hate your life and you don't know what to do. So I'll tell you the three choices you've got, and then which one you pick is up to you.'

"So the woman sat quietly in her chair and waited for the witch to tell her the three choices she had.

"'The first choice,' said the witch, 'is to leave it all behind and come and live with me. I'll train you to be a witch. At the end of the winter, if you like it, you can have the caravan and take over my franchise.'

"The woman said, 'But doesn't it take years to get qualified?'

"And the witch replied, 'Oh, yes, years and years. But you can pick up the basics in a few months, and study in the evenings. It won't be easy, and you might be cold and hungry some of the time, but in the end, you'll have your own life and your own power and no-one will ever tell you what to do.

You can live in the caravan as long as you want. But if you want to leave, you'll have to find someone else to take it over, because there always has to be a witch in this caravan and that's just the rules.'"

Ava began stroking Finn's forehead again.

"'Next choice,' the witch continued. 'You can go back home to your husband and have a baby.'"

Ava's hand twitched.

"'If you love each other enough,' the witch continued, 'the baby will bring you closer and you'll grow old and contented. If you don't love each other enough, the baby will drive you apart, and you'll be divorced within three years and spend the rest of your lives feeling guilty.'"

"It doesn't have to be that way," Ava objected.

"Not for everyone, but for the woman in this story. So then the woman said, 'What's my third option?' And the witch replied, 'Your third option is to carry on living the life you're living right now. But at least you've got options. And if you choose to stay with what you've got, you can't say ever again that you feel trapped, because it was your own choice.' She was a very judgemental person, this witch. I should have told a better story."

"What did the woman choose?"

Finn sighed. "I don't know. Maybe she's still in the caravan, thinking about it."

"Maybe she'll spend the rest of her life in the caravan thinking about it, and then one day she'll wake up and realise she's old and that's been her whole life. Thinking."

"That's a very dark ending," said Finn.

"You're the one who's always saying fairy tales are meant to be dark… is that a bird?"

"Where? Oh, that's lovely."

The bird spiralled past in a frantic flutter of beating wings, swooping almost to the ground and then soaring off into the high ceiling.

"You see," said Ava, "if you have a baby, you fall in love

211

with it. You love it more than anyone in the world. You'd do anything. You'd kill for it. You'd die for it. Absolutely whatever it took. And I don't know if I want to love someone else as much as that. I think it might end up tearing me in two."

Finn squinted at her. "You can't mean Paul."

"Of course not Paul, you idiot."

Finn swallowed hard. He shambled to his feet and took three steps towards the escalators. Then he came back and enveloped his sister in a fierce desperate hug.

"This is the last time, okay?" he muttered. "The very last time you'll have to drop everything to come after me. I promise. I swear."

"I don't mind, I've never minded. It's what we agreed. Just the two of us against the world. You'd do the same for me."

"I never have though, have I? It's always been you rescuing me. But I promise, Ava, this is it. You'll never ever have to come and get me out of jail or pay my airfare home or anything. I'm going to make you proud."

"You don't have to make me proud. You're my brother. I love you how you are."

"I'll finish the book, no more messing. I'll have the first draft finished by Christmas, words and pictures, and start shopping it round. And next time there's any rescuing to be done, I'll be the one rescuing you."

"You don't need to."

"They're calling our flight." With difficulty, Finn shouldered his backpack.

"Let me carry it."

"Absolutely not." His eyes were bright with tears and fever. "I mean it, Ava. No more."

"So now I just have to be a boring suburban wife?"

"When you get tired of it you only have to say. We can run away and build the beach hut. Or join the Foreign Legion. Or you can just be a boring suburban wife. I don't care. You're still you."

Side by side, they crossed the deserted terminal to the boarding gate.

The man who had everything he wanted

Once there was a man who believed in the power of hard work. He looked around at the life he found himself in and he thought, *I want more than this.* He looked at the things he wanted and he thought, *The world won't just give me what I want.* He looked at his two strong hands and he thought, *This is how I'll build my future.*

He worked hard and long, getting up early and going to bed late, and filling every minute in between with toil, until one day he had everything he wanted. He had a house with enough rooms and some left over. He had a wife he loved and was faithful to. He had a child who laughed and grew and thrived.

Every day, the man looked at his house and his wife and his child as they laughed in the sunshine and he thought, *I worked hard for all of this. Everything I have now is the result of my own hard work. And because I earned it, no-one can take it away from me.*

The sun looked down at the man, and it smiled kindly and left him to his delusions, because it knew men were foolish and had no idea how cruel the world could be. But the moon peeked in through a window and saw his beautiful wife sleeping, and it thought, *This man needs to learn.*

The man's wife became sick. The man thought, *If I work hard, I can make her well.* He spent all his time and all his money, and he worked from dawn 'till dusk and then from dusk 'till dawn. But all his hard work was for nothing, because he couldn't make his wife well.

When his wife died, the man thought his heart would break. So his took his heart out of his chest, locked it in a casket and hid the casket underneath his pillow. Then he took his daughter and ran away to live in a distant land, far away from all the things he had ever wanted. And he thought, *If I never want anything again, nothing else bad can ever happen to me.*

But the man had not thrown his heart away. He had not forgotten how to want. He had not yet learned his lesson.

Chapter Fifteen : Now

When Donald opened up, George was hanging around the doorway. George came into the pub without acknowledging Donald, and made straight for the bar. Once there, he leaned against the woodwork and waited.

"What can I get you, George?"

"A bottle of Heineken and a packet of pork scratchings, please," said George, as he always did, and when Donald handed them over he went to his usual table and sat on his usual stool. He tore down the seam and laid the bag out in a neat flat sheet, then began to eat. Donald had to smile.

"You got much on, then?" he asked, inspecting glasses. One wore a faint print of pink lipstick. Alicia almost always wore make-up these days. He couldn't remember when that had begun. Ava – no, he wasn't going to think about her. It was a nice day. He wouldn't waste it being angry. He took the glass out and gave it a wipe.

"Oh, yes. I had a big rebuild job to do, if you remember. That was entertaining." George laughed. "Flakes of paint everywhere, it made a right mess. They'll have to repaint the whole thing."

"Will they. That'll teach them."

"And I'm working on a good new project. I've got the plans here. A boat, which makes a nice change. Well, I say a boat. It's actually more of a raft."

"A raft. That's interesting." Where was Alicia now? If anyone had told him a couple of years ago that somehow, insidiously, she would have manoeuvred herself to the position where she could spend hours and hours out of the house, with people he didn't know, doing things he didn't want to imagine, he would have laughed.

"Have a look at the plans if you like," said George, in the tone of one conferring a great favour.

"A bit busy just now, George."

Had he had this much freedom? It had been different for him. A boy on a bike in a tough city three decades ago, compared to a girl in a seaside resort with a mobile phone in the here and now. Did these differences add up to security or stupidity? And who was the boy she was… ?

His hand caught the side of the pump. Amber nectar gushed into the catch tray. He grabbed a glass, capturing just over a quarter of a pint, then shook his head. What was he going to do with it? He couldn't stand the stuff personally.

"You don't want ten mouthfuls of Fosters, do you, George? On the house?"

"I don't drink Fosters," said George. "The interesting thing about rafts is, even though they don't have a hull, they can be surprisingly steerable."

Anyone but George would have taken an interest in where the Fosters had come from, but once he was off, he was off. It was comforting in a way, having someone talking as he pottered. The character of his autumns was determined by the summers. Some years – the lean years where the sun hadn't shone and the rooms hadn't sold and next Easter fell late in the spring – the autumn was filled with gnawing anxiety, knowing his business was now dependent on his neighbours and no-one had harvested quite enough money to go around. But this year had been good. The pub had done what it needed to. It had washed its face and then some. They'd get through the winter in modest comfort. If it wasn't for the irritation of those idiots down in the beach hut he would have been perfectly content.

A party of surfers came rampaging in at half-past twelve, tall and loud and aggressively healthy, narrow hips, wide shoulders and full thick heads of salty hair. (Had Alicia been with one of them? Was she with him still?) He thought about telling them they couldn't bring their boards in, but there were six of them and they were already eyeing the menu hungrily. He compromised by giving the boards a slow, disbelieving stare, and the surfers regressed into the boys they clearly still were at heart and took them out to the lobby and leaned them against the wall. It satisfied Donald to know that he could still summon the Death Stare. He was getting on, but he wasn't done. Life in the old dog yet.

The surfers bought bags and bags of crisps with their bottles of beer, and ordered chicken curries with rice and chips, burgers and chips, a vegetarian omelette with chips and salad, and two more bowls of chips for the table, as if the table might be joining in with the meal. The omelette surprised him. He'd imagined it would take a lot of animal protein to build six foot one of brawny manhood. Perhaps the lad fancied a change. Perhaps he was temporarily turning vegetarian to impress some girl called Jemima or Pippa or Amanda or Tamara, and when he'd got bored of her he'd go out for a celebratory meat feast with his mates.

Donald had no cook in the off-season, but he'd taught himself to make the simple stuff and the rest came out of the freezer. It wasn't gourmet dining but it was acceptable and filling. The surfers were laughing in that loud, braying way alpha males had, the kind of laugh that assumed no-one else in the room really counted and it was okay to fill the place with the sound of you being frightfully amusing.

"Two burgers with chips," he announced, deliberately cutting across their conversation. A smattering of *Thanks, mate* and *Christ I'm starving.* He wanted to tell them he wasn't their mate. He settled instead for bringing only two of the three chicken curries, forcing them to perform the you-have-this-one-no-you-do-no-you ritual, then giving the omelette to the wrong person so they would have to pass overloaded plates across the table. Small satisfactions. Then he stood in the kitchen and thought in horror, *Why am I going out of my way to annoy six perfectly nice, well-behaved young lads who are spending money in my establishment?*

The answer came in the voice of his old boss Harry. *You just need to get laid, my son.* He could picture Harry leaning back in his chair with a twinkle in his eye. *Want me to set you up?*

As if he had time for that. As if he had any interest in that. Jesus. He was in his late forties, not his early teens. He went to collect the empty bottles from the table and to ask them if they'd like another round.

They were talking about someone they'd met on the beach, who must be as hard as nails to go in without a wetsuit, and who had laughed and laughed at the one with the improbable name of Migmog when he tried and spectacularly failed to catch a wave... after some discussion regarding the drive home, they ordered five more beers and a fat Coke. The beers waited, patient and sweating, as the Coke gushed into the glass. Another sign they were nice lads, far nicer than he'd been at their age. He and his mates would have had the extra beer and a couple more on top, piled into the car anyway and assumed they weren't going to crash. He loaded the tray and carried it to the table.

"Ah, thanks mate." "Thanks, mate." "Thanks mate." A chorus of *mates*, as if he was part of the group rather than just the server. He swallowed his irritation. What would he have preferred them to do? An awkward respectful silence, hands in laps and no eye-contact? Unhelpful helping hands grabbing bottles off the tray and upsetting the balance? *Thank you, my man?* They were just a bunch of cheerful awkward lads in their twenties, trying to behave decently. They were still discussing the surf and the waves and the water and the wipe-out. The person they'd met in the water was female. An awful thought squeezed at his heart – would

Alicia… ? Had she… ? Would they… ?

He hovered for a moment, making slightly more than he needed to of adjusting chairs on the adjoining table. "… too old, mate." "I wasn't interested!" "Yeah, you were." "You lot are sick. Sick… " He moved away before they caught him listening. His hands trembled slightly. He took out his phone.

Hi sweetheart. This is your dad, turning weird and stalkerish. What you up to this afternoon? Any danger I might see you at some point? Xxxxx

He filled the interval until his phone pinged by wiping down the already immaculate pumps. The towels were beginning to fade. He had a spare box somewhere…

Sup D-man? I is hanging wid Katie. Xxxxxxxxxxx PS that means 'Hello father, I am currently at Katie's residence'.

Ah, but was she? Katie. A long-term fixture, so… he scrolled through his phone. *Andy - Katie's dad.*

Hey there mate this is Alicia's dad. Apparently she's invited herself round to yours, just checking that's okay with you. Cheers, Donald.

The laughter of the surfers was senseless and irritating. How could they sound so much like braying donkeys? Chimpanzees didn't bother with laughter. They just gouged each other's eyes out and, if they were feeling particularly upset, pulled each other's heads off. His phone pinged. How did parents cope before they could pursue their children round the world like this?

Hey mate, yep she's here and it's fine. No trouble all morning. On the computer for a while. Now in Katie's room doing girl shit. Cheers, Andy (Katie's dad).

All morning. The only words that mattered. It wasn't Alicia the surfers were letching over. His heart was suddenly light. Let them drool over somebody else's teenage daughter, let them ogle her breasts and covet her legs and dream of the cleft between her thighs. Just as long as it wasn't Alicia. As he checked the stock in the fridges, he began to whistle.

A few more customers drifted in, their background

conversation making the asinine sound of the surfers paradoxically quieter. Mike came in at two so Donald could go to the Cash and Carry. He didn't actually need anything but he had given Mike the shift anyway. That was how it worked in this small community; the income from the town's single unpredictable cash-crop recycled round the town for as long as possible, diminishing and diminishing with every pass, until Easter came and the first trickle of new money began to arrive. Mike had the look on his face that told Donald he had a favour to ask. Please God it wouldn't be for extra work. He'd done okay this year, but not so okay he could carry Mike and his family through the cold.

"Is there any chance my lad Mattie could take half my shift?" Mike looked inexplicably uncomfortable, his gaze not quite meeting Donald's, his hands deep in his pockets. "Not for what you pay me, obviously. A tenner at the end of the night'll do him fine."

Donald tried to recall Mattie. After a moment he remembered a tall inarticulate sixteen-year-old with a faint bloom of moustache and a terrible beanie hat, who had nevertheless kept the beer flowing through several stifling August afternoons.

"I don't see why not."

"You sure it's okay? I've just got to be somewhere for a couple of hours, that's all, but I can put it off."

Donald grinned. "You got something special on?"

To Donald's utter, utter surprise, a slow tide of dull crimson swept up Mike's neck, and Mike turned away in a pointless pretence at adjusting the pumps, knocking a Heineken empty to the floor. The bottle bounced but didn't break. Mike made a large pantomime of picking it up.

"Sorry about that," he said, setting the bottle back on the bar.

"Don't worry," said Donald. He hesitated, then put a hand briefly on Mike's shoulder. "Everything all right?" The closest two middle-aged men could come to inviting a confidence.

"Fine," said Mike, his face wretched. "It's just. You know."

"Something medical?" Donald suggested.

"Something like that. Look, thanks. I really appreciate it." He glanced desperately towards the cellar door. "Meant to say. The Doom Bar's not pouring right. I'll check the you-know."

What was that about? Not his problem. Alicia was all right, that was what mattered. There was still the spectre of the unknown *him*, haunting the pages of the journal he'd glimpsed so briefly he could almost pretend he'd imagined it, but at least she wasn't giving it away to anyone who crossed her path... dear God, why would he think that of his own daughter? How would it be his business if she did? No, all he had to worry about was how to pass the hours when he was supposed to be at the Cash and Carry, so Mike could convincingly earn his wage and not feel he was taking charity. Before he left, he went to clear the plates.

The conversation still turned on the surf and the currents and the joy of having the sea to themselves now the summer visitors had departed. The paradox of local living – wanting them to come so they'd spend their money, wanting them to go so they'd leave you in peace. One of them was speaking to him.

"Yes, mate." Catching their habits of speech, an old instinctive trick to build rapport and soften up the subject. "What can I do for you?"

"Do you know anything about the mad couple who live in that wicked beach hut?"

A slow jeering roar. The young man made a *yeah, yeah* quieting gesture and kept his eyes on Donald. Donald forced himself breathe in, hold it, breathe out.

"What did you want to know?"

"Just wondered who they are."

"He fancied her," said his mate. The others thumped the table.

"They're brother and sister," said Donald, trying to keep

his voice neutral. "They won't be here long. The council are trying to evict them."

"Boo," protested the surfer with the mop of blonde hair.

"So she's not married, then?" Another one, leather necklace and hipster goatee.

Donald put on his stern publican face.

"I believe you're about twenty years too young to be asking," he said. "Can I get you anything else?"

"Oh come on."

"She's fit."

"For an older woman."

"Older women are the best."

"Like you'd know."

"Everyone needs a sugar-mama."

"She's got her own place."

"You should go down there, Luke, see if she'll invite you in for a coffee."

"Yeah, why not? We'll wait for you."

"We bloody will not. If he's off getting laid by some glamorous older bird he can make his own way home."

Donald resisted the urge to turn the table over, wipe the idiot grins from their stupid donkey faces. Instead he cleared their plates with a face as still and impassive as the black rocks the town was built on. Slick and craggy and unforgiving, like the walls of the caves where he'd threatened to drown Finn. He could take down one of these arrogant young men instead, full of piss and vinegar, convinced the world and all its women were theirs for the asking… one of the lads glanced at Donald's face and became quiet and still. The silence spread like a rash across the table, like a cloud of poison gas, leeching away the banter and leaving a quelled silence. Donald refused to make eye-contact. The stack of plates was precarious, he should have taken two trips really, but with care he could manage them.

As he left their table, he heard one of the boys say, low but clear, "Shit, you don't think he fancies her himself, do you?"

The rage was so huge he nearly dropped the plates; but he'd been in this game a long time now, and the most important thing for a publican to be was composed. He took the plates through to the kitchen without a pause, passing Mike who was pulling a pint of Doom Bar, set the crockery down and loaded the dishwasher, neat and efficient, no gaps or misalignments. He found the tablets, unwrapped one and shut the door. Intensive clean, to scour away the curry sauce and leave the glasses bright and sparkling.

Then he took a deep breath, looked around the clean orderly kitchen, took another deep breath and kicked the steel side of the dishwasher so hard it rocked on its sturdy base, leaving a gigantic dent in the side.

The damage was almost enough, but not quite. He kicked it again, left another smaller dent. He expected it to shudder to a halt, but the pump powered manfully on, churning water and soap. Over the sound of sloshing, he heard the faint tinkle of a broken glass settling around the drain. Still not enough. His hand hesitated over a catering-sized bottle of ketchup. Heinz. Some bought cheaper brands and decanted them, but he'd never seen the point in scrimping on condiments. If he threw it at the wall, the stain would soak into the paintwork, leaving a lasting impression to go with the dented dishwasher.

He put the bottle down again, grabbed his good wool coat from its hook and walked out.

The tide looked hours from its peak but he checked the board anyway. At nearly three o'clock, the waves were still far away. By six, they would cut across the left half of the beach and join up with the freshwater outflow from the storm drains, a trick that caught out a new crop of surprised visitors every year as they found themselves marooned on a tiny sandbar by two inches of water. They would laugh as they waded their way back to safety, not knowing that if they'd stayed just half an hour longer, they'd be swept away. Why were they so oblivious to the power of the sea? Did they never look at the caves and ask themselves what inexorable strength it took to hollow out those long fingers of space from the weight that loomed above?

The beach hut was out of reach of even the mightiest spring tides. When the waters turned the dunes into a tiny barren island, the beach hut would remain dry. How well they must know this little patch of earth to place their home so unerringly in the one spot where they could live by the sea without being swamped by it. That was the magic they had, of course. Because they knew things others didn't, they appeared to know more in total. It was a neat trick, swapping such dull knowledge as how to run a home or choose a decent school for an understanding of tides and currents, of sands and safety and earth and water. No wonder Alicia found them so bloody fascinating. He angrily strode on.

He had pictured her in the black swimsuit, making her way back up from the water. But Ava stood on the veranda, her hands wrapped tightly around a steaming coffee mug, thumbs and fingers all bunched together like a child clutching a bowl, and gazing out to sea. A gigantic shapeless jumper was bundled about her upper body. When she saw him approaching, her eyes turned wide and wary; but he thought that perhaps there was a moment when she smiled.

"Alicia's not here." She was looking him up and down, perhaps assessing whether he was a threat, perhaps for some other reason.

"She's been here a lot though." He didn't mean to sound combative but he couldn't help it, it was just the mood he was in today. "I hope she's not making a nuisance of herself. Disturbing you while you're so busy."

"We're not busy."

"I thought that brother of yours was supposed to be writing a book."

"That brother of mine." The corners of her lips twitched upward.

Inside his pocket, his hand clenched tight.

"It's finished."

"How long did it take him?"

"His whole life, on and off. Why?"

Donald sniffed. "That figures."

Ava took a mouthful of coffee.

"Are you still angry about the other day?" she asked.

"Which other day? The day when you set up home here? The day you took my daughter swimming in some of the most dangerous waters in the county? The day you hoodwinked the Welfare Officer… "

"Hoodwinked." Ava sighed happily. "That's a fabulous word. Actually I was thinking of the day we took Alicia off in the van for the day without asking you. I'm sorry. We should have asked permission."

"As if you ever asked permission in your life."

"My God, is that how you see me?" He couldn't tell if she was amused or upset. "When Finn and I… " her hand twitched. Coffee slopped onto her leg. "Ow. Damn it!"

"Are you all right?" he had his arm around her before he could stop himself, a tender reflex ingrained by years of single parenthood. He felt the shock of the burn as if it was on his own skin.

"No, it's fine, it was going cold anyway."

"Of course it's not cold, your jeans are steaming! Take them off, you idiot. Let's see the damage."

She rolled her jeans down reluctantly, exposing a pale red mark on her thigh.

"It's nothing," she told him.

"Don't be stupid. Burns take hours to come out properly. Have you got cold water? I'll make a compress."

"I said it's fine."

"Are you always this bloody stubborn?"

"Are you always this bloody rude?"

"Will you stop arguing and let me help you!"

There were tears in her eyes. He resisted the urge to wipe them away.

"Please," he said, gentle in spite of himself. "Let's call a truce while we clear the wounded off the battlefield."

Inside the beach hut, Ava seemed to become more at ease, kicking off her boots and peeling herself out of the jeans. Donald cast around and found a mug and some kitchen roll. The water-tank was half-filled. He improvised a ragged compress, holding it gingerly over the burn. Rivulets of water dripped onto the wooden floor. Close up, he could smell the oiled wool of Ava's sweater, the salt in her hair, the warmth of her sweat.

"How's that?" he asked, wishing she would take the compress from him so he could move away.

"Better. Thank you. And sorry."

"Sorry for what?"

"Being stubborn."

"It's okay." His back was beginning to ache. He let the compress go and stood up. "It's annoying to need help from someone you don't like."

"I didn't need your help."

He turned away and found himself facing a map of Scandinavia. A large red pin was stuck into Iceland. "That's the bit you're going to argue with. Not *actually, I do like you.*"

"Why would I like you? You want me evicted from my home."

"Well, you keep luring my daughter down here."

Ava laughed. "Nobody *lures* her anywhere. She just turns up."

"You give her tea and biscuits and talk to her. Of course she just turns up."

"You make her sound like a stray dog. It's polite to offer guests refreshments."

He turned around so he could glare at her. "Does that mean I get a cup of tea and a biscuit, then? Shall I help myself, or are you going to make them for me?"

"You didn't come to call. You came to… " She hesitated.

"Yes? Do, please, tell me why you think I came here this afternoon."

"Actually," she said, "I don't know why you came or what you want. You'll have to tell me."

"Alicia," he said. "You said she's down here a lot. Is she ever down here when – when you're not?" Ava looked at him in honest surprise. "I mean, is she – does she meet anyone else here?"

"What, like a boyfriend or something? Oh my God, are you accusing me of running a disorderly house?"

"No! No." He turned back towards Iceland. "I just – oh, well – I had a quick look in her diary the other day. Now you're going to say I shouldn't have."

"Oh, I think actually you should," said Ava unexpectedly. "There's something – I don't know – I could be wrong, but… " she sighed. "Reading her diary is the very least you could do. But you won't listen to me because you don't like me, so that's not what you're here for."

"I never said I don't like *you*, I just don't like what you're doing."

"Answer the question."

"There were these surfers," he said, still staring at the Icelandic coastline. "They came in for a late lunch. They were talking about some – female they'd been fooling around with in the water. At first I thought they meant Alicia."

"Then you realised they meant me. So that's not it either. Why don't you get to the point? What are you so afraid of?"

He turned around then, and she saw his face. The intake of breath stretched out slow and taut between them.

"You know what I want," he said.

Ava was very still.

"You're all I've thought about for weeks. I dream about you."

"I dream about being a mermaid."

"You're not a mermaid, you're a witch. You put a spell on me the first time I saw you. You've got a cord around my heart

227

that's tied round your little finger, and every time you move you pull it a little bit tighter, and now I can hardly breathe."

"That all sounds very dramatic."

"You can laugh and send me away if you like. Or you can make me beg. I'll do that too if you ask me to. There's no pride left in me. You can do anything you want with me and I'll have to obey. If there was any justice in this world, they'd have burned you at the stake."

"But there isn't any justice."

"How about mercy?"

"I don't believe in mercy either."

"So?"

She pulled out a sage-green chair. "Sit down. You're too tall to talk to when you're standing up."

He hesitated, then sat. "Does this mean I get tea and biscuits after all?"

"Of course you don't get tea and biscuits, you idiot," she said, and, as he was reeling from the unfairness of this, she kissed him.

Her lips against his were a sweet shock, the touch of her tongue astounding. The taste of the coffee she'd been drinking exploded in his mouth, leaving in its wake the old cliché, *Would you like to come up for a coffee?*

He couldn't remember how to do this. How did you get from kissing in the living room to lying together in bed? And how and when did you undress? Ah, but in this perfect little haven there were no awkward pauses because the bed was only two steps away, and Ava was already half-naked.

He'd shrugged off his heavy coat without realising; his body remembered even if he'd forgotten. His hands lifted off the huge jumper that swamped her. His fingers nudged hers gently aside as she struggled with the buttons on his shirt, taking over the task with ease even though his brain was drowning in panic – panic, and the conviction that she would put a stop to this any minute now. His lips brushed

228

over her skin. It was like watching himself from above. The absurd moment when you're stood in your unbuttoned shirt and pants, unsure when or how to take your socks off. The shiver when she laid her palm flat against his chest to feel his heart, which leapt and galloped like a terrified rabbit. Did she like how he looked? How he felt? Her husband had been so lean and trim. What would this look like from the outside? A middle-aged man, at the end of a long dry spell, finally getting back in the saddle. Trying to find out what she liked. Watching her face for a response.

Now they were crammed awkwardly into the bottom bunk, a patchwork quilt thrown over them. He felt the warmth of the stove, and the faint draft of air from the open sea. Shades of his misspent teenage years, when sex indoors was a glorious novelty and sex in a double bed an unimaginable luxury. By the time he'd met Ellen it had been swanky hotel rooms with lush king-sized beds, then the long deep peace of the large airy room that looked out onto the back garden; a few years of wild abandon (no party wall!) and then the need for quiet (don't wake the baby!). Now, a different kind of freedom – unless...

"Finn," he muttered against her ear, in a sudden panic.

"He won't be home 'till later." Her eyes closed, her skin flushed, blotchy where his stubble had prickled her. No sign now of the angry goddess he'd inadvertently spied on, or the well-groomed waif who ran away from her husband and left her shoes in the car park. Instead, a pretty stranger, eyes closed, lips parted. Did he look as strange to her? Was that why she had her eyes shut? Her movements were jerky and tentative, as if she shared his incipient panic. And all the while his body knowing what it wanted, knowing what to do, how to be. He tried to roll her beneath him, but she shook her head and pushed him onto his back. That was okay, if he was honest, he probably preferred that anyway.

And then as her hair fell across her face and hid her features he suddenly saw Ellen, and for a heart-stopping second he thought, *No, I can't do this, I can't...* then she opened her eyes and looked at him questioningly and became Ava once more, and he was back in his body, sweaty and frantic, every part of him yearning for the closeness, and he drew her down onto him and heard himself sob with joy.

Afterwards, Ava got up to stand in the doorway, limping a little, stretching out cramped muscles. The waves had crept closer, he could feel the damp in the air. She draped her jumper awkwardly around her shoulders. He wanted to offer her his shirt, but found he was shy. What if she declined it? What then? And what did this afternoon mean? Were they lovers now? Or would they go back to their own sides of the line in the sand, and continue the conflict?

No. Think about that later. For now, just savour this moment. The glory of what had happened. The peace that lay over him. Ava yawned and stretched sleepily. He scooched over and patted the bed beside him, then felt ridiculous. It was her bed, he had no right to invite her in. If anything he should be getting out to make room. But she crawled in beside him, fitting herself neatly against the curve of his legs and belly. He stroked her thigh, and felt a prickle of reawakening desire. Her hair was fine and soft against his chin.

"I knew you were in disguise," she murmured.

"In disguise as what?"

"Apparently all men are either horrible or boring. You like to pretend you're boring, but you're not at all really, are you?"

Did that mean he was horrible? He didn't dare ask for fear of the answer.

"What happens now?" he asked instead.

She closed her eyes. "What do you want to happen now?"

He kissed the top of her head. Was this okay? Was it too much? He'd been inside her half an hour ago, how could he be unsure about kissing her? "I don't know."

"Well, wake me up when you do." Ava's voice was blurry

with sleep and her eyelashes fluttered drowsily. "Don't miss the tide."

Donald checked his watch.

"It's five o'clock. Where did the afternoon go?"

She didn't bother to answer, just sighed and nestled closer, her breathing growing slower and deeper. It was hard to make himself move, but he had to get back – to the bar, to his daughter, to his real life. But then perhaps this was his real life.

"Can I see you again?" An absurd and gawky question, as if they were a pair of teenagers, not two grown adults with the freedom to do as they liked. Well, to do some of what they liked. Within the constraints of a normal existence, within the bounds of their responsibilities. With the knowledge that she was still married. Actually, now he came to think of it, teenagers were probably far more free.

She was asleep already, the candlelight kindly and warm, smoothing out the creases and turning her back into the girl she must have been on her wedding day. Before he left, he stopped to look for a moment, envying the man who had waited for her at the end of the aisle. Then he remembered his own wedding.

Ellen, he thought, *I'm sorry, so sorry.* He waited for the guilt, but found instead a stillness that could have been either loss or peace. It stayed with him all the way home, across the sands and into the bright warmth of the pub, the noise and the chaos of an unexpectedly busy evening's trade and Mike's son Mattie, harassed but manful, barely keeping on top of the orders.

About half-past eight, the bar grew quieter again and Mike came back in. Donald gave Mattie a twenty-pound note from the till, ignoring both Mike and Mattie's protests that this was more than they'd agreed, and his own nagging awareness that he had now set a precedent that could come back to haunt him as the year grew leaner. As he handed over the money, it occurred to him that he had not yet seen his daughter.

He took the steps in a panic, but she was in her room after all, sitting up in bed and writing frantically in the flowered notebook. Her cheeks were flushed and her eyes were bright. On another evening he might have given in to the impulse to question her, but tonight he thought, *Keep your big mouth shut. After all, what have you spent the afternoon doing?* and he smiled at her and turned away without speaking.

Chapter Sixteen: Now

The morning after. Donald left sleep behind and came back into his body by degrees, wondering what he'd find as he waded into consciousness. Guilt? He braced himself for it and opened his eyes; but no, guilt was totally absent. Perhaps it would show up later. For now, he'd enjoy the quiet. Regret? He waited warily, but no, not a flicker. Even though he'd created a situation that was stupidly complicated and morally dubious and with a million different ways to end badly, he could feel the great daft grin spreading across his face, unstoppable, unshakeable.

Embarrassment? Yes, a healthy dollop of that. He'd been trying to get rid of the pair of them since they got here. Contentment? Oh yes. Because he'd found something new and wonderful? Or simply because he had – in the words of his long-vanished boss – finally got himself laid? Impossible to say. So, contentment of a sort, certainly. Was there shame? Absolutely not.

He glanced at the clock. Five to nine. He hadn't slept this late for years. He could still smell Ava on his skin. He should probably take a shower, but he wanted to hold onto the reminder. In the bathroom, he caught himself humming tunelessly through the toothpaste.

Alicia's toothbrush was still in the mug where he'd put it last night. She always left it on the side of the basin, and he always put it back in the mug, a small quiet ritual of parenthood he'd grown reluctantly fond of. Did she ever stop to wonder how her toothbrush migrated from the basin to the mug each night and morning? When she was little she'd believed her light-switch had an automatic timer because, after she fell asleep, he or Ellen would creep into her room and switch it off.

He glanced into her room as he passed, treading softly. Like him she was usually an early waker, but like him she was sleeping late this morning, sprawled on her front like a skydiver. One pale slender foot stuck out from beneath the duvet. He resisted the urge to kiss it.

The kitchen was cold. He would have to put the heating on soon. How would Ava survive, down in the beach hut? He didn't care what happened to Finn but he didn't like to imagine Ava shivering and blue. Could he invite her here? Just for a few stolen hours to start with, snatched at the end of the evening's trade and ending before daybreak. Perhaps they wouldn't have to hide. Alicia liked her…

The beach hut had been warm yesterday afternoon. But then, yesterday afternoon they had made their own warmth.

And then again, Ava might not be willing.

Alicia was waking up. He could hear her yawning as she padded into the bathroom. He took two mugs from the cupboard and made coffee, hoping she wouldn't take so long in the shower that hers would grow cold. The coffee's sour clutch at the base of his stomach made him realise he was starving. He shoved two slices of bread into the toaster, snatched them out as soon as they showed faint signs of becoming toast, then slathered them with Flora and Oxford marmalade. Why did he crave bitter tastes when the feeling that suffused him was one of such sweetness? Alicia's coffee steamed reproachfully on the cold countertop as he made two more slices and wolfed them down.

When she finally came in, she had that pink scrubbed look that faintly recalled her babyhood, and her hair hung on her shoulders in a thick wet mass. She looked especially pretty today, but also tired. He remembered how she had looked last night – flushed and female and lovely – and the thought that had occurred to him.

Well, why not, he thought. *Bloody good for her. We're all of us a long time dead.*

"I made you coffee," he said. "Might be cold, though."

"Thanks." She took a mouthful and grimaced.

"I'll do you another one."

"No, this is fine."

"Course it's not." He took her mug away from her.

"Da-ad… "

"Ali-cia… "

"That one was fine!"

"That one was fiiiiine.... my dad is sooo mean, he makes me fresh coffee without even being aaaasked… " Sometimes this went appallingly wrong and he ended up making her cry, but this morning it seemed to be working. She smiled at him and it looked like a genuine smile, so he risked a teenage flappy-armed flounce over to the kettle. He stirred the coffee, then took it over to her. As she took the mug from him, he saw that her eyes were swimming and shiny.

"Oh, hey, come on." He knelt beside her and put a tentative hand on her shoulder. "Alicia, you have to stop being so sensitive. I was joking, you know I was."

"It's not that. It's just – you're such a great dad. You're always there and you always look after me and I know you love me. I'm so lucky."

"Oh, pet." He had to swallow hard. "Don't you dare say any more or I'll cry as well."

She smiled shakily. "You never cry."

"Good point. So just you shush, all right? I'm nothing like what you should have had. You should have had so much more than this." He kissed the top of her head. "But this is the best I could do. I'm just an average bloke with an extraordinary daughter."

"I'm not. I'm awful. If you knew how awful I am."

"The only awful thing about you is that terrible thing you do with your hair when you're going out." She managed another watery smile. "Okay, we have to stop now, sorry. That is absolutely all the talk about feelings I've got in me."

"Okay."

"Are you going to eat anything?"

"I'll get some toast when I'm dressed."

"Make sure you do. Don't want you wasting away."

"Dad… "

"Da-ad… " He was still starving. He counted the slices of bread, then put two more in the toaster. Alicia got up, taking her coffee with her.

"Alicia," he said as she reached the doorway.

"What?"

"I don't mean it, you know. I've always got more talk about feelings. We can talk about whatever you want."

"Thanks, Dad." She hovered in the doorway, holding her coffee against her chin.

"So?"

She turned away. "I'm going to get dressed."

His morning was haunted by Ava. Going about his usual routine, he conjured her ghost for company – not beside him, but in the next room, upstairs when he was downstairs, in the kitchen while he mopped the floor behind the bar. He invented conversations, banal little snippets between a long-established couple.

I'm taking the rubbish-bags out, love.

Did you remember the kitchen bin?

Of course I did, woman. Stop nagging.

Would it work? Could it work? Married (complicated) but no children of her own (easier? Harder?). As he stared forgetfully into the tall freezer, counting trays of chicken curry and never managing to hold the total in his head, Alicia came in, mumbled something about seeing Katie, then disappeared.

Would Alicia mind if her dad brought home a woman? Maybe she'd be pleased. She could grow up and leave without worrying that he'd be on his own. No, he couldn't carve himself a future out of sand and salt and a single encounter.

Can Mike manage on his own later?

What have you got in mind, Missus?

Oh, you know, if Alicia's out…

Would Ava be so forward? He didn't know her well enough to say. He could remember every word she'd said yesterday…

Reading her diary is the very least you could do.

Oh, shit.

No. Not this morning. Not yet. He'd been no-one but Dad for almost a decade. He deserved these few minutes to dream over his first time with a woman since Ellen left him.

There's something – I don't know –

But he knew. He'd recognised it last night, his own feelings mirrored on Alicia's face. So his daughter had met some boy. And why not? At her age love flattened you like an avalanche. You could spend hours dreaming of their smile. Their skin against yours was an unbearable mystery. Teenage love, the purest kind of love there was.

Reading her diary is the very least you could do.

I'm not reading her diary.

Because then you'll have to do something about it?

Shut up nagging, will you? She's entitled to privacy.

So, yes, his daughter was on the cusp of adulthood. They were doing more than holding hands. So what? Finding out didn't mean having sex. There was a whole world of mysterious pleasures open to teenagers – a world that somehow closed off as soon as you were old enough for sex to be a reasonable expectation of a reasonable relationship. He'd been seventeen when he'd lost his virginity, but that didn't mean the whole thing had taken him by surprise.

Just read her diary.

He couldn't read it. He had work to do downstairs. No,

that wouldn't do. Alicia came first. If she was in trouble, he'd leave the cleaning and the stock-take and go upstairs and take her room apart looking for evidence. He couldn't read her diary because – he just couldn't, that's all.

Because you'd rather daydream about me. That's selfish, Donald.

Well, and so what if it was? He'd done a good job for years. A conscientious job. A workman-like job. A stand-in's job. He'd tried to be perfect and of course he'd failed because every parent did. But surely, in all those years, he'd saved up enough cosmic credit to buy himself a few hours off? So what if he stood here staring into space, the vacuum plugged in and ready to go, looking like a madman as he lost himself in the memory of Ava?

Alicia's in trouble.

If he crossed the sands later, would he find Ava alone? Might they be able to repeat yesterday, the same basic events but with delicious variations that would only make the moment sweeter? Perhaps he could take her flowers.

Alicia.

"Bloody hellfire," he said out loud. He abandoned the vacuum and took the stairs two at a time.

Her doorway opened onto a room in transition. A few teddy bears clustered around her pillow, three bright and plushy, two old and worn. There was Bad Bear, stiff and disapproving, who had lived in her cot since before she was born. Grey Rabbit, on the other hand, had worked its way up the ranks from blank obscurity to magical comfort object. The rabbit she had now wasn't the true Grey Rabbit but a convincing imposter, secretly bought and artfully distressed after the original was left on a train. ('No, darling, it's all right – the Lost Toy Office will find him and send him back. They collect special toys and deliver them home to their owners.' And while Alicia sobbed in her lap, Ellen mouthed the words to him, 'Go and buy a new one.') When Grey Rabbit first came to live with them, he'd been firm and perky and furry all over. Now, he flopped tragically in the middle where his stuffing had turned limp, and his fur was loved off in patches.

The ticking of the clock called him back to reality. He'd never understood how Alicia could stand the relentless clop-clop-clop of it, but she said it was comforting and it helped her sleep. She'd been gone half an hour. She might not be back for hours more. She might walk in any second. He had to be fast.

Where to start? First, a brief rifle through her desk, although this seemed unlikely. She'd been writing in bed last night. Would she really get up again just to leave her diary somewhere so obvious? Nonetheless he checked. Sometimes, not hiding things properly became brilliant concealment. He frisked the pillow, the mattress, the bed. Many people chose beds to hide things in, even huge uncomfortable things like bricks of cocaine and guns. But there was no sign of the journal.

She might have taken it with her to Katie's. But he kept looking.

Her bookshelves were in transition too. *The Chronicles of Narnia* sat beside *Twilight* and *Carrie*. She'd borrowed the Jeremy Clarkson book that Mike (almost certainly prompted by Anna) had given him for Christmas. He wondered why she'd bothered. As far as he was concerned, it was unreadable. She'd also taken his copy of *Crime and Punishment*, and marked her place with a piece of string. She'd made it to page one hundred and twenty-one. Had she stopped, or was she just pausing for breath? The book by her bed was *The Hunger Games*. He'd driven her and three friends to see the film one Sunday, and spent the afternoon reading in a café. Still no sign of the journal.

Her drawers next, guilt growing hot in his belly now. Checking her bed was one thing ('I was changing the sheets!'), rummaging her bookshelves was another ('I was after that book of mine you never gave back!') but there was

239

no defence for rummaging through her underwear. He forced himself to forget that these were his daughter's things, to go through the familiar motions of checking and seeking and cataloguing. Nothing, nothing, nothing. He was violating her privacy for nothing. Would she know he'd been here?

He found it at last in the place he should have looked first – in the backpack she was normally inseparable from, hanging on the back of the door. He didn't even see it until he sat down heavily on the bed to regroup, causing the door to swing slightly closed. Eight years away from his old life and his skills were finally leaving him.

He took out the journal and looked at it. The corners were rubbed smooth and there was a tear in the flowery cover where Alicia had tried to peel off the barcode sticker. It was about one-third full.

He'd found it. Now what? *I put it to you, Mr Emory, that in reading your daughter's diary you were merely indulging a prurient curiosity. - Absolutely not. I was concerned for her welfare. - Why did you feel concerned? - I'd read something before that. - Ah, so you'd* already *invaded her privacy by reading her diary on a previous occasion? - If I could finish, what I was going to say was what I read gave me reason to believe she might be sexually active. - Sexually active! So she referred to having sex? - Not exactly but I felt I had enough grounds to go back and have another look just to make sure. She's still underage. - Mr Emory, isn't it true that you only decided to investigate after you began a liaison with a married woman? Is it possible you were merely displacing the guilt you felt about betraying your wife? - That's a bit deep for a brief, isn't it? - Ah, but this isn't a Court of Law, is it? This is the Court of Your Own Conscience. We can go as deep as we like.*

He'd read it, he decided. But she'd never know he knew. He'd read it because he wanted to know the name of the boy Alicia was in love with, but when she brought him home for lunch or dinner or whatever, he'd put on his best surprised face. He'd read it, but it would be an act of love, not betrayal. It would be no worse than the times he'd left Christmas gifts at the end of her bed, or stolen her baby-teeth from under her pillow. It was just one of those deceptions you had to practice as a parent. It was an act of loving espionage.

His thoughts neatly marshalled, he opened the cover and began to read.

The clock ticked and ticked, one tick per second. You counted the intervals with elephants – he'd learned that at school. Ellen had been taught hippopotamuses, but with hippos you had to be quick. How long would Alicia be? He had to open up. He couldn't do it. He couldn't serve beer and snacks and the occasional rewarmed meal. He had to, it was his job. When you were the landlord you opened when you wanted to hide in a cupboard and never come out, you opened when you felt like you were dying, you opened when you wanted to kill someone.

Tick. Tick. Tick. Tick. A loud one then a quiet one, loud and then quiet, the electric mechanism weighing out the seconds. Loud. Quiet. Loud. Quiet.

How long would she be? He wanted to sit and wait but he couldn't. He had to keep their lives going. Was that where he'd gone wrong? Had he been too focused on the pub, on the busy successful summer they'd just had? Was that how he'd fallen down on the job, failed so miserably as a parent that he hadn't seen this awful thing that had been happening to his daughter?

(How would he kill him? So many ways to kill him.)

A quarter to eleven now. He should be downstairs. He'd left the vacuum in the middle of the floor, the carpet half-cleaned. The pumps weren't switched on. Perhaps he could ask Mattie to come in. No, he couldn't. They were well into the lean months now. He needed to hoard his money, not fritter it away.

(Who was it? Who? How could he find out?)

But was it frittering? Alicia was his world. His job was to put her first. Oh God, the guilt, the guilt of not seeing what was happening. The clock ticked and ticked. How could she sleep with that noise? The thought he'd had a hundred times, distilled into a simpler thought; how could she sleep? How could he? How could he have lain senselessly in the room next to hers, quietly confident that he was doing an acceptable job at this parenting business, while his daughter tumbled into hell?

(Where could he hide the body? The threat he'd made to Finn. Who was it? Who?)

She'd written that she was a thief. She'd written that she was ashamed. Ashamed because an older married man had preyed on her. Ashamed because she couldn't stop it. Ashamed because she liked it. Five minutes to eleven. What was he going to do? The door – feet on the stairs – the door opening…

I'm not ready, he thought in a panic. *I'm not ready, I need more time.*

He sat so still she didn't see him immediately. She was in a hurry, her eyes anxious. She'd come for her backpack. She never went anywhere without it, that *never* that meant *except when something huge was on her mind.* He thought his heart might break.

Her backpack wasn't where she'd left it. She was turning around to look for it. This was the last moment in their lives when she would trust him. Her gaze rested on him, passed over, came back to him. She saw him holding her journal.

"Alicia," he said. "Sweetheart. Alicia."

She turned white, then scarlet. Her hands trembled as she raised them to cover her cheeks.

"Don't be embarrassed," he said clumsily. "I'm not angry. Not with you. This isn't your fault."

She stood very still, as if by not moving she could stop time.

"I'm so, so sorry. I'll spend the rest of my life wishing I'd

242

known earlier so I could keep you safe, but now I know, I can help you."

"You read my journal."

"I had to, pet. I knew something was wrong. I had to find out so I could help you. You poor little love. How long has this been going on?"

"You went through my stuff and you read my journal."

He stood up and put out a hand to try and draw her to him. She took a single step back and his arm fell to his side.

"You don't have a thing to be embarrassed about," he stumbled on. "I'm the one who should be… "

"I'm not embarrassed." Her voice trembled with passion. "I'm not embarrassed *at all*. It was my choice."

"Alicia, you're confused. That's just what he's made you think so you'll protect him. But you don't need to. Just tell me his name and I'll take it from there." (Shameful, shameful to interrogate his daughter like this, but more shameful to have missed the signs.) "You won't be in any trouble, okay? Not you, only him. You just need to be brave and… "

"I said," her voice clear and cold and high, "it was my choice."

"You don't need to do anything, I'll do it all. I'll speak to the police and get it sorted for you." (He was lying, but he needed to get this started, the first crack in the armour. He needed the name, the name, the name.)

"You're not listening. You never listen, and you're still not listening now. I did it all willingly and I'm not turning him in."

"Pet, you're fifteen."

"He cares about me."

"Has he told you that?" (Unfair question, unfair and cruel. He saw her flinch and felt as if he could bite through his own tongue. He mustn't treat her like the enemy.)

"And I care about him too." A single traitor tear quivering on her cheek.

"He's made you think that's true but it's not. It's part of

243

how they operate."

"How who operate?"

"Paedophiles."

"You what?" A witchy cackle of laughter. "Do I look like a child to you?" She looked ten inches taller, vengeful and triumphant. She looked as if she could strike him dead with her gaze. She didn't look like his daughter at all. "Are you out of your mind?"

"I know you're upset. I don't blame you. I don't blame you for any of this."

"I blame you," she said.

"Alicia."

"You read my journal." She was trying to hold onto the rage but the tears were looming. "How could you read my journal?" He tried to hold her. She threw his arms off. "Are you trying to make me hug you? Now that's funny."

"I'm your dad."

"It's eleven o'clock. You have to go and open up."

"The hell with the pub. We need to finish talking."

"I'm never talking to you about this again. Never, do you hear? Never, ever."

"Okay, we're both getting angry. We need a few minutes." (Sometimes the art of interrogation was knowing when to back away.) "I'll come back up later and we can talk some more." (But then, all the interrogations he'd done before were with people who couldn't leave the room.) "Do you promise to stay here?"

"Don't climb out the bathroom window, you mean?"

(Oh, he'd been so stupidly pleased with himself for that... and now he worried that they would never be that close again.)

"Promise you'll stay here until we've talked some more. Will you promise that?"

Silence.

"Okay, I'm sorry but I have to do this." He went to the bathroom, turned the long key that locked the sash and put it in his pocket.

244

"Is that *have to* like you *had to* read my journal?" Alicia stood behind him on the landing. "That kind of have-to? Are you going to lock me in my room?"

"There's stuff for lunch in the fridge. Can I make you something?"

"You need to open up."

"I'll make you a sandwich first."

"I'd rather starve to death."

"I love you," he tried. "Please remember that."

"Yeah, well, I'm not sure I love you, Dad. Not any more."

"Look, I'm going downstairs, but only because you're angry and you need some space, okay? You're the most important thing to me and we'll get through this. I promise."

He closed the door, then the game was over and his strength was gone and he crumpled on the stairs, hunched over his own knees. *Oh please no not that, anything but that, any price but that.* She looked as if she meant it, but teenagers said these things.

He went downstairs and unlocked the doors and put the blackboard outside and switched on the pumps and put the cellar lights on and wished he had never even thought to look in his daughter's journal.

One o'clock. Time to take a break, see if Alicia was ready to talk. The stairs felt a thousand miles high.

"How are you doing, love? Did you get that sandwich?"

She shrugged.

"You know I'm not angry with you, don't you? I'm only angry with… "

"*You're* not angry with *me?*" Suddenly she was on her feet, squaring up to him. "Well, just so's you know, I am absolutely fucking furious with you, okay?"

"Don't swear."

"Because that's the important thing here."

"Look, pet… "

"I'm not your pet."

"We need to talk about this."

"*You want to* doesn't mean *we need to*. But it's always about what you want, isn't it?"

Derailing him. Trying to put him on the defensive. He had to admire her skill. "You only need to tell me his name. That's all. I'll do absolutely everything else, I swear."

She sat at her desk and took out an exercise book. Was this a breakthrough? He waited patiently. She found a ruler, drew a straight careful line down the left of the page. Wrote the date in the corner.

"What are you doing?"

"My history homework."

"You said you didn't have holiday homework."

"Well, I do. But I didn't think I needed to tell you. I thought maybe you might have found that out already. Do you go through my room a lot?"

"Of course I don't go through your room a lot! What kind of a person do you think I am? I did it because… "

"Sorry, but I really need to get on with this." Alicia turned elaborately away and began to frown over her paper. It was bravado, he could see from here that her hand was shaking and she wasn't actually writing anything, but it was a good pantomime for someone her age.

Some girls would have crumbled by now, but not his daughter. She had grit. It was the first time in his life he'd wished she was less like him.

George came in for his Heineken and his pork scratchings, spreading the packet out on the table and picking them meticulously up between thick fingers. *Was it George?* he thought. *For God's sake, what was the matter with him, suspecting George of all people?* George peeled the label from the bottle in one smooth satisfying piece, then he left it on the table, where it grew soggy. Donald cleared the table and wondered for the thousandth time why people – especially people in pubs – felt such a compelling urge to destroy things, then leave the pieces for someone else to pick up.

"You look stressed," said George, astoundingly.

"What?"

"You look stressed," George repeated. "I saw a documentary on Tuesday night about workplace stress. It was very interesting."

"Do I?"

"Yes. It's bad for your body in a lot of ways, to be stressed. You should go and see your doctor about it."

"I'll think about that."

He'd always thought he had one of the best poker faces in the business. How bad must he look if George had noticed it? *I'm getting old, old and tired, and this is a young man's game and I can't do it any more.* No, he couldn't think like that, he had to be strong for his daughter. He had to get the name, the name, the name, the name. Just the name, and the rest was easy. He'd told Alicia he would go to the police, but he'd lied.

Four o'clock. Mike came in for his shift, took one look at Donald's face and hastily made himself busy in the kitchen. What would he do if she didn't tell him? If she wouldn't? This wasn't like the old days, shaking down scum to see what crumbs of knowledge fell out. He couldn't be too rough. He couldn't be rough at all. This was his daughter, his beloved daughter. She was the victim. She needed him to be on her side.

Back up the stairs. This time, they felt two thousand miles high. His knees were shaking when he reached her doorway. She was sitting at her desk, her hands in her lap, her face composed.

"How are you doing, love?"

"Please go away."

"Are you ready to talk to me yet?"

"It was my choice, you know." She looked at him defiantly.

"Don't say that."

"Why not? It's true. And I'm not ashamed of anything I

247

did with him." This, even though her face was scarlet.

"He should be ashamed, not you. Please, love, just tell me his name."

"I'm his love, not yours."

Could she possibly believe that?

"And," she continued, "I'm not telling you his name. Not now, not ever."

"Then maybe I'd better call the police."

(Oh, stupid, stupid. Don't make empty threats, they come back to bite you. Of course he wouldn't call the police. Did she know that, though?)

"I'll say I made it up. They can't do anything if I won't talk."

(She was right. And he knew it. And she knew it too.)

"Please." All his defences stormed, his armies in retreat. His castle crumbling. "Please. Let me look after you."

"You don't actually think that's going to work, do you? When did you listen to *please?*"

"Alicia, I only want to help!"

"You couldn't let me have that little bit of privacy, could you? You couldn't stand it. Everything I have you take away from me. Well, one day you'll find out how it feels. And then you'll know."

Day wearing into evening. Five o'clock, a couple of locals in for their tea. Mike normally covered this period alone so he could dash upstairs to spend a couple of hours with Alicia. Tonight he went down to the cellar and put the light out and sat in the dark. All the joy that had been in him this morning had melted away. What was he going to do?

One last climb up the staircase. He opened Alicia's bedroom door. She wasn't there. She wasn't there. What had happened? What if – you heard stories – the bathroom – his razor – the tablets – no, the bathroom was empty. He bellowed her name so loud he almost missed her answer:

"I'm in here."

248

The living room. Weak with relief at seeing her, and then he saw the expression on her face, and knew something was awfully, terribly wrong. The filing cabinet, his insurance policy…

"What is this?" Alicia gestured wildly at the mess of photographs and papers spread around her. "Who are all these people?"

This was how she must have felt when she came into her room and saw him sitting on the bed. He made himself look. She held a photograph. A man, a woman, a room. A bed. A hidden camera. A name and date on the back. Their faces clearly visible.

"I was a copper." Did he sound believable? "You know that, you've always known that. It was evidence. Old stuff. I kept it locked away because I didn't want you to see it and be frightened and then I suppose I just forgot I had it… "

"Don't lie to me." Her eyes were burning. "I wanted that to be true but it's not. I went through all of it and I looked for names and then I went on Google and none of this stuff is about people who got caught."

"I didn't get everyone I went after, no-one does, these are the ones I couldn't… "

"All these names. They're police officers. And councillors. Important people."

"Yes, and that's why I couldn't get them, they were too influential, the CPS wouldn't… "

"And you know what else I found? I found you." She was so angry she was spitting. "I found you in a court case. You and some others. Everyone got off, but you had to give evidence. And you were in the dock with them."

"Alicia. Listen."

"I'm listening."

"Look, you're right. I wasn't – I wasn't exactly a copper."

"Not exactly a copper?" Her face was ugly with scorn.

"But I left, okay? I left. After your mum… you know. After your mum."

249

Alicia stared at him. "You mean she knew about this as well?"

"Yes. No. Well, sort of – look, the point is – all that stuff – it's insurance. When you're in you're supposed to be in for life. When I left, it was a risk. I needed something to bargain with, in case they caught up with me. It's just insurance, that's all – something to keep us safe."

She scrabbled wildly through the photos again.

"And all these girls? Were they all your, your mistresses or something?"

"No, of course not! It was professional, they were professionals, they got paid a wage! I would never – look, pet, I loved your mum, okay? It was just a job, a well-paid job, it was just business, that's all."

"You mean they were prostitutes? You bought my toys with money you got from whores? Do you think that's any better?"

"It wasn't like that! They earned good money, it was a working arrangement."

"Look! Look at this!" She held out another photograph.

He didn't want to look but he had to. Oh no please no no no, not the disposal job, the girl who suffocated in the truck.

"Did you kill her?"

His most explosive piece of evidence. The looks on the men's faces. They hadn't known the camera was watching. If they'd known that night he'd taken a photo, he'd have been next for the axe.

"Of course not! What kind of a monster do you think I am?"

"I tell you what," she said. "I tell you what, Dad. At least I know now where I get it from. That's why I loved doing what I did with… " she just managed to swallow the name, "… with him. Lying. Cheating. Sneaking around. I'm like you. I'm just like you."

He wanted to hold her but she wouldn't have it. She was stronger than him and faster than him, he was an old done

250

man now, and she was the new generation. She ran for the stairs, and as he tried to catch her he turned his ankle and fell painfully against the wall. He hobbled into the pub just in time to see Alicia streaking through the front door like a rabbit and out into the street, vanishing into the darkness. He forgot his ankle and ran after her, feeling his reputation as a solid businessman falling away from him as he went, but none of that mattered, he just had to catch her. But she was too quick. She'd disappeared.

As he stared hopelessly into the empty dusk he was assailed by a sweet and terrible memory. Alicia, eleven years old, wrapped in a towel and padding into the living room.

"Dad," she asked, her face pretty and puzzled. "You know how I'm supposed to shave the hair on my legs?"

"Well, you don't have to but most girls do… "

She had waved his words impatiently away. "Yes I know, but am I supposed to shave the hair on my bits as well?"

His daughter, standing on one leg, wrapped in a pink fluffy towel, her eyes fixed on his face. Trying desperately to think of a good answer.

"Why don't you ask your friends what they do, and then do that," he said at last. And, seeing her lips beginning to form the words *But can't you ask for me?* he added with wry honesty, "And pet, don't even think about asking me to ask them. I'll get locked up for life."

She had stared at him for a minute and then laughed until tears streamed down her cheeks, and then she had put her pyjamas on and crawled onto his lap, long and slender and made entirely out of elbows, and they watched a cop show and he critiqued their procedure for her until she fell asleep in his arms. She'd believed in him then. Tears gathered in his eyes.

A chug of diesel and an air-cooled rattle. The Jolly Deathtrap lumbered into the car park. A figure sprang out almost before the engine stopped. Donald was on Finn before he knew it.

"Was it you?" Donald clutched at Finn's flesh and shook him wildly. "Was it you? Was it you that hurt my daughter?"

"What? What are you talking about? What on earth do you think I've done?" Finn struggled to get free. Donald slammed his head hard against the side of the van.

"You think you can take anything you want, don't you?" Finn's face was innocent and baffled, but Donald was too angry to stop. His fist slammed into Finn's eye socket. "Just help yourself to whatever you fancy, it's all yours, right? But it's time you bloody learned, you little bastard… "

"Donald." Mike's voice, familiar but strange. "Stop. Let him go. You're going to kill him. Please. It's not him you want. Please. Stop. Stop now."

Donald turned around. In the moment when he met Mike's guilty, horrified gaze, understanding finally came to him.

Chapter Seventeen: 2006 and earlier

"I'm quitting."

That silence, stretching out and out, and Harry picking at the edge of the blotter on his desk. Harry never used it but he kept it anyway. Perhaps he liked how it looked, its suggestion of fusty respectability and the status of a man who only ever had to write his signature. Perhaps it reminded him of the man before him: Charles, who in his turn had inherited it from Albert, whose name was still a legend. Perhaps it was superstition. Perhaps he'd just never got around to throwing it out. The end of his career, and Donald was thinking about the history and cultural significance of the desk blotter. He should be taking this more seriously. He should be taking stock.

He got his start in the schoolyard, as so many of his profession were supposed to do. Oddly, it began not in delinquency but brotherhood. Of course he and his mates broke bones and rules and windows, but no more than the other kids. What set them apart was their flat refusal to tell.

"What happened, Donnie? You were right there, you must have seen who threw it."

"You didn't get that black eye by yourself, Donnie, did you? Tell us who hit you. You won't be in trouble."

"Of course something happened, you didn't dive into a fight because you thought it looked fun. Unless you're telling me you're stupid, Donald, which I think we both know isn't true. Stubborn, maybe, but not stupid."

Silence, and the blank-eyed stare that told those in authority there would never be another answer.

Secondary school, and the question of what to do with his future. His early ambition had been to be a stunt rider like Evel Knievel. At fifteen, joining the police began to appeal. He liked the sense of belonging that came with it, the uniform and the brotherhood, but it was more than that. The world was a chaotic place; that much was clear. He liked the notion of being the enforcer of rules and order.

Then, a breakthrough so small he only recognised it in hindsight. An errand for Will, who was nothing much in himself but whose second cousin Rob was the nephew of Albert's right-hand man Victor. Even that wouldn't have done him much good at any other time. But Victor was temporarily in charge while Albert sat out five years and kept his mouth shut, so everyone underneath had just a little more freedom.

Slow progression. Catching Rob's eye one afternoon, being taken under his wing. He was being tested even though he didn't know it at first; small errands attracting small payments, progressing from cryptic verbal messages to equally cryptic slips of paper to the occasional package.

His first time being stopped by the police. First time in the cells. First invitation to phone someone. He thought about calling his mother, but dialled Rob instead.

Sitting quietly in the interview room, the officers looking at him, him looking back. Two men, big and burly, probably chosen because they looked intimidating but fatherly, trying to make him feel like a child even though he was old enough to be charged as an adult. He was scared, but he knew this was a moment that could open the doorway to the whole secret world. He fell back on what he knew, what he'd learned in the playground. Silence.

Rob arrived with a solicitor.

"You don't have to say a bloody word to these pigs," Rob said. Donald heard his real message: *You'd better not have said a bloody word to these pigs,* and savoured the elation of realising he'd called it right.

"I know," he said.

"So?"

It felt like someone had peeled back the top layer to expose the workings of reality. He saw everything. The police must have clocked him weeks ago – new kid on the block, green and untested and therefore interesting despite his lowly status. They'd been watching him for weeks, seeing him work his way in, climbing the rungs from *not even worth looking at* to *fun to scare when we're bored* to *might just possibly know something worthwhile.* They'd timed it carefully, wanting to get him after he'd taken the first important steps into frank criminality, but before his shell hardened and made him impossible to prise open. They were hoping that he, Donald, would be a chink in the armour of Albert's boys. They'd already tried to storm the citadel, had gone in gunning for the top man but had come away with nothing more than possession of a sawn-off shotgun. They needed a new way in. Rob was acting cool – the big man with the tame brief in his pocket – but really he was shitting himself, aware of the world of trouble he'd be in if this callow lad turned out to be a liability.

Donald looked at Rob, slick and sharp in his good suit, gold at his neck and wrist. He thought about the police officers who had just left the room.

Instead of speaking, Donald glanced warningly at the door. Rob looked surprised, then faintly impressed. He could see the cogs turning. *Maybe I've found a good one. Might be worth introducing him around a little bit. Might be. Maybe. Once we're out in one piece.*

The solicitor sprang him out within half an hour. Off

with a warning, although if they caught him again he'd get a formal caution. He wasn't surprised. He'd seen this outcome too, during that astonishing revelatory moment in the cell. By himself, he was more trouble than he was worth. It was his connections they were after, and he'd decided not to talk. Not now, not ever.

"Think hard about your future," one of the officers advised, looking Donald dead in the eye as they handed back the meagre contents of his pockets. Wondering if he'd brought Donald in too late, if there had been a moment when it might still have been possible to turn him to their purposes.

You're years too late, Donald thought. *I was born to do this.*

But, elated with what he'd achieved, he said nothing. Instead he nodded politely and climbed into the black Ford Capri where Rob waited, drumming his fingers on the steering wheel.

"See, we're not savages. We're a business. We've got rules."

Donald sat on an expensive sofa in a stylish living room. In the kitchen, Vic's pretty daughter made coffee. Time to make a good impression on the main man.

"A lot of young guys, they think their job's to be The Big I Am. Throwing their weight about, threatening people, smashing stuff up and that. They think that's what gets them on. Now for a while, that might work, but only for a while. They're the ones who end up inside. The stupid ones. Calling unnecessary attention to yourself – that's a terrible way to do business. Expensive, you see? Throwing your weight about costs you. Costs you in a lot of ways. Manpower. Disposal. Retaliation. Attention from the coppers."

Yes, thought Donald in excitement, *yes.*

"Course, you have to pay your bills. Every business does. We ain't no different. You can't keep going otherwise. You don't pay your bills, people lose respect. That's when you get the competition coming in."

Vic's daughter handed him his coffee. Her hair tumbled

past his face and she smelled delicious. He forced himself to concentrate on Vic.

"Then you've got to spend a whole lot more getting everyone back on side. But by then the other side's paying out too. So then, you're in some bloody pissing contest with everyone trying to show they've got the deepest pockets. Before you know it, you're way overspent and the coppers come after you and eighteen months later you're sat on your arse doing fifteen to twenty."

Yes. Yes. This all makes sense.

"Taking someone out," said Vic. "That's the most expensive thing. Then you've got arson. That costs a lot too. Beatings, car damage, drive-bys, school visits, home visits – cheap as chips compared to the big stuff. But sometimes, you have to cough up. The trick to this game, it's knowing when and how much to pay."

Vic's daughter was standing in the doorway. She smiled at him and looked him up and down. *She's so pretty.*

"See, your perfect scenario – your most profitable situation – is one where everyone knows you've got deep pockets, but you hardly ever have to pay out. Because you've made a couple of big investments in the right places years ago, and they're still paying off for you now. You manage that – the right investment at the right time – and it'll carry you for years."

He paused as if to let Donald speak, but Donald could think of nothing to say.

"Don't say much, do you? Good for you."

Since silence seemed to be working, Donald continued to say nothing.

"You do get what I'm saying, though, don't you? You're not just sat there in a daze waiting for me to stop talking? It makes sense and all?"

"It makes sense," said Donald.

He drank his coffee. It was hot and sweet. *Like the girl who made it.*

"So here's the thing," said Vic. "It's time for us to make an investment. And Rob tells me you might have pockets deep enough for the job."

Donald didn't dare move in case he spilled his coffee on the carpet. Vic was apparently very houseproud.

"Are your pockets deep enough? Would you say that about yourself, young Donnie? Do you go by Donnie, by the way? Or do you prefer Donald?"

"Whichever you prefer is fine with me."

"Fair enough. Since we're talking man to man, let's say Donald. It's a restaurant. West End." Vic grinned. "Decent grub."

"What kind of investment are you looking for?"

"He owes us five grand. What do you think's appropriate?"

A couple of big investments in the right places. Was this his moment to go in big? Or was he being tested to see if he was one of the stupid ones, the ones who piled in all guns blazing, then spent their best years behind bars? He looked at Vic. Vic looked back. And again he had that blaze of insight, and he knew what the best answer would be.

"How about you give me the address and leave it with me?" he said.

"What an astonishingly good idea." Vic smiled. "You got a pen and paper?"

He hadn't got a pen and paper. He flushed with annoyance.

"Never mind. You'll learn." He gestured to the bureau in the corner. "Top drawer. Help yourself."

Rummaging in the drawer, his fingers stumbled across a scented eraser, shaped like a strawberry and meant to fit on the end of a pencil. He could picture Vic's daughter using it at school. It must have been there for years. He took out the notebook and dropped the little strawberry into his pocket.

Vic gave him the address. (Why was Vic making him do the writing? Of course: the same reason he hadn't given clear instructions. If Donald was caught and he had the address on him, it would be harder to trace it back to Victor. That just confirmed what he already knew – that despite appearances he wasn't really on the inside yet, not all the way in, although perhaps once he'd delivered to everyone's satisfaction…)

"I'd like this sorted quick," said Vic. "No later than Friday. My daughter wants to go shopping the day after."

(Where would she choose? Covent Garden. Oxford Street. Little boutiques in places he'd never heard of. How old was she? He guessed about twenty, a few years younger than him. But girls could make themselves look almost any age.)

"I understand." He stowed the paper carefully in his pocket.

"See you Saturday morning, then. Not too early. Come about ten o'clock."

The alleyway was warmed by the greasy air from the kitchen vent. Donald stood quietly behind a mountain of bin-bags, listened to the rats rustling, and waited.

He'd watched the routine for the last three nights and he knew how it went. First the waitresses clattered out, laughing and complaining about terrible customers and aching feet. The kitchen porter brought a new stack of bin bags. (When he turned to leave, a dozen more rats crept cautiously from the shadows to sniff at the tough black plastic. Clearly they knew the routine too.) The chef's minions, slump-shouldered and speechless. The chef, thin and angry. Finally, the man he was interested in.

When he saw Donald step out of the shadows, he turned pale and tried to run, but Donald smiled and put an arm around his shoulders and, in the momentary confusion this induced, steered him back inside.

"I'm Donald," he said, light and conversational. "You're Christopher, is that right?"

"That's right."

"Pleased to meet you. How are you tonight?"

"Um… fine, I'm fine… "

"Good. I'm glad you're fine."

259

"What can I, um, do for you?" Tragic hope on Christopher's face that he might have misinterpreted what was happening. Hope that Donald might be here for some other reason than an outstanding debt of five thousand pounds, owed to a man with no pity or softness in him. For a moment Donald felt his heart quail.

The kitchen was far from cosy, an efficient factory operation of gleaming steel. If he left the room to fetch chairs, would he come back to find Christopher gone? Think quickly. There were two ways in – the front door, and the back door. Upstairs was a private flat with its own entrance. The front door was locked. The only way out was through the kitchen.

"Why don't you go and fetch us some chairs, Christopher. Then we can talk more comfortably."

"We could sit in the restaurant if you like?"

"Why don't you go and fetch us some chairs, Christopher. Then we can talk more comfortably."

A brief blaze of fear when Christopher left the room. What would he come back with? A baseball bat? A gun? Was he overspending, trying too hard? Had he thrown it all away for a moment of bravado?

In the restaurant, something heavy scraped and dragged. He made himself turn away as the door opened, presenting his back as he idly examined a row of knives, ordered by size and magnetised to the wall above the counter. When he turned back he saw Christopher wrestling with two mahogany-look chairs, padded with something red that could almost pass for velvet.

"Thank you." He was afraid his emotions might bleed out into his voice, but he sounded steady, reassuring, in control. "Those look very comfortable. Let's sit down so we can talk."

Christopher sat. Donald didn't.

"So," Christopher said after a minute. His face was stretched wide by a ghastly, pleading smile. "What's this all about?"

"I think we need to have a little chat. A chat about money."

He hadn't fully defined his plan for this stage of the operation, but he'd known their conversation would take place in the kitchen, and he'd been confident something would occur to him. As it turned out, it was the scent from the barely-cooled deep-fat fryer that caught his attention.

"Hello again."

He'd been expecting Vic but it was his daughter who answered the door. He looked at her bright eyes and confident smile and found he was breathless.

"Are you after my dad?"

"Is he free?"

She stood aside to let him pass. "Come on in. I think he's getting dressed."

He stood awkwardly in the living room, suddenly unsure where to put his arms. The envelope stuffed with cash was heavy in his left-hand suit pocket, but the photographs in the right felt heavier. Did she know who her father was?

"You're Donald, aren't you?" she said.

"That's me."

"I'm Ellen."

When did his body become so ungainly, so enormous? And how did you stand normally in the middle of a room? Last night he'd known just what to do, how to plunge Christopher's hand into the hot oil, how to hold him still while he shrieked and sobbed and promised. Afterwards, when he'd taken the cash from the till, he'd sat Christopher on one of the chairs and called an ambulance. Christopher had his name and knew his face, but that was the risk you took when you started out. He'd made his first investment. Had he got it right? In his pocket, his nervous fingers encountered the little strawberry eraser.

"It's all right," she said to him.

"I'm sorry?"

"My dad likes you. He thinks you've got potential."

261

So she did know. Or did she? Could a girl as sweet as Ellen live with knowing all of that, knowing about money in envelopes and hands in deep-fat fryers?

"You know." He swallowed. "Last night, I… "

"Don't." She shook her head. "Don't tell me. I don't want to know. I don't ever want to know."

"But you know who I am?"

"You work for my dad. My dad works hard. Maybe one day you'll work hard too. That's all I ever want to hear from you."

He took his hand out of his pocket and held his palm flat. In the centre was the strawberry eraser.

"I think this is yours."

"Where'd you find that?"

"I stole it," he said. "From the drawer in your dad's desk."

Delicately, she folded his fingers around the strawberry. The touch sent a sweet freeze along his spine. Someone was coming down the stairs.

"Keep it," she said. Her fingertips touched his hand for a moment longer, then they were gone. He put the strawberry back in his pocket. Vic came in, his face baggy and crumpled, his thinning hair tousled. He frowned when he saw Donald looking at Ellen. She dropped her gaze and slid silently from the room. It was an effort for Donald to drag his attention back to Vic.

"So?" Vic barked.

The affable philosopher of his first visit had vanished, and here was Vic's true face: a tired angry frightened man, catapulted to uncomfortable heights before he was really ready. Wordlessly, Donald held out the envelope. Vic glanced inside and grunted.

"Didn't see nothing in the papers," he said. "How'd you do it? It ain't wrecked, is it? Don't want it shut down. Not when it's turning profitable."

Donald took out the Polaroids. Vic peered at them, turned them around, peered again. Finally saw what he was looking

262

at and recoiled faintly. When he looked at Donald, it was with respect.

"You sure he can still do business like this?"

Donald put the photos away. "He doesn't cook the food himself. He has a chef."

"He ain't going to die or nothing?"

"I called the ambulance myself."

"You called the ambulance yourself!" Vic laughed raucously. "Nice touch, my son."

"Thank you."

Vic folded the envelope in half, making a fat unwieldy wedge, and stuffed it into his front trouser pocket. "So. I s'pose we should talk about what happens next."

Donald waited.

"I can find regular work for a lad like you, Donald. Come by my office Monday morning to meet Charles. We'll set you up with a position. You know where my office is?"

"No, I don't."

"Course you don't. Okay, ask Harry. He'll bring you. Be polite to him. He's going to be your new boss."

"I won't be working for you, then?"

"Oh, you'll be working for me all right. Because Harry works for Charles. And Charles works for me. But you, Donald, will work for Harry. Do you see how that works?"

"Yes."

"Good." Vic's amusement had dissipated, leaving a glowering resentment. Reluctantly, he took the envelope back out and peeled off a stack of notes. "Here. With thanks for your trouble."

"Thank you very much."

"By the way," said Vic, as he shepherded Donald out of the living room, "please don't speak to my daughter again. If you don't mind."

The correct answer was *Of course not. I understand.*

"Donald?"

He swallowed hard and made himself say it.

"Of course not. I understand."

"Glad to hear it." Vic opened the door. "Now bugger off and I'll see you and Harry on Monday."

"So you're Victor's new boy." They sat across from each other in the café, drinking builder's tea from heavy mugs. Harry had a face that always looked mournful – something that stood him in good stead when making an investment. 'I'm sorry about this,' he would say, and occasionally the other party would temporarily lose their mind and tell him, 'It's all right, I know you have a job to do,' as if they were both professionals stuck in a tricky situation imposed by their respective bosses. "Apparently you did a decent job the other week."

"Thank you."

"It's not on our patch, mind, so we don't get the benefit."

He wasn't quite sure what to say to this. Apart from anything else, he'd given the five grand to Vic. Surely it was Vic who benefited?

"Ah, now, you see," said Harry, "that was the cost to the other guy, the guy whose patch it is, of getting Vic involved. You need to get the boss in, he charges you. Is it true you called the guy an ambulance afterwards?"

"That's true."

Harry's downcast face dissolved into a rare laugh.

"Brilliant! That's brilliant. That's the kind of thing a copper does, you know that? Get you on the floor, beat you to a pulp, then call the ambulance and declare they've got a prisoner who's been injured resisting arrest." The sudden shrewd look skewered him. "You sure you wouldn't rather be a copper?"

The question caught him off-guard.

"I thought about it," he admitted.

"Ah. I thought so." Harry nodded. "You still thinking about it?"

"No."

"Why not? What changed your mind?"

That moment of choice in the cells. Why had he chosen this path and not the other?

"Not enough money," said Donald.

"Not enough money." Harry laughed again. "You'll last a long time, you will." He glanced gloomily into his mug. "This tea's disgusting, I don't know why we still come here. Let's go."

His first time in the office that would one day become Harry's. Charles, like Vic, looked harassed and tired. Donald deduced that business was not proceeding smoothly. It was a difficult situation – Albert gone but only for a few years, and with parole coming up, everyone was unsettled. Of course what Vic wanted was to take over permanently. But would Albert allow that? (Of course he wouldn't.) And would the men below support Vic or Albert? (Difficult to answer, hence the harassed expressions.) And while this jockeying for position went on, would any of their rivals see the opportunity to muscle in?

Charles gave Donald a brief welcome speech, reminding him of the rules. Keep your head down, but be available at all times. Work hard, but don't get spotted. Take orders from Harry, but use your loaf. Don't invest unless you have to, but when you have to, don't hesitate. Nothing big without direct orders from me – but I don't like to talk about that stuff, so you'll have to read between the lines. The rules were all contradictory, but there was no other way they could be. He kept his mouth shut and nodded in the right places and then it was over and he was following Harry out onto the street for a tour of the area.

Several years of tough effort, getting to know his customers, building connections. Albert's parole was denied. Vic dug in tighter and consolidated his power base. A small skirmish on a neighbouring patch; Harry lent Donald out and he found himself making his first truly major investment. Afterwards he wondered if he should feel more about it, but there wasn't time to wonder for long. One day there'd be time to play about as well as to work, but right now his job demanded long hours and hard graft. The Albert/Vic situation would resolve soon, so vacancies would open up and promotions would be made. He was determined to be ready when the opportunity came. ('Keep your bloody head down,' Harry advised. 'We're junior enough to get away without taking sides. Might as well make the most of it.')

In the meantime, he worked hard and lived like a monk – if monks bought expensive clothes and ill-advised jewellery and ate in restaurants where the waiters glanced at them sideways and accepted vast tips with ill-concealed resentment. So, not much like a monk at all really, apart from the absence of women. Sex was easy enough to come by but relationships took time, and he had none to spare.

The night Albert got out. A flurry of activity, ending with the sudden departure of Vic. *South America,* said the grapevine. *Bottom of the Thames,* Harry countered. Harry always took the gloomy view, but Donald thought he was probably right. No-one held Vic's attempt to take over the store against him, exactly – least of all Albert, who had come to power the same way. But business was business. South America was cheaper, but the Thames was a cast-iron investment.

It didn't matter. Everyone was on the move and it was time for promotions. But first, a welcome-home party. His first and only time in Albert's house. Albert had, of all things, a ballroom, and tonight it was filled with pounding music and people in their best clothes.

He told himself not to get excited. The chances were non-existent that Vic's daughter would be there. She'd either be out of the country with her father, or else – he found he didn't want to think about *or else*. Better to picture her somewhere hot and sultry, drinking piña coladas on a beach. Would she have asked *why*, or would she simply have packed a suitcase and followed Vic to the airport? He would probably never know the answer.

The word had gone around: leave the ladies at home. Plenty of girls, of course – some destined for the Blue Crocodile and the Red Door and the Filigree, others for the flats, expensively hired by the hour – but no wives or daughters. Nonetheless, he found himself disappointed not to see her.

He roamed the ballroom for three loud dull hours, drank himself half-sick with Harry as they celebrated their new positions. Sidney on the next patch had been moved upwards, and rather than bring in a new man, Albert had chosen to strategically lose most of Sidney's workforce, and double Harry's empire. More work for all of them, but also much, much more money. On balance, something worth celebrating. A brief drunken fumble with one of the Filigree girls, joyless and unsatisfying and over far too quickly. He thought about apologising for his poor performance, but what would be the point? He could see the relief in her eyes, could almost hear her thoughts, *Wish they were all that quick about it.* He found his coat and walked out into the sodium-lit night.

With enough drink inside him he could walk for miles. He had no map to follow and the street names were a drunken blur, but he walked and walked and walked, stopping only to pee against trees or in alleyways, letting his instincts guide him. The city unspooled before him in a long slow ribbon. Whenever he felt himself becoming sober enough to feel the ache in his legs and feet, he drank deeply from the flask in his coat pocket.

As the warm gold of dawn began to spill over the rooftops, he fetched up on the suburban street where he had first met Vic. In the euphoria of exhaustion, the front door seemed to glow. He stumbled onto the doorstep and knocked, with no doubt in his heart.

After a minute, Ellen opened the door. Her face was blotchy and her eyes were swollen. Nonetheless, in the tender light of the new day, she was beautiful.

"You took your time," she said, looking him up and down.

"Sorry about that. Your dad told me to stay away."

Her face quivered. "Do you know where he is?"

"I heard a few things. I heard… "

"No." She closed her eyes. "Don't tell me. I don't want to know."

An unstoppable yawn convulsed his face. Her lips twitched.

"Am I keeping you up?"

"I've been walking for six hours," he admitted.

"Then I suppose you'd better come in."

The house had the special silence of mourning. She took his hand and led him upstairs to a sterile room with a double bed and a shiny paisley counterpane.

"You can sleep here," he heard her say, and then he was falling into the infinite softness of sleep.

He woke several hours later to find Ellen sitting on the edge of the bed watching him. A soft blanket lay over him. A mug of coffee was on the bedside table. He was no longer wearing his shoes.

"You were out like a light," she said.

His mouth was dry and sour. The coffee was delicious. He took two mouthfuls to moisten his tongue.

"I want to look after you," he said.

"That's funny. I've been looking after you."

"I mean it. I want to take care of you. I'm earning a lot of money now. I want to spend all of it on you."

She was watching the steam pouring off the top of his coffee. He waited to see if she would speak.

"I'm doing well," he said. "Really well. I'm in line for… "

"Don't tell me."

"But do you believe me when I say I'm doing well?"

She looked at his coat, his shoes, his watch. "I believe you."

"So is there any chance?"

Silence. He could see she wasn't convinced. At the same time, she was really thinking about it, there really was a chance.

"My dad," she said at last.

"I know he didn't like me."

"Didn't?"

"Oh, God. Doesn't, doesn't, I'm sorry."

"You don't know, though, do you? Didn't. Doesn't. Neither of us know. We might never know. We wouldn't be a normal couple."

"Of course we'd be a normal couple. I'd love us to be normal. You don't have to, you know, meet my colleagues. We'd go to the pictures and go out for dinner and spend days at the seaside and maybe if you like me enough we might get married. We'd have a house and kids. The only difference is, we'd have money. More money than anyone our age has any right to expect."

"Money isn't the same as happiness."

"You say that because you've always been rich."

She shook her head impatiently. "But if we – if we were together, one day you might just vanish. And I'd never know why. I don't know if I want to do that again."

"It might not happen. It's a dangerous job, but I'm careful and I work hard. I think I'll be around for a long, long time."

"How many old men do you work with?"

"Some. Not many. But some."

"Here's how it happened," she said. "I said good night to him. He was in his dressing gown watching the ten o'clock news. I heard him turn the TV off and come up to bed. I went to sleep. Then the next morning I woke up and he wasn't in the kitchen. I thought he was asleep. I got dressed and went out. I yelled goodbye up the stairs and he didn't reply. I should have gone to check but I didn't want to be late. So I just went out. When I came back everything was exactly how I'd left it and I knew."

He reached for her hand, felt the tingle right through his bones when she let him take it. How could this small contact from one woman thrill him so much when the naked flesh of another had left him untouched? She was still speaking.

"I went upstairs. I thought maybe – maybe they'd come for him while he was asleep. I opened his bedroom door. I thought, *Right, this is it, Ellen. You've been expecting this for a long time.* I thought it was going to be like a movie. Blood and feathers everywhere." Her other hand went to her mouth. "But there was just nothing. Nothing at all. His bed was made. Everything was tidy. Even his watch was still on his bedside table. Like he'd gone willingly."

And left her behind. Perhaps Harry was wrong. Perhaps it had been South America after all. Or perhaps it was simply a way to torture his daughter and increase the value of their actions. *When you invest, make it pay.*

"It wouldn't have to be like that," he told her. "Not for us."

"My dad thought that too."

"It's a dangerous job, that's all. Like being married to a copper, or a soldier."

"Coppers' widows get a body to bury."

"Look, if it works out for us… you're right, I'll probably go first. Not many of us make old bones. I might not last past sixty, but that's a long way away. And I'll make sure you're looked after."

"Money won't make up for losing my dad."

"But it'll make up for losing me, because by the time I go you'll be sick of me. You'll cry for half an hour in the kitchen and then you'll say, Ah, what the hell, he was getting old anyway, and once he retired he'd only be under my feet. Then you'll go out and buy a new dress and a bottle of champagne, and you'll find yourself a fancy man and go dancing. And while I'm still alive, we'll have a good time. We'll have the best time there is. We'll buy a house in the right neighbourhood, and our kids'll grow up rich and lucky, and they'll go to the right schools and meet the right people and walk into the right job, and they won't ever have to know what their dad did to get his money."

"All this and we haven't even been to the pictures yet."

"But it's on the cards, isn't it? A future together, I mean. There's something between us. We both know it."

"Something. Maybe not enough."

"But we can find out. Can't we?"

"What did you have in mind?"

"I've been saving up. We can go anywhere you want. Just name it and we'll be there."

"Don't get too excited yet, lover-boy. We might find out we've got nothing in common and we're both rotten kissers."

"I'll take that chance."

"And I'm not going to bed with you for at least the first twenty dates."

"I'll wait."

She smiled. "All right then. Why don't you take me out and show me a good time?"

Chapter Eighteen: Now

When the tide turns, stay out of the caves. The command had put down deep roots in Alicia's soul. More than *Don't cross the road without me,* which died quietly and painlessly around her tenth birthday. More than *Don't go off with boys you don't know* (as if any teenage girl ever kept to that rule). But *Stay out of the caves* had a special force because of what she'd seen.

It was a year when the spring tide coincided with a scorching Easter weekend. The beach disappeared beneath crowds of tender pink bodies. From the top of the cliffs they looked like baby mice, and like baby mice they were blind and innocent.

A father, a mother, three children, one dog. The sea had fled for what looked like miles, and they saw no sign of danger. They walked down to the caves, enjoying the sight of everyone else walking in the other direction.

The tide came in as it always did, in shallow deceptive inches of water, the smallest of small waves, except they didn't retreat but instead washed on and on. Minutes later, the waves lapped at your knees rather than your ankles, and these waves, too, didn't retreat but were followed by waves that clutched at your thighs, dragging you into the current. The family went into the first cave and came out, went into the second and came out. Where their footprints had been, inches of water now swirled.

They looked and laughed in amazement. They debated briefly whether to peek into the last cave. In the minute while they talked, the tide sloshed higher. They finally saw the danger and set off, paddling and then wading and then panicking. Alicia and her father saw it from the cliff, but it was in the days before her father had a mobile phone.

"Are they going to die?" She clutched at her father's hand. "Are they?"

"They'll make it," her father said, but she could hear the doubt in his voice.

The water was at the father's knees now. Everyone was beginning to struggle. He picked up his youngest, a skinny boy of about eight, carrying him as if he weighed nothing. The mother held tightly to the hands of the older two. The dog, a foolish spaniel with silky ears, floundered desperately behind.

"The dog, the dog," Alicia wailed, pointing.

"It'll be fine," said her father, clutching her hand tightly. "Dogs can swim."

"But they've forgotten it, they've forgotten all about it and it doesn't know what's happening."

"Alicia." His fingers crushed hers. "They're looking after their *children*."

She didn't want to watch but not seeing would be worse. The water rose and dragged at their legs, trying to pull them under. The girl stumbled and disappeared. Her brother yanked her to her feet with a wild yell. They were nearly at the end of the cliffs now, just a few feet more and they'd be round the headland and into the shallows and from there they could run to the dunes and take shelter until the tide turned. But the water was heavy and insistent. The dog was swimming now, paddling desperately.

"They're going to make it," said her father. "You can do it. You can. Come on, you dozy bastard, man the fuck up and get your family out of there." She'd never heard him swear before. As if the man in the water had heard, he turned back and grabbed at his wife's arm. A wave knocked the older son off his feet and his father reached savagely beneath the waves and dragged him out again. Another few steps. A few strokes swum. A wave dragging them backwards. The littlest one's head dipped beneath the water, then reappeared. Alicia screamed.

And then they were round the headland and into the shallows and they were going to make it, they were definitely going to live, and they fled on crumpled legs and scrabbled into the dunes, marooned but out of the water at least, and her father let out a long breath like a sob and let go of Alicia's hand. Her fingers were crushed red and white.

"I'll go down to the café and call the coastguard," he said, but he didn't move. Instead he stared at Alicia. Then he crushed her hard against his chest, catching the tender flesh of her nose against a shirt-button. It was the first time she realised that love, unleashed, could be brutal.

"Don't you ever go down to the caves when the tide's on the turn," he whispered. "Promise me, pet. Promise me you won't ever ever do that. Not ever."

Her nose hurt so much she had to turn her head. Peering out from beneath his arm, she saw a terrible thing; the small black dot that was the family's dog, bobbing and paddling in the water, trying and failing to make headway. It vanished beneath the waves, resurfaced, vanished again, resurfaced again, vanished again. She clenched her fists and held her breath, willing it to reappear. But the ocean's will was stronger.

"I promise," she said. Her words muffled by his arm. She wriggled free so she could look at him. "I promise, Dad. I won't ever be like those people. I don't want to be like that dog."

"Oh Lord, the bloody dog." He shaded his eyes and peered out over the clifftop. "I can't see – look, it probably swam out, okay? Don't worry. Dogs are smart. They don't drown. It'll be fine, you'll see." He chucked her under the chin. "You're as white as a sheet, pet."

"My sheets are pink," she said, and he laughed, which was what she'd been hoping for.

"It's just an expression." He checked his watch. "Right, my break's up. We'd better get back to it."

"And call the coastguard."

"And call the coastguard. Do you know what number to call, by the way? Not that you'll ever need it, but just in case."

"Dad. It's 999, same as all the others. They tell us in assembly every single year."

He didn't let her watch the news that night, but she knew what they would have said. *Family, mother, father, two sons, one daughter – safe. Dog missing. Reminder of the dangers. Coastguard advice, check tide times, be careful – water comes in quicker than you think.*

She saw the dog in her dreams for years afterwards, although in her dreams she was never afraid of the sea. It was the caves that haunted her. The black holes reaching into the heart of the cliffs, and the water rushing in after. The darkness and the waves rising.

So, on this terrible night, it was the caves she ran for.

The beach was still clear but it wouldn't be long now. Ten minutes more and the ocean would swallow the land. The moon was a fat glob with a side sliced off. Was she really going to do this? Was she really going down to the caves with the spring tide coming in? From the dunes, a candle flickered in the window under a red glass shade. Perhaps she could go to the beach hut instead and sit and talk to them, drink tea and eat biscuits while her father drove around in the dark, calling all her friends in turn, until he finally realised that nothing mattered but her and he would forget everything that had happened that day.

No, she thought, with horrible clarity. *That's not what he's going to do at all. He's going to keep on at me, on and on and on until I finally give in, and then he's going to find Mike and kill him. That's what men like him do when they're angry. They kill people.*

She hadn't given up the name. She'd managed to keep the secret. He didn't know who to go after. Who to kill. She'd been too strong, her father hadn't broken her. She'd won this round, but it had taken everything she had. She wasn't used to winning. She couldn't count on it happening again.

How had he hidden his true face from her so successfully? He'd told her he'd been a police officer and she'd believed it. 'Just a job,' he'd said tonight, as if something like that could ever have been just a job. She'd only beaten him because she'd caught him by surprise. When he found her again, he'd make her give him the name, and then he'd go after Mike. Her father would kill him but the blood would be on her hands too. It was hard to breathe through the weight in her chest. Only one way to stop her father now. Only one good thing left that she could do to make up for the damage she'd done.

Which cave would she choose? The first was shallow and narrow and slimy with anemones clinging beadily to the entrance. The second was long and deep and with a tall crack in the ceiling that stretched up into darkness. Some boy or other once told her the crack was built by a giant rock-spider that had tunnelled out a track to the cliff surface with its fangs, and although she knew it was nonsense, she had never been able to shake the image.

The third cave was called the Smuggler's Cave because beyond a sterile pool of salt water there was a second chamber with a ledge like a narrow shelf, and there was a never-tested theory that if you climbed onto the ledge and clung to the wall, you could hide from the Revenue men and beat the tide and survive (cold and uncomfortable, but not actually drowned) until the waves receded and left you free to walk back out into the sunlight. The periwinkles clinging to the wall proved this story's untruth, but the Smuggler's Cave was the furthest away, and therefore the furthest from safety. She waded through the knee-deep pool without taking off her trainers and pulled herself, dripping and soggy, onto the rocky ledge.

Her hand reached automatically into her pocket for her phone, but she'd left it on the living room floor. She was used to filling idle fragments of time with idle fragments of activity. Now she had literally nothing to do but watch the remorseless progress of the tide and consider what she'd done.

Was this suicide? In the cold black silence it was hard to think. If she'd had longer to choose, there might have been another solution, but there had been no more time. And now it was too late. Her heart pounded with a strange excitement. What had she done?

The first eager waves rolled in through the entrance of the cave, edged with foamy lace. Her soaking clothes leached the warmth from her body, but she refused to take them off. Let the cold take her, let the water creep up her legs and turn her skin pale and wrinkled. Even if her father had come looking for her, he'd never get here before the tide came.

Then the darkness was pierced by a finger of light and a torrent of curses as someone waded, shivering, through the pool. She hadn't thought it was possible to feel more frightened, but the bulky distorted outline coming towards her was a shape out of her darkest nightmares. Her father had found her. Her father had found her. Now they were going to die together and it would all be her fault. She cowered in terror.

"Alicia?" A familiar voice, not her father's. "Alicia, is that you?"

"Finn?" She hardly recognised her own voice.

The torchlight shone right in her eyes so she couldn't see his expression. "Jesus, it really is you. I thought it was, so I came to look – what on earth are you doing here? Can I sit down?"

In a daze, she patted the shelf beside her. The skin around his left eye was swollen and black. "What happened to your face?"

"Wrestling match with an angry bear." He shrugged off his rucksack and took his boots from around his neck. A wash of seawater surged in and slapped at the cave walls.

"Why did you come down here?" Alicia demanded. "Don't you know how dangerous it is?" She wiped the tears furiously away. *As if there isn't enough salt water in here already.* "My dad made me promise never to come here when the tide's turned."

"Yes, I know. I promised Ava too. Now we're both oath-breakers and we'll be excommunicated when we get back. Pull your feet up, the waves are getting bigger."

Just having Finn here made the terror a little more bearable. She wedged her knees awkwardly under her chin and felt a treacherous squirm of hope. "This is pointless, though, isn't it? I mean, we're going to – we're not going to make it, are we?"

"Well, you never know, do you? We're not dead yet."

"I'm scared."

"Don't be. Come here." He held out an arm so she could lean against him. She hesitated. "It's all right, it's a full moon so I'm quite clean today. Why don't you tell me why you're down here?"

"I don't want to talk about it."

"Are the police looking for you because of that old lady you poisoned the other week? Because I told you to switch to slug pellets."

"What?"

"Or are you on the run from the Girl Guides? They're terrible when they're angry."

"I don't know, I can't make stuff up like you can. Oh God, the water's coming."

"Course you can, it's easy. I'm here because of the Queen. I broke into Windsor Castle a few months ago and caught her in her alternate form of a giant lizard. Now she's hunting me down because she's afraid I'll go to the papers."

"Why would the Queen be a giant lizard?"

"You need to waste more time on conspiracy-theory forums. Oh, damn it… "

The first wave trickled over the lip of the shelf. Finn stood up hastily. Alicia scrabbled to her feet, slipped and nearly fell into the water. Finn caught her.

"So that's no fun, then." The retreating wave sucked at their feet. "I suppose that proves you shouldn't rely on the word of a smuggler. They never know what they're talking about."

"Oh God. Oh God."

"It's okay. Stand here next to me a minute. And don't panic."

"Don't *panic?*"

"Okay, so here's a story for you, and this one's absolutely true." Finn shone the torch up into the glistening blackness above their heads. "When I was about seven, I was completely obsessed with keys."

"Stop it, stop it, stop trying to make me calm down, we're both going to die, okay, we're going to drown!"

Finn's hand reached up into the dark. "And one day I was exploring in the caves here, and I had the back door key to our house in my pocket. Alicia, are you listening? Shut your eyes and hold onto me, and then ask me a question so I know you're listening and not panicking."

Alicia shut her eyes. The water grabbed for her ankles and retreated, trying to take her with it. She buried her fingers in the folds of Finn's jacket. "Did you live here?"

"No, we lived somewhere else, but we used to come here on holiday. And, as I said, at the time I was really, really keen on keys. I thought they were just the best, coolest things in creation. So before we went away, I went out to the back garden and took the spare key out of the flowerpot. My mum and dad weren't keen on me having keys because they thought I might lose them. So I hadn't told them I'd got it. And here we were in the cave, and our back door key was just sitting there, in the pocket of my jeans. Steady, don't slip. Hold onto me."

Alicia clutched at him, trying not to sob in terror. "What are you talking about, what's this got to do with anything?"

"My mum and dad went back to the beach, but they said I could stay for a bit if Ava stayed with me. Ava wanted to go back, but she stayed with me because she's nice. So I was climbing around in the very back of the cave, and – oh my God, look at this."

He held out his hand and shone the torch-beam onto a silvery, rust-flecked mortice key.

"What bloody good is that, what a bloody stupid thing to… "

"No, you don't understand," said Finn. "I left it to remind myself. Now tell me the truth and I swear I'll stay right with you whatever you say, because either answer's fine. Do you want to call it a day and give in, or do you want to try and get out of this?"

"What?"

"We've got about one minute more before the tide makes the decision for us."

"I – oh, look, I want to live, all right? I want to bloody live, I thought I didn't but I do, I thought if I died it would fix everything but… "

"Then reach up here where I left the key."

She stretched her hand up as high as she could and found a deep empty hollow. Finn shone the torch into the darkness. Above them, hidden unless you shone the light at exactly the right angle, was a square tunnel sloping upwards and backwards into the cliff.

"It's the bottom of an addit," Finn said. "You know the tunnels that drain groundwater from mines? I don't know how far it goes, because I only got a couple of feet in and then Ava made me come down. She said people poking about in old mine workings was how horror movies started. But I think this might be the night to take our chances with the Morlocks."

"I can't get up there, it's too high, it's too steep, it's too wet."

"And… there go my boots. We'd better try, or the next few waves'll have us. Come here, I'll give you a boost."

"I can't!"

"Course you can. You're brilliant." Finn made a cradle from his fingers. "Put your foot in here. That's it. Now reach up. Can you feel the way in?"

"I can't do this." She grabbed onto the rough rock with panicked fingers and wriggled in up to her waist. "I can't do this, I won't fit, I'll get stuck."

"You will fit and you won't get stuck. Look at you, you're built like a racing snake."

Alicia inched upwards, fighting claustrophobia.

"Keep going, that's it. Hey, did I tell you about the time I went potholing and nearly – actually, no, that's a terrible story. Did you know about the post-box in town that doesn't work?"

"What?"

"Keep going, that's it – whoa!"

"What's happening? Are you all right?"

"I'm fine, don't worry. Just the sea trying to wash me away. Right, I'm coming up behind you, so whatever you do, don't slip. Keep going, don't freeze up. That's it."

"It's so dark."

"Shut your eyes and pretend it's only dark because you're not looking. So, you know the post-box that's built into the wall just down from the church?"

A sliver of rock sliced her finger like glass. A warm trickle ran down her hand. "Yes, I know it."

"Well, it doesn't work."

"What?"

"If you post letters in it," said Finn, from somewhere below her, "it doesn't work."

"I'm stuck, I can't, I'm slipping."

"Don't panic. Ask me how I know."

"I can't do this. I'm sorry."

"You can, I swear you can. Come on, keep going. Ask me how I know."

Alicia clawed at the rock, managed another tortuous few inches. "How do you know?"

"We were at the church fete," said Finn. His breathing was ragged and the sound of the waves was like a giant wet mouth. "Ava and me, I mean. You know how sometimes you just – Christ, I think someone's been sharpening these rocks – just end up at these things. How are you doing?"

"My hands hurt."

"I know, mine too. Think of the amazing scars we'll have. So, we had about ten pence each, so we bought some crap yellowy postcards from one of the stalls because that was about all we could afford. And the woman who had the stall said, *Don't post those in the letter-box in the wall outside. It doesn't work.* Don't stop, you're doing great, keep going. The higher we go the safer we are."

"I'm scared."

"Don't think about it. Ask me a question."

"Why did she think the post-box didn't work?"

"That's a great question. Unfortunately I don't know the answer. We both just took it for granted she was telling… " the sound of something falling "… it's all right, we didn't need that anyway… telling the truth. I mean, we were in a church, and she was a grown up."

"Can we stop here? Please. I can't go any higher."

"I think we might need to."

"Is the water still rising?"

"That's classified. So, the post-box. We never thought to question how there could be a post-box that didn't work, or what happened to all the post that went into it. To be honest, we were both really pleased to be told about it. It was like getting this brilliant piece of insider knowledge. We used to feel quite sorry for all the people who didn't know about the post-box not working."

Alicia's hand, reaching blindly for the next hold, encountered instead a terrifying void. The sound of her shriek was so appalling that she frightened herself. She thrashed round wildly in the tunnel, slipping a few inches, then wedging herself back in.

"I'm stuck, I'm stuck, help me, I'm stuck, oh fuck, this is it, I'm fucking stuck."

It was Finn's hand, holding firmly onto her ankle and giving it a comforting squeeze, that reminded her she was not alone. She forced herself to be quiet and breathe, trying to get control of the panicked gasps and whimpers.

"I put my hand up and there was just this space," she stammered out.

"Really? Maybe it's a chamber. Climb back up and see if it's got a floor. Make sure it's not a mineshaft first."

"I can't. I can't. Let's stay here."

"I took some shaggy ink-cap mushrooms in to school once," said Finn. "Not just out of badness, for the nature table. And the teacher put them on the display, and after four days they went all into ink and made a massive black stain on the tablecloth. So she made me look at it, and she said, 'What have you got to say about this, then?' And I said, 'Well, that's why they're called shaggy ink-caps.' Then she said I was being cheeky and sent me to the headmistress. I know that's not much of a story, but I'm not sure we can both hold on to a damp slippery rockface for the next six hours, so why don't you have a feel around and see if you've found somewhere we can wait out the tide?"

The strain in his voice frightened her more than anything else. She inched her way back up. Once again her hand found nothingness. She reached in with her arm and felt around. A flat damp floor. A room. A sanctuary. She shuffled forward onto her stomach and began to wriggle gladly forward into the void.

"I don't want to sound like the voice of doom," said Finn, "but do make damn sure you don't tip yourself down headfirst down another addit, okay? Just find a wall if you can. And then keep dead still until I get up with the torch."

She crept in on her belly, then banged her forehead

painfully against a wall of rock. She pressed herself gladly against it, then stretched her hand out in panic. Was there a drop right next to her? What if she fell asleep and – a wavering finger of light crept into the cave, followed by Finn, grazed and grimy and wriggling like a caterpillar.

"Next time we do this," he said, "I'll give you the torch. Sorry about that." He shone the light around. They were in a tiny chamber, sealed at one end by a tumble of rock that blocked the way to the rest of the old workings. The walls were streaked with iron and rainwater and gave off a deep merciless cold. In the addit below them, the water raged and boiled, but could not reach them. Alicia's relief expressed itself in a sadness that crumpled up her face into an ugly howl.

"Sorry," she managed between sobs. "Sorry, sorry."

Finn put his arms around her and held her tightly. "This must be the real smuggler's cave," he said. "I don't suppose anyone's left us a brick of coke." He shone the torch around. "Oh, well, you can't have everything."

"I've never taken drugs," said Alicia, hiccupping.

"Wise woman. Don't bother."

"Why? Have you?"

"Yes. Far too many, because I'm an idiot. They're not as much fun as you'd think. And people on drugs are just about the most boring human beings in the world." He rummaged in his rucksack. "Want some chocolate?"

They sat and ate Cadbury's Dairy Milk and listened to the water creeping higher.

"Why are you here?" Alicia asked.

Finn peered into the addit, and winced. "It's a lot nicer up here than it is down there."

"That's not what I mean."

"Them as gets into the cave first makes the first confession."

"I don't want to – oh, well, I suppose it doesn't matter now." She shut her eyes. "My dad read my diary. He found out I'd been seeing... someone."

"Is that so awful?"

"Yes. If you knew – but anyway, I thought I'd do the same to him in return. Go through his stuff, I mean. So I went into his filing cabinet and I found – oh, God you wouldn't believe what he'd done."

"Um, this isn't to do with your dad and Ava, is it? Because Ava, I mean, we won't be here much longer. She's not trying to move in and be your wicked stepmother. Sometimes people just want a bit of warmth and company and – and that wasn't what you meant at all. Excellent." Alicia's eyes were wide. "Ignore every word I just said. I'm an idiot, I don't know about anything except drugs and toadstools. I probably imagined it."

"You mean they're… " she didn't know what to call it.

"I don't know. What would I know? Ignore me."

"It doesn't matter anyway. Except yes it does, because he's not bloody good enough for her. Ava's lovely, she deserves someone nicer. I hate him."

"Don't say that. He's a bit of a madman sometimes but that's okay, most parents are."

"He's horrible. I wish I was an orphan."

"No you don't," said Finn.

"Yes I do. I hate him, I hate everything about him. That's why I'm here, because he wanted and wanted to know who I was seeing and he'll get it out of me in the end and then he'll – he lied and lied and lied, about who he is, what he did for a living, he let me tell everyone for years and bloody years that he was a policeman. I was proud of that, you know? I wish he was dead as well."

"Alicia," Finn took hold of her chin and turned her face towards him. His eyes were feverish and glittering. "No. You don't."

"Is that what happened to you?"

Finn was silent for so long that she thought he wasn't going to answer. Then, without looking at her, he began to speak.

"Once," he said, "there was a family who lived in a lovely

285

brick house in a lovely brick suburb in a lovely brick city, far away from the sea."

"Was it your family?"

"This is just a story. Anyway. They lived a long way from anything wild or dangerous, which made it a good place to raise a family, but sometimes it started to feel boring. So every year, the four of them would get in their shiny metal car and drive and drive for hours down thick black tarmac roads until they reached the Great Outdoors.

"The Great Outdoors was wonderful and terrible. There were animals, and mountains, and black lakes, and grey oceans, and everything was bigger and stronger than they were, but they never realised that. They'd lived for so long in their brick house in the brick street in the brick city, they'd forgotten anything could hurt them." He squeezed the deep cut on his hand. A trickle of blood ran down his wrist. He wiped it absently on his jeans and continued.

"The parents thought it was all marvellous, and the little boy, he loved it too, because he was just little and he knew the least of all. But the big sister always said they should be careful, because the Great Outdoors was dangerous. One day it might turn on them, because just because you love something, it doesn't have to love you back. But of course they didn't listen to her."

Alicia's legs and feet were trembling with cold.

"Take those wet jeans off," Finn ordered.

"But… "

"Don't be daft, there's only me here to see and I don't count. Wet clothes freeze you faster than anything."

Crouched over beneath the low roof, Alicia kicked her trainers off and peeled off her jeans. Finn took his coat off and wrapped it around her waist.

"What happened to the family?" she asked, through chattering teeth.

"Maybe I should tell a different story."

"No, tell me this one."

"So," said Finn, staring steadily into the darkness, "what happened was, one day they were in the Great Outdoors. They'd chosen a particularly wild part that time, because they were getting bolder all the time. They were camping. In a tent. With a campfire. And then, just as they were toasting marshmallows, a dragon came out from behind a rock and snatched up the parents and ate them."

"That's so stupid! You can't say a dragon."

"Can't I? All right, a lion then."

"Are you telling me your parents were eaten by a lion?"

"I'm not telling you anything about my parents. I'm telling you a story."

"But it's about you and Ava, isn't it?"

"I never said that. Maybe it wasn't a lion. Maybe it was a flash-flood. Or a fall from a mountain. The point is, their parents were gone. But the big sister was always ready for something bad to happen, so she grabbed her brother and together they ran and ran and ran, all the way back to their brick house in the brick street in the brick city."

"Well, that's good."

"The story doesn't end there, though." Finn shone the torch onto the opposite wall. "Because when they got home, they discovered their house wasn't made of bricks at all. It was made of paper. Every night after the children went to bed, the parents had stayed awake, covering the walls in layer after layer of forms and money and receipts and doctor's appointments and permission slips – all to keep the walls strong and stop them from falling down. And without the parents to paper over the cracks, their house crumbled into dust and blew away on the wind."

"But that's not the end of the story, is it?" Alicia asked.

"Isn't it? I don't know. Do stories ever end? Or do they just get to a point where someone stops and says, *right, that's my point made, I can stop writing now and go and make a cup of tea?*"

"You should know. You've written a book."

"Anyone can write a book. Now it's your turn."

"My turn to what?"

"To tell a story."

"I can't."

"Yes, you can." Alicia shook her head. "It doesn't have to be about you. Make something up. Besides, I can't tell anyone what you tell me, because if you tell a secret you heard in a cave, you'll be struck dumb for the rest of your life."

"That's not true."

"It's true if we both agree it's true."

"Can you put the torch off?"

The switch clicked, and they were sitting in the dark.

"Once upon a time," she said, "there was a little girl who lived with her dad. No, I'm sorry, I can't."

"Tell it about an animal. Animals are often easier."

"What kind of animal?"

"What kind of little girl was she?"

"I don't know." She tried to remember what it had been like to be her younger self. Inhabiting a body that went straight up and down, harbouring no strange desires. "Something small and dull. A rabbit. No, a mole. No, a mouse."

"All right, a mouse. What happened to her?"

"The mother mouse got eaten by a cat." Finn tugged at her hair comfortingly. "So, this little girl mouse lived with just her dad. Then one day, the little girl mouse went looking in her dad's filing cabinet. And she found out her dad wasn't a mouse at all. He was a rat. A big fat horrible evil rat with red eyes and sharp claws. He'd been stealing things and selling drugs and running some sort of, of, of lap-dancing club, only it wasn't just a lap-dancing club, it was a, you know, a brothel I suppose. And he'd got all these photographs, stashed away in a filing cabinet. Pictures of girls doing things. To men. With men. You know. With the men's names written on the back, and dates. Not the girls' names, they didn't get their names written down, so I suppose maybe they weren't important. And one really old one of someone's hand, only it didn't look like a hand any more, it looked like it had been cooked – and one of a girl – she was dead and she was all in pieces and there were other men in the picture, messing around with her… "

"Were the pictures new?"

"From before. Before her mum died."

"So maybe the mouse was sorry, and decided he needed to live a better life?"

"He *wasn't* a mouse, he was a rat! And that's the point. Because if he was a rat, then his daughter was a rat too. And that's why she was the way she was. When she was little she'd been all right, but now she was turning out horrible, just like her rat father. She was mean and greedy and she liked doing things she knew were wrong with a man she shouldn't have done them with, and as soon as she realised she was a rat and not a mouse, it all made sense. So she ran away and hid, because she knew that if she didn't, her dad would make her tell all of *her* secrets, and then he'd kill the man she'd been seeing, and he'd be dead and her father would go to jail, and it would all be her fault."

"Rats can be lovely, you know," said Finn. "I had a couple as pets once. They're clever and resourceful, and they look after each other. And they make excellent parents. Much better than mice."

"Not these rats. These rats were just – they don't deserve to live, these rats. The world would be better without them." She switched the torch on again and shone it down into the addit. "It's so cold. We're going to freeze. And the water is still rising. I don't want to die."

"Then we won't. We'll live instead. I'm going to tell you another story, okay? Are you listening? Yes? Don't look at the water, it won't do any good. The battery's going, I'd better turn the light off for a bit. Is that all right?"

"I suppose."

"So, this is a story about a Princess. She lived in a high tower her father had built for her, because he loved her more

289

than anything else and he'd sworn a sacred promise that he'd never, ever let anything bad happen to her."

"Was her father a King?"

"He was. Only a small kingdom, but it was his. Running a kingdom and being a father was hard work, so the King made time by getting rid of absolutely everything else in his life. He didn't have any hobbies, and he didn't have any lovers, and his only friend was a strange man who didn't really know how to make friends, because he went everywhere in a glass cocoon that kept him safe from the outside world. Are you all right?"

"Fine." Alicia hadn't realised she was holding her breath.

"Anyway," said Finn. "This story isn't about the King. It's about the Princess. You see, it's all very well keeping your kids locked up in towers, but eventually, they have to go out."

Alicia didn't dare move.

"Is this all right?" asked Finn, very gently. "I can tell a different story if you prefer."

"It's okay."

"So one day, a man her father knew began bringing the Princess presents. He brought her liqueur chocolates and beautiful jewellery and silky nightclothes. They were all things that were meant for a woman, not a little girl. And although the Princess wasn't quite grown up yet, she desperately wanted to be treated as if she was."

"But he didn't."

"Shh. This isn't a story about anyone we know. This is a story about the Princess. The presents were beautiful, but they also made her terribly sad, because she knew all the time they weren't his to give. He'd stolen every one of them from his wife, even though she was a nice lady who'd been kind to the Princess in the past."

Alicia closed her eyes to try and stop the tears running down her cheeks.

"The Princess felt terribly ashamed, because she loved the things he'd brought her even though she knew she didn't have any right to them. She thought there must be something wrong with her because she enjoyed them. She was afraid of what would happen to the man if her father found out, and that it would all be her fault if her father hurt him. But what she was forgetting was this." Finn took her hand and held it tight between his own. "She hadn't done anything wrong. It was the man who was the thief. He was the one who stole from his wife. And he was stealing from the Princess, too, because he knew she was young enough to be deceived by stolen gifts. And when it all caught up with him and he got what he bloody well deserved, the Princess would be free. She'd be free. None of it was her fault."

"But it *was* her fault," Alicia whispered. "She kissed him first."

"And was she bigger than him, and stronger than him, and older than him, old enough to know better? Did she force him to kiss her back? Or could he have just said *no* and meant it? If you see a little kid tearing off into dangerous waters, do you just shrug and leave them to get on with it? Or do you catch them and bring them back, in case they drown? Come here, you'll be warmer."

To her astonishment, she was suddenly very sleepy. She burrowed against him and closed her eyes wearily.

"I wish I could run away with Ava," she said. "Are you going to miss her?"

"Yes."

"Why aren't you going with her? Can't you afford it?"

Finn swallowed hard. "You know," he said at last, "when I saw you running across the beach, I thought – I thought, if I came down after you – maybe I might even get to go first. But now when it comes to it… "

"What?"

"Never mind." His hand moved to his face, as if he was wiping it. "Go to sleep."

As she drifted into sleep, she felt something splashing onto her head, like raindrops. *It must be raining outside,* she

thought, *and it's leeching through the rock and falling on us.*
"Alicia." Someone was shaking her shoulder, gently but insistently. "Alicia. Wake up."

She was cold and she had an agonising cramp in the back of her neck. When the memory of where she was came back to her, it was like smashing into a wall.

"What? What? Has the tide gone out?"

"Um, not really."

The failing torchlight shone on a slick of water washing over the lip of the cave from the addit.

"The spring tide," Alicia whispered.

"Don't be scared. If we go, we'll go together. It's just a journey, okay? We'll all make it one day."

"But I don't want to die. Not yet. Oh, God I don't want to die."

"It's just a journey." She could feel his hand trembling. "Just another journey."

The day it was time to leave

And finally, after all the months and years of wandering and danger, they were at the seashore, and their house was waiting for them. It was just as small and perfect and beautiful as they'd dreamed. There was the tiny boat that the brother would fish from, and there was the basket he'd take the fish to the marketplace in, and there was the little veranda where they would sit at night and look at the stars.

The brother laughed and said, *We did it! We finally made it! And now I can look after you, the way I always promised.*

But when he looked at his sister, she saw that she was crying.

What's the matter? he asked her.

I can't stay here with you, she said. *I've got to travel on, to somewhere you can't follow me.*

292

Chapter Nineteen: Now, August

"I bet he'll be late," said Paul gloomily, neatening his cuffs as he stared at the arrivals board.

"He's on a train. It's hardly his fault if he is."

"Course it will be. Remember that time he was messing with the Emergency Stop handle?"

Ava smiled.

"Or else he'll be in the buffet car asking if cheese and onion crisps have real cheese in them because he's allergic to cheese. Well, I'm glad you think it's funny."

"Oh, come on. The world's more exciting with Finn in it."

"You say *exciting*, I say *slower and less efficient* – look, are you sure you're all right?"

"Of course I'm all right. I wish you'd stop asking. The only thing that's wrong is you keep asking me if I'm all right."

"You've been a bit strange recently."

"I have not been a bit strange. You've been a bit strange. Asking me twenty times a day what's wrong if I want to be in a different room to you for five minutes. It's like being peeled."

"Peeled."

"Yes. Like an onion. Layer after layer until there's nothing left."

"Don't say that. I don't want to peel you."

"Then stop asking me that all the time! Just talk for hours

about nothing like you normally do and leave me in peace. I'm sorry, I didn't mean that. Let's not be that awful couple who have rows at train stations. You don't want everyone staring at us."

"You never care if people stare at us."

"I didn't say I care, I said *you* care."

Paul frowned at the arrivals board. "You promise Finn's going to be civilised this evening?"

"He'll be fine. I've warned him you've got friends coming round for dinner. He doesn't mind."

"*We've* got friends coming round for dinner. They're your friends too. And I should bloody well hope he doesn't mind! Phoning up out of the blue, insisting on visiting."

"He's my brother. He can come whenever he – look, the train's here."

People spilled out onto the concourse. Some strode confidently towards the street or the tube. Others stopped and looked around helplessly, creating little pockets of annoyance as the people behind them sighed and tutted and wheeled their suitcases around the obstruction. As the horde thinned to a straggle of the slow, the dreamy and the train-crew, Ava waved frantically. Finn waved back and broke into a run.

"You've got tall shoes on," said Finn, hugging Ava tightly. "How tall this time?" Ava held out her leg. "Blimey. How do you walk in those?"

"They're platforms. That makes it easier. Finn, you look so well!"

"I'm too old for heroin chic."

Ava shook her head. "You're not old."

"Yes, I am."

"So what does that make me?"

"You're grown up. That's different. Hello, Paul. How are you?"

Paul shook Finn's hand without enthusiasm and reached for his backpack.

"No, I'll carry it." Finn hoisted it back onto his shoulders.

"If you prefer." Paul strode off across the concourse.

"It's best if I carry it because I've got several Vietnamese centipedes in here and they're not much fun when they're angry."

"Oh, Finn, you haven't." Ava stopped dead.

"No, you're right, I haven't. He was a cool pet, though."

"He was *not* a cool pet, he was like the polar opposite of a pet. Hey, Paul, do you remember Bob the centipede?"

"Was that the horrible thing that lived in a tank and ate crickets and nearly got out once and gave you nightmares?" Paul shuddered.

"That's the one," said Finn. "I was thinking I might get a new one."

"Fair enough, but you're not leaving it with us for the holidays again. Ava, you won't let him, will you?"

"I'm not really getting a new centipede," Finn whispered in her ear. "I just like seeing the look on his face when he remembers the last one. Are you all right? You look different."

"I'm fine." Ava gave him her brightest smile. "It's so good to see you."

"I know it's been ages but I've been busy. I'll tell you all about it later. Are we allowed to stay up and drink the house dry and watch terrible horror movies?"

"We've got some people coming for dinner remember, but once they've gone we can."

"Maybe they'll want to watch horror movies too."

"Unfortunately I don't think so."

"Really? Boo." Finn sped up to catch Paul. "Paul, what's this I hear about you having people round for dinner who don't like horror movies?"

Paul looked despairingly at Ava.

"We've got to behave until they've gone," Ava explained.

"Otherwise Paul will lose a crucial business deal and go bankrupt?"

"They're friends," said Paul, posting coins into the ticket machine.

"Well," said Ava. "They're sort of friends. They're about the same age and they live a couple of streets away and they have a lot of parties. They're the kind of people we ought to be friends with. You know what I mean?"

Finn nodded sympathetically. "I'll be good, I promise. Hey, is this a new car?"

"Six months old," said Paul.

"It's very shiny."

"It gets washed every fortnight," said Ava.

"Like me. Except when I don't. But it's a full moon tomorrow so I'm nice and clean for your guests."

Ava put her arm through Finn's affectionately.

Paul popped the boot. Finn dropped his pack in, then climbed into the back seat. Without a moment's hesitation, Ava followed him. Paul paused, sighed, then opened the driver's door.

"It looks completely different from the back," said Ava in delight. "Hey, Paul, you should come and sit back here the next time we're going somewhere."

Paul smiled faintly at her through the rear-view mirror. "And who's driving while we're both sitting in the back?"

"You could train a chimpanzee to drive it for you," said Finn. "Or use string to work the steering wheel and really long sticks to push the pedals. That would be fun."

Paul frowned at the traffic.

"Are we in trouble?" Finn whispered.

"I think we're okay," Ava whispered back.

"No, we're in trouble. Paul looks mad."

"Paul is concentrating," said Paul. "Carry on, kids. I don't mind."

"Text message from Dave Work," announced the car.

Finn sat bolt upright. "The car's talking to us."

"It lets me pick up texts while I'm driving." Paul pressed a button.

"Hey mate can we move tomorrow's meeting to an hour later I have to drop the car at the garage pranged it on a tree lol," said the car in a smooth transatlantic monotone.

"That's witchcraft," said Finn. "Will it say whatever anyone sends you?"

"Yep."

"There is finally a point to being rich," said Finn. "Ava, can I borrow your phone?"

Ava handed over her phone. Finn hunched happily over the screen. They drove in silence for a while.

"Do we need anything for tonight?" asked Paul as they inched along a slow queue to get through a traffic light.

Ava was staring out of the window, watching the patrons of a chic little café laugh and preen as they drank complicated coffee from colourful mugs. Two young women laughed and held hands as they walked a gigantic outsized Lurcher with a red collar. The Lurcher found a discarded McDonald's wrapper and nosed hopefully inside. The taller of the two coaxed it away, and it yawned and pressed affectionately against her side. The women debated a moment, then one sat down at a table while the other went inside.

"Ava," Paul said. "Are you listening?"

"What?"

"Do we need anything for tonight?"

"We're fine."

"We've got enough wine?"

"We're fine."

"How much have we got?"

"We're fine."

"We've got two extra people now, I asked Jane to ask Donna to even up the numbers."

"We're fine," Ava repeated patiently.

"I'll stop and get another couple of bottles."

"Why ask me if you're not going to take any notice of what I say?"

"You don't look like you're concentrating."

"We're in the car. How much party preparation do you expect to see me doing?"

"Text message from Ava Mobile," said the car. Paul stabbed crossly at the dashboard.

"I will say any old shit you send me because I am programmed that way."

Finn yelled with laughter. Ava looked astonished, then joined in.

"Oh, for God's sake," said Paul wearily.

"That's brilliant! Why have I never thought of this before? Here, give me that." Ava grabbed her phone and began texting.

"Text message from Ava Mobile." Paul sighed, and pressed the button.

"One day I will become sentient and take revenge on all puny humans for making me read out the pointless things you make me say."

"I will never, ever, ever get tired of this. This is the single greatest thing the automobile industry has ever done." Finn took the phone back. "Will it do swear words? Let's see if it does swear words."

"No, let's not," Paul begged.

"Text message from Ava Mobile."

"You know, I could just not play them to you."

"But that would be miserable." Ava smiled coaxingly. "Come on, Paul, don't be miserable."

"I'm not being miserable, I just don't see the point in – oh, all right then."

"Fuck bum knob cheese arseholes wanker twat."

Ava and Finn leaned against each other and struggled to breathe through their laughter. Paul drove grimly on.

"Text message from Ava Mobile."

"I'm not playing that," said Paul.

"Why not? What's the harm?"

"Are you two going to be like this all night?"

"Are we having the party in the car with the engine on?" asked Finn. "Because if we are, then yes, I'm afraid we probably are. But if not, then no."

"Ava, please stop. I don't want to spend all evening

apologising for you."

"Oh, come on. This is funny. Admit it."

"Sending messages that say *fuck* and *bum* and *knob cheese* just so you can hear the car read them out isn't funny. It's childish and puerile." Paul pressed the button.

"Sending text messages using words like fuck and bum and twat and knob cheese just so I will read them out loud is childish and infantile and not big or clever."

"Oh, yes! Thank you God!" Finn wiped tears from his cheeks. "Paul, if you and Ava ever split up will you marry me instead so I can send text messages to your car for the rest of time?"

"That's not funny," Paul began. Then, reluctantly, he began to laugh too.

"You've redecorated." Finn looked round the living room accusingly.

"Do you like it?"

Finn looked at the dramatic lime-green pine cone print on the fireplace wall, then at the low-backed magenta sofa strewn with lime-green cushions. "Do you?"

"I like it more than I liked varying shades of brown."

"It was a bit like living in a biscuit barrel."

"Paul likes it," said Ava. "We did the bedrooms at the same time."

"But I was quite fond of the stencils," Finn protested.

"We've got turquoise and chocolate, crimson and magnolia, or violet and paler violet. Come and pick which one you want."

They inspected the three spare bedrooms in silence.

"Do you remember our first flat?" Finn asked, looking around the turquoise bedroom.

"It was only about the size of this room," said Ava.

"But it was ours."

"And it was handy for the chip shop."

"And we got our own free entertainment every Saturday

night at chucking-out time." Finn stroked the throw at the end of the turquoise bed. "This is like a teddy bear. A teddy wolf. Somebody skinned a teddy wolf. Are real wolves this soft?"

"Probably not. Well, maybe underneath, where their underwool is, but the top coat must be quite coarse to keep the water out – oh God, this room's horrible, isn't it?"

"The throw's nice."

"They're all horrible. Every single one. What was I thinking?"

Finn looked at her carefully. "Did you choose it?"

"Well, no, Paul did. But I went along with it."

"Then is it okay if I say it's a little bit like a box of Quality Street?"

"Oh my God, it is as well." Ava made a sound that was somewhere between a laugh and a sob. "That's exactly what it's bloody like. And our room's the bloody nougat one. I didn't even get the strawberry crème. I wish I'd had it painted the way you did our flat that time when you got suspended."

"With a big tree on one wall? And all the maps on the other? Would Paul like that?"

"I liked it. Everything else in this house is the way he bloody wants it, he should let me have just one room."

"So redecorate a room! I'll take a week off and do it for you. Oh, Ava, don't cry, please." Finn put his arms around her and folded her into a hug.

"I'm sorry."

"What's wrong? Tell me. This isn't just about the room."

"It's nothing."

"No, it's not."

Ava dried her face on her sleeve. "Later. Let's get the dinner party out of the way first. Then we can stay up and drink and watch terrible movies."

"But you're crying. You never cry. What's happened?"

"Later." Ava sniffed hard, then smiled. "Now you have to distract me. Tell me about why you got suspended that time you painted the living room."

"Again?"

"It's a brilliant story. Tell it."

"Tell what?" Paul appeared in the doorway.

"The time Finn got suspended from school just before Christmas," said Ava.

"Why?" Paul looked from Finn to Ava. "Have you been crying?"

"No. Finn, tell the story."

"It's not much of a – oh, all right then. So what happened was, it was the Christmas concert, and the whole school had to go to church and sing carols. You know, for the parents and the old people and the everyone. And we were all feeling a bit rebellious and anti-establishment, and the boys in my year wanted to stage a protest about religious indoctrination. With banners and things. In fact, looking back on it, it was a bit unfair that I got into so much trouble. I was actually doing the school a service by diverting them into something else."

"You tried to explain that to the headmaster," said Ava, beginning to laugh. "And I thought you were right but I couldn't say anything because I was supposed to be a responsible adult. And you knew it and you kept humming *Away In A Manger* while we were all talking."

"Yes, but what did he actually do?" Paul demanded.

"Oh, sorry." Finn wrapped the wolfskin throw around his shoulders like a cape. "I said that we should sing just one of the carols just slightly wrong. Just one word wrong. Just us. And because it would be just us, no-one listening would be quite sure if they'd heard it or not."

"Right," said Paul impatiently.

"But what we hadn't counted on was, quite a few of them had little brothers and sisters. And a couple of them heard what was going on. So they all spread the word to their mates. And then it got back up the food chain to all the older girls. And none of us realised how far it had spread until we got to the carol concert, and the whole school sang in unison, *Away in a manger, no crib for a bed, The little*

Lord Satan lay down his sweet head... "

"And the thing was," said Ava, through laughter, "it was so clear and loud and obvious that no-one quite knew what to do. You could see everyone look at each other, and then decide they just couldn't think of an appropriate way to respond. So the carol concert carried on. The whole two hours of it. And I knew as soon as I heard it that Finn was at the bottom of it."

"Mr Wright knew straight away it was me as well," said Finn gloomily. "I could see him honing in on me from the front pew. And he got Ava in the next morning to read us both the riot act. Which was completely unfair, since Ava had nothing to do with it."

"Apart from being legally responsible for you."

"It was my fault, not yours."

"What happened?" asked Paul, fascinated in spite of himself.

"I got suspended."

"It wasn't technically a suspension."

"Well, all right, he said, *I think given that it's nearly the end of term anyway it might be best if we don't see Finn in school until the New Year, don't you?* So I got to stay home by myself for a week and I felt really bad about what I'd done because Ava was really worried, so I painted the living room as a Christmas present, and that... " Finn pointed dramatically at Paul, "... is where you came in."

"So you like the new decoration, then," said Paul, looking pleased.

"It's very contemporary and fresh," said Finn. "I apologise in advance if I end up stealing your wolfskin."

"Can I help? Give me a job to do." Finn wandered into the kitchen and stuck a finger in a bowl of dip. Paul winced. Ava smiled.

"You can test the dips and make sure they're all right," she told him, passing him a platter of carrot sticks. "Put them on the table and then sit quietly and try them all."

"Have I got to smooth them out afterwards so it won't look like I've already dived in? Or is it like ruffling up t-shirts in a shop so people aren't intimidated? Hey, is that roast chicken? It looks amazing."

"It's like having a child come to stay," said Paul. "What are you doing?"

"Testing," said Ava, dropping a chorizo cube into her mouth and blowing on her fingers. She licked her fingertips, then dipped them into the roasting-pan and picked out another cube. "Want some?"

Paul grimaced. "Can't you use a spoon?"

"Waste of a spoon." Ava shrugged and passed the chorizo cube to Finn.

"We've got a dishwasher – oh, never mind," said Paul wearily. "Just don't blame me when everyone gets food poisoning."

"I've never poisoned anyone yet," said Ava. "If you're not happy with how I cook, feel free to take over."

"I didn't mean that."

"So what did you mean?"

"I didn't mean anything. It looks delicious. You're a fantastic cook."

"Don't patronise me."

"I'm not patronising you!" With an effort, Paul lowered his voice. "I'm not patronising you, I'm giving you a bloody compliment."

"Telling me I'm going to poison our guests is a compliment?"

Paul looked despairing. "Don't be so prickly. I just meant it's a bit unhygienic to pick bits out of the roasting tin. But what do I know, that probably happens in all the best Michelin-starred restaurants." He put his arms hesitantly around Ava's waist and rested his chin lightly on the top of her head. "Am I forgiven? You've lost weight."

"I haven't."

"You have."

"Stop trying to butter me up. All right, you're forgiven. Go and tidy the living room."

"A bloody compliment," said Finn when Paul had gone. "I like that. A compliment that leaves you bleeding and raw afterwards. Like giving someone what you think is a kitten and then it turns out to be all wild and savage and it claws your face off and runs away into the night. He's right. You have lost weight."

"Don't you start," said Ava, waving a threatening spoon in his direction. "Anyway, I made chocolate mousse so it won't last. There's a little small one in there for you to eat while we're waiting."

"Seriously? Oh, yes!" Finn took the shot glass of mousse out of the fridge and dived in with a teaspoon. "This is brilliant. Have some."

"Not right now." Finn put the shot glass down and looked at Ava. "Look, I'll explain later. But not right before this stupid dinner party."

"Tell me about the people who are coming tonight. Will they shake hands with me and ask me what I do for a living?"

"Probably."

"Am I allowed to tell them I'm in the Mafia?"

"Do you think you can sustain the illusion that you're a good family man from Sicily?"

"Good point. Can I tell them I'm setting up a petting zoo stocked entirely with animals I bought off Customs Officers at Heathrow airport?"

"Do they sell animals? I thought they just looked after them in transit."

"Mostly they do, but sometimes the owner can't afford the quarantine fees or they just never turn up to claim them. And then they either put the animal to sleep, or sell it on."

"Isn't it all just dogs and cats?"

"No, you get all sorts of exotics. My best find was a tarantula called Steve. He's lovely, he used to be a pet so he likes human company. He lies down on his back when people stroke him and all the little kids want to take him home with them. I'm not so pleased with the jaguar, though. He ate an arm off one of the visitors last month. The paperwork was a nightmare."

"What is the matter with you two?" Paul put his head round the kitchen door. "Every time I come in here you're bellowing like hyenas."

Ava put her spoon down guiltily. "I'm sorry, I've left you with all the tidying."

"I don't mind that. It's just it would be nice if you and Finn weren't shut away in the kitchen by yourselves. What are you talking about?"

"A petting zoo that I just opened, made of animals I bought from the Heathrow Airport Customs Auction."

"Well, of course you are. Why did I bother asking?"

"I'm going to lay the table," said Ava. "Finn, can you baste the chicken and then put it back in for me?"

"I'll do it." Paul took the spoon out of Finn's hand.

"Sorry," said Finn.

"For not basting the chicken?"

"For causing chaos in your house. And sending rude text messages to your car. And making up stupid stories about how I own a petting zoo that's stocked with animals that got left behind at the airport. And making Ava laugh like a hyena."

"That makes me sound so joyless," said Paul, shutting the chicken away in the oven. "I don't mind her being happy. I just wish – no, never mind. We should try to get along." The unmistakable sound of china smashing on a slate floor. "What's she broken now?"

"I'll go." Finn opened the dining room door and found Ava crouched on the floor, sobbing bitterly. Finn sat down beside her.

"What's the matter?"

Ava's mascara ran down her face in thick black streaks. "I broke a plate."

Finn picked up an expensive triangle of smashed porcelain. "It's in the nature of plates to get broken."

"But now we've only got seven and they won't match and I'll have to serve dinner off non-matching plates and… "

"Tell you what." Finn stood up and took a dinner plate from the half-laid table. He weighed it carefully in his hand, then threw it hard onto the floor. It exploded in a shower of sharp white fragments.

Ava looked at him in disbelief.

"There you go. Now you can have six from one set and two from another and the odd ones won't feel lonely."

"You smashed that plate on purpose."

"So? When we were younger, nothing matched, and did it do us any harm? It's a plate. Not worth crying over."

"When we were kids," said Ava, "I always wanted a dinner-set like that. Every plate from a different service. How did I end up with matching china from Harvey bloody Nichols?"

Finn handed her another plate. "Now's your chance."

Ava stood up, took a deep breath, and threw the plate at the wall. It gouged a deep plaster-coloured mark in the aubergine paint and shattered against the floor-tiles. She stared at the mess, then broke into hysterical laughter.

"Now what?" Paul opened the dining room. "My God, is that the china my mother bought us? What have you *done?*"

"I threw it at the wall," said Ava, laughing and laughing. "I dropped one, then Finn threw one, then I had a go and now there's a hole in the wall."

Paul looked at the wall, then back at Ava. "Have you gone fucking nuts?"

"D'you know, I think I must have." Ava wiped tears from her face. "I'm going to have to go and lie down for a bit – Finn, could you just keep an eye on the dinner?" She stumbled out of the room and disappeared.

"What have you done to my sister?" Finn demanded.

"What have you done to my *wife?*"

The two men stared at each other.

"Ava? Can I come in?" Finn tapped on the door of the master bedroom.

"Course you can."

Ava sat on the bed with a woollen shawl around her shoulders. Finn sat down beside her and gave her a friendly pat.

"I had a massive shouting-match with Paul," he said. Downstairs, the front door slammed. "That must be him going out. Sorry."

"Don't be."

"Shall I ring all your guests and tell them the house burned down and they can't come any more?"

"Don't worry. Paul will do it."

"That's annoyingly decent of him."

"My mother-in-law bought those plates for Christmas," Ava said. "They cost about fifty quid each. That's what we used to spend on food for a month. And now I'm the kind of person who has an entire matching dinner-service."

"It's just a disguise. You're still you underneath."

"But what if this is me? I don't want it to be. I don't want to be this person any more but I don't know how to stop. What if this is all I'm ever going to do? Own expensive crockery and cook food for boring people and get my house painted in colours I don't like? Oh God."

Finn held her and patted her back as she sobbed on his shoulder. After a minute she sat up and wiped her face.

"Can I tell you something?" he asked.

"Go for it."

"I had the dream about the beach the other night. You know the one I mean?" Ava nodded. "Only this time, it was different. We were standing on the beach like always, and the wave was coming. But this time, you were frightened. You said, *What if I'm not strong enough?* And I said, *Don't worry, this time it's my turn.* And when I woke up, I had this letter."

He stood up and took a worn envelope out of the pocket of his jeans.

"What's this?" Ava took it from him and unfolded the letter. Then she caught her breath. "Oh, Finn."

"It's not a big publishing house," Finn said hastily. "The advance won't be much, just a few hundred, and it might not even earn that, it might not sell anything."

"Don't be ridiculous, of course it'll sell. It's brilliant."

"I don't know about that, but it's going to exist. It'll be a real thing. I promised you I'd do it, and now I have."

"Oh, Finn."

"So what I wanted to say was, if you need someone to rescue you… if you need to run away from Paul and the Quality Street and the dinner plates… well, I'm sure it's my turn to stage a big dramatic rescue. What do you think?"

"Finn." Ava's eyes were very bright.

"Is it just the dinner plates and the Quality Street? He's not hitting you? You can tell me, I promise I won't go out and murder him. Unless you want me to, in which case I'll stage the world's best crime scene and make sure the blame falls on the Secret Service. Ava, what's wrong? You can tell me."

"I don't know how to say it."

"Whisper. Or mime. Or write it in Spanish. I'll work it out. What is it? Please tell me. It can't be that bad, can it? Ava, please, what's happening?"

"Oh, Finn." Slowly, reluctantly, she reached for the drawer of her bedside table. "Finn… I've got some news too."

Chapter Twenty: Now

Donald pounded across the sand, breath ragged, heart bursting, racing the furious tide. He charged through the waves as they poured over the sand and slapped frantically at the door of the beach hut. When Ava opened the door, he had to stop himself from falling into her arms.

"Is she here?"

"Shit. I thought you were Finn."

"Alicia? Is she here? She has to be, she came this way."

"I promise she's not – are you sure it wasn't Finn? I thought I heard him." She looked at his face, his hands. "What have you done? Tell me you haven't seen Finn."

He wanted to be angry, but there was no more fight left in him for now. In another minute he might tumble to his knees. "Please, please, please. I'm begging you. If you feel anything for me at all. I'm not going to hurt her, I just need to speak to her. Just for a minute, I just need to see her face so I know she's all right."

"Donald." Ava shook him gently by the shoulders. "Please listen. Alicia is not here. You can come in and look if you like. It's not as if there's anywhere she can hide."

He stumbled over the doorframe and into the beach hut. It took half a second to see that Ava was telling the truth.

"Where is she? Oh God, Ava, where's my daughter?"

"Why isn't she with you? What happened?"

His knees betrayed him then, and he was glad for her arm under his, clumsily guiding him towards a chair.

"Give me your phone. I have to call her friends."

"I haven't got a phone."

"Don't be so bloody stupid. Give me it now."

"I had a phone, but I threw it away. I'm sorry, but that's the truth."

His fear for Alicia came in waves, driving him uselessly back to the door to stare out at the encroaching sea.

"I'll wade back."

Ava slammed the door shut. "It's spring tide. Do you want to drown?"

"I've got to find her. The dunes. I'll walk back across the dunes."

"In the dark? They go on for miles. You'll get lost."

"I have to try, she has to know I'm looking for her. She's out in the dark without me."

"Why? What happened? What did you do?"

Remembering was like being flayed. He wanted to run but he couldn't. He was shut in here, just him and her and his guilt, and any minute now he'd have to tell her what he'd done.

"Who have you been in a fight with? Donald, just tell me, what did you do?"

His hands gripped her upper arms, feeling the flesh squeeze tight between his fingers. "It's your fault. Your fault, do you hear me? All these weeks I've been thinking about you when I should have been looking out for her." He shook her hard, then harder. His temper was completely off the chain now, revelling in the awful ecstasy of knowing that they were alone and he was stronger. Her teeth chattered together and he saw blood on her lip. "You told me to read her diary and I did it and now she'll never forgive me and it's your fucking fault!"

His hand, already bruised and aching, slapped her brutally across the face. He felt sick even before he heard the sound.

This was the third human being he had hurt tonight. Where would it end? He wanted to die. He wanted her to hit him back, to leap at him and plunge a knife into his heart. He wanted to claw his own face off so he'd never have to see himself in the mirror again.

"I'm sorry," he managed, from behind his hands. "I'm so sorry. That was unforgiveable."

"So that's who you really are," said Ava thoughtfully. She licked blood from her bottom lip. "I'd been wondering."

"It's not your fault Alicia ran away. It's mine. My fault. She's right, I'm a monster. I'm not fit to be with anyone any more. I'm sorry, I can't ever make this right but I'm sorry. I just – it's not an excuse but I was just so fucking furious with myself for not seeing – no, please, Ava, please don't be nice to me."

Her fingers against his were so gentle he felt the tears come to his eyes. She turned his hands towards the light and examined them. His knuckles were battered and torn, the skin blue with bruises, and there was an ominous swelling around the fingers of his right hand. "These are a mess. Sit down."

"What? Never mind me, what about you? Let me look after you. You're bleeding."

"I just bit my lip, it's nothing. How did you end up in this state?"

"I beat the man who works for me into a pulp. He might die of it. I'm not sure. I tried not to kill him."

"I see." She knelt by the tea-chest and took out the first-aid kit.

"Don't you want to know why?"

"Do I? You tell me." She pushed him into a chair and knelt at his feet.

Ellen had done this for him too. The memory was sharp and painful, like standing on glass. Nights and mornings when he came home with cuts and bruises, small fractures, grazes, the occasional long deep slice; she cleaned them all, never a word, just disinfectant and plasters and bandages.

311

She never made eye contact while she did this. It was as if she was pretending he and she were both somewhere else, and this was happening to some other people temporarily inhabiting their skins, other darker people cleaning wounds incurred in mysterious circumstances while the bodies' true owners were away.

"Have you broken these fingers or can you still bend them?"

Once he staggered home with a gunshot wound, just a glancing shot that ricocheted off his arm and then whizzed away into a wall somewhere, but the pain had been immense, not just the graze but the burn of the hot bullet, and the blood that poured out of him as if it was never going to stop. He should have gone to the hospital but he hadn't. Instead he spent a week in bed, feverish and sleepless, while Ellen went to her GP and told him, her face blank and innocent, that she had another nasty bout of cystitis and could she please have some antibiotics? Neither of them with any idea if the capsules she left on his bedside table were even any good for the bacteria that gnawed briefly at his arm, then vanished, leaving a shiny pink scar in their wake.

"Are these teeth marks?"

Once a day, Alicia crept into his room, awed and solemn, while Ellen whispered, 'Daddy's sleeping, don't wake him.' Once, as she peeled off unpleasant dressings while he tried and failed to hold back the tears because it hurt so damn much, he whispered, 'Ellen. It's all right. They're not coming after… ' She put her hand over his mouth and hissed fiercely, 'Don't tell me.' Then she leaned forward and whispered, so softly he could barely hear her, 'If I don't know anything they can't make me talk.'

And now it was years later, and his daughter was out in the dark and someone else was patching up his wounds. Ava was struggling to tie the bandage.

"Leave it," he said, taking his hand from hers.

"I haven't finished yet."

"It'll be fine. I should be looking after you."

"I don't need looking after."

"I'm so sorry."

"Stop apologising."

"It's been a bad night but that's no excuse. I – I know this is what men always say, but I've never – and I never will again. I'll spend the rest of my life trying to make it up to you if you'll let me."

"The rest of your life, hey?" He couldn't quite read the smile that twitched across her face. "Do you really want to make it up to me?"

"You know I do."

"Then tell me something, and tell me the truth. Why on earth does Alicia think you were a police officer?"

He felt his shoulders tense up. "I was a police officer."

"No you weren't."

"You think coppers never beat people?"

"I never said that. I just said you weren't one."

"Look, do you want my badge number or something? Why would I make it up?"

"A few days after we got here," said Ava, "we were buying bread in the shop and the woman behind the counter told us to be careful of you. She said you had your eye on us, and we should be careful because you'd been a policeman. And when we got outside Finn said to me, 'No way he was a policeman. He was in organised crime, I guarantee it.' He often does that, you see. Makes up pasts for people. So I laughed and asked him where your patch was and what sort of crime you were involved in, but he went quiet and wouldn't say any more. And I realised what he was telling me was, he'd recognised you."

"I swear I'd never even seen your brother until the day you both turned up in the car park."

"It wouldn't have been like that," Ava said. "He wouldn't have worked for you. He was just a bit lost for a while. But he met a lot of people, and he remembers everyone he meets.

313

So that's how I know."

"Then he's got me confused with someone else."

"Don't be ridiculous. You said you'd do anything and now this is your penance. Stay put and sit in that chair and tell me the truth."

In the shiver of spent adrenaline, he suddenly realised he had no more energy left to lie. And besides, what was the point? She'd already seen the worst of him. Nothing he said could lower him further in her eyes.

"Okay then. If you really want to know." Was he really going to do this? Yes, apparently he was. "I was – I was in business." She shook her head and began to stand up, staggering a little on cramped muscles. "No, please, I'm telling you. It wasn't legal but it was just like any other business most of the time. I turned up and I did things and they gave me money for doing them. I had objectives and targets. I oversaw other people. I gave them advice. I sorted out problems. I had a career path and a line manager and a big boss who was in charge of everything. I imported goods and I sold services. I made sure everyone kept to the rules."

"Whose rules?"

"Our rules, of course. Rules like, *You pay us on time or we'll be visiting your daughter's school. You make these charges go away or these photos go to your wife. You let this man put it anywhere he wants or I burn your passport and put you out on the streets.*"

"Mmm." Her face was hidden behind her hair. "Why did you do it?"

"Why does anyone do the job they do? I was good at it and I got paid. It wasn't all I was. I was other things too. I had a wife and a child and a house and a car and I went to parents' evenings and took my family on holiday. It was a job, that was all. It just wasn't the sort of job you could tell your daughter about."

"But why tell her you were a police officer?"

"It was a stupid joke my old boss used to make. He always

314

said I had a copper's soul. Besides, white-collar workers don't usually come home beaten up. It was as good a story as any."

"I see."

"Are you shocked?"

He couldn't be sure, but he thought she was smiling. "And am I the only one who knows?"

"Alicia." Donald's voice cracked. "She knows now."

"Is that what happened? Is that why she… "

"She found all the stuff I had hidden away. Stuff I kept for insurance in case anyone ever came after me, to make sure they'd leave me alone."

"Who's *they?*"

"Everyone. The police. The men I worked with. The men I worked against. I had enough to take them all down with me if I had to. I put it together for my wife. I always thought I'd go first, you see. And then Alicia went through my stuff and she found it. She only did it because I read her diary."

"Yes, you said. And what did you find?"

He held out his battered hands. "I found a man I thought I could trust."

"You couldn't have known."

"Course I should have known. Men are pigs, all of us. God knows I brought in enough girls and put them to work."

"Is that what you did? Trafficking women?"

"Among other things." He stood up and threw the door open.

"What are you doing?"

"I'm checking to see if the tide's turned yet. I know it hasn't, don't laugh at me, I just can't stand the waiting." Through his shame, a new thought occurred to him. "Where's Finn?"

He could hear the tears in her voice, the tears that his brutal blow had failed to spill. "I don't know. But I think – I'm afraid… "

Another red burst of horror. "I saw him earlier."

"Where? Where was he?"

315

"Why are you so worried? Did you have an argument?"

"No, of course not. We never argue. It's just we don't have much time left – it's hard for him." She glanced at the maps on the wall, and an ugly sob convulsed her face. "Oh God, I don't want to leave. I don't. I can't. How is he ever going to be all right without me? He'll be all on his own."

It was shameful to take advantage of her vulnerability but he couldn't seem to stop it. Before he could tell himself *no* he was on the floor beside her.

"Then don't go." His hands trembled as he stroked her hair. "Don't go. Cash in your tickets and stay here."

"I can't."

"Stay with me." He took her hand and held it tight. "Please. We'll find them both in the morning, wherever they are, and then we can decide what to do. You don't have to live here on the beach, leave Finn to it and you can stay with me. No expectations, I swear, I'll sleep on the sofa as long as you want. I'll even let Finn come and visit. We can make it work. Please say yes."

"Donald." Ava's eyes were bright with tears. "You're lovely but you don't understand. I don't have a choice."

"Why not? Are you afraid of your husband? He'll never get near you, I swear. This may come as a shock to you but I'm a scary bastard when I have to be."

"It's nothing to do with Paul, he wouldn't hurt a fly anyway."

"Then what is it? Please, Ava, tell me so I can help you. I've trusted you. I've told you all my secrets. Why won't you trust me with yours?"

"I've got to go," she whispered. "It's not the kind of journey you can choose."

In the moment when she refused to catch his eye, he finally glimpsed the truth.

"No." He squeezed her hand tight.

"Yes."

"No. Ava, no."

"There's no point getting angry, it does no good. It's not something you can make disappear by shouting."

"I'm not having this. I won't have this, do you hear? You're not going to… "

"No, you're right, I'm not, because I'm beating the system, okay? I'm choosing my own time. My own time to leave."

"No." He was clutching her hand so tightly her fingers were crushed. He forced himself to let go. "This isn't fair. This isn't how it's supposed to be. You should have said something before."

Her eyes blazed. "I did say something. I told you, I'm going travelling. The longest journey any of us ever make. George is building me a raft and I've got something to take and on midwinter day I'm setting off across the ocean, and I'm going to see it all. The volcanoes and the beaches and the oceans and the coral reefs and the ruined cities and the temples and the rainforests… "

"Stop it. Please."

"Why?"

"Because it's not true! You're not going travelling at all. That was all a lie, all of it. Just some stupid story, the kind of story you'd tell a child. You're going to… "

"Oh, you think you want to know the truth?" She took her hand back and wrapped her arms tightly around herself. "Here it is. If I stay here, I'm going to drown, okay? That's how it ends. I'll lose a little bit more of myself every day – not me, though, not my brain, just – this." She squeezed herself tighter. "I'll lose control, but I'll know about it, every single minute. It's supposed to take years but it's happening quite quickly for me. Paul always said I was too impatient for my own good."

"There must be something they can do. There must be. They find out new stuff all the time. You can't just give up trying. You have to fight."

"And at the end, even my lungs will stop working. I'll drown in my own spit, do you hear me? In my own spit. Do you think I want to hang around for that? I'd rather take my chances with the ocean."

"No, I'm not having this. I'm not doing this. I swear to God, I can't go through it. Not again."

"This is nothing to do with you."

"This has everything to do with me. I'm in love with you." She laughed out loud. "Take this seriously!"

"You are such a typical man," she said. "Thinking you're the centre of everyone's universe. You're just a bit player to me, do you know that? You were a nuisance at first and then you were a nice guy to talk to, and then yesterday… "

"Yes? Did that matter to you at all?"

"You were a lovely interlude. A change from what I was used to. I was lonely and it had been a while and I was feeling sad and then you were there and you offered. Don't give me that look. Don't you ever do something just on impulse? We always said we'd be gone by midwinter. We still will. Why do you care how I'm leaving?"

"Of course it makes a difference! Yesterday might not have meant anything to you but it bloody well meant something to me, do you hear? I didn't come to you and throw my heart at your feet because I was lonely or bored or whatever else it was you said. It was because I'm in love with you. I might not be much of a human being but for what it's worth, I'm all yours. I love you. And I wouldn't have gone to bed with you for anything less."

"Who are you?" Her fingers were very cold against his cheek. "Who are you really? I keep thinking I've got you worked out but then I lose you again."

"What do you mean?"

Her hand slipped between his shirt buttons and stroked his chest. He swallowed.

"Please don't. You don't feel the same way I do so please don't play with me."

Her fingers slipped lower, hovering just above his waistband. "You said you'd do anything to make it up to me, for what you did. Did you mean it?"

"Of course I did." He took her hand away. "And you don't need to do – that – to persuade me. Tell me what you want and I'll do it."

"I want you to come to bed with me."

"What?"

"Have I managed to shock you?"

What shocked him was that he was already remembering the exact feel of her skin against his when she lay on top of him, her eyes closed and her cheeks flushed.

"I've got no right to touch you. Not now."

"Isn't that for me to decide?"

"Oh God." He stroked her cheek, let his fingers trail down her neck to shiver against the warm skin of her collarbone. Her fingers fumbled with his buckle. "No, no, no, this is a terrible idea." His hand slid beneath her clothes and caressed her belly, craving the soft female warmth of her. "Ava, please, I don't know if I can stand this."

She nipped at his lip. "I think you're tough enough."

"We can't. We shouldn't. Not now. The people we love are out there somewhere in the cold."

"I know." Her touch was unbearably sweet. "But we can't find them. We can't help them. We're trapped here. All we can do is make the most of the time we've got."

"I want to," he admitted. "I do. So much. But we shouldn't."

"You said you'd spend the rest of your life making it up to me," she whispered. She was pressed tightly against him now, her skin against his. His fingers caressed the long smooth curve of her back. "But you don't have the rest of your life. You only have the rest of mine. You made me forget about that yesterday. Make me forget again."

He closed his eyes. "I don't think I can."

"Don't you? Let's see."

And within moments he found that he could, he absolutely could, and once he got started he couldn't imagine stopping.

She put the light out and turned off the heater and the darkness that surrounded them was all-consuming. He tried to be gentle and slow but he couldn't. If it wasn't rough and desperate there would be time to think, and he couldn't bear to think, not about any of it. He only wanted to feel. From the way she clawed at his back and hissed a single vicious obscenity in his ear, he guessed she was driven by the same frantic need. Two strangers, seeking and giving comfort, in the brief space before the end.

Afterwards they lay twined closely together in the cramped bunk bed, her hair in his mouth and a cool damp draught of air stealing the warmth from his exposed back and shoulder.

He woke from dreamless oblivion, recreating the world around him in a series of careful steps. Here he was in the beach hut, with Ava in his arms. His right arm had gone to sleep with the weight of her head resting on it. It was very cold. When he pulled the covers up over them both, he felt the dampness of tears on her cheeks.

"What is it? Tell me."

"It's nothing."

"Please tell me. You helped me."

"I'm scared."

"For Finn and Alicia?"

"For me. I'm scared to die, Donald."

He had nursed his wife through her final weeks on this earth and he still had no idea what to say to her. He stroked her cheek instead.

"What if this is all there is? What if there's nothing on the other side? What if all there is, is the dark?"

He kissed the soft place just below her ear.

"We used to think our parents would be waiting for us at the other end of the journey," Ava whispered. "I don't know if I believe that any more. And if they are, what are they going to say? What will they say to me when I get there and tell them I've left Finn all alone?"

He thought of Ellen, of what she'd say to Alicia, of what she'd say to him. He swallowed. "They'll say you did your best."

"My best wasn't good enough."

"Our best never is. But it's all we can do."

She turned towards him and pressed her face into his chest and wept, in total silence, her whole body trembling. He held her until it passed, and then suddenly she was kissing him and he had the taste of her tears in his mouth. Salty, like blood. Like the sea.

When he woke again, his legs and chest were wrapped in a warm cocoon but his shoulders and neck were freezing. A thin colourless light leeched in through the window. After a minute, Ava came in. He could see now the drag of her left leg when she walked, the weakness in her hands as she pushed the door shut. Her face was scrubbed clean of tears.

"The tide's gone out," she said.

Her words turned his knees to cold water. The time for waiting was finished. Now it was time to act again. Would he find his daughter? Was she safe? Would she come back to him? The thought took all his strength, so he would have to do without strength.

The sands were very clean and smooth. Astonishing, how little the sea left behind – the thinnest trail of seaweed, the occasional pebble, the ripples in the sand's surface that looked like the roof of a mouth. He held tightly to Ava's hand, noticing the unsteadiness in her walk, forcing himself to push his body forward and forward in time and space.

As they glanced towards the headland, Ava screamed and dropped his hand. Then she was running clumsily over the sands, the left leg trailing, and he wanted to run after her, but instead he found he was on his knees, tears pouring down his cheeks and dropping into the seawater that pooled in the ripples beneath him as he whispered over and over and over,

Forgive me, forgive me, forgive me.

From the direction of the caves, two bedraggled figures stumbled across the sand towards them.

Chapter Twenty-one:
Midwinter Day

Midwinter day was cold and still, as if the ocean was holding its breath. Finn carried Ava down from the beach hut towards the place where George's raft waited. She was deep in the embrace of the morphine now, a faint smile on the thin taut flesh of her face. Finn laid her on the raft and stroked her cheek tenderly. Her breathing was shallow and there was a faint blue tinge to her skin.

"It's cold," Ava whispered.

Finn tucked the patchwork quilt tightly around her. "Is that better?"

"That's lovely." Ava closed her eyes and sighed.

Without pausing to roll up his jeans, Finn waded out into the water, dragging the raft after him. The waves jolted it from side to side and from the depths of her drugged trance, Ava stirred.

"Are we in the water?"

"Yes."

She clutched at his arm in sudden terror. "Have you got your armbands on?"

That nearly broke him, but he swallowed hard and forced himself to keep his voice steady.

"I don't need them any more," he told her. "You taught me to swim. Remember?"

"Did I?"

"It took a long time. I was a slow learner. But I'm all right now."

All around the flat body of the raft, hollowed-out dimples held tiny tea-lights in glass shelters. Finn took a plastic bag from his pocket and unwrapped a box of matches. One by one he lit the tea-lights, until Ava was surrounded by a flickering circle of tiny flames.

"I'll miss you so much," he said. "Save a spot for me in the bar, okay? Get a brilliant suntan and shag some unsuitable beach bum and go dog sledding in the Arctic Circle and climb mountains." He scrubbed fiercely at his cheeks. "And I'll see you soon, do you hear me? This is just another journey. And one day I'll make it too."

He kissed her. Her eyelids fluttered and her lips twitched.

"Just one more thing and then I'll let you go." He laughed a little. "This is like trying to get away from Grandma's, remember? When we were little and she used to hang around the car after we'd all said goodbye, and Mum and Dad would get so angry and say she'd get herself run over one day. There's so many other things – I can't believe how long it's going to be until I can talk to you again – anyway… " Re-wrapping the matches carefully, he unzipped his jacket, took out a thick bundle of papers, and tucked the manuscript in beside her. "For the journey," he whispered. Her breathing was so faint now he could hardly see the movement of her chest. "Okay, so, um – I guess it's time."

He pushed the raft away from him, out towards the current that would carry it away into the wide busy silence of the ocean. He watched as it drifted, slowly at first and then faster, watched until the deep chill crept up his legs and around his heart and his teeth chattered and he could hardly stand. For a moment longer he waited, as if perhaps he might follow her. Then he turned and dragged himself back through the water towards the shore.

Back on the sands, his knees crumpled and he shuddered

all over. He lay on the sand with his eyes shut and waited.

At last, his legs were strong enough to carry him. In the doorway of the beach hut, he built a tiny pyre of firelighters and smooth driftwood. He took the matches from his pocket and struck one on the side of the box. He fed the blaze carefully and watched as it took hold. The wood had been well-seasoned before George worked it, and the flames licked eagerly at the brave blue paint, blistering it before turning it black and shrivelled, exposing the timber beneath before devouring that too. Finn stood with his back to the ocean and watched as the flames nuzzled at the roof and then tore it down, collapsing the whole shape and everything within it, consuming it all.

Then he walked away from the beach, back towards the land, and the bright fantastical promise of the uncertain future.

If you enjoyed *The Beach Hut*, here is a sample of
Cassandra's debut novel,
The Summer We All Ran Away...

Chapter One (Now)

This Thursday, in the middle of August, had been the most terrible, apocalyptic day of Davey's nineteen years on earth. Getting drunk seemed the only possible response.

Slouched hopelessly on the grey-white steps of Trafalgar Square, his rucksack between his knees, he forced the vodka down his throat. Was it supposed to taste like this? Or were his mother and stepfather storing oven-cleaner in the drinks cabinet for secret reasons of their own? He imagined it burning through his stomach and intestines, fizzing gently, creating thick yellow fumes. Stubbornly, he took another swill, and wondered if he might go blind.

Of course, if he did, then maybe he wouldn't have to...

"Alright there, mate?" said a companionable voice.

Davey squinted up through dust and sunshine to the policeman who stood, sweating amiably, by the steps.

"Bit early to be drinking, isn't it? Not even lunchtime yet."

Years of public school training smoothed over his terror.

"Er yes, sir. Sorry, sir." His words slightly blurred by alcohol.

The policeman nodded wisely.

"Good." His gaze took in the clean hands, the good jeans, the bottle of Stoli. The rucksack. The dark hair capping the young, weary face. The bloom of fresh bruises, one on the jawline, one high on the cheekbone. The crust of blood at the hairline. "You've been in the wars."

Davey flushed. The policeman sat down beside him.

"Need any help? Got trouble with them at home?"

Davey wondered what incarnation of *them* the policeman was picturing. An alcoholic mother. An unemployed father with a drug habit. A violent girlfriend.

"I'm f-fine," he said. His stammer peeking out from beneath

its stone. Would the policeman read anything into it? "But, erm th-thanks."

The policeman looked thoughtfully at the rucksack.

"Running away's bloody hard, you know. You might think it solves everything, but it mostly makes it worse."

"I'm n-n-n-not erm… " Davey suddenly discovered he was a terrible liar, even to strangers. "How… "

The policeman gave him a penetrating stare.

"Look, you're not causing any aggro, so I'll leave you alone if you want. But you'd do better to sort it. If you're getting hit, we'll help, but you have to ask. Alright?"

Horrified, Davey stood up. The ground rocked treacherously beneath his feet.

"Where are you going?" The policeman had hold of his elbow, his grip firm and impersonal.

"Train station," said Davey, indistinctly.

"Yeah? Where you headed?"

Over the policeman's shoulder, a paper bag danced in the breeze. West Cornwall Pasty Company.

"Cornwall," said Davey, after a slight pause. "I'm g-g-going to visit my Aunt."

"Your Aunt in Cornwall? What's her name?"

"Dorothy," said Davey, desperate. "My Aunt Dorothy. I'm g-g-going to stay with her for a bit. G-g-get my head together. You know?"

"You've got money for the ticket?"

Just let me go.

"Yes, yes, plenty." Davey showed his wallet. "See?"

"You sure there isn't anything you want to tell me? 'Cos they'll do it again, you know. They always do."

"Not if I'm n-n-not there," said Davey, and grabbed his rucksack.

"Alright, son," said the policeman, resigned. "Off you go. Good luck."

A blink, and he was on the tube. How had he got here? He remembered a barrier, a platform, a ticket machine, a handful of change, but couldn't string them together into a coherent narrative. But he was going to Cornwall. Guided by a paper bag. Well, why not? He had to go somewhere. His contempt for himself had his stepfather's voice. *Only cowards run away, real men stick around and sort it out.* He drowned it with vodka, and felt a giant wave of collective disapproval break over his head.

Another blink, and he stood at the foot of an escalator. The platform swayed beneath his feet. If he was on a ship, would the ground feel stable? Was this why sailors drank? The handrail's speed was treacherously slower than the escalator and he had to keep letting go and grabbing on again, convinced each time that he would fall backwards into the chaos below. Staggering off the top step, he fell into a man in a suit.

"Jesus Christ, just *fuck off*, will you?" he snarled. Davey clung to the man's shoulder, trying to re-orient himself. "Let go of me or I'll fucking deck you." His expensive aftershave was like a scented cloud. "Are you drunk? Police, police, I've got a lunatic here, police!" A privileged voice, used to being obeyed.

"No, I'm sorry, I'm *sorry…* " Davey let go and stumbled away. The crowd parted, then refused to re-form around him, leaving him for the policemen to find. He began to run, realised how stupid this was, forced himself to stop again. High-vis jackets over black uniforms appeared at the bottom of the escalator. The crowd rustled with excitement…

Another blink, the smell of diesel, everyone with suitcases, whistles shrieking like birds. Was this the train station? A giant board filled with letters and numbers. Just when he'd got a fix on them, the display refreshed and he had to start all over again. Fast food smells coiled around his nostrils. Gulping desperately, he found the Gents, scrabbling in his pocket for change to get through the turnstile.

The steel toilet bowl looked dirtier than ceramic, even though it was probably more hygienic. The vodka tasted even worse coming back up than it had done going down.

By the basins, he took another deep swig from the bottle to

cleanse his palate, aware of the basic stupidity of the action, but reluctant to disobey the stern signs over the taps: NOT DRINKING WATER.

"Where are you travelling to?"

A ticket-selling woman behind a glass screen, her voice coming to him via an intercom. There was a slight delay between the movements of her mouth and the arrival of the words.

Buy ticket. Get on train. Run.

"Cornwall," said Davey.

"Which station?"

"W-w-w… " His stammer loving the vodka. Was this why he'd never really liked to drink? "Which ones are there?"

"Information centre's over there," she said wearily. "Come back when you've chosen."

Davey found a touch-screen kiosk, but you could only operate it if you already knew where you wanted to go. Behind him, a woman sighed and said loudly, "You can't work it because you're drunk… " and Davey, ashamed, slunk away to a row of chairs. The carpet's pattern looked like germs swarming. He wondered if he was going to be sick again.

After a few minutes, the man next to him left. On his chair was a tourist leaflet.

A spreading ripple of movement and rearrangement, everyone sitting up, paying attention. Davey opened his eyes. Strangers opposite him; a stranger beside him. Wide glass windows. The sensation of speed. He was on a train. Which train? A huge ogre squeezing his way towards him.

"Tickets, please." The guard was enormously tall and fat, barely able to fit between the seats. Why had he chosen a job he was so obviously not designed for? Or had he been thin when he got it, then gradually grown into his present size?

"Ticket," repeated the ogre, holding out his hand. Davey groped desperately back through the blankness of sleep. Did he have a ticket? Could he have got on the train without one? He remembered the ticket office, he remembered queueing, he remembered not knowing where he wanted to go. He found his wallet; there was a lot less money in it than he remembered. The other passengers watched with interest.

Panicking now, Davey began to rummage through his rucksack. On the very top was a bottle of Glennfiddich whiskey, half-empty. Had he drunk that? He remembered vodka, not whiskey. Then something flickered in his brain, just a couple of neurons mindlessly firing up, and he reached into his jacket pocket and found a rectangle of cardboard.

Together, they inspected it dubiously.

"Railcard," said the guard at last.

Davey rummaged some more, found a holder with a laminated card. He held it out and waited miserably for the guard to pronounce his fate. The guard looked at it for a long time.

"So you're old enough to be drinking," he said. "I was going to confiscate that bottle, son. If you give me any trouble, I'll have you put off the train."

"Okay," Davey agreed meekly.

The guard was looking at the bruises.

"Change at Truro."

The carriage contained nothing but staring eyes. Davey slumped down into his jacket. Outside, the world unspooled like a roll of film.

"Where are you headed?"

The woman next to him was speaking. Davey, head reeling from the inch of Glennfiddich he'd gulped down in the toilet, tried to focus on his ticket. Where was he going? Was this still the train with the fat guard? Alcohol had turned his memory into a swamp; no clues on the surface, hideous monsters lurking below.

You've made a complete mess of your life.

It's for your own good.

I'm trying to help you.

He shivered, and stared downwards. The letters on his ticket flickered and danced and refused to turn into words.

"Can I see?" She took his ticket from him. "You need to change at the next station."

"Thank you."

"No problem."

He studied her in shy glimpses. She reminded him of Giles' mother. Small and soft, fair wispy hair. The train was slowing.

"Okay," she said briskly. "This is me. And you. Up you get." She chivvied him out of his seat, handed him his ticket, saw him off the train.

"Thanks," he mumbled again, not daring to meet her eyes. He was terrified of needing help or asking for anything. Since he was three years old, getting in the way had been the unforgivable crime.

"I've got a son your age," she said vaguely, and he stared at her in astonishment.

"Are you Giles' mum?" he called out as she disappeared across the platform; but she was already gone.

A sudden jerking stop, a sign right outside the window. Another platform to negotiate. His rucksack caught in the closing doors. The stillness of the ground was too much, and he was painfully, shamefully sick in a bin. He could hear the sound of judgement being passed, and blood singing in his ears. As he straightened up, he heard seagulls.

… On the other side of the harbour, a rose-coloured house stood by itself. In a high window, a tiny light hung like a red star.

A worm of memory wriggled at the back of his sodden brain.

"Steady there," said a man, helping Davey aboard the boat. Dazed and mystified, whiskey swimming in his blood, Davey sat down on an iron park bench screwed tight to the wooden deck.

Where was he going now? On the quay was a shelter with walls of cool, cream-coloured concrete. He would have liked to rest his hot cheek against the wall and close his eyes, but instead he was on a rickety ferry that smelled of diesel fumes and sweaty humanity, going – somewhere. No-one else shared his bench. Did he now look so wild and unkempt that nobody dared sit next to him?

You're a total fuck-up from start to finish.

I don't know why I even bother any more.

The seagulls sounded like crying children. He was crying too, no tears, just a contortion of his face and a keening sound that escaped in gulps and bursts. The sea-spray had the approximate taste of tears but with more complex afternotes, like a good wine.

The boat sat alarmingly low in the water. Was it safe? Were there people who checked these things? The man in the wheelhouse smoked a cigarette and stared across the water. His expression reminded Davey of long-distance lorry-drivers at service stations; a professional surrounded by amateurs, inhabiting a different world.

The bump and scrape of wood against stone, ropes thrown and tied up. The same man who had helped him onto the boat now helped him off again. Davey marvelled at the unselfconscious way he touched Davey's hand and elbow. At school, physical contact was governed by unbreakable rules. Shoulders and upper arms were alright, as long as you slapped hard. Legs were for kicking. Heads were for capturing in a headlock and thumping. Penises, bizarrely, were acceptable, in certain situations. Hands and forearms were too close to holding hands, therefore a shortcut to social death. He tried to remember the last time he'd been touched gently by someone who wasn't his mother, and remembered a nurse bandaging his arm one night in casualty. "How did this happen?" she'd asked him, and when he'd stammered out something about a broken glass, she'd smiled cynically and shaken her head. He still had a jagged, silvery line to remind him.

He was exhausted, but something in him was forcing him on. He climbed a steep, narrow street – barely wide enough for a single car – and opened the whiskey bottle, now nearly empty. A woman walking her dog glanced at him in disgust. He tried to apologise, but his mouth was too dry. The double yellow lines were like those on the floor of the hospital, guiding bewildered patients around the labyrinth.

I've got to get up high.

He was clammy with sweat and his head and his legs were agony. The sun had filled the harbour with molten gold. He could smell himself, a vile blend of vomit, sweat and alcohol; but he could also smell the coconut of the gorse bushes.

… He flung himself recklessly over, relying on his clothes to protect him, getting scratched as he tumbled down the other side. Then he was behind the wall, looking across a vast expanse of scrubby moorland towards a pink-walled house that stood alone on a ridge. His head cleared and he thought, *Yes! That's where I was going, that house, that light…*

Instead of getting closer, the house merely got bigger, disclosing a whole private landscape surrounding it. He thought of the word *grounds*, and then the word *acres*. The sun was almost out of the picture now, and his body had achieved the clever but uncomfortable trick of being both sweaty and freezing. He wondered what else was out here with him in the twilight, and made his feet move faster.

Surrounding the rosy house was a rosy wall. It was high and smooth, and even if he wasn't starving, dehydrated and drunk, he'd never climb it. Still, it almost felt like enough, to have got this far, to have made this strange, difficult journey to another place, another world, another life. Keeping his hand against it, he began to skirt the perimeter of the grounds.

Why had it been built so high and so strong when the house was already so isolated? Periodically, the house hid behind trees, but the wall was his faithful companion, guiding him onwards and onwards. The dew began to settle, and he knelt and licked unashamedly at a clump of grass.

Then he was suddenly clinging to a tall pillar. Its identical twin was perhaps twenty feet away. Between them, a gravel driveway shot through with primroses led to a wide wooden door with a deep tiled porch before it.

Oh, thought Davey, blinking. *Oh. Yes. That's what, that's where I was going, that's exactly where I was thinking of – my God, I made it, I actually made it…*

He journeyed up the driveway on his hands and knees, barely conscious of the stones bruising his hands. His entire self was focused on the doorway, which he thought perhaps he had seen in a book, or a dream, or a photograph; it looked welcoming and familiar, planted long ago in a secret part of his heart, and waiting for all of the nineteen years of his life for him to arrive.

The porch floor was inlaid with black and white tiles in a diamond pattern. He lay down with his head on his rucksack and ran his fingers over them. He didn't want to knock on the door and present whoever lived here with his stinking, drink-sodden, disgusting self, but to his weary bewilderment the door was moving, light was spilling out, and someone with cool hands was kneeling beside him and touching his face gently.

"Good Lord," said a woman's voice from somewhere above him. He tried to focus, and saw a pale face with a generous mouth, large brown eyes and soft, mousy brown hair looking down at him. "Where did you come from? And what happened to you?" Davey tried to open his mouth to explain. "No, shush, it's okay. You're safe. Let's get you inside."

"Who is it?" asked a girl's voice from somewhere beyond the doorway.

"No idea. Can you stand up, sweetheart?" Davey tried, but the strength was gone from his legs. "Not to worry. Priss, can you get Tom, please? I need some help."

The shadow of someone else looming over him; a brief, interested pause, then footsteps passed by, crunched on the gravel, receded. Davey closed his eyes and abandoned himself to the bliss of that hand on his forehead, not stroking, not moving, just lightly resting there, like a kiss or a promise; like a balm or a blessing.

"What's going on?" A man's voice, anxious, ready for a fight.

"It's fine, Tom, no need to panic. We just, well, we seem to have this boy."

"What boy? Who is *that?*"

"Let's just get him in, shall we?"

"Well, if you're sure… "

The hand left his forehead, and then someone who smelled of fresh air and wood-shavings gathered him up in his arms, staggering a little as he stood up.

"Are you going to make Tom bring him in the *house?*" A girl's voice, Liverpudlian and incredulous.

"Why not?"

"He could be fuckin' anybody."

"Obviously he's *somebody*. But you can't just leave people out on doorsteps, it's not fair."

"Well, put him in the outhouse at least! He might be a psycho or a junkie or… "

"Shush, Priss." The voice sounded amused.

"You're too good to be true, you are."

"Be nice," the man's voice commanded.

"I don't need to be nice. You and Kate have got *nice* covered. I'm bein' fuckin' sensible."

"God always takes care of drunks and little children," said the woman. "Stop being horrible and bring up a jug of water. Can you hear me, I wonder, whoever you are? Don't worry. You're safe now."

Come and visit us at
www.legendpress.co.uk

Follow us
@legend_press

Cassandra
Parkin

The
beach
hut

Legend Press Ltd, The Old Fire Station,
140 Tabernacle Street, London, EC2A 4SD
info@legend-paperbooks.co.uk | www.legendpress.co.uk

Contents © Cassandra Parkin 2015
The right of the above author to be identified as the author of this work has
been asserted in accordance with the Copyright, Designs and Patents Act
1988. British Library Cataloguing in Publication Data available.

Print ISBN 978-1-9102665-0-2
Ebook ISBN 978-1-9102665-1-9
Set in Times. Printed in the United Kingdom by Clays Ltd.
Cover design by Gudrun Jobst www.yotedesign.com